Our house did not have a name until I was nearly five years old. Then, my hostling Cobweb (he that had brought me into the world) ordered that a board be nailed above the outer courtyard. It read 'We dwell in Forever'.

Cobweb is afraid of dreams and sees omens everywhere. His life is governed by a chain of complex charms, cantrips and runic precautions, leading from one day to the next. Perhaps he feared transience; to me the house became simply 'Forever'. Many things changed in my life at that time . . .

As the Wraeththu become pre-eminent, Swift, son of Terzian and Cobweb, will have a growing part to play. The simple days in the house called 'Forever' will dwindle into memory as love, politics and war come to rule his existence.

Also from Orbit by Storm Constantine:

THE ENCHANTMENTS OF FLESH AND SPIRIT:
The First Book of Wraeththu

STORM CONSTANTINE

The Bewitchments of
Love and Hate

The Second Book of Wraeththu

*With very special thanks to Valor of Christian Death
for creating the poems*

Futura

An Orbit Book

ISBN 0 7088 8274 9

Reproduced, printed and bound in Great Britain by
Hazell Watson & Viney Limited
Member of BPCC plc
Aylesbury, Bucks, England

Futura Publications
A Division of
Macdonald & Co (Publishers) Ltd
Greater London House
Hampstead Road
London NW1 7QX
A member of Maxwell Pergamon Publishing Corporation plc

*This book is dedicated to my long-suffering
colleagues at the library, especially, Lynda, Claire,
Karen, Michelle, Sheila and Gwyn. (See, you can
get your name in print as well!)*

*With thanks to Jag for locking me in the workroom
to get this finished, Sarah Wood at Macdonald for her insight,
Rhoda King for believing in me, Nick Green for providing
the hardware and software so promptly, to Sue Eley for
her invaluable help and everyone else who has offered help
and support and are too numerous to mention.*

Energy is ecstasy. When we drop the barriers and let power pour through, it floods the body, pulsing through every nerve, arousing every artery, coursing like a river that cleanses as it moves. In the eye of the storm, we rise on the winds that roar through mind and body, throbbing a liquid note as the voice pours out shimmering honey in waves of golden light, that as they pass, leave peace. No drug can take us so high; no thrill pierce us so deep because we have felt the essence of all delight, the heart of joy, the end of desire. Energy is love, and love is magic.

STARHAWK
The Spiral Dance, Harper and Row, 1979

BOOK ONE

BOOK ONE

CHAPTER

1

Made into Har
*A lie from the lips of a hostling
Swimming in the irony
Gasping for breath of perfect wisdom
Whilst disgorging the relics.*

O ur house did not have a name until I was nearly five years old. Then, my hostling Cobweb (he that had brought me into the world), ordered that a board be nailed above the outer courtyard. It read, 'We dwell in Forever'.

Cobweb is afraid of dreams and sees omens everywhere. His life is governed by a chain of complex charms, cantrips and runic precautions, leading from one day to the next. Perhaps, he feared transience; to me the house became simply 'Forever'. Many things changed in my life at that time. I was now old enough to receive tuition, although Cobweb had been imparting his own particular brand of education for some time, so that now I habitually crossed my fingers and said a little rhyme whenever black birds flew from right to left across my path, and I never wished evil out loud upon anyone, in case the spirits heard and punished me.

'Each day has its own special character,' Cobweb told me. 'Today, for example, is a day of sharpness and crystal; you must learn to recognize the smell, the *ambience*.' It was true that the sky did look particularly brittle that day (could it really break?), and everything looked hard and shiny. On a metal day, my whole body would ache and the taste in my mouth would set my teeth on edge. By the time I was ready for schooling, other matters had taken precedence in my imagination, although I never confessed it to

Cobweb, and the taste of the days would only come back to me on extremely summery days or extremely wintery ones.

Forever was enthroned upon a hill in the north of the town Galhea, my father's stronghold. We had farms to the west and in the valleys, hidden behind Forever's hill. In the summer, I could look from my bedroom window and see herds of cattle grazing the lush grass and the rippling seas of grain, green and silver, that were never still. In the autumn my father's house was filled with the smell of mown hay and wagons would come from the east, bearing produce from tribes who needed our grain and meat and leather. I once attended an autumn market in Galhea, shrinking against my hostling's legs, frightened by the noise and bustle. Cobweb gave me a newly minted coin that had come down from the north and I bought myself some sugar sweets with it that had come from a village on the other side of the great forest. Tribe leaders from miles around brought my father gifts, seeking favour in his eyes. It was usually in this way that our wine cellar became stocked for celebrations later in the season. Similarly, the larder shelves would become so full with preserves, delicacies, sweetmeats and cheeses, that jars would have to be stacked on the floor beneath. After the markets, it was customary for the people of Galhea to join together in the dusk to dance the harvest away from the town. It was a cheery lamplit procession of wagons and oxen and skipping feet. Blood-red flowers shed petals beneath the wheels and the air was full of music. Back in Galhea, the great doors to the grain stores would be closed, now half empty, but still holding more than enough for our needs.

Although my hostling could teach me to read and write (along with other more secret knowledge that Terzian would certainly not have approved of), it was not enough of an educati n for the son of a high-caste har. I was not allowed to attend the college in Galhea with other harlings my own age. Terzian, my father, preferred to find tutors whom he could trust, whose intelligence he respected, and who were happy to imbue my supposedly eager little mind with knowledge at home. I was not as intelligent as my father thought. It did not take my teachers long to realize this, but they were shrewd enough to continue entertaining my father's fancies by praising my progress. I suppose I was a late developer. Terzian lived by logic and strategy; I lived happily in a world of totally illogical imagination, inherited, no doubt, from Cobweb. I'm sure it always grieved my noble sire that Cobweb had ever had to have anything to do with my procreation and if he could have found a way to cope with reproduction all by himself, he most certainly would have done. He suspected every other har but himself of foolishness and fought constantly to discipline Cobweb's superstitious nature. Conversations at mealtimes were habitually punctuated by Terzian's impatient outbursts. 'Clouds are clouds, Cobweb! That is not an avenging spirit, neither does it seek to recruit souls from my house! For God's sake!' and other such denials.

Forever is such a big house and so few of us lived there, yet I was never lonely. Cobweb once told me that he used to be afraid of it. 'This house has been lived in for a long, long time,' he said.

'Who lived here?' I asked.

'Oh, the *others*,' Cobweb answered darkly and would not explain what he meant. 'You are young; it might spoil your innocence to know,' he said. I was used to my hostling's somewhat grey remarks and had learned at an early age that some of my questions were not to be answered, at least not by him.

One day, I was playing at being a big, black animal in the green conservatory at the side of the house. Someone was paid to look after the plants there, but they did not seem to notice and continued to grow in unruly defiance all over the windows. The door to the garden could not be opened because vines had grown through the lock. It was one of my favourite haunts, a place where, when I was very little, Cobweb and I used to spend a lot of time together. The plants must have absorbed many secrets; Terzian hardly ever came there. But that day, he pushed open the window-door and stood in the darkness of the room behind.

'Swift,' he said. 'Come ... Swift, what *are* you doing?'

Guiltily I told the truth because I was too surprised to think of a suitable lie. 'I'm a big, black animal,' I said nervously, and I could

11

see my father gritting his teeth.

'Yes, well, the time for games is over!' he said with his intimidating air of authority. 'Really, Swift, at your age, you must begin to put aside these infant habits.'

I picked myself up off the floor, brushed down my clothes and went to stare up into his face. I have heard people call him wickedly handsome, but how can wickedness be seen in a face that is usually so cold? Although I was always conscious of displeasing him in many ways, I adored my father. Most of the time he paid me little attention, but when he did my whole world would light up with his special radiance. He was very different from me in ways I could not understand; there was something about him that made him seem very far away, but to me he was simply Magnificence Incarnate. I wanted him to like me. Most of the time, I was confident that he did. After all, Cobweb made a hundred mistakes every day that made Terzian angry and I had no doubt that my father was fond of him. I was canny enough to learn from Cobweb's errors. Terzian would never catch me making the secret signs, or talking to myself or watching the clouds; usually, I could sense his presence rooms away.

'Swift, I have chosen two hara to attend to your education,' Terzian told me, drawing me into the dark room and closing the conservatory door. 'The time has come for you to study properly, as befits a har of breeding.'

'Yes, Tiahaar,' I said meekly. We rarely spoke to each other. Questions always died on my lips when he turned his eyes upon me.

He took me to another room, at the front of the house, where sunlight came in during the morning and the roofs of Galhea could be seen from the window. Two hara stood with their backs to the light, but I could still see their faces. One of them was smiling at me, one looked only at my father. The one who smiles will be the kindest, I thought, unconsciously shrinking back against my father's side, although I did not touch him.

'Moswell, Swithe, may I present my son Swift,' Terzian announced grandly. I knew I was not at my cleanest and could feel my face uncontrollaby twisting into an idiotic grin. I wanted

Cobweb. Swithe looked at me for the first time; he still did not smile.

'Lessons begin tomorrow,' my father said.

Afterwards, I ran straight to Cobweb. I found him upstairs, in his own room, where the light fell in so pleasingly, and everything was comfortable. He was sitting at a table by the window, painting strange faces on porous paper with black ink. I just ran to him and threw my arms round his neck. 'Swift, be careful!' he said, but he turned to take my face in his hands with inky fingers. I was distraught, but I didn't know why. Dimly, I thought my father wanted to take something away from me, change my existence, yet I couldn't see how. Secrets can never be kept from Cobweb; he does not need words.

'He wants you to learn things,' he said gently, 'that's all.'

'Will things be different?'

'Different?' He absorbed my fears and contemplated them. 'Sometimes, Swift, it is better that Terzian does not know exactly the way we think and feel. He finds you teachers; listen to what they say. They are probably wise in their own way, but do not take their words as Truth, just because they are older and wiser than you. Just listen, that's all.'

I crawled onto his lap, although I was nearly too big for that. 'Things will change; I can *smell* it!' I said.

'Everything changes eventually,' Cobweb said. 'That's just the way of things. Not all changes are bad.'

Not all, but more than half. Cobweb neglected to mention that.

'My father rules Galhea,' I said to Moswell. It was the first day of my official education and I had been roused from my bed earlier than was usual. Moswell and Swithe had both eaten with Cobweb and myself in the dining room, though my father had not been there.

'Terzian is a great har,' Moswell said stiffly. 'And you are a privileged little harling to have him as your father.'

Moswell was scared of Terzian. It was not until much later in my life that I learned of my father's reputation as an enthusiastic and callous warmonger. I knew that he was a warrior when he wasn't with us in the house, but I didn't really know what that meant. It didn't concern me, so I just never thought about it. Questions like 'Whom does he fight with?' and 'Does he really *kill* people?' never crossed my mind. Terzian would disappear from the house for months at a time, and the house would feel different then, more relaxed, and let itself get rather more untidy. Then he would be back; the big front doors would be opened and in he would come with the cold air and a dozen other hara, all dressed in black leather and talking in gruff, grown-up voices. Sometimes he would be scarred; once above the left eye, which made Cobweb moody and short with him. At these times, home from the fighting, he and Cobweb would be at their closest. I did not understand the needs of adults, but was intrigued by their brief caresses and the different tone in their voices, the exaggerated grace of their bodies. Cobweb was rarely to be found in his own rooms when Terzian came home.

Moswell's task was to instruct me in the history of Wraeththu. It was the first time that I heard of men.

'Before the rise of Wraeththu, another race ruled the Earth,' he said. 'Humanity. As Wraeththu are called hara, they were called men.' I was instilled thoroughly with the knowledge of man's intrinsic badness; his pointless aggression (Wraeththu aggression, of course, was never pointless), his short-sighted pillage of the world and more than this (horror of horrors), his two separate *types*. Moswell struggled grimly with the necessary delicacy to impart this information; not an easy task as I was (naturally) ignorant of Wraeththu sexuality at that age. Humanity had male and female, their bodies were sort of *split*. This made me feel cold. How could humanity ever have felt whole? Half their natures simply did not exist. I was not sure whether I believed what Moswell was telling me. It was an inconceivable idea. The first lesson was merely a glamorous alleluia on how wonderful Wraeththu were and how vulgar and vile men had been. None of it seemed real, or even relevant, to me. I had been born in Galhea, sheltered in my father's house; the outside world was a mystery I had no inclination to penetrate. 'You are just young,' Moswell intoned, noting my impatience and wavering attention. 'But your father would have you know these things, so, uninteresting as they appear, you must commit them to memory.'

Moswell did smile a lot, but this was merely to cover up a numbing tedium of manner. What he told me should have been exciting. Wraeththu, after all, were a comparatively new race and their escalation had been thrilling, the foundation of legend.

After the first lesson, I looked for Cobweb; he was in the garden. It was the time of year when spring begins to get warm.

'What are men?' I asked him. He was dressed in palest green, some floating stuff, and his hair was braided to his waist. His skin looked very luminous that day.

'I was once a man,' he said.

'You were once a man?' I repeated slowly, unsure that this was not one of my hostling's oblique jokes. He sighed and touched my shoulder.

'Ah, Swift, I would protect you from all this if I could. I cannot even see the purpose for you knowing it yet, but Terzian ...'

An eloquent pause. He led me into the greenest part of the garden, where there are few flowers and the shadows seem alive. Sometimes there are lizards there. Paving stones beneath our feet were viridian with old moss.

'You mature so quickly,' Cobweb said and we sat down on a wooden bench, which would undoubtedly leave licheny stains on our clothes afterwards. 'When I was your age ... well, I was just a baby.'

I snuggled up close against him. That way most fears would disappear, but I could feel an unnameable sadness within him and our fears mingled. 'I was human ...' he said.

'When? When? Was I there?'

He laughed and squeezed my shoulder. 'You? No, no. If I was human I couldn't have been your hostling, could I?'

'Why not?'

He took me on his lap and stroked the hair from my eyes. 'Why not? Well, because, long ago, when I wasn't Wraeththu, when I wasn't har, I was the half of human that can't bear children,

15

harlings ... oh, do you know what I'm talking about?'

'No ... I thought ... what? What are you talking about?'

'It's so hard to explain.' He sighed again and I pressed my head hard against his chest where I could sense his heart beating. 'Swift,' he said. 'When Wraeththu began, we weren't born as hara like you. We came from human stock. We were mutated from human stock. I did not have a hostling like you. I had a mother; it's different. When I was sixteen years old, I became har. I was *made* har. That's when I stopped being a half and became a whole ...'

'I don't believe you,' I said. Time before my own simply did not exist for me and I could not imagine Cobweb as anything but my father's consort, gracing Forever with beauty and being there for me to run to for comfort.

'If I was human and you a human child,' he said, 'then I would be your mother and that's all. But as I am har, it would be quite possible for Terzian to be your hostling and me your father.'

'But you're not!'

'No, but I could be. Oh God, now is not the time, Swift. One day you'll understand. Just see it like this ... oh, like what?' He laughed. 'Later perhaps.'

'What's "mutate"?' I asked.

'Change,' he answered, and I became alarmed.

'Change? Does changing mean you become something else?'

'Sometimes, but don't worry, you won't ever change physically the way I did. That's in the past now.' He sighed again. 'I'm not very good at explaining things, am I?'

'Not really,' I agreed.

'Look at the animals,' he said, pointing vaguely at the unseen birds twittering above our heads. 'Terzian's dogs, your puppy Limba ...' He looked at me strangely. 'Men are like that.'

'Like animals?'

'In many ways!'

'Did they have whiskers, tails and fur?' My mental image of mankind was becoming a purring, cosy thing.

Cobweb laughed. 'You are too young,' he said mysteriously, but he did not answer my question.

For several days after this, I became interested in the concept of male and female. Our cook Yarrow had a tabby cat named Mareta and apparently it was a female. Females are 'shes', although we habitually called Mareta 'he'. I wandered around the kitchen driving the staff crazy, saying '*She* has she's kittens!' and considering myself worldly and clever. (Mareta watched me condescendingly from a cushion beside the stove.) One day Ithiel, my father's equerry, was at the kitchen window, taking a mug of ale, leaning on the sill, and he said, '*She* has *her* kittens, Swift, you little moonfly!' and everyone laughed at me. I never said it again after that, but mulled over the concept of 'her' for half an hour afterwards, in my private den among the shrubbery, beyond the grey garden wall. 'Her' sounded suspiciously like 'har' to me; was there a connection?

About this time (a natural progression from what I had learned), I began to wonder where harlings came from. Cobweb told me that Terzian and he had made me, which was an intriguing idea. Had I been formed from mud and sticks in the garden, perfected by one of Cobweb's secret charms? I preferred to think that Terzian had climbed the highest tree and found me inside an egg in a bird's nest. I fantasized them carrying the egg carefully back to the house (it would have been a moonless, windy night), and laying it gently on a fur rug before the great fire in the drawing-room. Terzian, his chest swelling with the emotion of fatherly love, would have put his arm around Cobweb's shoulders and maybe even touched Cobweb's face with his mouth, which he did sometimes. Perhaps, creeping from the darkness outside, some little, furry men had pressed their whiskery noses up against the window to catch a glimpse of the infant as it hatched in the glow of the flames. They would have silently vowed me their king and would come back some day to take me to their secret land.

I told Cobweb all this one evening as we sat in his room, with the curtains drawn against the night.

'Terzian would never climb a tree!' he said, riffling through piles of different-coloured paper. 'Here is a picture of you when you were very young.' He handed it to me, and I put my head on one side and squinted my eyes.

'I don't like it!' I said.

Cobweb shrugged, 'You are vain, Swift,'

'What's that?'

'You!'

'Oh, Cobweb!' I ran to him and squeezed him hard, so full of love for him that I felt sad.

Moswell bored me to tears. He droned on and on every morning about Wraeththu this and Wraeththu that; I never really listened to him. It was far more interesting to watch the way the light changed colour as it came in through the schoolroom window, dust motes dancing like insects upon the rays. My rangy hound Limba would lie against my legs and yawn, his yellow eyes appraising Moswell speculatively. Unfortunately, my father had trained him too well for his instincts to get the better of him. He would never bite Moswell, as I'm sure he longed to do. My tutor said that the world had once been full of people that had only wanted to take things away from each other. How could that be true?! Men were *so* bad, he said, and yet I secretly pitied them. I could vividly imagine shambling lines of pathetic, furry little creatures, leaving their homes with sorrowful backward glances, heading for the bleak north. That was when Moswell brought me books from my father's library and showed me the pictures of men. 'Oh,' I said, disappointed, 'but they look just like us!'

'No,' Moswell insisted patiently. 'Men are crude, often ugly beings. The ones in the photographs are nothing to go by. Most of them are not half as attractive.'

Physical ugliness was another new concept for me to ponder. Of course, I wanted to see it, but it was a few minutes' walk back to the library, and Moswell didn't want to go.

'Another time,' he said.

'But what *is* ugly?' I wanted to know.

'Your questions are tiresome and mostly irrelevant!' Moswell said.

In the afternoons, Swithe took over as my mentor. He was a shy and introverted person, uneasy in my presence, but his head, like mine, was full of dreams. I could see that, no matter how hard he tried to conceal it. The first time we met he said, 'What do you know, Swift?' with a shaky smile.

'Oh, lots of things,' I answered airily. 'I know the names of all the plants on the estate, the secret names that is, and I know where the spirit lives in the lake (it's near the drooping tree), and how to call him up to grant you wishes. I haven't tried it yet, but Cobweb told me how.'

Swithe had difficulty maintaining a smile. He always looked as if someone was after him and I wondered if he had done something terrible somewhere else. Perhaps hara or even (with a shiver of delight) *men* would come looking for him some day. Perhaps he was a sorcerer. He had sorcerer's eyes. They changed colour with the weather and Cobweb said that was always a way you could tell. I don't know what he was supposed to teach me, but mostly we spent our time together discussing the ponderous statements Moswell came out with in the morning. That was how I came to memorize what Moswell taught me. I needed to know just so that I could tell Swithe about it later. Swithe never actually criticized his colleague, but I could tell he did not like Moswell.

'You, and others your age, are the first pure Wraeththu,' he told me, and I asked what he meant.

'Well, some time ago, but not that long, only men lived on the Earth. They had lived here for a long, long time and they changed gradually over the years. Not *all* of them were bad.'

'I'm glad,' I said. 'Have they all gone?'

Swithe made a noise of amusement. 'Well, hara like your father would like to think so, but no, they haven't.'

'What happened to them?'

'To be honest with you, Swift, I don't know for sure. When it happened, and I became Wraeththu, I was too young and too inter-ested in the newness of being har to take much notice of *exactly* what went on. It was important that I should have done; I can see that now. One moment, we were living in cities, hiding from men and killing them when we could and then suddenly ... I realized. There were more hara than humans. The cities had died around us. It happened ... silently.'

'You were once a man then, like Cobweb?'

Swithe nodded. 'Like everyone. Everyone but for our children.'

As time went on, I began to learn more quickly, more from my interest in knowledge than any natural aptitude for study. Like all Varrish harlings, I had been taught to read and write at a very early age. It surprised me to learn that human children were not developed enough to understand these things until they were much, much older, nearly adult, I thought. Then came another surprise. Humans were not considered adult until they were about eighteen years old! How sluggish their brains must be. No wonder Wraeththu had taken their world away from them.

I had had little contact with harlings of my own age. Once, in a moment of outstanding bravado, I had mentioned it to my father and he had murmured obliquely that some day he hoped I would have brothers. He could not specify when. I wanted to go into the town because on those rare occasions Cobweb went there and took me with him, I had seen other harlings playing in the sun, laughing, running barefoot over grass. They had seemed so free and I could never join them.

'Swift,' Terzian said to me, 'the harlings in the town are ... well, they do not have your *breeding*. You would gain nothing from mixing with them.' Happiness, laughter; to my father these things were apparently nothing. 'Anyway,' he said with a smile, ruffling my hair, 'you have Limba to play with.'

This was true, of course. Limba was a good companion and fond of fun, but I couldn't talk to him, could I? If I did, he would just smile at me with his tongue hanging out of his mouth, but I don't believe he understood what I had said.

'All hara belong to different tribes,' Moswell told me and then went on to explain what a tribe was. 'Your tribe is the Varrs. You are a Varr, Swift.'

Of course, I had heard this word before, but now it took on new meaning for me. I belonged to something, a great something. I was one of many. Swithe expanded on this for me later.

'All tribes live in different ways,' he said. 'They have different *cultures.* (Write that down, Swift.) Some of them live in deserts in the south and they do not look at things in the same way that we do. They are influenced by the desert. They are sort of *dry*, like snakes; deadly and quick. Some tribes care a great deal about magic (like Cobweb does). I'm afraid the Varrs are not one of them. Varrs have no religion, they shun the gifts that have bloomed within us, following man's path of fighting and greed.' He remembered hastily where he was and whom he was speaking to and smothered the glaze of fervour in his eyes.

Swithe's often barbed remarks about my tribe and my father did not pass completely over my head. Terzian would of course have been furious if he had known. I said to Swithe, 'You do not completely like the Varrs, do you?'

I could see from his face that he longed to tell me why, and I wanted him to tell me, but all he said was, 'It is not my place to tell you about your father, Swift.'

This did not frighten me as it should. It only added to Terzian's mystique. I never told Cobweb what Swithe said.

Naturally I was curious about Swithe's old home, where he and Moswell had come from. Swithe seemed reluctant to tell me, but I gathered they had sprung from a minor branch of the Unneah (who I later learned were allied to the Varrs only through prudence — or fear). Terzian had ears everywhere. He had heard of my tutors' reputation and had whisked them from under the nose of their tribe leader, whose sons would doubtless suffer from inferior education because of it.

All through the long, hazy summer, I stored knowledge from Moswell and then got Swithe to explain what it meant. Moswell neatened up my writing and polished up my ability to read. I could tell that he considered the tuition Cobweb had previously given me in these directions to be sloppy and undisciplined. Swithe said that my scrawly, illegible writing cheered Moswell up, because it gave him something to moan about. In the afternoons, we would sit in the garden and Swithe would tell me what to write in my notebook. Once, he recited a rhyme he had made up and I learned it by heart and then wrote it down.

From ashes stumbled, whitened by the crumbled stone
Of all Man's fears and exclamations
Wraeththu rise and take the sword.
Though we are red-pawed,
Still panting from the kill,
We say: 'This is not sin but justice,
This is neither shame nor pride.'

Where then the darkness
Whose shadows we present as light?
Must it not be buried with the debris,
The earth stamped down in triumph.

Ignored then, this black-hot cone,
Suppressed beneath a grin of victory,
But always pulsing, hidden:
The lights within the tomb,
Visible only to those who pass
Its granite door, at dusk, alone.

Cobweb was not impressed by this. I chanted it to him in the evening and when I had finished, he threw down his book and turned on the light. 'God, Swift, that's horrible!' he said. 'Don't ever say it to me again, especially after dark!' He was not very pleasant to Swithe the next morning at breakfast. I insisted that the poem had only sounded horrible because of the way I had said it. 'It is vile and unfit for harlings to hear and that's that!' my hostling declared vehemently.

After this Cobweb often used to sit with us in the garden, a somewhat icy presence which was unusual for him. Swithe would stare at him and he would throw back his head, gaze at Swithe haughtily and then go back to his reading, never turning the page. Blind I was to the implication of this behaviour. It was part of a ritual dance I was yet to discover in life.

Near the end of the summer, my father had to go away for some weeks and Forever breathed a sigh of relief and happily sagged in its foundations. Even Moswell became more likeable. The four of us, my tutors, Cobweb and myself, took to spending the evenings together downstairs in the house. We played games with cards and dice and talked. Moswell liked to steer the conversation in adult directions. Once he said, 'No doubt Terzian has heard the whisper of Gelaming activity in the south.' He wanted to appear clever and politically minded to Cobweb.

My hostling had been idly juggling a couple of dice in his hand. Now he threw them at the wall.

'In this house,' he said darkly, 'we shall have no talk of Gelaming!'

I could not understand why the atmosphere in the room became so cold after that. I knew that the Gelaming were another Wraeththu tribe for I had once heard Ithiel talking about them in the kitchen. Why the mere mention of them should anger Cobweb so, I could not guess. Moswell muttered an excuse to go to bed early and left the room. Cobweb sighed and rubbed his eyes. Swithe was hunched precariously on the edge of the sofa; Cobweb sat near his feet on the floor.

'I'm sorry,' Cobweb said to the fireplace.

I had a feeling that one of those times was approaching when I would be reminded that it was time I went upstairs, so I tried to make myself invisible in a corner of the room. Swithe reached out gingerly and put his hand on Cobweb's shoulder, sensing what he thought was distress. Only I knew it was rage. Cobweb leaned his cheek upon Swithe's hand and said, 'Terzian is my life.'

'Terzian is not here,' Swithe suggested and Cobweb smiled. That, of course, was when they noticed me.

'Go to bed now, Swift,' Cobweb said.

When my father returned, when the leaves had begun to change their colours on the trees, Swithe's behaviour became most eccentric. Several times I had to upbraid him, 'Swithe, you are not listening to me!' and he would smile wistfully. I once went to his room and found it littered with scrunched-up pieces of paper, scrawled with verse which he would not let me read. I could not understand, for it was beyond me to work out the connection between my father's return and Swithe's behaviour; beyond me to see the

23

similarity between the discarded, savaged balls of poetry and Swithe himself. For Cobweb, the incident was over; his lord had come home.

Terzian had sustained a nasty wound in his thigh and had to rest. Cobweb never left his side, and Moswell and Swithe did not come to sit with us in the evening again for quite some time. One night, as I was lingering over my hot drink before bedtime, Terzian said, in a low faraway voice, 'Cobweb, do you remember ...?' and Cobweb had interrupted him.

'Please ... don't!'

My father sighed, touching his thigh. 'It's just the leg ... this wound, like yours ...'

'I know.' Cobweb went over to where Terzian lay on the couch and stroked his brow. 'If it's any comfort, mine was a lot worse than that.'

I was longing to scream, 'What? What?!' sensing something agonizingly interesting.

'You've changed so much since then,' Terzian said, taking a lock of my hostling's hair in his fingers.

'Perhaps we both have.'

'Do you blame me for what happened?'

Cobweb shook his head. 'You thought I was dead.'

'Not just that ... the other thing. It still makes you angry ...'

'Not really. I think I was more angry for you than for myself.' I recognized immediately an outright lie on my hostling's part.

There was a moment's silence, which gradually filled with tension.

'Cobweb, you know so many things. Do you know if ...?'

'It's unfair of you to ask!' Cobweb answered sharply and my father sighed and nodded.

The next day, I just had to question Cobweb about this conversation. He pulled a face and looked at me hard, deciding whether or not to answer me.

'You might not remember, you were so young,' he said.

'Remember what?' I asked impatiently.

'When the Strangers came here; two of them. They stayed here in the house. Pellaz and ... the *other one*.'

It was one of my earliest memories. People had been either hot or cold to me then, young as I was, and I vaguely remembered the dark-haired Pellaz and his golden warmth. I remembered also his companion, who had had yellow hair and the feeling of ice and who had not liked me.

'I remember them,' I said and Cobweb nodded.

'In a way, we were talking of them last night,' he said.

'I don't suppose you're going to explain it all,' I said hopelessly, weary with the experience of someone who is always too young to be told things.

'The one with yellow hair (I cannot speak his name), he caused your father grief,' Cobweb said, making the sign of the cross of power on his brow, his lips, his heart.

'He had the evil eye?' I enquired knowledgeably.

Cobweb wrinkled his nose. 'Not *exactly*. He is just Trouble, standing up and walking about in a body!' We were in the drawing-room. Cobweb walked over to the long windows and threw them open. Air rushed in smelling of smoke and ripeness, birds flapped noisily off the terrace in alarm. 'Sometimes I am so afraid,' Cobweb said, in a soft, sad voice.

'Of what?' I asked, running towards him. He bent down and put his hands on my shoulders.

'You're growing up,' he said. 'I suppose I still think of human children when I look at you. You are five years old, yet you look twice that age.'

I sighed. 'Afraid of *what*, Cobweb?'

'Let's sit down,' he suggested and we curled up on the couch together.

'They brought me back home when I was hurt, those strangers,' he began.

'How did you get hurt?' I demanded. 'Where was Terzian?'

Cobweb pulled a face; his expression comprised bitterness, wry humour and disgust.

'Where indeed! Let's just say I was alone and they rescued me.'

'Pellaz was nice. He talked to me,' I said.

'I know he was ... it was the other one.' He began to scowl and his eyes shone with the kind of hatred that can quite easily destroy someone. I kept quiet, waiting for him to go on.

'I hate to say this, Swift, but I shall. Your father fell in love with him.'

I did not think this was terrible, only understandable, because my simple grasp of 'love' was then concerned wholly with what was pleasing to behold and what was not. The *feelings* were beyond my understanding. The yellow-haired har had been beautiful, in a cruel, lazy sort of way. This was clearly why my father had loved him.

'Was that bad?' I asked timidly.

'Bad?!' Cobweb screwed up his eyes and snarled. 'It might have gone very badly for both of us if *he* had stayed here.'

'Why?'

Cobweb looked down at me. 'You love your father very much,' he said, 'as you should. But you are too young to understand him.'

'It seems I am too young for anything at the moment!' I retorted hotly, mightily sick of hearing that particular phrase.

'Alright,' Cobweb said, 'Alright. If *he* had stayed here and given Terzian sons, there might have been no room in his life for us. He worshipped C — he worshipped *him*!'

'You're wrong!' I cried, pulling away, facing a Cobweb I felt I no longer knew. My hostling was too wise, too tranquil to come out with things like this.

'Oh, Swift, you know so little. One day, you'll understand.' He stood up and walked back to the window. 'Terzian needed me when they left here; his heart was broken. I suppose he's become fond of me over the years, but I am not deceived. That is why I am afraid.'

'Why?' I pleaded, feeling tears building up inside me. Cobweb had never talked like this to me before; he had always protected me from things he feared might be upsetting.

'He … might … he might *come back*!' Cobweb pressed one slim, white hand against his eyebrows and leaned against the window. I could see his shoulders trembling, oh so slightly. I ran to him, snivelling and afraid, and we sat on the floor and hugged each other.

'Never speak his name, *never*!' Cobweb warned. 'Never whistle in the dark for it summons evil and he will hear it. In the treetops, the feathered ones will know. Watch them, Swift, watch the birds!'

That night I had a terrible dream. In the dream, the yellow-haired har was standing in a wreath of shadowy flames and his beauty was ugliness. He saw me and snared me in horror. 'Call me,' he whispered and held out his hands, which were dripping red and shaking. I tried to turn away, run away, but I could not move. His eyes transfixed me. 'Call me!' A terrible whine started in my throat, a sound I could not control. When I woke up I was shrieking, 'Cal! Cal!' and lights were being turned on hurriedly in the hall outside my room; voices, and footsteps, running.

Next morning, I went alone to the long gallery on the second floor of the house, miserable and haunted. Cobweb had been very upset by what had happened in the night and Terzian very angry. They both blamed each other. I had heard my father shout when they had left me once more in darkness. The sound had come right through the walls. He had shouted, 'What possessed you to tell him that? What possessed you?'

And my hostling's answering cry, 'Are you ashamed that he should know?'

I could remember that things had changed when Pellaz and Cal had left Galhea. Of course, at the time I had not understood why. At first the house had held its breath, everyone speaking in hushed voices and looking over their shoulders. Ithiel had skulked about looking very embarrassed, but on hand in case my father needed him. He had wanted to go after them, I suppose. He had wanted blood; Cobweb too. He and Ithiel had had low, heated conversations together when they thought no-one was listening. My father had stayed alone in his room for three days, refusing food, accepting only wine and hot, potent sheh. After that, he had appeared once more downstairs, grey as with the aftermath of illness. That part I remember well. Cobweb and I had been eating breakfast together and my father had come into the room. He had stood in the doorway and no-one had spoken and then Cobweb had risen from his chair and Terzian had walked towards him; they had embraced.

27

Since that time, I had sensed them drawing closer to each other as the memory of the blighted Cal faded. We had built for ourselves an emotional haven within the walls of Forever; father, hostling, son. Now Terzian had come home from his fighting, sick and tired, and he had had too much time to think of the past, lying around the house all day. Now I had dreamed and called Cal's name. Now I feared I had opened the door to let him back into Forever. We had not thought of him for five years.

Swithe came to find me. 'They guessed you'd be here,' he said and squatted down beside me. I thought to myself, He is my only friend. I can tell him anything, and told him about the dream and then, after a split second's consideration, about the dreadful episode of Cal and how he had spurned my father. I suppose I should have been prepared for the warm light of respect that came into Swithe's eyes when I explained how Cal had refused to share Terzian's life, but I was still quietly outraged. 'He would have made Cobweb and me leave the house!' I added venomously, forgetting that only yesterday I had denied that was possible.

'Come downstairs,' Swithe said. 'Moswell is fretting.'

Later, I tried to apologize to my hostling for the dreadful thing that I had done, speaking the forbidden name, but he had only waved my apologies away with one quick movement. 'I should never have spoken as I did,' he said. 'No wonder it gave you nightmares.'

'But are we *safe*?' I begged.

'Yes, of course,' Cobweb answered shortly.

CHAPTER

2

Coming of Age
Radiant angel; magnificent black hair
Prostration at his feet
Overwhelmed by the loveliest Har
Under the concave firmament.

Some weeks passed and then news arrived for my father from the north. There were cities there, Varr cities that had been seized from men. Varrs of high caste ruled in those places (of castes higher than my father's anyway), and sometimes their eyes wandered in the direction of Galhea and they would send emissaries down to see how things went with us. Terzian was never pleased about this.

One morning, three polished black horses trotted out of the mist, past the follies, the fountains of Forever's gardens, up the drive to the great, white steps where my father's dogs leaped up and howled and bounded round the horses' legs. They had been riding through the night. The riders' garments of thick black leather and metal were glistening with dew. Cobweb said that northern Varrs were hardy to the point of masochism. I was in the hall when Ithiel strode into the house, when he went straight into Terzian's study without knocking. They left the door open and I could hear my father's abrupt noise of irritation when Ithiel said, 'There are three of them. Ponclast has sent them.' Ponclast was Nahir-Nuri, the most elevated of hara. Normally, his name was heard only in oaths; my father resented Ponclast's interest in his affairs.

They were received in the red room that overlooked the lawns at the back of the house. It was the most uncomfortable room in Forever. I hung about by the door and one of them patted me on the head as he passed. Food was ordered, ale and sheh. I went into the kitchen where everyone was hurrying around looking harried. Limba was with me and he nearly made Yarrow trip over by getting under his feet. Yarrow boxed my ears and yelled at me to get the hell out of his kitchen. That was when Moswell put his nose around the door. I had hoped lessons would be forgotten for the day, but he dragged me off to the schoolroom and I did not see our visitors again until the end of the afternoon.

That evening, my father, looking much relieved and uncommonly cheerful because of it, made an announcement at dinner. We were eating off the best silver because the northerners were there. 'Swift,' my father said, and I turned red because I was uneasy with strangers then. 'Swift,' he said, 'I know you'll be pleased; Tiahaar Ponclast's son Gahrazel is coming here to Galhea to stay in the house, to study with you.' He addressed his guests. 'My son has often wanted company of his own age.' (I mentioned it once, I thought angrily, just once!) If the northerners hadn't been there I would have asked, 'But why?' However, paralyzed by everyone's attention upon me, I was too shy to speak. It had nothing to do with manners.

Cobweb had a flinty look about him, caressing the smooth silver handle of his fork (maybe thinking it was a knife). He said in a clear, cool voice, 'But why?'

One of them, who had sleek black hair and the face of a hawk (his name, I think, was Mawn), said, 'Compared to how you live here, it is no place for harlings in the north. Ponclast feels the situation up there might adversely affect Gahrazel's development. He has always admired Forever, and is aware of Terzian's excellent choice of tutors.' If Mawn was aware of the veiled hostility in Cobweb's manner, he forgave him. Cobweb, because of his charm and his beauty, could get away with murder. Mawn smiled toothily at him, helplessly enthralled.

'Swift's tutors are the best,' my father said, rather unexpectedly. Cobweb looked at me and I could tell we were sharing the same thought. Ponclast's eyes in Galhea, in Forever, looking out from the face of his son. Cobweb smiled, partly because he saw in my recognition of that fact a developing maturity.

Later, I heard them talking, Cobweb and my father. I lay in my bed and their voices reached me through my open door. Since the nightmare, I was too afraid to sleep with it closed. Cobweb spoke with sarcasm. 'You seemed almost *grateful* and so *pleasant!*'

My father answered irritably, 'I have to be pleasant; we all have to be, damn them!'

'He's had trouble with this Gahrazel, I feel,' Cobweb said.

'Who, Ponclast? Hmm, perhaps.'

'Why else send him away from home? You don't believe that fawning rubbish about Forever being so *admirable*, do you?'

'He will be company for Swift. The child spends too much time alone.'

I lay there, listening, in two minds about whether I was pleased or not. New people meant changes; I would have to talk to Cobweb about it.

The next day, all my hostling would say was, 'It'll do you good, having someone else here your own age. Terzian is right, you live inside your own head too much!'

Feeling betrayed, I went to look for Swithe and he said, 'Cobweb is right. Anyway, it'll make lessons more interesting, won't it?'

'Hrrmph,' I consented glumly. 'Anyway, what did they mean by it not being "right" for harlings in the north?'

Swithe looked perplexed. I sensed him carefully preparing an answer for me. 'This country ... it is not ... a *peaceful* place, Swift.'

I must have looked completely blank. Galhea, after all, was very peaceful.

'There are two kinds of darkness,' Swithe continued, still struggling. 'Remember them now, even if you don't really understand what I'm saying. One darkness is the natural kind, like when the sun goes down, what you find inside a locked cupboard or the deepest glade of a forest. The other, well, it is a darkness *inside a person* and it can eat them whole! It can eat entire cities away, until

31

only dust and shadows are left. It is what men called evil and the darkness in the north can be like that.'

How could I understand his words? I couldn't; not then. But the feelings behind them struck deep. I never forgot them, nor how the room had seemed to chill as Swithe spoke, the sun beyond the windows to grow briefly shadowed.

Gahrazel was about a year and a half older than me, but he could not write as neatly and was always horribly restless. He was deposited one morning, without ceremony, at the gates of Forever, and Cobweb and I watched his hunched figure, carrying a single, bulging bag, trudge wearily up the wide, gravelled road to the house. 'It seems they are glad to be rid of him,' Cobweb remarked drily. I thought so too. Gahrazel had seen fighting, real fighting. He had seen hara die and had actually touched the dead body of a man. 'I cut some of his hair off,' he said confidentially. I showed him all the secret places in the garden, including the corner of the lake where the spirit lived, which Gahrazel appeared eager to invoke.

'If I am to stay here, I suppose we must be friends,' he said grudgingly, and went on to tell me how he would miss the hara he had known back home.

Lessons were over for the day and in the garden it was becoming quite dark. Nearly all the leaves were gone from the trees now and we had to wear coats when we went outside. 'This *is* a beautiful place,' Gahrazel said, 'there is nowhere like this where I come from.'

We had known each other only a week or so, yet already communicated in an unselfconscious manner. This was mainly because of the way Gahrazel was; spirited, confident and, to me, surprisingly mature. He had been sad to find himself in an unwelcome situation, but was prepared to make the best of it.

'Why did your father send you away?' I ventured carefully and he snorted angrily.

'Why?! You know what fathers are like,' he answered scathingly.

I did not want to appear ignorant so I said, 'I know what *mine* is like,' and we laughed.

'I am near my time,' Gahrazel told me. This was obviously something momentous.

32

'Oh?' I said.

'You know, Feybraiha, the coming of age.'

'Oh, yes ...'

'You *don't* know, do you!'

I shrugged helplessly.

'There was ... someone, someone a lot older than me. That was why Ponclast decided to bury me in the country. He disapproved of my choice, and I knew I would disapprove of his! Our tastes have never coincided. There was an argument, so' (he threw up his hands) 'here I am!'

Feybraiha: so, another new word for me to ponder. Was this another changing? If so, what? Pride prevented me from revealing my ignorance then, but something about it worried me deeply. A feeling of vibration; a sting. Presentiment perhaps?

For the first few days, Gahrazel was sullen and uncooperative. I tried to imagine how I would feel if Terzian ever sent me away to live with strangers. I strained to be tolerant. Gahrazel disliked his room (one of the best in the house), complained the food tasted strange and was sarcastic to Cobweb. It infuriated him that Cobweb didn't get annoyed. On the third day he joined me in my lessons, and to my delight, contradicted Moswell constantly. 'This har knows nothing. He is a fool,' Gahrazel whispered to me. From that day forward, the most crucial aspects of my education came from him.

Terzian gave Gahrazel a pony, solid and swift as my own, and we would often ride together, over the wide fields beyond the town and into the edges of the dark forests. My father did not approve of young harlings being out alone in the forest; stray men or hara of different, unfriendly tribes might lurk there, so either Moswell or Swithe would always accompany us. Gahrazel complained bitterly, once even to Terzian himself. 'I go away for days by myself at home!' he said.

My father smiled. 'It is not my wish, Gahrazel, to deliver you back to your father in pieces, however unlikely that might seem to you.'

I had been brought up in Forever without ever feeling threatened by danger. I was not brave like Gahrazel, only ignorant. My

33

father knew what lay beyond the fields of Galhea; I did not. Gahrazel knew too, to a degree, but it did not frighten him. In fact, he wasn't afraid of anything.

One night, Gahrazel came to my room when everyone was asleep, and we climbed out of my window, down the creepers. Outside, everything looked white and ghostly beneath the light of a round, white moon. I was terrified of the dark places, rustling with shadows that might not just be shadows, but it was an exquisite fear. Under the trees, we looked back at the house, standing huge, silent and grey, moonlight made the windows shine. Gahrazel said, 'Do you know *all* of that house?'

I thought about it. 'Well, no, I don't suppose I do,' I replied, which seemed odd. It was my home after all.

Gahrazel put his arm around me. 'Soon, we'll both know all of the house,' he said.

And oh, how Gahrazel came to know the spirit of my father's house, what lurked in the shadows, much sooner than I did.

At mid-winter, there is a festival. Mostly it is to celebrate and welcome in the new year, but Gahrazel said that it was just another thing that Wraeththu had stolen from man. 'It was once a religious holiday for them,' he said. We were with Swithe in the schoolroom. Swithe always listened patiently to Gahrazel.

'In a way, I suppose it is for us too,' he said. 'A new year is a magic thing. We are still here and for the future, all things are possible. The rituals bring us together and it is good to have a time when hara can relax in each other's company and look forward to better things.'

Gahrazel cast a cynical eye at our tutor. 'I would say it is only an excuse for too much drinking and eating. In my father's house I would imagine that the future is seen only as a ringing head in the morning.'

'You'll find it's different here,' Swithe said gently and I noticed his pity of Gahrazel with amusement. Gahrazel turned his attention to me, his face brightening.

'Once, I heard some hara of the Uigenna tribe actually ate a roasted man at Festival,' he said.

34

The weather gradually became colder, the days shorter, and one morning, when I woke up, the ground outside was frosted with snow. Festival was but two weeks away, and the house was warm and vibrant with preparation. Exalted citizens from Galhea had been invited up to Forever to eat with us on Festival day, and the house would be decorated with branches from the evergreens in the garden. Cobweb supervised the stocking-up of the larder with a cool, efficient air. Moswell and Swithe took a holiday to go back to visit their own tribe further south, accompanied by an escort of Varrish warriors, should hostile tribes or stray humans be abroad, braving the weather. Gahrazel and I now had time to explore the upper regions of Forever, where I had never been before. Gahrazel was puzzled by this, but I explained that I had always preferred to roam outside. Forever was the warm place to run back to when I was hungry or tired; at the top of the house it was neither warm nor welcoming. We found a way into the attics and it seemed we were in a different place; a house that shared the same space as Forever, while at the same time being in another dimension. It was forgotten, crumbling, resentful. One day we took food with us and ventured further into the cobwebbed rooms and corridors than we had ever been before. I took Limba with me because it made me feel safer. Gahrazel was never scared. 'A madman must have built this place!' he said excitedly.

'Did men live here, do you think?' I asked in awe.

'Of course,' Gahrazel said condescendingly. 'This house is old; Wraeththu are not. Forever is just another thing hara have taken from men. Galhea too; it hasn't always been called that. It was a man's town once.'

(I should have known that, I thought.)

'Imagine,' Gahrazel whispered, 'imagine if we found men still living up here, if they had been here for years, eating rats and waiting...'

I cried out and touched his arm. 'They may want to kill us!'

'They may want to eat us!' Gahrazel added with relish.

We found no men, though. The attics were full of rubbish and treasures; a table whose legs were carved in the shape of hounds, a box of tarnished dress jewellery with half the paste stones missing, hampers of clothes that turned to dust when you touched them, bundles and bundles of papers and heavy, dark furniture with useless mirrors that I could not imagine ever having been downstairs, or even how anyone could have dragged it up there.

We came upon a grimed window that looked out over a flat roof and Gahrazel forced it open. Limba leading excitedly, we climbed out into the frosty air and, sitting with our backs to the sloping eaves, unwrapped our parcels of bread and cheese and apples, staring out above the chimneys.

'Swift, how old are you?' Gahrazel asked.

'Oh, nearly six years old,' I answered importantly.

'Feybraiha is some way off for you then,' he said. 'Have they chosen for you yet?'

'Chosen? What do you mean?' I asked, no longer embarrassed when Gahrazel knew something I didn't.

'Someone for aruna. You know; the *first time*.'

'No, what's that?'

Gahrazel looked at me queerly, then laughed. 'You are nearly six. In as little time as a year you may come of age, and you don't know what aruna is?'

'No,' I admitted sheepishly. It seemed, in comparison to Gahrazel, I knew next to nothing.

'Then I'll tell you,' he said gleefully.

I could not believe it; I had known nothing about sex. Suddenly, it became all too clear what had occurred between Terzian and Cobweb to occasion my appearance in the world. Gahrazel asked me if I ever touched myself and when I looked blank, went on to explain in what way. 'No!' I exclaimed, horrified. Could our bodies have this strange life, this strange need, of their own; something we had no control over?

'All Wraeththu need aruna,' Gahrazel said. 'It is part of us; we are part of each other. I was told this long ago.'

I hated the thought of it. I had spent so much time alone in my short life that I was perhaps too modest. But this concept of aruna seemed so sordid; something messy, without order. Two hara coming together, with utter lack of privacy, invading each other's bodies in their most secret places. It reminded me, strangely, of cutting. I kept seeing huge hunks of raw meat slapping down on the kitchen table and the great, sharp knife that the cook would plunge into it.

'It is supposed to be a wonderful thing,' Gahrazel said earnestly, having grown up with the idea, but I was not convinced. I tried to imagine myself naked with Ithiel or Swithe and just the thought of it made me blush and I had to make a noise, like a growl in my throat, to make the thought go away.

'How do you know when you come of age?' I asked, and Gahrazel wrinkled his nose.

'I'm not exactly sure, but it's a kind of change, I think,' he said.

'I might have known; a change!' I cried.

'Your father or your hostling will choose someone for you,' Gahrazel said. 'Someone has to teach you these things. It is usually one of their friends.'

'Ithiel?' I squeaked, appalled. It would have to be him; there was no one closer to my father.

'Maybe. Would you mind? He's very slim, I like his arms, and he has hair the colour of fur,' Gahrazel said wistfully.

I shuddered, not sharing this sentiment. 'I most certainly would mind!' I said.

We went back through the attics, Gahrazel happily oblivious of my confusion. I was anxious to return to my room, to curl up on my bed and think about what Gahrazel had told me. I would have to familiarize myself with this knowledge; maybe then its sting would lessen. When the time came, would Cobweb and Terzian really force such a thing on me?

We scrambled, sneezing, out of the attics into a disused room that had no carpet on the floor and no curtains at the window.

'We haven't been here before,' Gahrazel said. He was nosing around the walls, looking as if he knew what he was doing.

'What are you looking for?' I asked irritably, hovering at the door, holding onto Limba's collar, looking out at the carpeted corridor.

'You never know,' Gahrazel answered mysteriously. He squatted down on the floor. 'Ah, your father's room is below here.'

'I'm not allowed in there,' I said, unnecessarily.

'Look at this!'

I joined him. Limba whined and put his wet nose between us. There was a small, splintery hole in the floorboards. Gahrazel bent lower, his fingers splayed out on the floor.

'Don't!' I cried and tried to pull him back.

'Why not?' he asked reasonably, and I could not think of a suitable answer. 'You can see his things; there is his wolfskin coat with the tails on. You can see quite a lot; look.' He tried to drag me forward.

'I don't want to!' I hissed, thinking, he will know! He will know! Gahrazel's eyes narrowed. He would think I was afraid of Terzian.

'One day,' he said, 'coming here, looking down here, you may learn quite a lot.' And then he laughed and I smiled back nervously, thinking, Never!

Of course, I had bad dreams again that night, of imagined violations, my body breaking. I woke up sweating, tangled in the sheets, too hot and yet my breath misted on the cold air in my room. We had heating in the house, but it was never turned on at night. I needed to talk with Cobweb badly. I wanted to ask him why he had never told me about aruna. He had taught me so much, things I could never have learned anywhere else, and yet, this most private, crucial information he had kept to himself. Did he ever look at me and wonder? Had he and Terzian discussed whom they would choose for me when the time came? It is because he thinks I am too young to be told! I thought angrily, yet I was sure he would have a reasonable explanation when I confronted him. ('Oh, *that*, Swift! I didn't want to bother you with *that*' or something similar.)

I went to Cobweb's room, but it was cold and in darkness, the bed smooth, and the curtains had not been drawn. I stood there for a moment thinking and then crept stealthily back down the corridor and hovered outside my father's door. An impish voice in my head whispered, 'Upstairs ...' but I visualized a gigantic NO! and denied the forbidden thought before it could form properly. Pressing my face against the door, I could hear nothing; then it opened silently beneath the pressure of my hand flat against the wood and I jumped back in alarm.

The room was empty, silent and cold as Cobweb's had been. Where are they? I thought frantically, suddenly too aware of the dark, the cold. Running, I went to the stairs and leaned over the bannisters. The hall lights were off. The staircase looked wide and mountainous, the hall beneath massive and shadowed; above me, glass in the chandelier clinked eerily in a breeze I could not feel. I thought that my father must be in his study; he often stayed up late in there. A dim light glowed from the drawing-room. No doubt Cobweb was in there, reading beside the fire, dogs and cats sprawled along his side. I wanted only to feel his strong, slim arms around me and hear his soft, low voice soothe away my night terrors. The marble floor of the hall was so cold beneath my feet, it hurt.

The door to the drawing-room stood ajar. I had already decided to creep in quietly, tiptoe to Cobweb's side and curl up against him. I wouldn't have to say anything; he would *know*. He would sigh and say, 'What, dreams again, my little pearl?' and stroke my hair. Then I could tell him. I put my head round the door, one foot over the threshold.

They were together beside the fire. My first thought was, No, not now! Why now, this precise, immediate now? and my second thought was, I'm still dreaming. I didn't want to look, but I had to, to be sure. I remember thinking, they are truly one creature; there is no division. It was slow, sinuous, like snakes sliding over each other in the summer, on the flat, grey rocks beside the lake. Cobweb's fingers lost in my father's hair. Terzian's lips upon my hostling's white neck. They did not see me. I don't know how long I stood there; a second, an hour, but they didn't see me. Perhaps it *was* a dream. When I woke up next morning, in my own bed, warm and rested, it certainly seemed that way, but on my way to break-fast, I saw Cobweb coming out of Terzian's room, putting his hands to the back of his head, lifting up his hair, and his neck was bruised. I can say nothing to Cobweb now, I thought. He is part of it.

Gahrazel was consoling and sympathetic when I told him about it, but eager for explicit details, which I was reluctant to give. 'At first,' I said, feeling important and grave, 'I was disgusted, yes, disgusted! Now ... well, I'm not so sure.'

'Your hostling is perhaps the most lovely har I have ever seen,' Gahrazel mused, having been pursuing thoughts of his own.

I nodded, still playing at being the sombre keeper of knowledge. 'Yes. Perhaps I have never seen him properly before, not all of him, not as a separate living thing. Now I know that people are still doing things when you're not there. Before it used to seem that they only existed when they were being watched. I thought I knew all of Cobweb, but I don't, obviously.'

That morning, I felt as if a lot of questions I had not been aware of asking had been answered. It was a day of thin clouds, racing in wisps before the wind.

'How uncanny that you should have seen them like that,' Gahrazel said, 'after what we'd been talking about on the roof.'

'No,' I answered. 'The truth is that it is not the slightest bit uncanny at all.'

CHAPTER

3

The Flesh
Coalesce the flesh; a splendour
Momentarily eclipsed by
The phenomena of the spirit.

On Festival eve, we heated wine with spices over the fire in the drawing room. Ithiel and some other of my father's officers came up to the house, stamping snow off their boots in the hall and grabbing hold of members of our household staff as they flitted past, for festive caresses.

Gahrazel drank two mugs of hot wine too quickly and sat, glazed, by the hearth staring dreamily at Ithiel, who did not notice. Cobweb, whose favourite colours were habitually pale, unexpectedly wore loose-fitting trousers and a shirt of deep crimson material, sashed with gold. Ithiel said to me, 'Remember this time last year, Swift? You seemed such a baby then. Enjoy your childhood while it lasts; I feel it will be brief.' It was the first time Ithiel had ever talked to me properly, yet I could not answer him intelligently. When I looked at him, I could only clench my fists behind my back and make the banishing growling noise. Ithiel laughed, surprisingly not surprised and brushed his hand against my face. I fled to Gahrazel's side by the fire, but of course he would not speak to me.

At midnight, my father called to Cobweb across the room. I heard him say, 'Share breath with me,' as they stood face to face with people all around them. Cobweb said, 'This is an old custom, Terzian!' and their lips met. I had to look away. Was I to be faced with this kind of intimacy all the time now? Perhaps I just hadn't noticed it before.

Festival day means eating, and that is precisely what we spent our time doing. This year, hara from the town seemed to notice me for the first time and they were exceptionally polite to Gahrazel, who had gone to bed the night before sulking but was now back in a good humour. We ate our main meal seated around a gigantic polished table in the largest room in the house. It was only used for functions and was, therefore, only opened up a couple of times a year. Terzian rarely entertained on a grand scale. Seated next to Gahrazel, I asked him, 'Do you miss your home?'

He shrugged. 'I haven't been here that long; things *are* different here. It seems Forever is my home now.'

After dinner in the evening, Terzian summoned Gahrazel to his study. Helpless with curiosity, I begged Gahrazel to come up to my room afterwards to tell me what it had been about. Had Gahrazel done something wrong? Was he to be sent home? I had got used to his company; we rarely argued and I did not want him to leave. I sat in my room, in darkness, on the window seat, staring out at the white garden. It is true that when a new year starts, everything does seem magical and sort of sad as well. It seems that everyone is given another chance, another year to get things right, the slate wiped clean. New beginnings. I sighed and misted up the windowpane. Already I could feel that unconscious childhood innocence slipping away from me. Outside the grey shadows were becoming just that. The spirits waved goodbye to a child who was solidifying, who would have to think about different things in future, until his casing cracked and a different being stepped out into the light. I had seen insect chrysalises hanging in secret places around the outbuildings in the garden. That was how I felt now. Insect! Insect! I thought angrily.

Gahrazel burst into my room about an hour later. He looked flushed, excited; I knew it could not have been bad news.

'Well?' I asked, and he threw himself down on the seat beside me, gripped my shoulders, shook his head, almost speechless. 'Gahrazel, what?!' His excitement was infectious; I found myself smiling. He had become the light in the room; I could no longer see outside.

'Your father,' he said.

'My father what?'

'We talked,' Gahrazel said, settling down, letting go of me.

'Talked, yes … about what?'

'Well, he asked me how I was getting on, polite stuff, so awkward. As if he cared! He gave me a letter from Ponclast to read. It was quite boring, you know, "Are you behaving yourself?" Things like that. He'd obviously got someone else to write it for him. But he must have sent a letter to Terzian as well, because after I'd finished reading, Terzian said, "Well now, Gahrazel, your father feels the time has come for me to talk to you."' (He mimicked Terzian so well.) 'I knew straight away what it was, of course: Feybraiha. I tried so hard not to be embarrassed, but it was difficult.'

I nodded vigorously in sympathy, only too aware of how he must have felt. I dreaded the day when my father would call me into his study to talk to me about such things.

'What did he say?' I asked.

'Well, after a few moments' temporizing, he told me that soon I would begin to notice changes about myself, physically and in mood. He said if anything worried me, I was to go to him, any time. As if I would! He asked me if I knew what Feybraiha actually was. Thank God I did. There's no way I could have sat there and let him tell me. I think I'd rather die! I explained I had been taught all that before and he said, "Then you know I shall have to choose someone for you. Gahrazel, you have not been with us long, so I was concerned that there's no one you'd prefer it to be. I realize it will be hard for you, having to take your first aruna with someone who will be a virtual stranger to you, but I shall choose wisely, and naturally, once your coming of age becomes apparent, its symptoms obvious, you will spend some time in his company, which may make it easier." Oh, Swift, I couldn't help it. Maybe I shouldn't have asked, but I had to. I said, "Who is it then? Do you know yet?" Your father raised his eyebrows and gave me what they call a scorching glance. He smiled, but not at me. He said, "It is

43

obviously important to you. Is there a reason?" I couldn't answer. He let me squirm for a few minutes, just looking at me. Then he said, "Oh, I'm not blind, young har. Not much goes on around here I do not notice. Therefore, I feel sure it will meet with your approval that my equerry Ithiel is the har I consider most suitable for the responsibility." I could have jumped up and hugged him!'

I winced. 'I hope you didn't!'

'No ... He said, "Run along now. Go and tell Swift all about it!" and laughed.'

'He knows I know then?' I asked quickly, breathless.

'What do you mean?'

'He knows that I know, about aruna, about ... oh, he just knows, that's all!' Suddenly I felt irritable and exposed.

'Swift, it will be a long time before ... well, before any of this happens to you. You'll be surprised how different you'll feel when the time comes,' Gahrazel said, reaching to touch me. I shrugged him off and looked out again at the garden. We were silent for a while.

'It will snow again,' I said. Gahrazel moved closer to me on the seat and put his arms around me. I did not draw away.

'You're a funny little thing!' he said. I looked at him, his open, rather cheeky face radiant with pleasure, his long, curling dark hair. Gahrazel was nearly adult. Just a few hours into the new year and I could feel him growing away from me.

'Don't forget me,' I said, thinking aloud.

'Forget you? How serious you are!' Gahrazel put his warm, smiling mouth against my cheek.

'Why do things have to change?' I asked as Gahrazel and I scuffed through the snow. Festival had come and gone; now we were faced with the rest of bleak, sunless winter before the spring came.

'Swift, you've become melancholy recently,' Gahrazel said.

'You seem to thrive on change,' I remarked.

Gahrazel considered this. 'I don't really notice it. I suppose it's because I get bored easily, so I must *like* changes. I think you've had an easy life so far, living here. Why should you want anything to change? It's so perfect for you, isn't it? Being Cobweb's baby, being spoiled, not having to make decisions ...'

'Oh, Gahrazel!' I cried, but not too stubborn to recognize the truth.

We came to the tall trees where the crows lived. Cobweb had told me they were birds of ill omen and, when I was very tiny, their coarse, squabbling cries had always frightened me. Gahrazel looked up at the sky.

'Winter!' he exclaimed miserably. 'Everything's so quiet, isn't it? Everything's sleeping.'

'Or dead,' I added. We stood among the gaunt, black trunks staring up at the untidy nests. Suddenly, the sky seemed to flash and I felt sick, so sick. 'Gahrazel!' I screamed and sank to my knees in the snow.

'What is it? What is it?' he demanded in alarm. 'Swift ...?'

'Look! Look!' I squawked, waving my arms.

'What? What?!'

'The *birds*!'

'What birds?'

'That's it!' I reached for him, half crazy. 'There are no birds!'

'No birds?'

'Gahrazel, it's something I made happen! It's something I did! Oh God!'

I pressed my face against my hands. Suddenly the world seemed far too large. Gahrazel tried to make me stand up.

'Come back to the house,' he said gently.

I told him everything. Perhaps I should have done so before. 'The birds are gone,' I moaned, 'and now *he* will come back. Cobweb said so.'

'Oh, come on, it may be just a coincidence,' Gahrazel said reasonably. 'There are a hundred reasons why the crows could have gone. Something may have killed them all, anything may have happened. Anyway, if they are birds of ill omen, it can hardly mean something bad if they decide to leave.'

'You don't understand,' I said grumpily. 'They are trying to tell us something. *They know.* They are magical birds and the har with yellow hair is jinxed. That is why they left.'

'Alright, alright, I *do* know about these things!'

45

'Do you think I should tell Cobweb?' I asked nervously.

Gahrazel shook his head. 'No, it's obvious what we must do.'

'It is?'

'Yes. We must protect the house.' Here he smiled smugly. 'I'm surprised you didn't suggest it yourself.'

'But how?'

After lunch, Gahrazel went to the kitchen and asked the cook for a bag of salt. He must have made up some fantastic excuse for needing it, for Yarrow handed it over without question. For someone whose tribe supposedly shunned the use of magic, Gahrazel had a surprising grasp of occult lore. Perhaps he, too, had had a Cobweb figure in his formative years. In his room, we made protective talismans from herbs wound with horsehair and sanctified them with drops of our own blood. Then Gahrazel intoned a prayer over the salt and we were ready.

Outside, the afternoon air stung our faces with cold and the snow beneath our feet became really deep once we had left the neat garden behind. My trousers were soaked, my flesh smarting with chill. We trudged doggedly to the boundaries of Forever's lands, starting at the gate. Limba, who I insisted should accompany us, bounded ahead apparently unaffected by the cold. Gahrazel pinned one of the talismans to the gatepost, which was difficult as they were made of sandstone. 'We must use only bent nails, made of iron,' Gahrazel said. I was in awe of his knowledge. Then we made a trail of salt (very thin, to conserve the supply) from the gates along the edge of the high wall that hugged Forever's country. At intervals, we pinned up one of the talismans to the wall.

By the time we had got back to the gate again, it was really dark and well past dinnertime. We heard horse's hooves on the drive, and then Ithiel appeared out of the shadows of the overhanging yew trees, saying, 'What on earth have you two been up to? Terzian's had people out looking for you!'

Naturally, Gahrazel and I were not exactly taken by surprise when we received a thorough scolding, first from Terzian, then further upbraiding from Cobweb. 'Don't you realize how vulnerable you are?' Cobweb snapped.

No, I didn't! I couldn't see what harm could have befallen us within Forever's boundaries. It never crossed my mind that, because of the season, outsiders, enemies, might be drawn to the town, seeking food or shelter.

'Terzian is very protective towards you, Swift,' Cobweb continued. 'You are his only heir ... at present. He is concerned for Gahrazel's safety as well. Can't you see that anybody could have come in off the fields? Anybody could have been hiding in the trees.' He shuddered expressively.

Terzian decreed that, until lessons resumed in a few days' time, Gahrazel and I must be kept apart. This was humiliating, but inside myself I was once again contented. Nothing, nobody, that wished us ill could cross the magical threshold we had made. I longed to tell Cobweb about it, but knew instinctively that part of the magic was its secrecy.

More snow fell. Messengers came once again from the north. Now, my father considered me old enough to be included in the conversations at dinner. He said, 'It seems the Uigenna have just disposed of yet another of their leaders. Sometimes, I wonder whether they are really quite sane.'

'Are any of us?' Cobweb said drily. 'Are we real, even? Do you think it at all unlikely that one day we might waken up in our beds to discover that all of Wraeththu was just a dream?'

'Well, I certainly do!' I answered hotly, and Terzian laughed, gesturing at me.

'There you are then,' he said. 'Did you dream up hosting the pearl that gave us Swift?'

Cobweb smiled. 'No, at least I hope not. If I did, I expect I should wake up, not in my own bed, but in some kind of asylum!'

'They are all rather insane in the north,' Gahrazel said then, in a thoughtful voice. He had been silent for most of the meal. 'My father enjoys killing things. Do you know, it is a public spectacle when hostages are brought to the citadel. If they're human, some are incepted, made to be Wraeththu, some are just butchered. I saw it, many times. From my room in the tower, I heard it more times than I saw it.'

My father looked at Gahrazel with embarrassment. 'You must know that humanity has to be dealt with the most expedient way. Not all of them can be kept by Wraeththu.'

'Oh yes, I am well aware of that. Another thing that I've heard many times. I also know that the humans would kill us all, if they could. Perhaps it is the only way, killing all of them. I can't answer that; I don't know. What I can't understand is why they have to suffer, why their screams are as music to my father's ear. They may be our enemy, but they're not animals.'

Words cannot convey the stunned silence that followed that little speech. I was dumbfounded, not sure whether to believe what I'd heard. How lucky we were that Terzian would never allow such things to happen in Galhea.

After a while, Cobweb pushed his chair back and stood up. 'Well!' he said brightly. 'Swift, why don't you ask Swithe if we could all go riding together this afternoon? Look at the sun, the snow; we shouldn't miss it. Soon it will be raining and thawing and unpleasant.'

'Alright,' I said, still looking at Terzian, who was discretely observing Gahrazel with speculation.

Wrapped in furs, kicking up sprays of snow, we galloped our horses to the lake's edge. I looked at my hostling and thought, Gahrazel is right, he *is* the most beautiful har in the world.

Swithe pulled his horse to a halt and said, 'Just look at this place! How hard it is to imagine we are struggling through a time of fighting, uncertainty.'

'Oh, and are we?' Cobweb asked archly.

'Terzian keeps Galhea very ... safe,' Swithe replied in an unpleasant tone of voice.

Cobweb dismounted and walked towards the frozen edge of the water. Brittle, dead reeds rattled in the breeze like bones. I looked at the expression on Swithe's face and realized, Of course, they are ...

A revelation that was cut, only half-formed in my head. All that followed was simply a flowering of this realization. I had been within the flower; now I could see the sky.

'Swift, come here!' Gahrazel called and I jumped from my

pony's back, running over to him, but reluctant to leave Swithe and Cobweb alone.

'What is it?'

'Look!' He poked something with a stick. Something dead. Its beak spread wide in a last obscene denial of death, a bedraggled black bird poked halfway out of the ice. I was chilled.

'Do you think he's noticed?' I asked numbly.

'Who? Noticed what?'

'Cobweb ... about the crows ...'

Gahrazel glanced over to where Cobweb stood staring into the ice, Swithe some distance away, arms folded. 'Who knows ...' he said.

Gahrazel and I walked back to the others. I felt on edge for some reason, nervous and twitchy. I could hear whistling in my head. Someone was watching me.

'Let's go back,' I said and my voice sounded slow, echoing. Cobweb turned towards me slowly, his lovely, pale face smiling, a reflection of the wild, frozen landscape, his hair lifted by the breeze like wings. He began to speak, then a vague puzzlement came into his eyes; he winced.

'Cobweb?' I said, cautiously, and it echoed around us: 'Cobweb! Cobweb!'

He shook his head once, as if something had got into his hair. 'No ...?' he said.

'What is it?' Swithe asked harshly, still behaving in a way so that Cobweb would know that he'd been hurt.

'Nothing.' Cobweb straightened up and began to walk back to the horses. I wanted to run to him, but my limbs were paralyzed. Above me, livid darkness was crawling across the sky from the south. Gahrazel was staring at me. Some feet away from us, Cobweb dropped to his knees in the snow. I could not move. He screamed. Swithe turned his head.

'No!' Cobweb slammed his fists into the snow, which flew up in glittering spurts. When Swithe went to him, Cobweb smashed his hands into Swithe's face.

We all called, 'Cobweb!' me softly, Swithe indignantly, Gahrazel wonderingly. Cobweb sprang to his feet and ran to the jostling horses. Not bothering with stirrups, he threw himself over his animal's back and urged it furiously back towards the house. I still could not move. Gahrazel shaded his eyes with his hand and squinted at Forever. Swithe rubbed his chin thoughtfully, putting his foot in his stirrup, remounting his horse. 'There's some kind of activity at the house,' Gahrazel said.

I was first back at Forever after Cobweb. Leaving my pony loose in the yard, I ran, slipping, sliding into the house. I could sense the strangeness immediately. The house was outraged, holding its breath. I ran into the hall and I remember thinking, They have let the cold in; it is cold. Everywhere seemed empty, I could not hear anything. The drawing room, my father's study were deserted and the fires were low. I went to the kitchen. All the household staff were in there, talking in low voices. They went quiet when they saw me standing in the doorway. 'What's going on?' I demanded. 'What's happened?'

Yarrow spoke. 'In your father's room,' he said.

I ran out, up the stairs, stumbling. Of course, the door was closed. I could hear voices inside, speaking quickly. I could not go in.

Cobweb and I must have been guided by the same instinct. I found him in the conservatory. It was cold in there, colder than it should have been, and I was afraid that it might kill the plants. I put my hand on the radiator and it was hot. I rubbed my hands and shivered. Cobweb was slumped at one of the wrought-iron tables we had in there, elbows on the table, his head in his hands. I went to him and put my arms around him, resting my chin on the back of his head.

'Don't kiss me,' he said, 'not from behind; it's unlucky.'

'Cobweb . . .' I began.

'No,' he said, quite emphatically. 'No.'

'Tell me, you must tell me!' My voice sounded alien to me, somehow stronger and older. Cobweb raised his head at the imperative tone.

'Can't you guess?'

I squatted down beside him and looked into his eyes. A single tear spilled and fell on my hands where they clasped his own in his lap. I knew; there was no way I couldn't have.

'Oh, Cobweb!' I said, and suddenly it didn't seem as bad as before, when it had been only a threat. This was real. This we could fight. 'Tell me.' My voice was calm.

'They *found* him, somewhere ... I don't know. I don't know! He's here! Who the fuck cares how!' I had not heard my hostling swear in my life before.

'But he can't be,' I insisted. 'Gahrazel and I, we protected the house ...'

'Swift, are you joking?' Cobweb spat sarcastically. He pushed me away and stood up. He laughed. 'Destiny!' he said.

It was later, from Ithiel, that I heard how it happened. I cornered him in the kitchen, long after dinnertime (none of us had eaten), begging food and coffee off Yarrow. Limba was in there, crouched mournfully against the stove. Ithiel started guiltily when he saw me and said, 'Oh, Swift.' A brief wave of shame washed over me, for I was still troubled by my discovery of the existence of aruna, but I ignored it.

'Tell me what's happened,' I said. It was one of those rare, magical times when I felt twice my age and others even treated me as if I was. Ithiel sat down again on the edge of the table, nursing a hot drink. I went over to the window and drew the blinds and turned on another lamp. Evidence of confusion was everywhere; unwashed pans in the sink, breadcrumbs on the table. Usually, this room was spotless. The cook was sitting by the stove, drinking a large measure of sheh and absently scratching Limba's back with his foot. 'Yarrow?' Ithiel said and he replied, 'This is my kitchen. If you want to talk in private, go somewhere else.'

Ithiel inclined his head and ushered me out into the hall.

'My room,' I suggested. 'No-one will disturb us there.'

It felt strange, preceding Ithiel up the stairs, feeling him tall behind me, passing hurriedly the closed door to my father's room. The first thing he said was, 'Cobweb will need you now.' He sat down on the bed and I on the window seat.

'Not just me,' I pointed out and Ithiel looked at his hands and shook his head.

'No-one can predict what will happen now,' he said.

'Who found him?'

'A patrol, three hara, south of Galhea. He was lying in the snow. They thought he was dead at first. God, maybe five, ten minutes later and he would have been!' Ithiel looked up at me. 'They would have just left him, even finished him off, but one of them had to recognize him. That's when they sent for me.'

'Ithiel,' I said. 'You needn't have brought him back here. No-one would have known.'

He laughed. 'You can't mean that! Three hara *did* know and is there any har in Galhea who doesn't know what that devil was, what he is? The patrol knew and I couldn't guarantee their silence. If Terzian had ever found out …' He shook his head and we both pondered the terrible consequences of that.

'What condition is he in?' I asked. 'And why has he come back after all this time?'

'His condition is poor,' Ithiel answered, with a bleak smile. 'But I shouldn't raise your hopes too high. As you know, we're a resilient race and difficult to kill. As for why he's come back, well, your guess is as good as mine at the moment. I just think it means trouble, that's all. Terzian's always been obsessed with him and that worries me. It's unnatural.' He stood up and looked at the door.

'How is my father?' I asked and Ithiel rubbed the back of his neck, flexing his spine.

'Oh, he behaves in his usual cool, contained way, but …'

'Perhaps we should kill him,' I interrupted, 'kill the devil that calls itself Cal!'

Ithiel grunted in derision. 'A thought, I imagine, that will cross more than one person's mind. Anyway, I have to go. I have things to attend to. Our defences must never slip, must they?'

He paused at the door, frowning and burrowing in a pocket of his jacket. 'Oh, Swift, I meant to show you this,' he said. 'I found two of them on the gate this morning. Is someone casting spells on us, do you think? I thought I'd better take them down.'

He threw them down on my bed. Two of them, bound in horse-hair, blessed with blood. Our talismans.

After Ithiel had gone, I sat looking at my hands, afraid to look at the talismans. Eventually, I knocked them to the floor without turning my head. A sudden wave of anger made my eyes hot. I thought, I'm not going to skulk in a corner like everyone else! This Cal is just har. How dare he come back into our lives and destroy the harmony of this house? I stood up. Young though I might be, I was not going to let this upset me. I am Terzian's son, I thought, and I shall face this beast with his strength.

Hesitating at Terzian's door would have made it too difficult. I knocked once, loudly, and walked right in. My father was sitting at his desk, writing. Two hara stood by the bed, fussing over what lay in it. Terzian looked round as I walked in. It was the first time, that I could remember, that he seemed genuinely pleased to see me. Perhaps, because of that, I was more self-assertive than usual with him.

'Swift,' he said. 'I was beginning to think I was a pariah in my own house. Has Cobweb sent you?'

I shook my head.

'Come here,' he said and I went to him. 'You've grown up so much lately,' he continued. 'Perhaps we still treat you too much as a child.'

Oh God, I was thinking, don't get emotional; I couldn't stand it! 'What does this mean?' I asked clearly. 'To Cobweb and me? What does it mean?'

My father bit his lip; not a gesture common to him. 'Cobweb is naturally angry,' he said.

'We want to know where we stand,' I said stiffly.

Terzian laughed. 'Oh, I see! Cobweb's told you that now Cal has come back, you and he will be cast aside, perhaps even thrown out of the house, hasn't he?'

I could not answer. Looking at my father's face, I realized that our eviction was probably the least likely thing in the entire world. Terzian touched my shoulder

'You are my first-born,' he said, and that was reassurance enough. 'Swift, a long time ago, when Cal was here before ... and afterwards, I explained to Cobweb how things were. Cobweb is your hostling and my consort and because of that, my people are fond of him. He belongs here, but if it hadn't been for Cal, well, maybe I would have had other hara in the house to give me sons as well. Cobweb's had it easy; I've spoiled him. There is no reason why his life should change now except that he shall have to learn to share his home.'

'And you,' I pointed out.

'Yes, that too,' Terzian agreed.

I thought to myself, Father, you have no heart.

'Go and look at him, Swift.' Terzian stood up and, clamping a firm hand on the back of my neck, half steered, half dragged me over to the bed. I thought, How lucky he has good bones. Starvation has barely marked him.

'Are you sure it's him?' I asked. 'I remember him differently.'

'It's him,' my father said shortly.

Cal's eyes were closed, his head turned to the side. I could see so clearly the long line of his neck, the caress of hair against his cheek, his brow, the dark circles beneath his eyes. I could see his arms, outside the blankets, laid along his sides, smooth as sculpture, his long, sensitive hands. My first impression was unashamedly this: he is made to be touched. I hated him. I remembered a fairy tale that Swithe had once read to me from an old, old book, a man's book, about a magic mirror.

The beautiful witch queen had asked the mirror, 'Who is the most beautiful in the land, magic glass?'

And the mirror had always replied, 'It is you, O Queen.' Until one day it had clouded and it had seen someone else, more beautiful still. When the witch had asked the mirror, 'Who is the fairest in my husband's kingdom?' it had answered her differently and dark poison had flowered in her heart. Someone else, and here it lay, on my father's bed, and yes, more beautiful still. A Wraeththu child of snow and thorns whom we could not kill, because fairy stories just don't end that way.

The following morning, Cal was moved from my father's room, ironically, back to the very suite that he had occupied once before, with Pellaz. A circle in time; we begin again. Cobweb would not speak to Terzian, except with his eyes, which radiated contempt and fury disguised as pain, and all gatherings of the household became fraught affairs, where silence could be cut with a knife and knives glinted sharply.

Gahrazel and I philosophized endlessly about what all of this meant, the complexities of relationships, the capriciousness of feeling.

'Is Cal *really* evil?' Gahrazel asked me.

I had to admit, 'I don't know. We all hate him because he broke my father's heart when he left and yet his staying here was the last thing in the world Cobweb wanted.'

'Poor Cal,' Gahrazel remarked cynically, 'whichever way he turns the path is wrong!'

'We shall really have to wait,' I said. 'When he has regained his strength, then we may see him as he really is. Then he may try to bring about all the terrible things Cobweb is afraid of.'

'But Swift,' Gahrazel said, 'Does anyone know for sure that Cal *was* trying to get back to Forever?'

I shrugged. 'It does seem rather a coincidence ... and the talismans, Ithiel *did* break the circle ...'

That night, Gahrazel went to bed early with a violent headache and I was more or less compelled to spend the evening with Cobweb in the drawing-room. By now, his martyred silence was beginning to get on my nerves. Had we been cast out into the wilderness? No. It seemed to me that my hostling was only driving Terzian farther away from him. His tactics were all wrong; it bored my father, which was perhaps the gravest error. Cobweb was displeased with me because Terzian talked to me at mealtimes, but that was only because he could not talk to Cobweb. Secretly, I thought that Terzian might need Cobweb more now than he had ever done.

On my way up the stairs that night, I heard Terzian and Ithiel talking in the study; low murmuring, the chink of glass. All the lights in the house appeared to have been left on; there were no shadows, anywhere. The corridors upstairs were tense and still, burning brightly. I could always sense the house holding its breath. Now I would go to the enchanted room; there are secrets there, an oracle ... Outside the door, I was alert for changes in atmosphere (would it be cold there? A spirit breath?). He lay as before, inert and splendid, carved from ice, asleep for a hundred years. Now I was the prince of valour come to wake the sleeping beauty with a kiss. I found myself chanting, 'Here is the room, the room of death!' At that time, I am quite sure, I was not wholly rational. I went to his side and said, 'And what are you, white beast?'

His eyes opened, his hand shot to my wrist; not the grip of illness. Fathomless power, a sense of timelessness, burned right through me, but he could not have known it. His voice was husky, as if long unused. He said, 'Pell, come closer, I have to ... I have to tell you something ...' and fell back on the pillows with a sigh, his eyes rolling upwards.

I ran back to my room, I sat down on the bed, I stood up again and walked to the window. 'Must you always sit in darkness, Swift?' I said to myself, but I did not turn on the light. I flopped down, on my back, on the bed; strangely thrilled. In a month's time, it would be my birthday, I realized, wondering where the thought came from. I remembered Moswell telling me that at the growing stage, one of our years was equal to two of man's. I am a twelve-year-old human, I am a six-year-old har, I thought. When the time comes I shall be be fourteen, I shall be seven ...

That week Gahrazel was confined to his room, afflicted by strange pains. I once heard him whimpering in the night; his room was not far from mine. Swithe told me that Gahrazel's coming of age was upon him, which sounded most unpleasant. 'Men grow hair upon their faces, upon their bodies; we are not quite the same,' he said. 'Your flesh shall become furred with down as you mature,' he went on, 'beneath your arms, a thicker growth and between your legs, the silky mane that marks you as adult. Don't blush and writhe so, Swift! I am not your father after all.'

I wondered what it was that caused Gahrazel pain. Swithe explained that certain internal organs (known as soume-lam) were coming alive, flexing, preparing themselves for the accommodation of aruna and pearl-hosting. 'The phallus, the ouana-lim of Wraeththu, is a complex and wonderful thing, Swift,' Swithe said, thankfully with his back to me. 'Treat it with respect.' (God forbid that I should do otherwise! I thought.) 'Of course, some time from now you will be given thorough instruction concerning aruna and procreation,' Swithe continued airily, 'but if you are ever curious about anything, you can ask me. Of course, by that time, your friend Gahrazel will doubtless be answering all your questions!'

I went to visit Gahrazel in his room and his behaviour was manic, more restless than ever. He said he itched unbearably all over and I charitably rubbed his back for him. The skin was taut and hot.

'How does it feel, this change?' I asked.

Gahrazel rubbed his arms, shivering, sweating. 'Horrible!' he cried. 'Horrible!'

He mentioned terrifying dreams that had been ruining his sleep, dreams about my father. At the time I thought nothing of it. We all have strange dreams occasionally; not all of them are prophetic.

Cobweb, nudged out of his self-indulgent moping, prepared steaming elixirs for Gahrazel to drink, which made him sleep. 'I wonder how long this will last?' I wondered.

'Oh, not long,' Cobweb answered vaguely, and by that, I guessed he had no idea.

Soon Gahrazel began to feel much better and told me that Terzian had been to see him to arrange for his coming-of-age celebration. 'I suppose you're going to spoil my birthday,' I complained. 'Coming of age and having the lissome Ithiel to court you.'

His face changed a little when I said that. I realized he was not quite as confident about his Feybraiha as he liked me to think.

'Will it be alright, do you suppose?' he asked. 'I think about it often. It's an invasion and I'm afraid of conquest ...'

'I hope it kills you!' I said and for a moment we stared at each other in silence.

'Is there a fate worse than death?' Gahrazel asked, and we both laughed.

All the snow had melted, the ground outside was dark and rich, green shoots sprouting beneath the trees. But no crows came back to their ragged nests in the high branches. Cal was brought downstairs in the afternoons to sit in the conservatory, which outraged Cobweb and put me off going in there. Terzian would spend an hour with him every day. Once, I crept to the door and eavesdropped on them. Cal said, 'What am I doing here?' in a voice that was barely even a whisper, and my father answered, 'Must you ask that every day?'

I peeked around the door, hidden in the curtains, and saw my father reach for Cal's hand, but it was snatched away instantly.

'Don't! Cal cried hoarsely. 'Not ever!'

'It's alright,' Terzian soothed. I was amazed by this reaction.

The idea of Cal fascinated me. He was a creature of mystery. We all presumed that only Terzian knew where Cal had been going, where he came from, when the Varrish patrol had found him. And what Terzian knew he told no-one. Not even Ithiel. Gahrazel was now allowed to spend some hours several times a week in Ithiel's company, under Moswell's watchful eye. I pressed him to drill Ithiel for information, which must have been difficult with Moswell there, but although Ithiel was not loath to divulge what he knew, it wasn't anything we weren't aware of already. One evening, afire with the spirit of rebellion, Gahrazel and I appropriated a decanter of sheh from the dining-room and consumed it lustily in the privacy of Gahrazel's bedroom.

'I wish I knew what was going on!' I exclaimed. 'He won't let Terzian touch him; I saw!'

Gahrazel was already rather drunk. 'Why bother squeezing useless information out of everyone else?' he said. 'Why not go straight to the source, the one person who will know. Ask Cal, ask him outright. It's your home too.'

'Yes, you're right. Tomorrow then ...'

'What?' Gahrazel snorted. 'Tomorrow we have no sheh, tomorrow we are sensible and shy. Do it now!'

Spurred on by a tide of drunken bravery, I cried, 'Alright, I will!' and rolled onto the floor.

Leaving Gahrazel giggling helplessly on the bed, I went to look for Cal. Of course, he was penned in his room. That was where they kept him at night. They had even locked him in. I turned the key and went right through the open doorway.

He was lying on the bed, dressed in a heavy, woollen robe. The curtains were drawn, the light dim. Books were scattered around him. We stared at each other for quite some time before I spoke. 'What are you doing here?'

He smiled faintly; my voice was slurred. 'And what are *you* doing here?' he replied

'It's my house,' I said. 'It's my father's house.'

'Ah, you are Swift,' he said. 'I remember you.' A dry remark which made me uneasy.

'You did not like me,' I accused.

His smile is constant, words move around it. 'I was afraid of you.'

'Afraid!' I laughed and went to sit next to him. 'What are you reading?'

'Tales of the night,' he said.

'Why did you come back?'

'I didn't. They brought me back.'

'I don't believe you,' I said. Until I looked at his eyes, close up, I still felt strong. Now I was a child again. He smelled of smoke and flowers.

'Where's Pellaz?' I asked and he shrugged, bland as a cat.

'I don't remember.'

'Where have you been? Why are you ill?'

'Who knows? Who cares? Give me the strongest light and I shall carve an axe for you.'

'What?'

'It was in the book.'

'Oh.' One thing that is remarkable about Cal was that he was so easy to talk to. He appeared to have no side to him, communicating as easily as water running over stones. People did not perplex him and he cared about nothing then.

He said, 'I have sobered you!' and laughed.

'My father's sheh,' I explained. 'My friend Gahrazel has come of age and we were celebrating together.'

'I *see*.' He sat up and rubbed his face. 'Be a friend to me, little monster, little reptile child, and bring me some of your stolen sheh.'

'Alright,' I said, and swung my legs over the edge of the bed.

'They lock me in,' Cal said. 'Lock the door behind you. The stairs are very steep and oblivion is heaven to me at the moment.'

Strange he should say that when we both knew he would never kill himself. I smiled uncertainly, pausing at the door. 'Cal,' I said, and his name felt strange in my mouth. 'Why were you afraid of me?'

'I told you,' he answered. 'You're a monster; you shouldn't exist. Men can't bear children, it's not possible.'

'But we're not men!' I protested.

'Aren't we? Sometimes I wonder,' Cal said.

I went to fetch the sheh and Gahrazel, reassured that Cal wasn't about to attack us, insisted on coming back with me. I was afraid Terzian would find out, convinced he would be angry. Gahrazel and I sat on Cal's bed and watched him gulp down the sheh, holding the glass with shaking hands.

'Aren't you bored?' Gahrazel asked.

Cal screwed up his face. 'Bored? I can't feel anything. Only the evidence of my eyes persuades me that, in fact, I possess arms and legs.' He held out his glass and I filled it dutifully. 'This will make me sleep,' he said. 'The little death.'

'Cal thinks we are monsters,' I remarked to Gahrazel.

'My father thinks that too,' he replied. 'He often called me a little monster.'

'Varrish brats,' Cal said good-naturedly.

When Cal got sleepy, Gahrazel and I went back to Gahrazel's room. 'He doesn't seem evil,' my friend said thoughtfully. 'Only rather pathetic, rather hopeless.' I could say nothing. I was no longer sure of what I thought about Cal.

Gahrazel's coming of age was now just a week away, my birthday but two days. Terzian told Gahrazel to cut his hair, but Gahrazel told me he had no intention of doing any such thing. Among Varrs, only those hara whose life-work has been designated as hostlings wear their hair very long. Later, I learned that this was seen as a sign of femininity. Like men, Wraeththu want the bodies that carry their children to be lovely. What I did not know then was that among other tribes, all hara are considered equally masculine and feminine; anyone can host a pearl and it does not matter how you dress or how long your hair is or whether you're a soldier or a clothmaker. To a man, someone like Cobweb might appear superficially female, because that side of his nature has been unnaturally encouraged. Terzian was obviously worried that Ponclast's son might be too feminine. Ponclast wanted to breed warriors, not hostlings. Gahrazel and I discussed this and, of course, his disregard for authority meant that his hair stayed long.

Messengers came frequently from the north now and sometimes they would bring a letter for Gahrazel from his father. I began to sense something huge, an uprising, great activity, in the world beyond Galhea's fields. Terzian would sit at mealtimes with a frown on his face, ploughing his food with his fork. I think Cobweb was almost disappointed that the arrival of Cal had prompted no dramatic change in our lives. Now he had nothing to complain about. Naturally, I had told him what I had witnessed in the conservatory and this had made him smile.

One day, I said to my father, 'What *is* happening in the world?' We were in the stables. One of Terzian's horses had gone lame and he was supervising the application of poultices.

'Rumours, rumours,' Terzian replied vaguely and I knew he could not be bothered to tell me.

'What rumours?' I insisted.

'Rumours that Thiede is becoming active,' he said.

'What's Thiede?'

'Not a what, a who,' he said. 'And a very dangerous who at that. Of another tribe; Gelaming.'

'Oh, Gelaming,' I said, remembering the incident with Moswell and Cobweb the year before. 'Will they come to fight you?'

My father laughed. 'It is suspected that they covet this land. There is a possibility we may have to fight to keep it.'

'Oh,' I said. I was used to my father disappearing and I had a vague idea what he got up to on those occasions, so I was not unduly alarmed. To me, he was omnipotent. I could not imagine him ever being beaten.

'I understand you've been to see Cal,' Terzian said carelessly, but I could sense the slight tension in his voice.

'Sometimes,' I admitted. 'He's strange.' Terzian did not comment on this.

'I think perhaps he is well enough to eat with the rest of us now,' he said carefully. 'Perhaps it would be better if you informed Cobweb of this.'

As I grew older, I discovered I had a new role in life; that of intermediary between my parents. I realized that, although Terzian considered Cobweb to be alive solely for his personal use, he was also slightly afraid of him. Cobweb lived in a strange, magical world, but because he believed in it, the strangeness became power. When Cobweb became angry, he was a thing to be feared, because his power was invisible. I told him what Terzian had said and he smiled fiercely and said, 'I see.' That was all. I dared not tell him that I sometimes went to visit Cal in his room, but it was more than likely that Cobweb knew about that already. Because of his art, it was virtually impossible to keep secrets from him. I was torn two ways. Curiosity, and loyalty to Terzian pulled me one way, devotion to my hostling the other. Whomever I sided with, there would be unpleasantness. Cobweb and I had always been close, now he was reserved with me. I had a suspicion that the friendship with Swithe had been resumed as well, but I could not be sure.

Our first meal with Cal was a nightmare. If I thought the atmosphere had ever been bad before, I was now horribly enlightened. Cal, with a definite air of self-preservation, treated Cobweb's hostility with light amusement. I cringed when he had the nerve to say, 'Well Cobweb, you've certainly changed since we last met. You're quite stunning now, aren't you! How lucky that injury to your leg didn't leave you with a limp. Did it scar? I seem to remember that the last words you said to me were something like, "You'll be back some day". I never thought you'd be right. Here's to your gift of intuition!' And he raised his glass, sipped daintily. If Cobweb had been a cat, he would have fluffed up his fur to twice his normal size, but he was har and therefore only simmered silently with rage. Gahrazel and I dared not look at each other, for fear of giggling. My father had a tight, uncomfortable expression on his face as he stared at his plate.

That was perhaps the only reference Cal had made to his past. I noticed that his hands still shook, although he tried to hide it, and his eyes were still shadowed, but he was no longer locked in his room at night. I wondered what had transpired between Cal and Terzian that my father should no longer worry about Cal trying to leave. It was hard to imagine them actually talking to each other.

I had got into the habit of seeking Cal's company virtually every day. He fascinated me so much, I couldn't keep away. I never got the impression that he didn't want me around, but at the same time he never said anything *important* to me. He asked me questions about myself and my family and his mordant sense of humour always made me laugh, but he never talked about himself. It wasn't that he was being secretive, it was more as if his life had only really begun once he had woken up in Forever. It didn't seem as if he was interested in what had happened to him before. He would never stare out of the window with a faraway look on his face, or stop talking as if a memory had walked across his eyes. His whole existence was simply 'now'. This irked me because my curiosity about his past was overwhelming. I wanted to know why he had left Terzian before, what had happened to Pellaz and, more than either of those things, why he had come back. He had evaded that question once, and I didn't believe the answer he had given me then. Was he evil? Sometimes I was troubled by my fascination for him. Alone, at night, I was often afraid of him, but I was always drawn back, for I had met no-one like him before. Each time we met it was as if I learned something new about the world that would never be put into words. It was as if I was learning his secrets, not through concrete ideas, but just from feelings that were nearly smells and sounds and tastes. On several occasions, after I had left him, fleeting pictures would flash across my inner eye, like memories, but they were of places and people I had never seen.

I once remarked upon Cobweb's hostility towards him and Cal laughed and said, 'He is lovely now. Who would have thought it!'

'He will never like you,' I said swiftly. Cal ignored this.

'I would like,' he said wistfully, 'to bind him naked with green, shining ropes of ivy and cover him with kisses.'

I went cold, a strange, numb feeling. 'More than you would like to touch my father's hand?' I snapped, a question which had come out before I could think better of it. Cal looked at me startled for a second, then he made a noise of amusement, as if at a private joke.

'In dreams, Terzian and I may be together. Is that what you wanted to know"

Heat suffused my face; I could not look at him.

'If you want more of an explanation,' he continued, 'then let me say that reality may make me come alive, and I fear life. Can you understand that?'

It was the first time he had ever spoken to me like this, and I was unsure of his motive. 'Do you mean that aruna may make you remember?' I asked cautiously, hating the feel of that word on my lips. Would he answer me? Cal wrinkled his brow and twisted his mouth to the side as he considered what I'd said. He did not appear embarrassed and chose not to show me he knew that I was.

'Aruna will open up all the blocked circuits in my head, I'm sure of it,' he said. 'It's an electric thing, after all.'

'But can you live forever like this, now knowing?'

He shrugged. 'I never think about it.'

I wondered if that was true.

I was given gifts on my birthday, small things, and Cobweb and I had a small party with Swithe, Moswell and Gahrazel. My father was away for the day and Cal kept to his room. I knew he had started to write, but he kept the subject a secret. He spent most of his time writing now. Later, when it began to get dark, Ithiel joined us in the drawing-room and Cobweb mixed us drinks of sheh and herbs and piquant essences. We all got happily drunk. Moswell, in a rare mood of abandonment, stood up and capered and sang. Everyone laughed till it hurt. I was sure that Cal would be able to hear us in his room. Did he throw down his pen in annoyance or think wistfully, If I was with them …

The day of Gahrazel's Feybraiha arrived; a sunlit morning, where yellow flowers glowed brighter than ever before under the trees and young leaves of an acid green colour filtered all the light and made the garden secret and exciting. As Varrs don't hold much with religion and ceremony, Gahrazel had neither to fast nor pray.

I understood from Swithe that in other tribes, Feybraiha was surrounded by ritual and meant a lot more than just losing your virginity. Cobweb plaited flowers into Gahrazel's hair and Terzian invited friends and officers of his guard to share our meal at lunchtime. The table was strewn with greenery; hara murmured in Ithiel's ear and laughed. Clear sunlight streamed in from the garden, making the curtains look transparent at the edges and spinning magic gold in Cal's glorious hair, where he sat with his back to the light. Cobweb forgot to be angry that Cal was there and I saw Terzian take Cobweb's hand and they looked into each other's eyes, smiling, half ashamed. I could not tell what Cal was thinking, watching them. He had a faint smile on his face and drank wine at a steady but consistent pace. Terzian made a speech and congratulated Gahrazel on reaching the lofty state of adult. 'Today, you are no longer harling. Today you have a caste. I pronounce you of caste Kaimana. Your level is the first of that caste; it is Ara. You are Aralid, Gahrazel.'

In the evening, much to everyone's surprise (and I'm sure, Gahrazel's horror), Ponclast arrived from the north. Terzian and he embraced and slapped each other's backs.

'My little Gahrazel is no more!' Ponclast boomed. He was a big har, though not fleshy, and had short, dense black hair, like fur. His nose was the fiercest I had ever seen and his eyes could have seen through steel. It was clear that, like my father, he made no concessions to the feminine side of his nature. 'So *you* are the one!' he exclaimed to a white-faced Ithiel. 'Take care of him!' When Terzian introduced him to me, he picked me up bodily and shook me as a dog would do with a rat. 'Fair of face, as both his parents!' he shouted, close to my ear.

We had music and dancing in the big room. My father persuaded Cal to dance with him (which embarrassed me), and at the end they hugged each other. Cobweb hissed at my side.

Then the time came for Gahrazel and Ithiel to leave us and repair to the room that Cobweb and the house-hara had strewn with grasses and flowers. My heart was thudding so, it was almost as if it were me who would walk up those stairs with Ithiel, not Gahrazel. He came over to me and we pressed our faces together,

65

cheek to cheek. I could smell sandalwood and fear.

'It's almost like goodbye,' I said, surprised to find my voice was shaking. 'You are leaving me behind.'

'No,' Gahrazel said. 'No, Swift.'

I could not imagine that one day, a celebration like this would be held in honour of my Feybraiha. On that day, my body would come alive. Another har would touch me and nothing about me would be private any more. I knew that aruna was more than just a communion of bodies; my mind as well as my flesh would have to be surrendered.

Must we do this? I thought. Can we never be alone?

After Gahrazel and Ithiel had gone upstairs, accompanied by ribald cheering and shouting (which disgusted me), everyone forgot about them and the music seemed to get louder, the lights brighter. Cal sauntered over to where Cobweb and I were sitting, looking this way and that like a cat. I wondered if he would sit down and begin washing himself without looking at us, but he said, 'Cobweb, I would like to make you dance.'

'Over my dead body!' was the predictable response.

Cal looked thoughtful. 'To dance on your dead body, hmmm ... An attractive prospect perhaps, but impractical; too lumpy. Maybe you are too drunk to stand?'

'I have changed since we last met,' Cobweb hissed icily. 'In those days, I would have told you to go fuck yourself; now I am contained and civilized and merely shake my head with a condescending smile. Now I visualize your extinction, now I dismiss you from my attention.'

He rested his chin on his hand and gazed glassily at the dancers. Cal smiled as he always smiles, relishing any contact with my hostling. After he had gone I said, 'Why do you hate him so, Cobweb?' and my hostling answered.

'Outside the trees are alive. I can see them moving, although the garden is dark. All trees have spirits ...'

It is a wonder I was ever born sane.

CHAPTER

4

Enigma of the Beast
Incarnate war, captives clamouring,
Pangs of Trojan endurance.
Never suffering the distant humility
Of the human incarcerates.

Our house, throughout the ages, may always have been a place of secrets. Among the curtains, whispering, all the long corridors rustling with the confidences of unseen lips. We that lived there eventually got to hear everything. We were close-knit, and at that time, Forever was our only world.

Ponclast and my father spent several days after Gahrazel's Feybraiha locked in Terzian's study, deep in conversation. (Not just for his son's coming of age, then, had the mighty Ponclast left his northern realms.) I had often wondered what it was like in the north; what it would be like to have to live there. My imagination supplied dark visions of Hell; smoke, livid flame, shattered build-ings, creeping forms, faraway howling. I could not imagine daylight in such a place. (Later, I learned that my visions were not that inaccurate.) Gahrazel had always been reluctant to describe in detail his old home, yet I could tell he had never been really unhappy there. I knew the names of his friends, that he had two rooms of his own in his father's palace, that his relationship with Ponclast was not as bad as he sometimes made out and that he did not know the har who had been his hostling. I knew all this, but very little else.

Through Ithiel, via the house staff and finally from Cobweb, I learned most of what my father and Ponclast had discussed.

Because of my ignorance or because of the security I felt surrounded me, I was neither shocked nor worried by what I heard. It was unreal to me, only words, and the meaning of them could not touch us. I felt we were distanced from everything, that Galhea existed only in its own universe. To a degree, I suppose this proved uncannily true, for my home was never marked by true conflict, but I was wrong if I supposed what lay beyond our fields could not summon me out to meet it. Our country, which the Gelaming (and finally all Wraeththu) called Megalithica, was controlled for the most part by the Varrs and the Uigenna. In the south, other tribes held sway and northern Wraeththu had little congress with them for they were sorcerers and, while uninterested in accruing more lands, people to be wary of, for it was said that their currency was souls. Swithe said that the southerners did not seek conquests in this world and that even the Gelaming might avoid confrontation with them. I knew that Cobweb's tribe had travelled south all those years ago, when Cobweb had turned his back on them and remained in Galhea. I asked him if he knew about the currency of souls, but he only laughed and ruffled my hair. 'And how many souls would it take to buy meat to fill the belly of my child?' he said, but I could tell that he knew. Cobweb knew many things and some of them he would never speak of. He said, 'Swift, the rumours are true.' He had known that for a long time.

For nearly a year, snippets of news had been filtering through to Galhea about the Gelaming. Terzian had no doubt that one day, they really would descend on Megalithica. 'They are too powerful not to,' he said. Now it was true; they were here, a long way to the south, just north of the desert, but too close for comfort. Some said that they had come across the sea in long, pointed ships that sailed against the wind, powered by silence, and others said that they had travelled through the air by means of magic.

Terzian scoffed at these ideas. 'However they damn well got there, one thing is sure,' he said, 'they mean to take Megalithica away from Varr control. Mission of peace? Bah! That is rot, and the first to believe it will be the first to die. If they take control, the pestilence of their beliefs will infect us like a plague; masculinity repressed, all this talk of peace and harmony … They will leave us half dead, like a race of women, twittering helplessly, seeking maleness, until the next tribe crosses the sea from the east and makes slaves of us! Can we allow that? It will happen if we don't fight and I shall fight until my last breath!'

It was in the town that he said that, and it is now quite a famous speech. All the people cheered him as he stood there so tall, so handsome, with the fires of courage and action burning in his eyes. Cobweb stood at his side like a queen, dressed in a robe of green. Afterwards, hara came to kneel before him and kiss the jewelled serpent's eye he wore set into a ring on his left hand. It was lucky. They gave him flowers. Cobweb the witch; they entreated him to pray for victory. Inside every Varr, it seemed, the seed of religion still waited to be nurtured. Terzian's sarcasm might turn them away from the light, but the light was patient. It could wait.

The Gelaming were giving no sign of what they intended to do next. They had installed themselves in the south and had so far, made no move towards the north or even tried to communicate with anyone. The Varr leaders refused to be discomforted by this, treating it as a rather obvious ploy to engender panic. I asked Cobweb why the Varrs and their allies didn't move first and drive the intruders back across the sea.

'Why?' he replied mysteriously. 'Why indeed! It is because of Fear, little pearl, no other reason. Now Terzian and his friends may come to regret turning away from the path.'

'The path?' I queried.

Cobweb smiled. He lifted one hand and twisted the fingers. Out of the air three colours merged and danced for a full half-minute before fading away.

'Imagine such a thing as that, Swift, but more powerful by a thousand times. Enough to take off your head! Now do you see why they are afraid?'

For a while, I too was scared by this, but then, as the days passed and nothing changed in the house, my apprehension faded. Terzian was all-powerful. The Varrs could repel any threat; we were safe.

Once Ponclast returned to the north, Forever closed its doors and again turned its back on events occurring beyond its walls. As before, we, its little occupants, became more interested in the convolutions of our daily lives. Terzian was absent much of the time, but I never thought to ask why. I was more interested in the blossoming of Gahrazel and asked him endless questions about the practices of aruna. He infuriated me by refusing to answer, saying, 'To tell you would spoil it for you.' He enjoyed annoying me, smug beast, and would only laugh when I lost my temper with him. Sometimes, Ithiel would stay with Gahrazel in his room and because I was excluded, I would get angry and bored. I bullied Swithe and Cobweb to take me into Galhea with them and occasionally they would relent and we would go into the town, perhaps to eat at the best inn, where they treated us like royalty, or to walk in the market where traders would respectfully entreat us to inspect their wares. I would see other harlings watching me curiously, whispering among themselves. I had learned to be haughty and kept my nose in the air.

Predictably, Swithe became friendly with Cal and they had long conversations about our race, most of it meaningless to me, all of it dull. Cal enjoyed arguing and I noticed that he often completely changed his opinions from day to day. This confused Swithe, who sometimes found himself defending a point that previously he had argued against fiercely. Cal would catch my eye and wink at me while Swithe spluttered for words. I was glad Cal had someone else to talk to, for it worried me that he spent so much time alone. He *seemed* to have recovered from his illness, but I could sense that not all was well with him and that he put a lot of energy into appearing healthy. The mask may have been convincing, but it was brittle. Once, it nearly broke completely. Once, we nearly saw him as he really was. I have found that in our house, a lot of important things were revealed during mealtimes. An idle remark, a seemingly innocent occurrence. This time was no exception.

Terzian had just come home and Ithiel had joined us for dinner. Outside it was dusk although the days were lengthening. Everyone was talking when suddenly Cobweb said, 'Cal, you never told us, but what did happen to Pellaz? Did you fall out?'

Nobody else even stopped their conversations; it was perhaps only me that heard it. I looked at Cal. His fists were clenched on the table. He was staring at Cobweb, who stared back, a gentle smile misting the challenge. It happened so quickly. Cobweb said, 'I see death in your eyes.'

My father stopped talking to Ithiel, mid-sentence, and looked at them. Cal made a noise. Cobweb said, 'Well?'

Cal cried, 'Don't! You are ... you are ...!' He had lost the words; he couldn't speak. Terzian, reacting quickly, anticipating trouble, reached for Cal's taut hand. Cal barely winced; his face seemed to ripple, like wind over water. He picked up the nearest object, the nearest weapon, fumbling as if he was blind: a silver fork. His face was blank. Suddenly it was in his hand, my father was speaking his name, and suddenly Cal had plunged the pointed tines into Terzian's hand where it lay over his own on the white tablecloth. Ithiel stood up, pointing, making a sound. My hostling laughed and Cal ran from the room, knocking over his chair as we went. My father stared in amazement at the sharp fork still half-hanging from the back of his hand.

It was all so quick. Of course, Ithiel wanted to go after Cal. One does not attack the person of the ruler of Galhea and get away with it, but my father shook his head. 'It is not as bad as it looks,' he said and carefully removed the sharp points from his flesh. It did not bleed at first. Terzian looked sharply at Cobweb, who blithely offered his napkin, which Terzian wrapped around his hand.

None of us felt much like eating after that. At the end of the meal, my father said to Cobweb, 'Don't ever say anything like that to Cal again. We can't guess what he's suffered to be the way he is!' But Cobweb only smiled. He was as aware as I was that Terzian had not gone after Cal to comfort his distress.

Naturally, I was the one that finally went to look for him. He had only gone to his room and was reading through some of his notes at the desk that my father had brought into the house for him. When I asked him if he was alright, he laughed and said, 'Of course!'

It occurred to me that he might have forgotten the whole incident, but I said. 'You stabbed my father's hand with a fork!'

'Yes,' he agreed.

I was exasperated. It was like trying to communicate through a mist. 'Why? Why?!' I shouted. 'What was it that happened to you? Where *is* Pellaz?'

Cal turned his back on me, adjusted his lamp and went on reading.

'You *are* mad!' I cried.

'Very possibly,' he said quietly. 'Get out, Swift; I'm working.'

But I had more to say. 'Cobweb knows everything. He *knows*, Cal. He will have seen it in your mind and he will use it to destroy you. Can't you see that?' That thought must have been in the back of my mind for quite some time; now it seemed blindingly obvious.

'I don't want to talk about this,' Cal replied. 'Cobweb knows nothing about me.'

I rushed forward, tried to take his shoulders in my hands, turn him towards me. His body felt rigid. His eyes were inches from my own and cold as death. I couldn't speak. He smiled.

'Do you see it too, Swift?' he said.

After this, I said to Gahrazel, 'How does Cal sleep, do you think? Is he troubled by dreams?'

Gahrazel and I spent a lot of time discussing Cal. 'I should imagine he sleeps very well,' Gahrazel replied. 'I don't think he remembers his dreams.'

I watched Cobweb warily. His acceptance of Cal into our household had been too easy, too quick. What was he plotting? I had no doubt he knew a lot about what had happened to Cal and *would* use it, but carefully. It would have to be in a way that Terzian could not notice or even suspect.

One day in the late spring, one of the ever-vigilant patrols cornered a group of humans south of Galhea, some miles away from the town. No-one knew why they had been there, where they had been going, or why they had forsaken their cover. My father had been summoned to the town after Ithiel's troup had rounded them up. Inevitably, several humans had been killed. Now Terzian would decide the fate of the survivors and supervise their interrogation. Gahrazel and I were delighted. Men! At last, and in Galhea. Gahrazel had seen humans before, of course, but only as flitting shapes in the dark or dead bodies. We were both eager to see living humans. They were some kind of strange animal to us. I knew that, years ago, there had been human slaves in Galhea, but they were no longer around. I could only guess at what had happened to them.

Terzian was approached, first by me and then by Gahrazel, both of us requesting that we might see the captives, but he shook his head. He did not want to be bothered with harlings and our demands annoyed him. He would not give us a proper reason.

Gahrazel said that my father had looked almost guilty when he refused our request. He was so angry at having anyone saying no to him that he devised a plan. 'We must sneak out of the house at night,' he said, 'and go to Galhea ourselves.'

At first I protested violently. It would be too dangerous, my father would find out, we would be caught and punished. Gahrazel sneered at my objections and argued with me until I gave in. He was restless and craved adventure and I really wanted to see a human. I tried to imagine what it would be like speaking with one. Would it be astounded by my wisdom?

Gahrazel managed to find out that all the humans were kept penned in a fenced enclosure near the soldiers' quarters, where I had never been. This was not too far from Forever and we could walk there within fifteen minutes. Gahrazel planned our adventure down to the finest detail. He charmed, bribed or threatened the guards who would be on duty to let us approach the enclosure. We would be able to get really close.

When the night came, I could not sleep for excitement. Gahrazel waited until he was sure the whole house was asleep before he came to my room. We dressed in dark clothes and clambered down the ivy outside my bedroom window, as we had done many times before. This was the first time I was scared of being caught. I was unsure of my father's reaction. I could equally imagine him being furious or amused; it was impossible to guess his mood.

Running through the dark, I held Gahrazel's hand and the town below me glowed softly with the memory of light.

The guards did not know who we were. I waited while Gahrazel spoke to them. It was not a cold night, but I could see that the humans had built themselves a fire. They were sitting miserably around it, making very little sound, hunched shapes against the flames. The earth looked raw where the stakes of the fence had been punched into it. Behind the enclosure I could see the outlines of the soldiers' buildings against the sky, sounds of merriment and music reaching me from the open windows.

Gahrazel beckoned me over. He was speaking to two tall hara, resplendent in dull leather of deepest black. Gahrazel's voice was low and confident. 'Can you get one of them to come over? I've never seen a human close to.'

We approached the fence. If only I did not feel so small and nervous. A voice behind me, one of the guards. 'Get one to the fence? Do you think they want you looking at them? How do you think we can make them do that?' He was laughing at us.

'Can't you offer them something?' Gahrazel asked indignantly. He hated to be laughed at.

'What, like throwing sugar to a horse?' the other guard joked. 'Maybe they'd prefer a few handfuls of hay. Have we any hay?'

I could only think, 'They do not know who we are. I must not be afraid.' I could not turn round and look at them, but I could feel them behind me, slightly threatening, slightly wild. The one who had first spoken to us walked forward and put his hand in Gahrazel's hair. Gahrazel did not move; I jumped for him. 'Share breath with me and I'll offer the rest of my sheh to them. It is said they crave alcohol.'

I could tell he didn't think Gahrazel would say yes. But he did not know Gahrazel. My friend, whom I trusted to keep me safe, folded his arms, wrinkled his nose and then said, 'Alright.'

'Gahrazel!' I squeaked with horror.

He looked at me like a stranger. 'Don't panic, Swift,' he said and to the guard, 'Afterwards, OK?'

I thought, Ah, this is a trick, and partially relaxed.

The guard cheerfully shouted a few insults at the humans by the fire and then made the offer of the sheh. One of them called back, 'What is this?' I had expected human voices to sound completely different to ours, like animals perhaps, but they weren't. It could have been a har calling out.

'Whoever comes to the fence gets the sheh! Two of our citizens want to have a look at you!'

'We are not animals!' an angry voice shouted back, but two of them stood up and came towards the fence. I was almost too scared to look. I was afraid of their difference, but one of the guards laughed and said, 'Kids!'

Their appearance was dreadful, but not alien. We could look like that, if we were half starved and filthy, dressed in rags with ragged spirit. I could smell them and it was the stink of stale bodies and wretchedness. They were young, but I could not guess what age or whether they were male or female. (Was the difference apparent on the surface?) Their arms were thin like flesh-covered sticks, hands like paws on the fence. Only their eyes showed any sign of brightness and there I saw the strength of humanity, the instinct to fight until weakness or death prevents it. One of them put its fingers through the slats and said, 'Sheh!'

The guard looked at Gahrazel. 'They are little more than children,' he said, 'but probably ten years older than you. This one's a female.' He poked through the rails with the butt of his gun. The female did not move but reached towards us with her eyes. Perhaps sheh could ease her misery, perhaps she craved numbness more than anything. For that she would let us make fun of her; us, in our fine clothes, flaunting our clean, well-fed bodies before her poverty. For a moment she looked me in the eye and I was nearly physically sick. For the first time in my life, I felt truly ashamed. We should not be here. I could see myself tearing down the fence. I could see it so clearly, but all I did was lower my eyes.

'Where have you come from?' I heard Gahrazel ask.

'We are from nowhere,' she answered in a clear, high voice. 'We having nothing; you know this. We are nothing to Varrs!'

'The Gelaming!' the other human, a male, said suddenly and the female turned on him like lightning and pummelled him with her fists.

'Shut up!' she cried. The male backed away, panting.

'They're going to kill us,' he said, pointing through the fence with a shaking hand.

'Will you?' the girl asked, pressing her face against the slats. 'Are you going to do that?'

'We might!' The guards laughed.

'Oh, we are nothing!' she screeched, shaking the fence.

'The beast will come! The beast will come!' her companion raved madly.

'That's enough!' One of the guards slapped the fence with his gun. The humans hissed like animals and withdrew a few paces. A bottle of sheh landed in the dirt at their feet. I was surprised that the guard had kept his word. The female leaned down, picked up the bottle and wiped it, strangely fastidious, on her ragged clothes. I found myself against the fence with my mouth open. I said, 'Female.' She looked at me. 'What is your name?' I asked.

She smiled, and nodded, almost imperceptibly. 'Bryony.' They both turned back to the fire.

'Wait!' I called. Their pale faces stared at me through the darkness, but they would not come back to the fence. I wanted to ask, How much do you hate us? How much? Something foolish. I wanted them to say something bad to me. I wanted to say, 'I am different.' They walked away. Gahrazel touched me on the shoulder.

'The guards are called Leef and Chelone,' he said. 'They have more sheh in their rooms, and the guard is changing now. They're going off duty. Come on.'

'No, I think we should go back now,' I said, uncertainly.

Gahrazel laughed. 'Are you joking? Go back alone then! My adventure does not end here!'

He knew I would not go back alone.

Their rooms were in a house shared by several other hara. A splendid creature, dressed in blue and gold, opened the door to us. His face was heavily painted, jewellery hung heavily from his throat and ears. 'Hostling stock,' Gahrazel whispered to me confidentially. 'Only the best for your father's warriors!'

We were offered sheh in crystal glasses. The painted har served the drinks and then left the room. It was a sumptuous salon, all comforts provided for. I was desperate to get home but too scared to do anything but stay by Gahrazel. Chelone unlaced his leathers and shook the creases from the linen shirt he wore beneath. 'I am hot,' he said. 'Later, I must remove these as well.' He stroked his black-clad thigh and Gahrazel laughed. Leef told me to sit down and I balanced myself on the edge of a chair. I felt my presence invaded the room; I was not supposed to be there and the room knew that but the guards did not. Leef asked me how old I was and I told him. He looked over his shoulder at Gahrazel sitting next to Chelone on the couch and back again. 'Where do you live?'

'I ... somewhere ...' I shrugged helplessly. At the time I was more afraid of Terzian's wrath than what the soldiers could do to me. All I could imagine was these strangers telling Terzian what we had done. Shaking with a cold I could not feel, I drank some of the sheh. It was rougher than the drink I was used to. Leef took the cup off me when I winced.

'I think you're too young to be out taking sheh off strange hara,' he said.

Why must they always laugh at us? I wondered angrily.

Leef leaned against the wall and stared at me. All my limbs felt enormous. I know the way back, I thought. There is no reason why I should stay here. I know the way back. I will leave Gahrazel. The door seemed a hundred miles away. When I stood up, Leef put his hand on my arm. Apprehension turned to terror in my heart. I was so young, but would that be important to him? Meat cutting ... I looked at Gahrazel, frantic, but he did not notice. He had his arms round Chelone's neck, his mouth on Chelone's mouth; I felt queasy watching them. Leef's hand slipped under my hair. I froze.

'You're afraid,' he said. 'Don't be.' He tried to pull me against him. I could not resist; he was much stronger than me. With my head against his chest, my body shuddering as he stroked my back, I spoke the only words that could save me, 'I am Swift. I am Terzian's son.'

Leef hesitated for only a moment before he virtually threw me away from him. 'Terzian's son!' His eyes rolled upwards. He laughed. 'Do they know where you are?'

'No,' I said miserably, close to tears. 'No!' I wanted to make the growling noise and run, but snared by shame, I only backed slowly towards the door. Leef watched me speculatively. Then he shook his head and reached for the sheh bottle. My fingers touched the glossy wooden panels of the door and then I was in the hall, running towards the main entrance, and outside, gulping air, hurrying as if the devil's own hounds were on my heels. Someone shouted out as I ran past the humans' enclosure, perhaps one of the other guards stood up, but then there was only cruel laughter and the dark mouth of the avenue that led back to Forever. My mind kept repeating, 'What if ... what if ...' and I growled and growled and growled.

Half a mile up the road, my chest aching, I slowed to a wobbly walk. Damn Gahrazel! I thought furiously. I shall never speak to him again! Never! Some moments later, I heard the pounding of hooves on the gravel behind me and slipped in among the trees at the side of the road. 'No-one can see me, no-one,' I chanted under my breath and leaned against one of the smooth trunks. Looking up, I stared through the waving branches at the stars and the dark, dark sky. Up there are eyes, I thought and felt the warmth of a tear escape my blinking eyes. Am I safe? Am I? How far is it back to Forever? Do I have to go past anyone? When the horse slowed down and snorted, I dropped to my knees and pressed my face against the tree. Will I die? I thought. Somebody touched my shoulder and I turned and snarled and lashed out with my hands.

'Hey!' the shape snapped and I knew it was Leef, that he had followed me, and though I was Terzian's son, I was in the dark, alone and helpless, and if I was dead I could say nothing.

'Don't touch me!' I screeched.

'Don't hit me!' Leef said, laughing. 'Stop it! If you are who you say you are, you have nothing to fear, do you?' His voice was not threatening. I stopped striking out.

'That's better,' he said. 'Now, my lord Terzian will not thank me for letting his beloved son roam the streets of Galhea all alone, will he?' He took my hands in his own. 'Come on, I'll escort you home.'

'Don't tell him!' I cried, pulling away. 'Please don't!'

He laughed again. 'It might be dangerous for me not to,' he said reasonably. 'If this was ever found out ... well!'

'It won't be!' I pleaded desperately. 'Please, it won't be. Just let me go. Go away. Forget you saw me. Please!'

He thought about my fear. 'Don't be foolish, get on the horse!' His voice was sharp. When I wouldn't move, he sighed. 'Alright, alright, I won't say anything to anybody. Not a soul. Just come with me, *please*.'

He held me in front of him on the saddle and we cantered back along the avenue, all the trees rushing past us in a blur. At the gates of Forever he said, 'What possessed you to do this?'

'I only wanted to see the humans,' I said. 'My father wouldn't let me.'

His hand tightened on my waist a little. 'Humans, was it! Your friend didn't seem very interested in them. He seemed more interested in Chelone.'

'Yes,' I agreed quietly.

'I wouldn't go wandering with him at night if I were you,' he said. 'At least, not for a while ... God, Terzian! You must be brave!'

'No,' I said. 'Can I get down now?'

He hesitated a moment and then said, 'What a pity. Alright, off you get!' When I stood on the ground, he added, 'I'll watch you for a while, OK?'

I nodded, and because I was safe again, I remembered and asked, 'The humans, will they be killed?'

'Killed? I doubt it, not yet. We need the labour.'

'Labour?'

'A nice way of saying slavery,' he said. 'But never mind that! Start walking up that drive, now!'

I smiled at him shakily. 'Thank you, Leef,' I said and slipped between the gates of Forever. Soon the dark limbs of the trees hid him from me. I looked back twice. I could hear the horse snorting and stamping by the gates, but I could not see him.

Next morning, I went early to the kitchen. Yarrow was surprised to see me before breakfast. Our meal was already prepared, waiting to be taken to the dining-room. Yarrow was now concentrating on lunch. 'Yarrow,' I said, walking around his huge, worn table. 'How often I've heard you complain you do not have enough staff! Always you complain the house is not kept up as well as it might be.' Yarrow looked at me suspiciously, still slicing vegetables at the speed of light.

'And what is this to you?' he asked.

I shrugged carelessly, watching him. 'Oh, nothing really. I was just wondering; I might be concerned for you.' I picked up a crisp finger of raw potato and chewed it thoughtfully. 'Yarrow?'

'Now what?' He stopped slicing, pushing back his hair, which he always tried to tie back, always unsuccessfully.

'I need you to do something for me.'

'Do something ...' Yarrow repeated ominously.

'What do you think of humans?' It was one of our cook's privileges that he could virtually say what he liked to any member of the household, even Terzian himself to a certain degree. Cobweb said it was because Yarrow was an artist and the best cook we could ever possibly hope to get. He was young and he sometimes got too drunk, but even if our tempers often got sick of him, our stomachs were in love with him. Now he narrowed his green eyes at me and said, 'Why?'

'If the opportunity presented itself, would you have them working for you?' I asked carefully.

Yarrow sighed and went back to his slicing. 'Do I like the sound of this? I think not!'

'But *would* you?' I insisted.

'What, do you mean preparing food?' He wrinkled his nose. 'No, I don't think so. Would you eat it? They are different from us. As for working about the house, I don't know. They're not supposed to be trustworthy and the fact that they loathe Wraeth-thu must be taken into account. Why, Swift, what is all this?'

Now I would have to trust him. First making him swear not to tell anyone, I told him about the humans in the town, that they might be killed, that I wanted him to get round my father and have two of them brought to the house. 'There is only one person who can get his own way with Terzian over something like this, and that is you,' I said.

Yarrow was flattered. 'Mmm, maybe. Are you sure you wouldn't prefer another puppy instead? Mareta will be having kittens again soon. Won't a dog or a cat be less trouble than humans?'

'I don't want them as pets,' I said. 'I feel sorry for them.'

'Really! This is worrying, Swift. How did you get to see them anyway? How do you know about them?' I smiled and shook my head.

'I just know, that's all. Will you do it?'

'They are children?'

'Yes ... well, not that old.' I walked around the table once more and put my arms around him. 'Yarrow, if you do this, I will love you forever, I promise!'

'Ha! Love me, will you?' he said and laughed, and by that I knew that he'd agree.

'One of them is named Bryony,' I told him. 'One of the guards will know. His name is Leef.'

'Leef!' Yarrow exploded, obviously knowing more about Leef's reputation than I did. 'Swift, what have you been up to?'

'Hush!' I said. 'Nothing. See my father after breakfast. I shall be especially well behaved to soften him up.'

It was a tribute to Yarrow's powers of persuasion and my father's fear of upsetting Yarrow that within two days, Yarrow and two of his staff went into the town to choose human slaves to work at Forever. I was a little worried that Leef would not cooperate. After all, he would be afraid that my father might find out that he had spoken to me in the dark, and thought of me as older than I was and put his warm, forbidden hands on my waist when we were on the moving horse. He might say, 'Terzian's son? What are you talking about?' and laugh. There was a very good chance he might do that and then Yarrow might bring the wrong humans back to the house. Not that it mattered, I suppose, a charitable act was a charitable act, whoever it was that benefited, but I was particularly interested in those two.

I had been ignoring Gahrazel very thoroughly for the past two days and Swithe and Moswell could not understand what was going on. Gahrazel had said the next morning, 'Look, Swift, I'm sorry that —' But I had not let him finish and had walked away, head in air.

Cobweb said, 'Have you and Gahrazel quarrelled, Swift?'

I just shrugged and said, 'He's changed.'

Cobweb smiled and touched my hair. 'Poor little Swift,' he said and went back to his painting.

One evening, I went to see Cal in his room and, even though he looked even more tired than usual, told him all about it. He laughed. 'Oh, Swift, all that trouble, all that secrecy! If you wanted to see humans, I'd have taken you myself, in daylight even!' and I thought, Of course, why didn't I think of that?

'Cal, do you like my father?' I asked, knowing he would have taken me to Galhea because he cared so little what Terzian might think.

'Your father is a complicated har,' Cal said obliquely.

'But do you like him?'

'Like him ... like him ...?' Cal tapped his lips with a pencil, thinking, his eyes glowing like coals in dark, ravaged sockets. 'I think perhaps I do. I don't dislike him, certainly. Pass me that green pen, Swift, will you?'

'Can I read what you're writing, Cal?'

'No,' he said.

Yarrow spoke to me about the humans. 'I told them if they tried to run away, or steal anything, or not work hard, I'd have Ithiel slit their throats,' he said. 'Their names are Bryony and Peter and they are brother and sister.' He told me that the rest of the staff were rather pleased about the new arrivals because it meant that all the most shunned, arduous or unpleasant tasks could be allotted to them.

I wondered whether the humans were pleased that they had been saved from death or working for someone worse than Yarrow, who, although he exacted hard work from his staff, was never deliberately cruel. He might treat the humans differently, of course. When they had first arrived, Terzian had told everyone about it at dinnertime. 'Yarrow is behaving strangely,' he said. 'He's asked for human slaves! Cobweb, do you think that latest batch of sheh was tainted or something?'

Gahrazel looked at me slyly while everyone laughed politely at Terzian's joke. Cal saw me going red and said, 'Well, Terzian, this does dispel an illusion! There was I thinking that the only human you'd tolerate within a mile of your august presence was a dead one.'

Terzian's responsive laugh was a little strained for some reason. Cobweb refused even to smile.

'Oh, you know how Yarrow is,' Terzian said. 'We suffer his whims. No doubt he'll get sick of trying to discipline them and get rid of them.'

'We must examine carefully then all the meat we are served in future,' Cobweb remarked drily and I saw Cal look at him. Did Cal ever tell the truth? I wondered.

A few days afterwards, my father was summoned north by Ponclast and we all looked forward to a relaxing few weeks while he was away. I thought the humans were quite attractive once they were cleaned up. Good food and comfort would restore their flesh. I was glad that they did not appear to recognize me. Yarrow suddenly found jobs for them to do that had been building up for ages. There was a cupboardful of linen to be repaired and all the silver and brassware needed a good polish. His racks of herbs needed labelling; the list was endless. Sometimes we could hear Bryony singing while she worked, that strange, high, female sound. Perhaps they were not too unhappy. Once, when I went into the kitchen, she was sitting by the hearth with Mareta on her lap, peeling vegetables (so Yarrow had relented about the food). She looked up and said, 'You are one of the pure-born, I can tell.' Then she said, 'The Varrs live differently to how we imagined.'

I was quite surprised that she dared to speak to me, and without any shyness, too. 'And how did you imagine it?' I asked.

'Oh, we thought that with all the killing and because you have no craft, you'd live like pigs!'

'You're not afraid of us, are you?'

'No,' she said. 'I'm not afraid of anything any more. This house is like a palace and you're all like people from a story. Peter and I thought Cobweb was a woman at first. Will they incept my brother, do you think?' She gave me a dazzling smile.

'I don't know.' I was not sure what she meant. 'You don't seem to mind being here; do you?'

'No, I don't mind being here. Isn't it strange? Our tormentors

83

are now our saviours. We were foolish to get caught, though. The winter made us foolish.'

'Where were you going?'

She didn't answer for a moment. 'Oh, south,' she said finally.

'Are there humans in the south?'

'Not many.' She had finished the vegetables and carried them over to the sink. It looked so natural, the sunlight coming in through the window onto her face, the brightness splashing from the taps over her hands, as if she had always lived here in this man's house that Wraeththu had taken for themselves. Her face was shiny and she pushed back her hair. 'You don't seem much like your father,' she said. (They must have been asking who I was, then.)

'They say I resemble my hostling more,' I replied, missing her point.

'Hostling,' she said and laughed. 'I can't remember my mother. It must be really odd having two fathers!'

'I don't. I have a father and a hostling.'

'Oh, I know. It's just that Wraeththu look more like males to us. Strange males, like angels and elves and demons all mixed up together. Some of them are angels, some of them are demons. In the north, there are more demons than angels, that's for sure!' She carried the cleaned vegetables back to the stove and began dropping them into a saucepan.

'This was once a man's house,' I said.

'This was once a man's world,' she replied. I could imagine Cobweb saying that.

'I don't think you're that different from us,' I said.

'Perhaps not, but you're supposed to be. Our father (his name was Steven), he said that Wraeththu came into the world because men and women had forgotten how to open their eyes properly. I was younger when he said that and I didn't understand. He said it in church and everyone was angry with him and after that, the Wraeththu came, and they took away our homes. They only killed the ones that tried to fight them; they were not one of the very bad tribes. My father spoke to the Wraeththu, he wanted answers, and sometimes people would throw stones at us because of it. But it wasn't too bad until the Varrs came on their black horses and the Wraeththu began to fight. Things happened ... we knew we had to leave.'

'Wraeththu fighting *each other*?' I asked in a small voice.

She looked at me strangely. 'Well, yes. Varrs kill nearly everything, don't they?'

'Not here.'

'Well, you're all Varrs here, aren't you? And I suppose you're a sort of prince and you haven't killed anybody at all yet, have you?'

'Cobweb said ...' I began and then couldn't continue. I had been about to say that Cobweb said that to kill was an extremely bad magic and one for which I would have to pay dearly if I ever did it. Just to wish someone dead was bad. But I couldn't say it because Bryony had seen Wraeththu kill Wraeththu and Wraeththu kill men and saying it was pointless. Bryony had seen all this, yet she could still sing and be happy. She had no proper home and had lost most of her family, yet still she smiled. I thought she must be very strong.

'Swift,' she said. 'Can we be friends?'

I looked up startled. 'Don't you know your position?' I asked sharply, not really offended but just surprised.

She nodded. 'Yes, I know my position, but I also know that I owe you my life. That's why I know I can suggest it.'

'You *do* recognize me!'

She smiled. 'How could I fail to do that? When I first saw you, I saw a girl and a boy superimposed over each other with the most wonderful eyes I had ever seen. I felt your shame. When you asked my name, I knew. I only had to wait and then Yarrow came. I want to thank you. We never thought we'd find someone like you this far north.'

I was too embarrassed to speak.

'Friends?' she said.

I nodded. 'Bryony, what is the beast?'

Her face clouded. 'What do you mean?'

'You know, your brother said it, when I first saw you. He said, "The beast will come." What did he mean?'

She looked at me hard and I could see she didn't want to answer.

'It is just evil,' she said.

But it was more than that and I didn't learn its form for a long time.

One day, hara came to the house with Ithiel and one of them was Leef. It was early summer and the weather was already very warm. I didn't know where they had been, or what they were doing at Forever, but they were very dusty. Leef had stripped to the waist and was washing himself at the pump in the stableyard. Gahrazel and I had just finished lessons; we were going into the house for tea with Swithe wandering behind. I stopped and looked at Leef, intrigued by his lean, tanned body. He sensed he was being watched and looked up. 'Oh, it's you!' he said. 'Been wandering among the common people again recently, have you?'

I looked around nervously but the others had gone inside and no-one was listening. I couldn't think of anything to say to him and yet I wanted to; it was very strange.

'Have you still got those humans here?' he asked, and I nodded.

'Yes, I can't understand it, they seem quite happy.'

Leef laughed in a not altogether pleasant way. 'Wait until you see the world outside, son of Terzian. Maybe then you'll understand only too well!'

I wished it was not always so obvious that I knew so little about the world. If I felt strong, it always happened that I was made to look foolish and it kept me in a childlike state. I wanted experience. I wanted to stand up and say to someone, 'Oh, one day you will understand,' complete and smug with my own special knowledge. I was the only person I knew that never did that. Leef put his shirt back on, but left it open. Now, most of Ithiel's guard affected the fashion of wearing their hair long at the back while still kept short over the crown. Leef tore the band from his hair with a grimace and scratched it loose. Was it a sign of growing up, I wondered, that he fascinated me? Yet if I dared to nurture any fantasies about him, I was too young to realize them, and by the time I was old enough, perhaps he wouldn't be around any more or would still see me as a spindly harling. Uncomfortable thoughts like that seemed to be springing into my head with uncontrollable regularity nowadays. Leef was no longer paying me any attention. I said, 'One of the humans told me that up north Wraeththu are fighting Wraeththu. Is that true?'

'Why don't you ask your father?' he replied, and stung by a shame so deep I could not understand it, I turned away and ran back to the house.

That evening, Cal did not come to eat with us. After the meal, I went to his room and found him lying on the bed, staring up at the ceiling. 'What's wrong?' I asked. 'Don't you want anything to eat?' He turned his head in his lazy, Cal way and looked at me with his lazy, Cal eyes.

'Maybe I don't feel too well,' he admitted. I sat next to him on the bed and put my hand on his face. He flinched so slightly, I barely noticed it.

'Do you hurt?'

'My head's black inside,' he said.

'I could read to you,' I offered cautiously.

He sighed. 'No ...'

I didn't want to leave him. To me he was like an injured wild animal that had been brought into the house. I couldn't understand him, it seemed unlikely we could heal him properly, he didn't really belong here, yet still I did not want to open the door and let him out. Half of me thought, Only what's outside can heal him. I was not exactly right about that.

Inspired by a memory of infant sickness, I said, 'Turn over.'

'Why?'

'You'll see. Something Cobweb used to do when I felt ill.'

Sighing, reluctantly, he turned onto his stomach and I lifted his shirt and pushed it up above his shoulders. He laughed and said, 'Swift?'

'Hush, now listen. I will draw you a story.' His skin was hot beneath my fingers as I began a tale of creatures living in the dark and eating only sticks and mud.

'Do they hate the light?' Cal asked sleepily.

'But of course!' I answered. 'Here is the big stone they use to block the entrance to their tunnel.'

'It is my story you're telling then!'

87

'No, they are ugly creatures. They have little sense of humour and they don't know how to write.'

'How do you judge ugliness?' Cal asked suddenly, half turning over and looking at me.

I shrugged. 'I don't know. When you can't bear to look at something, I suppose, or worse ...'

Cal shook his head. 'No! You can't see true ugliness,' he murmured and his eyes looked past me. 'It is on the inside. It is always hidden ...' Our eyes locked. 'Always!'

'Cal ...' I said softly and he replied, 'No, no,' just as softly. What was he denying? He looked dazed, almost delirious, turning his head this way and that on the pillow.

'What can I do?'

'I'm being attacked.'

'But there's no-one here!'

'There's no-one here. Look! Look!'

It was on my mind to fetch Swithe or even Gahrazel. I was afraid. 'What is it, Cal? What is it?' I shook him, and his hand crept beneath his pillow.

'I'm being attacked,' he said and pulled something out to show me. A card. On the card someone lies prone in the mud pierced by ten swords. A divining card and one of evil omen. Only one person would put that there. I took it from him and tore it to pieces. He watched impassively. We said nothing. His face twitched and he pressed himself into the pillows. His voice was muffled. 'Draw me another story until I fall asleep,' he said.

The next day, as it was the end of the week, we had no lessons, and Gahrazel and I went out into the garden to talk. I had eventually come to forgive him for the incident in Galhea although I still harboured a prudish disapproval of his behaviour. We never talked about it. It was a strange day, hot and close. The kind of day that makes you nervous and I could taste it clearly. It tasted salty and sour. 'There will be a storm later,' I said. Gahrazel rolled onto his back on the grass, looking lovely and wild and secretive. Sometimes I could not control my jealousy of him, although our relationship did not appear to have changed that much since his Feybraiha.

'I want to stretch and stretch and stretch!' Gahrazel cried.

'You!' I snorted. 'All the secrets of the world are yours!'

He laughed and sat up. 'You are growing up to be another Cobweb,' he said.

'What? Because I shall be a dark and wondrous beauty, or because I shall be slightly mad?'

'Oh, both, I think. Definitely!'

We saw Peter come into the garden and start digging around in the flowerbeds. Gahrazel called to him and demanded that he bring us refreshment because it was so hot. I knew Peter disliked talking to hara or even being near them. Gahrazel enjoyed making him uncomfortable.

'Peter could be har,' Gahrazel said.

'Could he? How?' I hoped Gahrazel was not making fun of me.

'Like our fathers, like Cobweb, like everyone,' Gahrazel replied, in a reasonable voice that was not the slightest bit mocking. 'Do you think Wraeththu came from nowhere? Most of them were human once.'

'Oh, I know that!' I said scornfully. 'How, though? How do they do it?'

'It's our blood,' Gahrazel explained, stroking the blue vein just visible on the inside of his arm. 'It makes humans become like us. Male humans develop female parts as well. It can't work the other way. I saw it once at home.'

'But how do they change? Is it really possible?'

Gahrazel laughed. 'Give Peter a cup of your blood. Let's see!'

I shuddered. 'Ugh, no. Gahrazel, you're disgusting!'

When Peter brought our drinks out, Gahrazel laughed because he would not look at us. I felt embarrassed. I did not want the humans to hate us.

'There may be thunder,' I said, squinting at the deceptive sky.

'And great tearing gouts of lightning!' Gahrazel added enthusiastically. By lunchtime, the sky had become green and boiling.

Looking back, I can't decide whether it was the tension of the approaching storm or some kind of presentiment that made me so jumpy. I could barely eat my lunch. My head was full of strange,

89

high-pitched sounds that I could not hear properly. Sometimes, ghostlike zigzags of light would flit across my vision. Cobweb ate daintily as usual, but I could feel the power in him and he scared me. I kept thinking of the Ten of Swords. A black sky, blood and despair. Gahrazel chatted with our tutors, sensing nothing.

After lunch, I went to my room and sat on the window seat. Vague growling echoed deeply in the sky from the east and the air was very still, as if holding its breath. The eerie green light outside made the garden darker, untamed and sentient. I pressed my face against the cool glass, feeling my heart flutter in my throat, the sound of blood in my ears and the dull pain that echoed it. Something is going to happen, I thought, and with that acknowl-edgement, another thing, shapeless and wild, released its terrifying grip on me. I opened up and let it flow into me; the power of the storm and something else, something more controlled and yet less understandable. My body shook, my throat was dry.

Outside, a white shape flickered through the gloom, passing beneath the mantle of the evergreens, into the darkness that lay beyond, towards the lake, towards the summerhouse, out in the living air. My skin prickled. Was it someone? Was it? While my mind still seemed to hover at the window, my body launched itself across the room, out of the door, down the corridor, dark and silent, down the stairs, towards the outside. Beyond the door, in the garden, the air was still hot, yet moist and scented. I ran into the trees, not looking back, sure-footed. I could see the white shape ahead of me. It was not running or even hurrying. By the time it reached the summerhouse, I had slowed to match its pace, and I could see that it was Cal.

A crooked finger of light snaked across the sky, flashing off panes of glass, off Cal's hair, off the water through the trees. The ground beneath my feet was moss. I crept towards the summer-house and Cal opened the door. Was I so totally silent that he did not hear me? Inside, the summerhouse was strangely dark. There was a shallow stone basin in there, full of water, where orange fish lived among the lilies. It was in the centre of the summerhouse. A stone animal curved uncomfortably out of the water. It was a fountain, but it was not turned on. Seated on the edge of the basin, holding something in his hands, on his lap, looking more lovely, more pale, more smoky, more deadly than I had ever seen him, was Cobweb.

I stood in the doorway and watched Cal walk towards him, his feet barely lifting, his head hanging. Cobweb looked only at him. If he knew I was there, I was of no importance and no hindrance. Cal stopped moving. Cobweb stood up. Cal looked around him, as if suddenly unsure of where he was or how he had got there. My sorcerer hostling smiled. 'I am pleased you came,' he said.

Cal looked confused; he said nothing.

'I knew you would come back one day,' Cobweb continued in a conversational tone and he began to walk, around and around the basin pool. 'I knew this, as I know many things. I know *you*, Cal, perhaps better than you know yourself. I have never liked what I have seen.' He stopped and hugged closer to him the secret he held in his hands. 'Sometimes when I look at you, Cal, when you sit at my table, drinking from my crystal goblets, using my silver knives and forks, with my Terzian's heart on your plate, I think to myself, "There is blood on his hands," and I can even see it. It is thick, dark blood. Blood from somewhere deep; lifeblood. And I can't help wondering how it came to be there. Can you tell me perhaps?'

I looked at Cal. His face was grey, his body strained and tense as wire, shaking as if it would break. Cobweb would wind him tighter and tighter, and then … a single touch would … I think Cal tried to speak. He made a noise. Cobweb laughed.

'It seems to me that you are no longer beautiful, Cal. Look into the water. See how I have brought all the foul ugliness that is within you to the surface. Look …' His slim, pale arm gestured towards the pool. His hair, unbound, was like creepers of ivy. I thought, I should stop this, shouldn't I? But how? I could no longer feel my hand where it gripped the doorpost.

Cobweb spoke again, so low, I could barely hear it. It was a lover's voice, caressing, reassuring. 'I will make you remember, Cal,' he said. 'Will you thank me for it, I wonder?' He paused and tapped his lips thoughtfully. 'The past, the webs, the fragments, all there. Like a locked chest full of treasures.'

Cal tried to shake his head. 'No,' he croaked, but he could not move.

Cobweb revealed what he held to his breast. He held it up and in the green light I could see liquid in glass, moving slowly, like thick waves on a tiny sea. There was a mark on my hostling's arm, a thin smear of dried blood. Cobweb's eyes flashed. Lightning outside; lightning within. From his lips came words that hurt my ears, that I could hear and that were without sound. He raised his arm, higher. The mark on his skin cracked as if a great force from within had burst its seal. A single drop of red peered from the whiteness and began slowly to investigate the length of his arm. I tried to run forward, but it was too slow, as if all the world had become too slow. A hundred visions of my hostling's arm flickered down to the lip of the stone basin, a sound like a soul in torment, splintering, laughter; shards of light spinning outwards. My slow hand had closed on Cal's arm and it was cold and shuddering. Cobweb saw me and in an infinite space of time, recognition stripped the triumph from his face and made it anger. He screeched. He raised his arm. I tried to pull Cal away, but it was too late. Red lightning arced across the room, splashing down on Cal's face, his clothes, the floor behind him.

For a second, for an hour, there was only stillness and the phantom of a booming sound in the sky outside. Then the infant patter of raindrops. I think I said, 'Cal ...' or I thought it. Cobweb stared at him, his dark eyes immense, the whites of them showing all around.

Cal raised his hand. He looked at it almost inquisitively. He touched the redness on the front of his shirt, rubbed it between finger and thumb, sniffed it, tasted it. He looked at Cobweb, puzzled ... for a moment. Then he looked at his hand again, it was wet and scarlet, and it started to shake. Cobweb and I were held in stasis while the terrible thing happened, while the thunder crashed in Cal's head and the lightning spurted out of his eyes. He threw back his head and the howling raised the hair on my head. His hands flew to his face. They *clawed*.

I was crying; I couldn't help it. I screamed, 'Cobweb! Cobweb!' helplessly, impotently.

My hostling did not even look at me. His voice was hoarse, his clothes, his hair seemed to billow around him. 'Know yourself, Cal!' he snarled. 'Know yourself! You are evil and death, the lord of lies!'

Cal twitched as if the lightning had coursed right into him. His face was the face of a demon, twisted, gaping. Through the glass above, the sky crawled with fingers of light.

'Go to the elements!' Cobweb screamed and Cal was blown past me, a scrap of flesh, light as air, into the rain, into the thunder, and my hostling laughed. 'Not even all the hosts of Heaven can save him from himself!'

I heard it in my head as I ran out into the rain. Whether Cobweb had actually spoken it, I could not be sure.

Lightning had carved a great, seeping, pale gash in one of the gnarled yew trees by the lake. Perhaps at the same moment as the lightning struck, Cal's shuttered mind had opened up to him. I walked to the water and looked around me, still sobbing, tears and rain on my face. I was dazed, unsure of what had happened except that Cobweb's insane jealousy had been appeased. I called Cal's name, not really expecting an answer. Thunder was my only reply. I was soaked to the skin, my hair flat to my head. Cobweb would wait in the summerhouse until the rain stopped.

I knelt in the soft, damp earth at the water's edge. Last year's dead reeds had not yet been cleared away. Among the stronger, greener shafts they juddered beneath the firing-squad bullets of the rain. I looked across the water, towards the half-tumbled temple folly that nestled into the trees on the other side. I could see a patch of white there. Before I realized what I was doing, I had started wading out into the water, mud and reeds swallowing my legs. Splashing, panicking, I turned round, waded back and scrambled round the sucking banks towards the stones.

He lay among the grey, licheny rocks as if he had been thrown there, his shirt torn off, his skin filthy with leaf mold and dirt, scratched and bleeding. I hurled myself towards him, wrenching my ankle, feeling the arrow of pain shoot up my leg. 'Cal!' It was a scream.

He moved feebly. He curled away from me and put his arms around his head. I was so relieved to find him alive, I tried to pull his hands away, but he pushed me back and hit my face. 'Fuck off, Varr brat!' he snarled, but I am sure he did not really know who I was.

I thought I would know madness when I saw it. The face that looked at me was not mad. There was anger, pain, despair, but also frightening sanity. 'I'm sorry,' I said feebly.

He sneered at my tears. 'Get out of here!' He tried to lift himself and his face creased with pain. He punched the rock. 'Get out of here!'

I put my arms round my knees and howled. Cal said nothing more. I didn't even know if he was watching me. After a while, I lifted my head and he was sitting with his knees up, his elbows on his knees, the heels of his hands pressed into his eyes. 'Cal,' I said again, hopelessly.

After a moment, his hands dropped and he looked at me. It seemed he was saying, 'Go on, look at me. This is grief. I weep real tears and only I have the right to.'

'You're all dirty,' I said in a small, husky voice. Cal swallowed and blinked.

'Swift.' It was just a whisper.

'Yes?' Only the leaves dripped around us. Long, pointed, shiny leaves. It was still dark, but the rain was stopping. Cal's face was a pale glow. He was filthy and haggard, attenuated, perhaps the ultimate evil, and yet ... Can this be? I wondered.

'Swift,' he said again and again I answered, 'Yes ...'

'I never really forgot everything you know, at least ... I don't think so.' He held out one hand and looked at the water. 'Little monster, little friend, come here, sit beside the lord of lies. I shall tell you such tales ...' I did not move and he turned his face towards me and smiled. 'Please don't be afraid of me; that's absurd!'

Scrambling, I tumbled over the stones down to him and came to rest against his cold side. He put his arm around me. 'Cobweb —' I began, but he put his other hand over my face and I could smell the rich, dark earth smell.

'No,' he said, 'don't try to apologize for him. He was only doing something he thought was right, and he may *be* right...' Whatever result my hostling had hoped to achieve, I did not think it was this. Perhaps Cobweb thought that Cal was dead, destroyed by magic or by his own hand.

'Swift, you must understand, I don't think I am consciously wicked, but I have done wicked things. Some of them nobody knows about, but others, they have driven me across the land, this way and that, always wandering...' He sighed and closed his eyes. 'What brought me back here? What?' His fingers squeezed my arm. 'I must admit, my travels have brought me to good places sometimes, where good things can happen, things that can ... touch me somehow. I'm here for a reason. What is it? Oh, Swift, you are the special one here, I think.'

'Me?' I could not follow his ramblings. What did he mean?

'You remind me of someone I once knew,' he said. 'Not in looks, certainly, for there is too much of Cobweb in you, but that crazy, totally misguided, idealistic, childish view of things, *that* is very familiar to me. Very.' He sighed and looked at me. Part of my soul seemed to melt right out of me into the ground. 'This is the part of the picture story where I draw my confession on your skin, I suppose.'

'You don't have to,' I said quickly, for I was afraid of hearing it.

'But there *is* only you!' he said. 'Who else could I tell? I have to tell someone, don't I? That's the way things happen, isn't it? Now I've regained the burden of my lost memory, I have to share it with someone.'

'Terzian will be back soon,' I said, glumly.

Cal laughed. 'Oh, Terzian!' He leaned his head back against the rock and I stared at his throat because it looked so long. 'Terzian,' Cal continued, in a thoughtful tone. 'My confession would bore him. He is not here to absolve me, no, not that. I've been out of my mind and out of my body, now I'm back again. If I returned to Galhea because of him ...' He trailed off and smiled secretively.

'I'm cold,' I grumbled. Cal snickered and I wondered, if like Cobweb, he could see into my mind. His free hand cupped my neck.

'Little Swift,' he said.

95

'Let's go back to the house,' I suggested, afraid that he was laughing at me.

'In a moment,' Cal replied and before I could blink, he had me thoroughly in his arms and his mouth was on my own and my mind was full of red and black and rushing air. It was like dreams. I could see flames, only beyond the flames was a field of golden corn caressed by sunlight. I could smell it through the fire. I was not afraid. After a moment, it returned to merely flesh on flesh and the aftertaste of his tongue, which was like fresh apples. He put his lips against my closed eyes and held me to him.

'I once dreamed of you,' I said. 'In the dream you made me speak your name.'

Cal rested his chin on the top of my head. 'Did I?' he said.

We did not speak of what had happened in the summerhouse. I did not know how badly he had been hurt, but I had realized his strength was immeasurable, perhaps more so in spirit than in body. He was cut and bruised, but his injuries appeared to be only superficial; a scraped elbow, scratched shoulders. I wanted to lick his blood, I wanted to be like him. We walked back to the house.

I was afraid of meeting Cobweb, but Cal wasn't bothered about that at all. 'So let him see me. What harm can he possibly do me now?' When he first stood up, Cal had complained of dizziness but by the time we walked in through the back door of Forever, he had completely recovered. The house was full of the smell of fruit cooking and I could hear Gahrazel's laughter coming from the drawing-room. Sunlight filled the hall; the storm had passed us. I followed Cal into his room. 'Just wait here while I take a bath,' he said.

After a while, I plucked up the courage to go over to his desk and look at the papers lying on it. If I thought I'd find answers, I was wrong. I could understand nothing of what he'd written. It was complete gibberish, but dark in mood and disquieting. It was inevitable that he should come back into the room, a towel round his waist, rubbing his hair with another, and catch me red-handed, but he did not seem to mind.

'If you were older,' he said, 'we'd have taken that bath together.'

I looked away. 'But I'm not.'

'No. I forget how old you are sometimes; you look much older. I'm sorry, it must have been confusing for you.' He sat down on the bed.

'You mean what happened at the lake?' I asked, hesitantly.

'Yes, the legendary, essentially Wraeththu sharing of breath. Don't tell your father. It was very impulsive of me, and no doubt very corrupting.'

(Don't tell your father, he said. Of course not. No. That part of Cal, the hands, the lips, the eyes, that was reserved for Terzian alone. I have not enough to offer; I am empty.) I tried to smile and watched him stand up and stretch. Magnificent, and forever beyond me. I turned to the window.

'I don't understand you, Cal. How come you always spring back like this? Nothing bad ever seems to affect you.'

He shrugged. 'Oh, I wouldn't say that. But I'm not self-indulgent, if that's what you mean. Anyway, as I said before, I don't think I'd really lost my memory. Cobweb just made me face things and it was for the best. I'm glad that he did now.'

I had to smile at that. 'Cobweb will be furious. None of that was supposed to help you, you know.'

'But it did.' He looked over his shoulder into the mirror and examined his back.

'You're incredible.'

'Years of effort have gone into that effect,' he said and winked at me.

He went back into the bathroom to dress and I sat at his desk. Soon I laughed out loud. Perhaps we were still at the lake; perhaps this was just an illusion and we were still melded mouth to mouth, living dreams. (If I think hard enough, can I make it true?) Cal walked up behind me, but he didn't touch me. I had the absurd feeling that he never would again, but at that moment, I felt too intoxicated to care.

'What are you laughing at?' he asked.

I shrugged helplessly; I couldn't explain.

'Pellaz is dead,' he said.

I turned in the seat and looked at him. 'Dead?' Cal saw what I was thinking and shook his head quickly, frowning.

'No, no, *I* didn't kill him. That's not the death the incomparable Cobweb saw around me. Let's sit down together, Swift. I want to talk to you.

'You are virgin in every conceivable way,' he said. 'Untouched, unmarked. Incredible really, when you think that you're a Varr and Terzian's son at that, but then, he's always looked after his own. Pell and I noticed that when we were here before. The Varrs are cattle and Terzian is the big, black bull!' Cal told me something of how he had met Pellaz, who had been unhar at the time, totally human. 'He seemed about the same age as you then, but of course probably eight or nine years older.' I learned about the Nahir-Nuri whose blood had made Pellaz har, whose name was Thiede. My skin prickled. I remembered my father speaking of him. Cal's eyes seemed to go black when he talked of Thiede. 'It was he who murdered Pell!'

'You *saw*?!'

Cal shook his head. 'You don't understand. I saw Pell die, and the person who did it, but it wasn't Thiede who fired the bullet. He's too clever for that, but I do *know*.'

'Why would he want to kill Pell?' I asked.

Cal laughed bitterly. 'Why? Oh, who can understand Thiede's reasons for doing things? One day I shall know the reason. Unfortunately (and here it comes, Swift), I killed the one person who could have told me. That's the blood your charming hostling sees dripping from my hands all over the dinner table.'

I looked at his hands, but I could not see death in them. They were the hands of love, if anything. 'Beautiful, aren't they?' he said, lifting them up. I knew that; I had felt them upon me.

'Were you in love with Pell?' I asked. Perhaps that was impertinent, but I had to know. Cal did not hesitate.

'When someone says they are madly in love, there is no more fitting description for it. Madness, yes. It is worse than dying to lose it. It's like having your brains unravelled and squashed back into your head the wrong way. I loved him, I still do, very much.' He thumped the bed with the flat of his hand and smiled and sighed. 'Of course, out there, in the wonderful real world, love is an outlawed concept. Pell had a teacher once upon a time. His name was Orien, he was my friend; I killed him. It took me a long time to get Pell to unlearn all the pious things Orien taught him about love.'

'I don't understand,' I said.

'No, of course you don't. Let me illustrate it. Your hostling is in love with Terzian and then I come along and Cobweb is so scared of losing Terzian that he wants to kill me, or at least drive me insane. Now Wraeththu don't like that kind of thing; it's messy. The real Wraeththu that is. We're supposed to exist sublimely together, scorning the passions of jealousy, seeking aruna as a spiritual exercise and beaming with tranquillity over everyone. It's a horrendous idea! So dull.'

'Are all Wraeththu like that except for us?'

'Mostly, I suppose they're scared of becoming too much like men, yet you are pure-born and born with the ability to love. That proves they're wrong, doesn't it? OK, so my heart isn't exactly overflowing with positive feelings, but I *do* know what I'm talking about.'

'I don't think I do,' I confessed.

He laughed at me. 'It *is* gibberish, isn't it? How can I illustrate it?' He twisted his mouth in thought. 'Ah yes. You'll have to pretend. Imagine we are Gelaming and this is Immanion, not Gahlea. Immanion is the first city of Almagabra; the Gelaming capital, if you like. For a start, Cobweb would have welcomed me with open arms, delighted to have someone to smother with concern, and by now, he would be very worried that I'm not taking aruna with Terzian yet. He would want me to. In fact, I'd probably be sleeping with both of them by now. That's the difference.'

'And that's bad?!'

'You don't understand,' he said. 'I'm not saying it is; I'm just explaining the difference. The thing I hate about the Gelaming and their kind is their hypocrisy. They can't be perfect; it's not possible. All that fawning niceness turns my stomach.'

'Does that mean you prefer evil?' I asked in a small voice.

'What?! Oh!' He sighed and closed his eyes. 'What the fuck am I talking about? It's so complicated. Today, I remembered. My beloved and one of my best friends are dead. One murder I had to watch helplessly, the other was by my own hand. Do you know what I did? We argued, I hit him, he went away. Does a sane har cool down after an argument and go after the other person and apologize, seeking comfort, take aruna with them and then murder them in cold blood? Does a sane person do that? God knows! I don't. They are good people, they are knowledge-seekers and I'm just a dangerous crazy!'

'What did you argue about?' I asked.

He was looking around the room. He was remembering.

'Cal?'

'I think,' he said slowly, 'I think that Orien watched Pell drift into some kind of trap because he thought that as Thiede was Nahir-Nuri, everything he did must be right. If Pell was to die, then that was right as well. I think Orien could have warned us, a long time before Pell was in danger.'

For that, Cal had sentenced him to death.

It was starting to get dark. We stretched out on the bed and were silent for a while. There was one more question to be asked. I waited until the room was at peace.

'Tell me about my father, Cal.'

He did not open his eyes. 'I can't, Swift.' The tone of his voice chilled me.

'Why not?'

He shook his head. 'I just can't. Decisions have been made. My decision is to stay here …'

'A lot of hara hate him, don't they, even here, like Swithe.' I hoped to prompt him, but he would not respond.

'The Varrs are hated everywhere. Let me tell you about Varrs.'

'Is there a difference?'

'In this case, yes.'

I already knew it was us versus them; the timeless formula. Cal told me that the Gelaming are the peacemakers, who want only to restore harmony to the world (did the world ever have it, I wonder), while my own tribe, the Varrs, just want to own it. Varrs kill everything, and what makes it worse is that they enjoy doing it. Apparently, it wouldn't be such a bad thing if they killed with distaste. Cal hadn't been there, but he'd heard that northernmost Megalithica (the stronghold of Ponclast) had been reduced to a scorched wasteland, punctuated only by ruined cities and stark fortresses. Obviously, the Gelaming were concerned that once the Varrs had exhausted Megalithica, they would turn their attention upon the east, the countries across the ocean, Almagabra in particular. More than assuaging the oppressed minorities of our country, I suspected that the Gelaming were, in fact, worried by eventual invasion of their own territories. It explained a lot.

Cal was scathing about my tutor. 'Swithe is an intellectual. He takes your father's money while privately deploring his obsessions. I despise him.'

'Yet you talk to him, often.'

'Yes,' he admitted, 'but it doesn't stop me thinking he should leave here and go to the Gelaming. He's living a lie if he doesn't.'

'What about you, Cal?' I asked. 'What are your beliefs?'

'I don't care,' he answered. 'I just hope I'm with the winning side when it's all over!'

I lay down again on the bed, in the creeping twilight, and let the silence form around us and thought, Out there …? No more than that. Why couldn't I understand? Why couldn't it become real in my mind? I had no fear, yet I knew that the Gelaming were here already, only to the south of us, and they had come to take our lands away from us. So near, and they had magic … The name of peace. Would it be soon? No, I couldn't imagine it. Tomorrow would dawn fragrant with the smells of yesterday, until tomorrow becomes yesterday and so on. Nothing changes in Forever, nothing. Something had happened to me. It seemed that Cobweb's storm magic had opened up my mind as much as Cal's, but in a different way. I stared into the darkness, I felt powerful, my body brimmed with a nameless joy that was sharpened by sadness. That night I had the first dream.

Before dinner, I went to see Cobweb. I left Cal asleep on the bed and walked slowly to my hostling's room. My mind was still buzzing. It was as if I was afraid of something I'd forgotten about, that could come back to me at any moment. Cobweb opened the door to me; we looked at each other. He reached out and touched me lightly on the face, the arm, the chest. I knew what he was thinking.

'I thought I'd lost you,' he said. I shook my head and went past him into the room. He observed me carefully, alert for changes.

'Swift, don't be taken in.' So, he was prepared to be magnanimous, perhaps recriminations would come later.

'Then tell me the truth!'

'About what?'

'I don't know!' He watched me sit down miserably on the end of his bed. Did he know about my father, the secrets? He must do. What were they?

'You shouldn't have seen that this afternoon,' he said, incapable of controlling the cold that crept into his voice.

'I had to.'

'Cal is stronger than I thought,' he conceded reluctantly.

'Perhaps he is just different to how you thought.'

'I'm not beaten yet,' my hostling said.

The first dream:

I am drowning. There is water in my mouth, but I am calm. There is no pain. Through the water, I can see something shining, far away. Two lights. That is all. I woke up laughing.

CHAPTER

5

Shrinking out of touch
Belief in magic,
Of a power over zenith
Asphyxiation of the lesser legerdamain.

Two days later, Terzian returned from the north, with a face and a mood like thunder. His only welcome to me, as I lurked conspicuously in the hall, was a kind of surly growl. He stalked into the house, trailing bewildered hara in dusty uniforms, and bellowed for Cobweb, going directly to his room and slamming the door. Some moments after, my hostling ran through the hall and up the stairs, two at a time. We saw neither of them until the next morning.

It was from Ithiel that Gahrazel and I learned the reason for my father's ill humour. The talks with Ponclast had not gone well. Apparently, Ponclast had attacked the other Varrish leaders for their lack of foresight. He had ridiculed them for abandoning the powers inherent in our race. For some time, he had been grooming his own occult abilities and now was the time to fight fire with fire. The fire of the Gelaming was magic, the power of the mind, will pitted against will. Then he began to speak of a tribe that dwelled in the southern desert, the Kakkahaar. The tales of their art and cunning were widespread, and it was professed they had no love of Gelaming. Ponclast spoke carefully, each word chosen to instil fear into the hearts of his generals. As the Varrs stood now, the Gelaming would defeat them effortlessly, for the Varr's powers had been neglected, but with the Kakkahaar as Varrish allies, the invader would not find such an easy defeat. 'I propose,' Ponclast boomed, 'that without delay, representatives are sent south to contact the kakkahaar, with a view to combining our strength!' He delivered this final statement with gusto and sat down.

For some moments, the other Varrs had not moved to speak, only whispering among themselves. It had been Terzian who had eventually stood up and I could imagine vividly all eyes turning towards him. It was no secret how highly Ponclast valued Terzian and most hara would have expected Terzian's opinion to sway the vote. It must have been a hushed moment as he arranged his notes to speak. How would the Varrs' brightest star react to Ponclast's suggestion? From the moment he opened his mouth, Terzian lost no time in vehemently protesting against Ponclast's idea. Eloquent as ever, he said that he understood that different methods of warfare would have to be employed against the Gelaming, even to the extent of reassessing the worth of the effect of magic (the sarcasm would not have been missed there!), but he could only stress that in his opinion any alliance with such as the Kakkahaar would simply prove disastrous. The Kakkahaar had always been regarded with the highest suspicion by my father and his supporters. He reminded Ponclast that this was not the first time that an alliance with them had been suggested. As before, he could only urge that this proposition be abandoned. The Kakkahaar could not be trusted and it was not inconceivable that they might already have some arrangement with Thiede. 'Both tribes are sorcerous,' Terzian said. 'How simple it would be for us to trust the Kakkahaar, have them privy to our plans, only to find ourselves in the midst of battle with our powers deserting us, with the Gelaming embracing the Kakkahaar triumphantly! I cannot support such a foolish intention!'

Ponclast must have been expecting Terzian's opposition. He had let the clamour die down before rising from his seat. My father had sat down again, staring at the table. Ponclast began by arguing reasonably that the Kakkahaar would never be allies of the Gelaming for the simple reason that Kakkahaar stood for everything that the Gelaming deplored. True, they were both masters of the occult, but their approach to it was entirely different. The Kakkahaar were not a large tribe. Ponclast thought that they would welcome an alliance with the Varrs. 'Standing alone, both tribes are too weak to resist Thiede's advances, but together we can combine the physical might of the Varrs with the occult strength of the Kakkahaar. To an intelligent person it is obvious; this is our only chance!'

Ponclast had sat down again amid a burst of cheering. He had given the Varrs hope. Terzian could offer nothing better. No doubt my father's face had been black with fury. He would probably have stormed out of the hall. It was not often that his peers questioned his judgement. Ponclast had insulted his intelligence. Ponclast had won. Emissaries from the Varrs would ride south to contact the Kakkahaar. This in itself would be a hazardous venture. No-one was exactly sure how widespread the Gelaming were in the south. Many of the Varrish agents who had been sent to investigate had not yet returned. It was likely that the Gelaming had intercepted them.

Ithiel said that after the meeting, Ponclast had spent many hours arguing with Terzian alone. He must have been very persuasive. When the time came for my father to ride back to Galhea he had reluctantly conceded his support to Ponclast's action. Their farewells had been frosty, however.

'The Kakkahaar are dark creatures,' Ithiel said ominously. 'I, for one, would never trust them. They care for no-one's welfare but their own.'

'A concept alien to the Varrs, no doubt,' Gahrazel said acidly.

'For all we know, they might already be strong enough to protect themselves from attack,' Ithiel continued, oblivious of Gahrazel's remark. 'Why should they want to assist us?'

It was shortly after this that Terzian informed Gahrazel that the time had come for Gahrazel's instruction in caste progression. Perhaps this was another thing that he and Ponclast had discussed. Among other tribes, notably those further south, this would involve rigorous and protracted spiritual training, but for a Varr it meant becoming acquainted with the regalia of warfare, the gun, the blade and the stomach required to perform the act of killing. I knew Gahrazel was far from happy about this and I sympathized deeply. To progress to the next level of his caste, he would not only have to learn how to fight, but how to survive in the wild, and, perhaps worst of all, how to endure pain. Further progressions would involve concentration of these activities and to reach a higher caste, that of Ulani, Gahrazel would have to kill. Now, for three days a week, Gahrazel was taken to the training yards of the warriors in Galhea and I continued my lessons alone. Swithe made one or two tight-lipped comments disparaging to the Varrs, while Moswell intoned that soon Gahrazel would be truly adult and that being able to take a turn at aruna was nothing to do with it.

Missing Gahrazel's company on those days when he was away, I took to spending more time with Bryony in the kitchen. I feared Terzian's disapproval of this, but he had much more pressing matters on his mind at that time. The humans had been warmly accepted by the other household staff, mainly, I suppose, because of their youth, together with the fact that they were willing workers. They were survivors, and somewhat manipulative in their charms, I think. It continually surprised me how alike our two races were (sometimes I forgot that Bryony wasn't har); our thought processes seemed entirely similar. Before, I had been taught to think very differently. As far as I could see, the main contrast between us was entirely biological, the division of male and female in the human. Bryony explained to me that it was more than that. 'Wraeththu don't grow old like we do,' she said and then explained it in more detail. I found this hard to believe. Looking at her tanned, healthy face, I found it impossible to imagine her shrivelling up until she died. 'You are much stronger than we are,' she said. 'Not just physically, but in your resistance to disease and the control you have over your emotions. Less fear, more confidence. Mankind was always plagued by self-doubt.'

Peter never joined in our conversations. He was a loner and shunned contact with everyone but Bryony. He was sixteen years old and feared that my father would force him to become har. I couldn't understand his terror, knowing as I did about the shrivelling-up process. 'Once, every man who was unhar and under the age of eighteen was incepted by Wraeththu if he was caught,'

Bryony told me. 'Now, they don't seem to bother about it as much. Since hara like you have been born, I suppose. They don't need to steal human children any more.'

Her attitude puzzled me. Humans who became har were the fortunate ones, that was clear. Why should her brother be a slave when he could be made har, ageless and beautiful? Bryony could not answer me when I pointed this out. After a while she said, 'I'm not saying I agree with Peter, but it's his life, isn't it? Perhaps it's fear of the unknown ... Our time is over, we know that. Wraeth-thu is the only future. If I had the choice, I know what I'd do, but of course, I don't.'

One thing I learned from Bryony without her telling me, is that there are really three races upon the Earth, Wraeththu, Man, and Woman. I think that out of the three, men are the odd ones out. Manliness is the side within ourselves that causes us most trouble. It is the fire principle, while feminity is the water principle. Water is magic, mystery and passivity. Fire is war, aggression and activity. Marriage of the two principles should produce a perfect, rational being: Wraeththu. Perfect theories are rarely perfect when put into practice, I thought cynically.

High summer unfolded around us. Terzian went away again to visit other Varr settlements in the east, and I arranged for Bryony to become friends with Cobweb, as I thought it would be good for both of them. My hostling had never harboured any particularly strong feeling against humans; he accepted all living creatures as individuals and I felt the girl was similar to him in many ways. He enjoyed sharing his wisdom with her, for she was eager to learn, and also found in her an ally in the house when everyone else had got fed up with being hostile to Cal. Bryony was frightened of Cal. Now, our soirées in the drawing-room had expanded to include both of them, which created amusing atmospheres. Cobweb would pretend that Cal wasn't there, which was an art form in itself. Once I overheard Cal say to him, 'I should thank you. You have made me well.' Cobweb didn't even blink, only turning to speak to Moswell with a smile. Cal caught my eye and smiled ruefully. I disliked the way Cal looked at my hostling. I disliked even more the way Cal would not hate him, because I didn't understand it, and I thought I should have done.

One day, Gahrazel asked me to walk with him in the garden, something we had not done together for some time. He seemed preoccupied or troubled, but I was not as close to him as I had been so he could not speak as freely as once he might. 'Peter is going to be incepted,' he said. I looked at him aghast.

'What has changed his mind?' I asked. We were both aware of Peter's previous sentiments about becoming har.

'I have talked to him,' Gahrazel replied rather frostily.

'I did not notice.'

'You don't know everything about me, Swift!' he said.

After this, I tried to observe more carefully the transactions between my friend and Bryony's brother. Why hadn't I noticed before? Both of them nurtured very strong anti-Varr feelings, for different reasons, but it gave them a common ground. Gahrazel didn't care what happened to mankind; he cared only what happened to Gahrazel-kind. Peter was naturally bitter and restless, but since coming to Forever, perhaps he had come to understand more about what Wraeththu was. Perhaps he realized it was really absurd not to become har. However, I thought that Gahrazel's and Peter's encouragement of each other's hatreds was dangerous. They lived in Terzian's house, after all.

When I talked to Bryony about it, she told me that her brother had gradually withdrawn from her. 'He is on fire and it is a strange fire that he cannot share with me,' she said. 'He is like the picture Cobweb showed me on one of his divining cards. Spears falling to earth and their descent is accelerating. He seeks a goal, but I fear for him.'

'I didn't notice him becoming friendly with Gahrazel,' I said.

'No,' she agreed. 'The secrecy of that is disquieting.'

'You're worried about him,' I said.

She smiled a small, sad smile. 'As I said before, he has his own life to lead. He is flying away from me. I can do nothing.'

So many of the inhabitants of Forever seemed disloyal to Terzian. There was Swithe with his wordy, arm-waving speeches,

Gahrazel and Peter, hot in their fervour, and Cal, who didn't care about anything; we were not a large household either. One day, I felt sure, Terzian would stand still for long enough to notice, and then there'd be trouble.

When Terzian came home again, he consented without interest to Peter's inception. Swithe, who had taken charge of the proceedings, asked Cal to donate his blood. Cal laughed when he told me about it, but, I noticed wryly, he had still said yes. It was not the choice I would have made in Swithe's position. Cal was a wonder to me, but because so much of him was beneath the surface to be seen by no-one, I would have been very wary of putting his vital fluids into anyone. I am sure Peter had a worse time than was usual because of it. He fasted for a day before Swithe conducted the inception ceremony in the garden, beneath the canopy of the trees. I thought Cal looked like a white, shimmering spirit. His veins were blue and luminous, the life within them dark and poisonous. We could hear Peter's screams throughout the house for days afterwards.

It took a fortnight for him to recover fully, instead of the usual three days, but at the end of that time, his mutation was successful. Now he had a dash of Cal's weirdness to complement his revolutionary zeal. Gahrazel initiated him into the mysteries of aruna and the first time I saw them afterwards, Peter's eyes were full of prophecies that made me shiver. I saw Fate there, with a sharp knife held against the thread of life. Never again, that I know of, did Peter go to visit his sister in the kitchens.

At the end of the summer, we learned that the Kakkahaar, after some initial reticence, had agreed to combine their strength with the Varrs. High-ranking Kakkahaar would be travelling north for talks with Ponclast and his Nahir-Nuri. Because of its convenient position, Galhea had been chosen as the location for the meeting. Forever was an ideal conference centre. Suddenly, the house was full of strange and important hara, and extra staff had to be engaged from Galhea to cope with it. Terzian surprised everybody by promoting Bryony to the position of housekeeper, which she said was to appease his guilt, while I thought it was more because

Terzian realized the girl was capable of organizing the household to show him off in the best possible light. All the visitors thought it was a great novelty, as if we had a talking dog, walking on its hind legs, carrying the keys to the house and telling the staff what to do. I know that many of the northerners gave her tips in the form of money or trinkets, which was especially unusual, for the northerners had even less tolerance of humankind than most. Bryony affected an air of competent superiority, and what jealousy she might have aroused among the household staff was dealt with discreetly.

The Kakkahaar rode Arabian steeds. Cobweb and I watched their arrival from my bedroom window. I was intrigued by their strange, swirling clothes and their dark, interesting faces. 'Their hair is so long!' Cobweb exclaimed, touching his own with a nervous hand.

Meals were always laid out in the main hall now, although Cobweb and I often ate in the kitchen with the staff. We did not like formality and were also wary of the Kakkahaar. I had been eager to meet them at first, but when their leader, Lianvis, turned his stone desert eyes upon me, I was chilled to the bone. I could see why Terzian was opposed to the alliance. I did not know the name for the darkness that came from their eyes, but I felt it touch me, and the touch was cold.

The Kakkahaar claimed to have had no contact with the Gelaming yet. They had monitored the invaders setting up their headquarters, but had made no overtures towards them, either conciliatory or hostile. No-one seemed quite sure what the Gelaming were actually doing, but their arrival had certainly caused a stir, and in more than one way. Reports were coming through that other, weaker tribes and even straggling bands of humans had been slowly, but consistently, making their way to the Gelaming base. Many people, human and hara alike, had very good reason to hate the Varrs in Megalithica, and it was only natural that they should seek the protection of the Gelaming. However, the Varr leaders were not oblivious to the fact that a lot of stragglers eventually become one large unit, all feeling righteous, and vengeful towards the Varrs. Security was increased across Varrish territories and anyone found making their way south was killed without question.

Bryony told me that her own people had been on their way to seek sanctuary with the Gelaming when Ithiel's patrol had intercepted them. Only a few months later and they would have been shot on sight.

Ithiel told me that he didn't think anything would happen until the new year. Preparing a campaign takes time. Our house was never free of strangers nowadays. Sometimes I would come across a strange har wandering round the corridors, lost. If it was a Kakkahaar, I would turn the other way and run.

I don't think anyone was too pleased to learn that we would have Kakkahaar with us for Festival. Most of them had returned south once the weather became colder (including their horrifying leader), but two of them had been elected to stay behind. I felt quite sorry for them because they found the cold so disagreeable, but I could never feel at ease with them. I always got the feeling they could eat you whole, if they had a mind to. Still, nothing could really dampen the mounting feeling of celebration. Snow fell and the garden was transformed into its winter fairyland of frozen marble. The house was fragrant with the smells of spice and cooking; the shelves in the larder were filled with Yarrow's creations.

One day, out of an upstairs window, I saw Leef in the stableyard, laughing with other hara, their breath like smoke on the air. I put on my coat and went down to speak with him. It pleased me that he did not recognize me at first. This meant I must have changed since we had last met. 'You are taller,' he said. I asked if he would have to go south in the spring and he replied, 'I expect so. Nobody seems to know what exactly is going on at the moment.'

'I hope you come back,' I said, realizing immediately the tactless tone of this remark. Leef smiled, and I liked the way his face changed when he did so.

'I shall be here at the house at Festival,' he said. 'I've been promoted, so that means an automatic invitation to your father's celebrations.'

'Congratulations,' I said, 'I shall look forward to seeing you.'

Leef had a faintly puzzled, amused look in his eye.

'Me too,' he said.

Events took a rather dramatic course before then, however. It was a week before Festival; each night the air was crisp with the anticipation of celebrations to come, and all the curtains and corridors seemed alive with the ghosts of songs brought back from other winters, other happiness. My father had invited a few friends up to the house, a social evening, to sample the festive sheh and for hara from the town to meet the Kakkahaar. Everyone was in high spirits; noisy hara tramping through the front door, trailing waiflike consorts, dressed in furs. Cobweb crimped my hair and gave me new clothes to wear. 'Quite the dashing young har!' he said and stroked his throat with perfume. He seemed nervous that night, and his smiles were forced.

Downstairs, among the lights and the perfumes, we were all intoxicated by a wild kind of happiness, because deep inside we knew that everything could change in our lives in the near future and our merriment was tinged by a desperate flutter of hysteria. I had not expected Leef to be there, for most of the guests were long-standing friends of Terzian's, but when I saw him standing rather awkwardly in our grand drawing-room, I knew that his presence was right and sort of preordained, suiting my teetering euphoric mood. I think I was trying to convince myself to be like Gahrazel was over Ithiel and perhaps Leef guessed something of what was on my mind, but he was not stupid enough to try and find out.

I asked him to come out with me into the hall to sit on the stairs, and he looked quickly at my father before following me through the door. I said, 'He will not mind, you know.'

'Who? What?' Leef asked and I replied, 'Terzian; that you're with me. Don't worry about it. He's not that fierce, or that bothered about what I do for that matter.'

'If you believe that, which I doubt, you are wrong,' Leef remarked, but he let himself relax a little.

We sat down on the stairs, but we were not alone. Hara seemed to be everywhere that night. Leef said, 'The atmosphere is strange. I don't feel comfortable.'

112

I thought about this. 'Perhaps you are right. I've felt strange all day but I thought it was just me.'

We looked at each other and Leef said, 'Well!'

I realized I must have changed quite a lot since the first time I had met him. Now he seemed to be nervous with me. Most of his reserve, I felt, could be blamed on who my father was.

'In the spring –' I began

'Yes, in the spring!' Leef interrupted, rather sharply. 'Not one of us is free from fear. Thiede has almost won before we even face the Gelaming. He has been cultivating his reputation for years for just this moment.'

'What, us two sitting here?'

Leef did not smile. 'Everything,' he replied. He looked at my hands resting self-consciously on my knees for several minutes before he dared to take one of them in his own. 'Pampered hands,' he said. 'Aren't you afraid that Thiede will come and make you work for a living?'

'No,' I answered. 'Does everyone think like you?'

Leef shook his head. 'I don't know. I shouldn't be talking to you like this.'

'Because of my father, I suppose! Do you really think I ever talk to him properly?'

'Don't you?'

'No, not about real things. We may discuss the condition of the meat at table, or the weather, or horses, but not much else. I think I am just a possession to him; like this house, like my hostling. Can houses or whores have opinions?'

'Swift!' Leef exclaimed, hurriedly scanning the hall to see if anyone had heard me.

'Can you deny that it is true?' I asked.

'Stop this conversation, stop it!' he said in a low but vehement voice. 'We must be happy!'

'Alright,' I agreed. It must be Cal infecting me, I thought. Perhaps I was becoming more like him, talking as he did. Was it me that had started this conversation? 'I want to find out what my father thinks of you,' I said and Leef looked at the floor and smiled. He knew what I meant by that.

Someone called my name and then Gahrazel was breathless on the stairs beside me. 'Swift!' he said excitedly. 'Come back into the drawing-room. Now!'

'Why?'

'I think it will happen tonight,' he answered mysteriously.

This was a kind of code between us. Ever since Cal's memory had been restored to him, both Gahrazel and I had been anticipating the day when Cal would give himself a shake and lower the defences he had constructed against my father. It had always seemed inevitable. We could tell that Cal was naturally a sensual creature, and, although I thought that he had grand, if futile, designs on Cobweb, Cal would one day respond to my father's advances. I could not understand what was holding him back now. Terzian had never given up, and sometimes, his subtle, essentially Terzian method of wooing became rather too blatant; through sheer desperation, I think. Everyone knew, yet my father had not become angry. Another puzzle. Being made to look foolish was not a state that Terzian normally accepted gladly.

Leef followed me reluctantly back into the drawing-room, with Gahrazel leading the way. I was suddenly angry at Gahrazel's eager curiosity, that all this was so entertaining to him. What was happening was a stately dance that had fallen into disorganization; it was not a joke.

My father was standing by the fire, leaning on the mantelpiece, caressing an empty glass, talking to the Kakkahaar. Cal was listening to Swithe on the other side of the room. Disappointed, I turned to Gahrazel. 'I thought you said that—'

'Hush,' Gahrazel interrupted, smiling, both hands on my arm. 'Just watch them; absorb the atmosphere. You'll see.' Still laughing, he sauntered away, no doubt to find a good viewpoint in the room.

'What are you up to?' Leef asked, once more nervously scanning faces.

'Oh, the Big Thing is about to happen,' I explained. Leef shook his head.

'Is it? Will it hurt?'

'Who knows!'

I looked at my father. He is lithe, I thought, and tonight he looks so young. His heavy, golden hair was falling into his eyes. He raised his hand to push it back and glanced quickly across the room. I felt that look pass straight through my body like an arrow. I did not have to turn my eyes to Cal. I felt it. My father was like a stranger, no longer familiar to me. My head began to swim and I realized I'd knocked back two glasses of sheh without noticing. Is this what it's like? I wondered. This power, this hidden fire? Is it waiting for me some day? I looked slyly at Leef. Will it really be you …?

'I've drunk too much,' I said and Leef glanced at me sharply. He was so uncomfortable; I felt sorry for him.

'Swift …' he said and I could not see all of his face, only his mouth talking or his grey eyes, but not together.

'What?'

'I want to …' He put his fingers lightly on my mouth and shook his head. 'Terzian's son!' he said and smiled.

Now it was me that felt uncomfortable. 'I want to watch my father,' I said. Leef followed me over to the sofa and we sat on the floor.

'Do you often watch your father?' he asked, wondering what kind of joke I was playing on him.

'Never!' I replied. 'Leef, have you ever *wanted* Cobweb?'

'Stop it!' Leef hissed in a low voice.

'Another thing that is Terzian's … He is smoke and ivy.'

'And you are three-quarters sheh at the moment!'

'This is how we live; we are all quite mad. Don't be annoyed with me.'

Leef shook his head and drew his mouth into a thin line.

I could see Cobweb talking to Ithiel, and his face was white and wild, his hair unbound, which always signified that he wanted to feel his own power around him. Ithiel looked as if he knew that he might have physically to restrain Cobweb before too long. Has anyone else noticed? I wondered. Desire in the air, so strong, it smelled like burning. I could feel it in my lungs, my head, behind my eyes. How can they stand it? I thought. Their need for each other is another being in the room, almost visible.

Eventually Terzian could stand it no longer. I saw him put the empty glass down slowly on the mantelpiece, rub his face, glance once more at Cal. He excused himself politely to the Kakkahaar, and began to make his way across the room, stopping to exchange brief conversation with other hara, smiling, gracious, signalling the staff to bring more drinks. As he passed me, he looked down and grinned and I grinned back; but we were strangers. I had no part in this event.

Cal was standing quite near to where Leef and I were sitting. I heard my father say to him, without deferment, 'I have been waiting for you,' and Cal's reply, 'Yes, I know.'

There was a pause, then Terzian said, 'I know what happened while I was away.'

'Of course you do, Terzian. You know everything,' Cal replied, rather coldly. 'What surprises me is that you haven't mentioned it before.'

'Hmm.'

They were so awkward with each other I began to think Gahrazel had been wrong. Leef said, 'What's the matter?' but I waved him to silence.

My father said, 'You're still afraid, aren't you?'

I could imagine Cal shrugging but I dared not look round. 'Afraid? Not exactly. Alarmed, perhaps. I expect your terms haven't changed.'

'Terms?' Terzian's voice was raised, then he remembered he was in a room full of people, some of whom had turned their heads. 'I am not so callous,' he said quietly.

'You are! You know you are.'

'*You* know how much I wanted you before. It wasn't just to sire harlings with you, perfect though they'd be ...'

'But it's part of it, Terzian. Why can't you admit that?'

'Admit it?' My father's voice was almost sad. 'You're a fine one to talk about admissions. Maybe you should admit to yourself that you're made to host sons, to sire them. You are Wraeththu. Admit that, Cal!'

Can no-one hear them? I wondered. Leef was staring at the carpet while my blood was in flames. Cobweb was a thin ghost, distant and in chains.

116

My father said, 'I would never hurt you, Cal.'

'I know that.'

'It's in your blood; you need me. It's been too long.'

'I know that ... There is one thing you must do.' I heard the steel come into his voice, but I knew, if I looked, his face would be innocent.

Sensing triumph, my father said, 'Yes, anything, anything.'

There was a brief silence and I knew that Cal was looking round the room, making sure the right people were watching.

'If you want me, you must prove it. Nothing sordid. I think I deserve the status and demand recognition of my position.'

'Cal, what are you talking about?'

'Don't laugh, Terzian. I know what your people think. Cobweb is like your queen. He's respected. I don't want anything less.'

Perhaps it was only me that knew Cal cared nothing about things like that. This was just another move in the game and, of course, Terzian would fall for it, because it was the language he understood. Cal said, 'Terzian, I want you to take me in your arms.'

'Here?'

'Now! Share breath with me, here. Let them all see. I must be equal to Cobweb, nothing less.'

'Is *that* all?'

All! I thought. Their embrace will take the form of a blade, more than one; ten. Who will lie face down on the bloody soil, pierced by swords, now? Terzian's consort, to be shamed before the elite of Galhea, that's who.

I sensed the silence fall around me and realized I had closed my eyes. I heard Leef mutter, 'Good God, look at that!' His surprise was tempered by amusement.

The first thing I saw was Ithiel, trying to hold a feral Cobweb in his arms. Cobweb, with eyes like black saucers full of obsidian fire. He made no sound, struggling silently. I could not turn to look. I stood up, Leef tried to pull me back, he made some palliative sound, but I did not listen. I went straight to the door, across the carpet, past the faces who did not see me, a hundred miles away.

In my room, alone, sitting in darkness, I licked tears from my face, listening to the noises downstairs. There was still laughter, the buzz of voices, perhaps more so than before. The tension had disappeared. I voided my mind, letting it become a great and silent blackness, and into that emptiness I formed my hostling's name. Before too long, I heard the door open behind me and light from the corridor shone into the room.

'I had to walk past your father's door,' Cobweb said.

'Already?' I asked and my hostling nodded silently. I must have been sitting alone for longer than I thought.

'You did this!' I pointed out cruelly.

Cobweb shut the door. He leaned upon the door and slid down it. I wanted to go to him, but I had no energy. I couldn't tell how I felt about anything any more. Cobweb was crouched against the wall, his hair touching the floor, beaten in so many ways.

'What is happening?' I asked the room.

'If it should happen tonight, then we shall feel it. We shall feel the soul when it comes . . .' Cobweb's voice was a whisper in my head.

I uncurled my feet from under me, touched the window with one hand. It was cold, much colder than the room.

Cobweb didn't resist when I went to help him up. He felt light, as if all his substance had drained away. I could smell moss in his hair. I led him over to my bed and he lay down on it. Standing there, I looked at the spidery, dark locks creeping over my pillows, his face that is a wood-creature's face, and I thought, So many times Terzian has stood as I am standing now and seen that lying there. Then I thought, My father is so greedy! and then, No, he is just very fortunate!

'Has the spring come already, Swift?' Cobweb asked. 'Is it all over?'

'Not for you,' I answered.

Cobweb laughed, an ugly, bitter sound. 'It is the real magic that comes from within,' he said. 'We are all under its spell. It destroys us, yet we need it . . . We should have destroyed it first. We are all tangled up, here in Galhea. We're not reaching out.'

I understood some of what he was trying to say.

'It is said we are getting caught in the same traps that men once set for themselves,' I said, and Cobweb sighed.

'We are all spiders; without the webs we cannot feed.'

'You tried to kill him, didn't you?'

Cobweb turned his head slowly on the pillow, dark and lovely as a velvet poisonous flower. 'I think my child attempts excuses for what has happened. Cal does not want Terzian. He seeks only to attack me. I need your support, Swift. Where is it?'

I fell to my knees beside the bed and took his long, cool hands in my own. 'Cobweb, it is not a question of support! You tried to kill him! You're intelligent enough to realize that this is only the most predictable of reactions. You caused it yourself. You should have let well alone.'

Cobweb threw his arms over his eyes. 'I hate him! He makes me let darkness into my soul! I want him dead!' He sat up, wild-eyed, reaching with clawed hands for my shoulders. 'Can't you see what he does to me? Worse than leaving me lonely, he extinguishes the light in me. It is a battle that sometimes I am too tired to fight and I let it come, and I let it take me over and then I hate him and wish him dead and find my hands around the things that could make him dead. He damns me!'

'No, it is you!' I cried. 'You damn yourself! It is in your head!'

Cobweb pushed me away as if I repulsed him. 'I'm going to Swithe,' he said.

'No!' I would not let him stand. 'Stay with me!'

'Why? Why should I? When I look at you, I see your father in your eyes; the same madness. You're as obsessed with that dark beast as your father is!'

I could say nothing. Immediately, 'he is right' formed in my head. I lowered my eyes and a pane of ice was between us.

'I knew it!' Cobweb growled, very quietly.

And then emotion was bursting up, like a spire of blood, through my heart. I threw myself against him, curling my arms around him, very tight.

'I love you!' I cried. His body was cold and unyielding. 'I do! I do! I swear it! I will never betray you!'

I felt his hands on my back, flexing from paws to hands to paws. I felt his leafy sigh through my hair.

'Mine,' my hostling whispered. 'Mine ... Mine!'

119

Another dream:

A voice says to me, 'It is nothing. Outside is the real Hell. This is nothing.'

I must have been crying. My head is on my knees. When I look up, there are two eyes in front of me. I cannot see the face, I say, 'Oh, I will never go outside!' and even in the dream, I know that this isn't true. I put up my hands. I shout, 'I don't know you! I don't know you!' but I want to look into those eyes forever.

That is the way of dreams; they are never logical.

CHAPTER

6

Straw in the Wind
Straw in the wind
Blowing in my dreams.
A birth in the Spring
Sinking into pillows.

So for some of us, Festival was to be devoid of merriment that year. Admittedly, the house was full of hara blissfully ignorant of the dreadful stirrings in Forever's heart, and food and drink were in plentiful supply, everyone was smiling, but there was still Cobweb's gaunt and haunted silence to face every day. Terzian chose to ignore it. For various reasons, mostly, I like to think, because of loyalty to my hostling, I decided to stop speaking to Cal. Predictably, this only made him laugh. 'Close ranks, Swift,' he said. 'The wicked seducer is loosed among you!' He knew, as we all did, that it had been Cobweb who had freed him from his fear of aruna.

At dinner, in the evening, I found that I was sitting next to Leef. He made several brave attempts at conversation and then commented drily on my sullen silence. I didn't want him to think I no longer liked him, but I was powerless to speak. I wanted to look at him helplessly, so that he might ask me what the matter was, but I could only stare at my plate. I couldn't understand myself, why I was locked in such a strange depression, and I wished desperately someone would notice it and say the right words that would release me, but Leef only sighed and turned to speak to someone sitting on his other side.

The new year had started with everyone in a sour temper, and that was a bad omen. The atmosphere did not improve when my father announced that he expected Gahrazel to accompany him to the south when the spring weather allowed it. I knew how Gahrazel felt about the approaching campaign. It wasn't that he was torn between loyalty to his tribe and loyalty to his beliefs; he just craved peace, an easy life, more than anything. He was angered by cruelty and killing appalled him. He knew Terzian was seeking to change all that about him. My father also sent Peter to work for Ithiel and we all knew that Ithiel and his staff would be remaining in Galhea when the Varrs set off to confront the Gelaming.

I had come to hate movement and rarely left the house. My sleep was often disturbed at that time by troubling dreams, whose main feature seemed to be the enigmatic eyes I had seen before. In a short time, I would celebrate my birthday. In a short time, I could expect to come of age. It was a prospect I anticipated with dread. Since Festival, I spent more and more time alone. My love was knowledge, not flesh. Swithe gave me books to read, and I virtually devoured their pages with my eyes, so eager was I to scour them for information, for answers. I learned a great deal about the world and about the past, but little about my own condition. Wraeththu had not been in existence long enough for anyone to have had the time to write serious books about our singular, wondrous estate. When I grew older, perhaps I could be one of the first to begin the analysis. That was when I started to keep notes, to write down my impressions of what was happening to us. The foundations of my life had become unsteady, the sacrosanct haven of my home soiled. Cobweb had become an icy and tragic figure, haunting the upper parts of the house or scrawling horrific, black pictures with splintered charcoal in his room. The faces he drew came into my dreams, the aftertaste of their anguish flavoured my days. Even Gahrazel had become a bitter, fevered thing. The intrigues of Forever no longer seemed to interest him and he had learned how to kill. He gave Peter a Wraeththu name, Purah. They were together always, for their days together were numbered.

All I can say of Cal is that I could only look at him with painful anger. He would look back with smiling, knowing eyes. I heard him whistling in the corridor outside my room on those nights when he would go to my father. His presence burned me, and I tried to avoid him. It was clear he felt no remorse for the pain he had brought into the house, nor that he had lost me as a friend. I could not believe that he returned my father's feeling as strongly. It was all a game to him, to pass the time, to eliminate boredom. Time and again, I told myself to hate him.

As a fitting punishment for our ignorant behaviour, Cobweb and I were the last to hear of the momentous news when it came. It happened only a few weeks after Festival and it was Bryony who told us. Cal was to host a son for Terzian; Phlaar had confirmed it. Just hearing about it made me see them together, in my father's bed, in that room. I was glad in a way, because I knew Cal would hate it. He was not made to be a hostling, no matter what my father thought.

Cobweb did not scream or rage as I expected. He took the news quite calmly, and I did not ask bewildered questions. We were quite, quite dignified, like something out of the history books. I remembered Cal once likening Cobweb to a queen and that was how I saw us now. The imprisoned queen and her son hearing news of the king's new wife; out of favour, out of mind. Cobweb and I drew closer together. I was wrapped in his ophidian hair, his inky eyes, and we caressed each other's black hearts with pungent fires and dark, whispered words. We nurtured our powers and found satisfaction in occult promises. 'We too shall host a pearl,' my hostling said, 'the blackest pearl of regret!' It was a promise that was never realized.

When the first shoots found their way up into the light and the garden stirred and stretched into the spring, we watched them leave. Black, shining horses and the finest of Varrish hara. Terzian leaned down from his horse and embraced Cal for the last time, looking up to glance at Cobweb's expressionless face as he stood on the steps of Forever. My father called to me and offered his hand, which I took. 'I shall bring you home a beautiful Gelaming slave,' he said with a smile.

I grinned back weakly. 'Good luck,' I said.

Terzian raised his hand and they turned their horses towards the gate. Cal stood near to me but I did not look at him. Terzian turned in the saddle once and waved to us, before quickening the pace to a canter. It was an impressive sight. The main body of his army would be waiting for him in the town.

Afterwards, I paused on the steps of Forever and gazed up at its worn, white walls. It seems my story has ended already, I thought wistfully. All the happiness has gone from this house. Now it is forbidding and its secrets are cruel. Now, as long ago, a woman, a daughter of man, holds the keys to its rooms. Perhaps there was only Bryony left really to care about the place. To Cobweb, Forever had taken on the ghost semblance of a ruin of stark, poking rafters; a charred remnant of a home. His touch had palpably withdrawn from the rooms. Now he claimed only the darkest corners of the garden and his own suite on the second floor.

The previous evening, I had sat in Gahrazel's room and watched him pack away his belongings, as if he would never return to Forever. He is truly adult now, I thought. His enthusiasm is contained, his fire quenched. I watched him cut off his hair and burn it. There were few times we could reach each other now. After all, I was still just a child. Perhaps I bored this new, sophiscated Gahrazel. The Varrs, the state of being Varr, had come between us.

Not long after my father and his army had gone south, Cobweb and I celebrated my birthday together. Yarrow baked a big ginger cake, but no-one came to eat it with us. We sat in my room, drank sheh, and Cobweb cut my arm with a knife to take some of my blood. He made spells for my protection and put his hand on my face and said, 'Some day soon, the animal sleeping inside you will wake up.'

I remember I made an angry, bitter noise. 'And what will happen then?' I demanded. 'What will happen when my body takes over and there is no-one to take hold of it?'

Cobweb took me in his arms. 'I would keep you as a child forever if I could,' he said.

At night, lying awake, I would think of my father and of Gahrazel, wondering what they were doing and if they thought of home. Then I would drift off to sleep and the dream presence would visit me, the wondrous eyes, the hint of alien breath. In the

124

morning I would wake afraid, but at night, in the dark, I felt comforted.

Sleeping late one morning, I was woken up by a female scream, coming from the Hall. Bryony's white face looked up at me when I leaned over the bannister, half dressed. 'Swift, come quickly!' she cried.

Cal had collapsed, half way through eating his breakfast. When I saw him, my heart missed a beat. Could he be dead? Could we be free once more? But he moved in our arms as we carried him up the stairs to his room. When we laid him on the bed, he moaned and threshed, curling and uncurling as if poisoned. Cobweb? I wondered. Someone had sent for Phlaar and I was left alone with Cal, while everyone raced around the house as if the end of the world had come. (Already he was Forever's heart.) He opened his eyes and saw me standing there. I stared back haughtily into his twisted face. We know each other now, I thought.

'Do you know what's happening to me?' he croaked.

'No,' I answered, 'but whatever it is you deserve it!' I was uncomfortable, thinking how not long ago, I would have been soothing him or stroking his face, craving his attention. It would have felt natural to go and do that now, but I controlled myself. 'How things change,' I remarked coolly, walking over to the window, so that he could not affect me. I could hear him groaning softly. When I could resist no longer and turned to look at him, he was clutching his stomach. His face was damp.

'Swift ... don't hate me ... please, not now.' I began to speak, but he rolled around and shouted, 'I need you! I need you! Swift!'

Even as I went to him, I was thinking, Surely you're strong enough to resist this?

His face was hot and wet between my hands; he was weeping. 'You are witness to a miracle,' he said, and laid his head in my lap. I put my hand on his arm where it lay across his stomach.

'What is it?' I asked.

'Life, I think,' he said.

Cal was in torment for two days while his body sought to expel the pearl that would become Terzian's son. Phlaar did not seem unduly

125

concerned about Cal's condition, and I shuddered to think that this agony was normal.

Only Cobweb had no interest in this momentous birth. Everyone else in the house was fascinated. Someone had to sit with Cal all the time as he struggled feverishly with his body. Phlaar would not risk leaving him alone, because sometimes he got violent and Phlaar was afraid he would try to damage himself. Bryony was particularly intrigued by Wraeththu birth, for the bearing of life had previously been a female prerogative to her. Near the time, when everyone was sitting up all night waiting for news, Bryony took me to the kitchens. We curled up in the darkness next to the stove, drinking strong, sweet coffee and talking of the mysteries of life. How intrigued she was (without actually saying so) about the secrets of Wraeththu physiology. I evaded her subtle questions for it was something I preferred not to think too deeply about. Not so Bryony. She explained with great candour a lot about woman kind and how their bodies worked. Then I learned about human procreation, so similar in some ways to our own, yet so different in others.

'The whole rotten business has been drastically improved in Wraeththu,' she said. 'I can see that, and it takes so little time. It's so unnoticeable. Women do not have it so easy. Oh no! We have to lumber around for months, growing and growing. It's something I've never cared for ...'

Human reproduction did seem messy to me, and how inconvenient to have to look after such a helpless creature for so long. (No teeth, no hair!) Like little rats, I thought. I had seen Mareta's kittens take milk, but it seemed inconceivable that intelligent beings could be brought up the same way. What if they were separated from their mothers? How would they survive? Did many babies die?

During those strange grey hours before the dawn it was my turn to sit with Cal. 'It will be soon,' he said to himself and clenched his fists along his sides.

'Cobweb will hate me for this,' I said, hoping to make him smile.

Cal barely recognized me and kept calling me Pell. 'I've always lied to you!' he said. 'You don't even know me, not really, but in spite of all that I've done … I do love you, Pell.'

I sat beside him. He looked weak and helpless. His body was merciless; the personality was irrelevant at this time. His mind, set free, wandered at random. 'Cal, you're a wicked, wicked person, but enchanting all the same!'

He did not hear me. 'Pell, do you remember … that time … when was it? When I found you. Oh, there's something I've always longed to tell you … about the first lie, and it's so important … I must tell you!'

I put my hands on his face. 'Hush, I'm not Pell. Be quiet.' He tried to shake free of me.

'You must hear this, you must!' he whined pettishly. 'It's important, because I mustn't lie to you any more. I want you to know everything … about Zack …'

'Zack? Who's Zack?'

'You know … have you forgotten? Years … years …' He lay back on the pillows, his eyes searching the ceiling frantically. 'I told you he was dead, didn't I? I did say that, didn't I? Well, it's not exactly … true. I don't know. Not when I went back for him … he was alive then …'

'What are you talking about?' I asked to humour him. 'Who's not dead? Pellaz?'

'*No!*' he said, as if angry with my stupidity. '*Zack*, before I met you. I ran away. I left him … I told you he was dead. It was a lie.' He closed his eyes.

Thinking he'd be quiet for a while, I fetched a damp cloth and bathed his face. His eyes flickered, half open.

'There is no-one on this earth more lovely than you,' he said, his hot hand seeking to curl itself around my wrist.

'Who, Pellaz …?' I dabbed at his temples.

'No, no, Pell's dead. I mean you, now that he's gone … it's you, even though you hate me …' He sighed. His voice sank. 'Unbind your hair, all over me. Fill me with your perfume, let me taste you …'

My hair grew only to my shoulders; I never braided it. Incensed, I threw the cloth back into the bowl of water and stood up, wrenching my wrist out of his hold.

'Why can't you see *me*?' I complained. 'I'm Swift and I'm alive and I don't hate you, at least, not at the moment.'

He looked confused. 'Oh Swift,' he said. 'Yes … Swift. I was just thinking of a time, oh, it was a long while ago, before I met Pell. I was with someone else. We were in trouble and I left him for dead. I could have helped him, but then, maybe we both would have died. I had to save myself, don't you see? I told Pell I'd hurt my arm in a fall. Look …' He took my hand and ran my fingers over the long, white scar. 'That was a lie as well. There was no fall, no. It was Zack's knife that did it. His curse and his knife thrown at me, while I saved my skin … ah well.'

At dawn he was wholly lucid, the fever had gone, but his breath came quickly. 'Fetch Phlaar!' he cried. 'Quickly!' When I reached the door, I heard his voice behind me. 'Don't come back in here, Swift.'

They took the pearl from him and it was black and gleaming with the essence of his body. I saw them carry it down the hall like a holy relic. It was tested for life and washed. I wanted to look but they made it clear I was in the way, so I wandered back to Cal's bedroom to find him lying drained and relieved among the pillows.

'So, it's over,' I said.

'Yes, it is.' After a moment, he laughed quietly to himself.

I wanted to know how much it hurt him.

'Quite a lot, I suppose,' he said, 'But the memory of pain fades so quickly. It wasn't as bad as I thought …'

'You are pleased,' I observed, conscious of a vague kind of prickly, edgy feeling within me.

'I'm pleased that it's over, certainly,' he replied, but I knew it was more than that. His eyes were alight.

Not long afterwards, they brought the pearl back to him. It appeared to have nearly doubled in size already and its surface seemed to have toughened over. Now Cal would have to incubate it with the warmth of his body. He will hate this, I thought, he hates having to lie around. But he curled himself around it like a great, contented cat and closed his eyes. I once came from a *thing* like that, I thought. It was disorientating to think about it, so I chanted three words of terrible power to empty the mind and went down into the garden to think of other things.

We had had no news of my father. Rumours reached us, of course, but we guessed that most of them were untrue. From one source we heard that the Varrs had successfully exterminated the Gelaming with little effort, the Kakkahaar allies wreaking havoc with their elemental force. From elsewhere, we heard that Terzian had been defeated and been taken prisoner, that Thiede now held him in Phaonica, subjecting him to torture, and that the Gelaming were marching on Galhea. It was said that they also possessed vehicles that ran without fuel and vomited demonic flames capable of incinerating whole cities. The Varrs had no fuel for vehicles. We knew that in the north, Ponclast had some kind of wide, black car that growled like a tiger, but his fuel conserves were precious and the car was only used on ceremonial occasions or to ferry Ponclast to executions of particular interest. Swithe told me that not all of the Earth's natural resources had been depleted, but that it would be a waste of time for us to try and go back to the old ways. 'Now is the time for Wraeththu to seek a new way, a new source of power,' he said excitedly. 'Maybe the Gelaming have already found it. The less time spent fighting and squabbling over land, the more time we have for research, for rebuilding!'

I studied hard, using books from Terzian's library, marvelling at the sparkling metal cities that men had left behind them, touching the photographs. Had it all gone forever, this world of metal and glass? Gahrazel had once told me that the land was growing back over the cities of men, that vines had dragged down the buildings that once reached towards the sky. Often, he had said, only the creepers still stood, with stems as thick as oak trunks. Inside the cage of leaves, the buildings had crumbled away already.

'Things changed rapidly during the last forty or fifty years of man's rule,' Moswell explained loftily. 'Perhaps they advanced too quickly for their own good; their minds could not keep up with their technology. They lost control so that they craved extinction and sought depravity. In truth, men became demented by ennui, unnerved by so much leisure time, driven feral by lack of money. Their brains had been neglected for centuries, their spiritual lives were barren; they could no longer create through thought. Is it any wonder they turned on each other and their environment?'

I could not accept this explanation without question. It was too easy for Moswell to stand there and say all that, but I knew he had missed so much out. I wanted to know how Wraeththu had begun and what had made us happen. Was it a Grand Design or just a grand and cynical joke, or even merely an accident? Were we fooling ourselves that we were created to inherit the Earth?

Bryony was not so confused and she talked more sense than Moswell. As she was human herself, I valued her opinions and wanted to know how she felt about what had happened to her people. Had she looked for reasons? Her father, a devoutly religious man, had thought that most men were disgusting and selfish and godless, and that Wraeththu had been sent by God to punish them for their sins. Bryony said that she shared this belief to a degree, but she was not so sure about the wholly religious aspect. Perhaps humankind had just worn itself out. Her people had been seeking the Gelaming because everyone considered them to be the Great Saviours who had come to make everything better. Gelaming were thought of as the true Wraeththu, the pure strain. The Varrs and their like were considered deviants from this. Perhaps this was true. I lacked objectivity, I know, because I had never met any Gelaming, but one thing I was sure of: I felt very strongly about anyone coming to take our lands away from us, whatever their reasons.

'But it is not your land!' Bryony protested. 'It belongs to everyone! Can't you see how wrong it is for your tribe to kill anyone they feel is weaker than themselves? They are in the position to be charitable, but no! They enjoy killing and making people suffer. They want slaves and sport ... and worse!'

I couldn't be bothered to argue. I still thought the Gelaming were interfering and hypocritical.

'You wouldn't believe some of the things I've seen,' Bryony said in a low, dark voice, 'and yet now, I work for a leader of Varrs looking after his house, feeding his family. I should be ashamed of myself!'

'Run away then!' I snapped. 'Go back to the wilderness. Take your chances there with a clear conscience!'

Bryony looked at me helplessly. 'Don't think I haven't considered that,' she said bitterly, 'But the truth is, I like it here. I've found a home. I like you all. I'm treated well and I'm trusted with a position of responsibility. What's worse is that I've earned that trust. Me, a woman! Many would see me as a traitor to my race.'

'You are like us then,' I said, 'Like Swithe, Like Gahrazel was before, like me, even. We philosophize about the state of the outside world and we argue and rant, but Forever is still our home and it keeps us safe. We don't want to go out there into the cold and *do* anything!'

'Forever is an enchanted place,' Bryony observed wryly.

Just over a week after Cal had suffered delivery of the pearl, its shell became brittle, almost transparent, and a young, mewling har burst it asunder from within and crawled out into the world. So, Terzian had missed the hatching of his new son. He could have delayed riding south to be with Cal at this time, but to a Varr war always comes before life.

I had been out with Ithiel when the great event occurred. Ithiel always took me with him when he went about his duties, for he understood how I would have to learn about the administration of Galhea. We could talk together freely now and I came to realize why my father placed so much trust in him. Ithiel was thorough and economic and diplomatic in his dealings with other hara. He always introduced me as Tiahaar Swift, never Terzian's son. That day, when we got back to Forever, in the haze of a beautiful evening, everything stained red and gold, Bryony was waiting for us on the steps of the house, peering down the drive, still wearing the long apron she was rarely seen in outside the kitchen. She had matured recently, I thought.

'Where have you been?' she asked crossly. (We had paused in an inn on the way home for refreshment.) 'You have a brother now, Swift.'

A brother. I hadn't thought of it that way before.

Cal was in the drawing room waiting for me. He didn't have the harling with him. The room was cold; it did not seem the place I had grown up in.

'Ah, Swift,' Cal said when he saw me.

'Congratulations!'

He smiled at my sarcasm. 'Would you tell Cobweb that I'd like to speak to him?'

'Do you give the orders here now, then?'

'Would you *ask* him then?'

'You're wasting your time!'

'Maybe, maybe. Just ask him.'

We looked at each other for a moment. Cal's face was inscrutable.

'Alright,' I said. 'But I'm warning you. Direct contact like this might provoke him into further unpleasantness.'

'His unpleasantness is exhilarating!' Cal replied.

Cobweb was still punishing me in subtle ways for restoring my friendship with Cal. I was not sure how he would receive my news. On hearing Cal's request, he rose from his window seat and went to the mirror. 'What for?' he asked, and it was impossible to tell whether anger or suspicion coloured his voice.

I shrugged. 'He didn't tell me, but I said it was a waste of time asking you anyway.'

Cobweb slunk over to his table and aimlessly shuffled piles of paper in his hands. He was silent, but his silence lacked character.

'What shall I tell him?' I asked. 'How shall I tell him to go to Hell?'

'He asked for me?'

'Yes. I was surprised at his nerve. Obviously, you can't see him.'

'Ah, Swift,' my hostling chided gently. 'Never presume to anticipate my actions.'

He was out of the door before I realized. I called, 'Cobweb, wait!' hearing his laughter ahead of me. He was already down the stairs by the time I looked over the bannister.

They had not really confronted each other since the incident in the summerhouse because there had always been other hara around. Now, they were nearly alone. I was unconvinced whether I was worthy of refereeing this encounter and wondered whether I had time to look for Ithiel, but I was scared to leave them. Cal was soaking up the sunset by the long windows; his hair looked red. I heard him say, 'Cobweb,' very softly.

I paused at the door. My hostling said nothing. He kept a distance between them and folded his arms, his eyes like flints.

'Thank you for coming.'

Cobweb still said nothing but I could sense his excitement.

'I want you to do something for me,' Cal said in a careful, reasonable voice.

Cobweb made a noise like an explosive snort. 'So, the thief who stole my house requires something of me, does he!' he said, which was not quite the sort of thing I would have expected him to say. Cal turned away from him, as if he could not bear the sight of all that cold dislike.

'Yes, the thief who stole your house requires a favour,' he said. There was a silence. I held my breath. Cal sat down on the edge of a chair. 'Cobweb, I'm not a fit person to bring up a child, as I'm sure you'll agree ...'

My hostling sighed through his nose. 'Somebody thinks you're entirely fit, that's obvious!'

'Yes,' Cal agreed bitterly. 'Cobweb, I want someone to care for my son, someone who'll bring him up to think in the right way. I want it to be you.'

Cobweb laughed, coldly. 'Me?'

'You've done such a good job with Swift,' Cal pointed out, somewhat ironically.

'You're mad! Can you really trust me with such a precious thing?'

'Yes,' Cal replied simply. 'There is no reason for you to hate the harling; he has never harmed you.'

'But he's half yours!'

'Half Terzian's ...'

'Half yours! I hate you!'

'I know, but I still want you to do this.'

'You're the most impossible, insane thing I've ever met!' Cobweb raved, momentarily over the top in his indignation. 'You want the child; you look after it! You took Terzian away from me

133

to achieve it! I don't even want to see the creature! I can't believe your nerve!' He turned grandly, in a swirl of braids and ribbons, and stalked towards the door.

'Cobweb,' Cal called softly. My hostling stopped. His head was up and I could see his fists clenched at his sides. 'Why did you come?'

My hostling did not turn for a moment. 'Curiosity,' he said at last.

'You liar,' Cal said, smiling, and my hostling's face twitched. He made a growling noise and stormed out, towards the stairs. 'Don't you *know* everything, Cobweb?' Cal called after him.

This was the time I learned that it is possible to argue about one thing while really meaning something completely different. Words are flexible. Tone speaks more eloquently than words. Another move in the game.

I went to see the child and he was beautiful as expected. Cal took him in his arms, which I must admit looked unnatural. 'Who could wish for better?' he asked, wondering.

'Yet you do not want to care for him,' I remarked. Cal handed the harling to me, and he squirmed in my hold, sensing my nervousness. What disquieted me most was, despite his lovely face and small, perfect limbs, cherub-pale, his sentience was still only half formed, and his eyes were filled only by a kind of animal intelligence. 'What shall you call him?' I asked.

'Perhaps I ought to wait for Terzian to come home before I decide.'

We looked at each other, but neither of us could face saying the obvious. Eventually, I thought of, 'Oh, but that could be ages yet. What are you going to call him till then?'

'I haven't thought.'

'Do you really want Cobweb to look after him?'

'I want my son to be like you,' Cal said and touched my face.

The harling reached for his hand.

Before I went down to dinner that evening, a little later than usual, Cobweb came into my room. 'Tell him yes,' he said shortly. I had to turn away so that he could not see me smiling.

'You're an enigma,' I said.

'I'm not sure if that's the word I'd use,' Cobweb replied acidly. 'I know you're laughing at me, son of my flesh, my faithful one.'

'I'm sorry, it's just ...'

'I always wanted another child,' Cobweb said, uninterested in my remark, 'but it was never ... right, never possible. I agree with Cal in that I can't stand by and watch an innocent being indoctrinated by *his* sicknesses and cruelties. The harling is your brother, part of this house, another Varrish heir. I know I'm capable of rising above personal feelings. I was trained once, not all of it has deserted me ...' He turned his lambent eyes on me. There was more, both of us knew that, but it remained unspoken.

At dinner Cal said, 'I'm sure Cobweb will feel happier now, and without guilt too. Quite an achievement on my part, I think.'

I was appalled. 'You're an absolute beast,' I said.

'No, I'm not.'

'You can't repair what you've done!'

'I don't want to ... More wine?'

'You knew Cobweb would accept, didn't you?'

'I wasn't sure, but I thought it was worth a try.'

'I can see through you,' I said uncertainly.

'Oh, can you? Do you understand my motives?'

'Implicitly!' I replied, but he didn't believe me.

Cobweb decided that the harling should be named Tyson, and baptized him into our tribe, although Swithe commented that this was a worthless practice. As soon as the child was delivered into Cobweb's care, Cal appeared to lose interest in him. Occasionally, pricked more by my reminders than conscience, he would come into the nursery that had seen generations of human children grow up and the first harish childhood, mine, and half-heartedly perform acts of what he supposed was affection. Tyson always looked wary and confused. In just a few weeks, he had learned to wobble around, careering off furniture, and say 'Obbeb' and 'Wift', which was how he addressed my hostling and myself. It was true that he helped to seal up the scars left in our household by recent traumas (even my nightmares began decreasing in frequency), for he possessed an inner glow of happiness that could not be affected

135

by moods on either Cal's or Cobweb's part, but could only encourage to dispel them. I could see that Cobweb unashamedly adored him from the start, perhaps convincing himself that it was indeed his own child. In the afternoons, I would lift Ty out of his bed and wake him up and breathe in his wonderful, clean smell. Now his brown eyes were beginning to fill up with an eerie, knowing wisdom. I would hold him and hug him and he would nestle against me and whisper childish nonsense into my ear. It made me want to have sons of my own. Children are miracles, the living proof of the infinite. I had been told by Cobweb that only a special, vitally intense kind of aruna can bring about conception. 'There has to be an utter mingling of souls for it to happen,' he said, and then added drily, 'Terzian has never found that easy.'

One day, a messenger rode into Galhea and some hours later the news he bore reached us at the house. The Varrs were returning home. Cobweb went pale when Ithiel told us. I caught a glimpse of the visions of terrifying injuries and death that flickered across his mind's eye. But Ithiel could soothe his fears.

It would seem that the Gelaming were trickier than we thought. The Varrs could not even reach them. This demanded more explanation and Ithiel told us that there had been strange and potent spells cast upon the country. Places once recognizable had become territories of uncharted weirdness and the army had been travelling in circles. Their supplies and morale had dwindled. There had been one or two minor skirmishes with bands of marauding humans seeking to steal guns and food, and others with hara of hostile tribes, but these had just been irritations helping to cast a veil over the whereabouts of the enemy. Eventually, sensing the rising hysteria and depression among his hara, Terzian had ordered the retreat home. Ponclast would be summoned; there would have to be further debate. The Varrs had not been expecting this.

'The Gelaming do not want to fight,' Bryony said. 'It is because they know the Varrs would have no chance. Now, do you see, Swift?'

'We won't know what really went on until Terzian gets here,' I said testily.

They returned in the mid-afternoon of a warm, glorious day. Terzian did not come up to the house for some time. I sat with Ty on the lawn and told him about his father. He would not listen, only chuckled and reached for my hair with handfuls of torn daises.

Everyone in Galhea was relieved that the army had returned alive, and there was great celebration that night. Terzian looked tired, but he managed to smile and take his new son in his arms. Tyson was frightened by all the noise and strange faces, and fretted until Cobweb came to take him away. Terzian looked after them speculatively. Leef came to find me and he looked thinner and exhausted. I suggested we went for a walk in the gardens. I was eager to question him, but waited for him to offer the information himself.

'I feel as if I've got someone to come back here to now,' he said as we walked along.

'I did think about you sometimes,' I said, which was not untrue, but there had been no sentiment involved.

'The whole thing, all that distance; it was a waste of time,' he said bitterly.

'We heard something like that,' I replied cautiously.

We had come to the lake. It looked eerie, with insects chirruping and the water shifting lazily in the darkness. I put my hand on Leef's arm, feeling his sadness.

'I really wanted to fight,' he said. 'I needed to. We all just wanted to *do* something. At night I could feel them watching us, but they never showed themselves. Terzian was furious.'

'I can imagine,' I said tartly.

'Everything got worse and worse. We crossed the great marsh Astigi but could get no further. Some of us became ill and there was the constant harassment of attacks by men and hara of small tribes. Things were always being stolen. It was so *strange*. Took a few days for us to realize what was happening. I began to recognize a tree we would pass every day, late in the afternoon. At first I thought I was mistaken, but no, we really were travelling in circles. The scouts' compass needles spun as if in a wind. Soon after that, Terzian gave the order to turn back. Every one of us was relieved ...'

137

He sighed and rubbed his hands through his hair, smiled weakly. 'You've grown again, Swift.'

I had been standing uncomfortably silent. Now I shrugged. 'Well, I have no control over it.'

'Out here, in this weird place, you look just like Cobweb.' He laughed. 'You see, I'm becoming used to magic!'

I wondered how long it would take him to get round to touching me. Leef was so hesitant, as if Terzian was always standing behind us, watching.

'I wasn't much fun at Festival, was I?' I joked.

'No, you weren't, but I know why now. It must have been very ... stressful.'

'Not compared with real things, what goes on out there.' I waved my arm vaguely at the trees.

'Perhaps not, but troubles are always relative, aren't they?'

I sat down, on the spongy moss that is always a little damp. Leef hovered at my side. 'Sit down,' I ordered. 'What's wrong with you?'

He sat. 'You know, don't you? At this moment, I want to pour torrents of my breath into you, but I have to be careful.'

'Not Terzian again!'

'It's easy for you to scoff; you don't know him in the same way that I do.'

'You must have at least shared breath with a hundred hara. Am I so different?'

He sighed. 'He may already have chosen for you.'

I shuddered. That was quite, quite possible. Terzian would probably not think of consulting me. I stood up. 'We'd better get back,' I said.

I walked to my favourite yew tree. Once it had seemed such a long way to the nearest branch. Now I could reach it easily. Hanging upside down by my knees, I could see Leef smiling at me.

'Get down,' he said.

'I feel like climbing to the top.'

'Get down, now!'

He hauled me out of the branches and we ended up rolling in the springy, sharp leaves round the base of the tree. I wanted to taste him because it had only happened to me once before and that had been Cal. I needed to compare that time with someone else. Leef's breath was all dark, beating wings and feathery darkness. It reached right into me. I broke away and said, 'Tell me how I taste.'

'Of gold,' he said huskily and sought my mouth once more, melding into me. My body felt strange. It almost hurt. It was the beginnings of desire and I was unfamiliar with it.

'You are near your time,' Leef whispered, touching my face and neck all over with his lips.

'What will it be like?' I asked.

'Like heaven,' he replied.

Terzian was worried and it was impossible not to be affected by it. Ponclast had been summoned and representatives from the Kakkahaar were expected any day. I kept trying to look at the situation objectively, to face the seriousness that might be hovering, waiting to surprise us with drastic change and discomfort at any time, but all that seemed real to me was a strange, half-waking, dreamy state where all that mattered was my own body, newly graceful, newly aware. My books were sadly neglected.

'Well, you've certainly changed your tune recently,' Swithe observed caustically, but I could see that his eyes were smiling.

The Kakkahaar, whose names were Aihah and Shune, brought us gifts from the south. Exotic, spicy sweets, aromatic with honey and bitter, pungent nuts; glass beads that changed colour in the light and dried herbs with arcane and special properties for Cobweb. I was intrigued by their strangeness, more aware of their presence than I had been before, when other Kakkahaar had visited us. They weaved and braided their thigh-length hair in convoluted styles and their eyelids were tattooed on the inside so that they never had to wear Kohl. Of course, our lack of occult development must have been held in utter contempt by these adept practitioners of magic, but it was never shown. They were always gratingly polite. Aihah obliged me with special attention and from him I learned that they were still in communication with their tribe in the desert. I realized it must involve a similar practice to the one Cobweb and I used occasionally, when our minds could touch, but how much stronger the Kakkahaars' ability must be to be able to cover so many miles. Aihah corrected me about this. 'Distance has nothing to do with it,' he said. 'We communicate *laterally*, not head on. Do you understand?'

'I'm not sure.'

'It is something like visualization. A calling, and something more.' He smiled at me. 'One day, it might be possible for you to come south and learn with us. There is much we could teach you.'

I had no doubt of that and thanked him warmly, but I couldn't imagine it ever happening.

CHAPTER

7

Seasonal Affliction
Tears of belated remorse
Swung from lashes
Worshipping manifestations within
    sexual glands,
To catapult assassins of beauty into
    erogenous zones.

I had always believed that the majority of harlings came of age in the spring, with the rising of the sap and the burst of new life. Perversely, I began to feel my Feybraiha approaching with the advent of the autumn. Since my father's return and my brief encounter with Leef in the garden, I had started to be aware of my body more than before, but that had been sort of exciting and secret, like hugging myself in private. Gradually, my advancing maturity began to get uncomfortable. Cobweb noticed it before anyone else; I had said nothing, half hoping it would all go away and I could resume my life peacefully. Blossoming sexuality raged within me like a fast-growing, strangling vine. I had no control over it. My moods swung like a great and sickening pendulum. One moment I was happy to the point of lunatic hysteria, the next plunged into a depression so black, only the thought of death could comfort me. As Swithe had once predicted, unexpected growths of hair seemed to burst from my skin overnight, beneath my arms, between my legs, and in those places the skin was hot and sore. I remembered what Gahrazel had gone through the year before and wondered whether I should talk to him about it, but ever since he had come back from the south, he had been like a stranger to me, no longer the elfin beauty with whom I had shared secrets and childish dreams, but a tall, tanned intruder that looked vaguely like a Galırazel I had once known. He looked at me with different eyes now and appeared to shun coming into the house.

Cobweb made an ointment for my skin, using some of the herbs that the Kakkahaar had brought. Aihah expressed polite interest in my coming of age and taught me some relaxation exercises to try when I felt too manic. I think Cobweb would have liked the Kakkahaar to have given me some instruction concerning aruna and its practices, but my father was against it. I never knew for sure whether Cobweb had suggested it, but sensitive as I was at that time, I guessed some of what went on behind my back. As it was, Swithe and Moswell were entrusted with my education, as usual. Cobweb knew that the Kakkahaar could have taught me much more than either of my tutors could ever know.

Swithe was the most informative, which was not surprising as Moswell could never be termed a particularly sensual creature. 'You must learn to understand your body in an adult way,' Swithe told me. 'It can no longer be simply a thing to giggle over in the dark. You must bring your sexuality to the forefront of your being and examine it carefully.'

He told me that in humankind, where the sexes had been split into two different kinds, men and women were attracted to each other because of their opposite polarities, the positive aspect of male and the negative aspect of female. 'They sought to make themselves whole through the act of copulation,' Swithe explained. 'We do not possess that confusing, desperate yearning; our desires are centred upon different aspects. As we contain both negative and positive elements within our own bodies, we can express through aruna a fusing of these elements to previously unattainable satisfaction. Men were unaware that through sex they could reach a higher form of consciousness. To us it is virtually commonplace. In the simple act of sharing breath, the minds of two hara can mingle and rise. During aruna, the manifestation of ecstasy can accomplish anything. It creates a living force that may be harnessed and used. If such an effect is desired, we call aruna Grissecon, which is aruna to perform magic. Varrs seldom practice it.'

At night, I could rarely sleep. My skin burned, the moon called me with a soft, white voice and I sought the dew-soaked coolness of the shady trees outside. One morning, at breakfast, Cal said to me, 'God, you look awful! What's the matter with you?'

Raging irritation made me run from the room, virtually in tears. Behind me, I heard Cal say sarcastically, 'Oh dear.'

Some time later, he came to my room. Swithe had obviously explained what was going on. His inquisitiveness was part ghoulishness, part concern. 'Never was puberty so grim!' he said, pulling a face, which I guessed was supposed to make me laugh. 'This must be one of the prices we pay for being so goddam perfect!'

'And what are the others?' I asked.

'One of them's learning, I suppose. A little of it is a dangerous thing, as they say. God, what a wreck you are!'

My face was red, the skin scaly, my eyes puffed and sore. It seemed to hurt me physically if anyone looked at me. Cal was interested in the concept of Feybraiha and what it entailed, but I shrank from explaining.

'So your honourable father selects some worthy har for the purpose of deflowering you,' Cal enthused while I cringed with shame. 'Who will it be, I wonder.'

'Probably Leef,' I said, surprised at a strange kind of anger that had crept into my voice. There was no way I could know whom my father would choose.

'And do you like him?'

'He's alright.'

'Is that all?' Cal laughed. 'How disappointing! I would have thought that for the first time you would have to be with someone who set your head on fire at least!'

'I've heard that soon just about anyone will be able to do that to me!' I said bitterly. I still spent a lot of time resenting the way my body was behaving, sailing happily on in the special life of its own that it was enjoying.

My little brother, Tyson, seemed more aware than most of what I was going through. He looked at me with strange, fearful eyes, bringing me presents in a pitiful, childish attempt to cheer me up. I now had two strips of rag, a pink stone and some of Cobweb's earrings (all mismatched) lined up on my windowsill. When Tyson thought I was particularly downhearted, he would grab hold of my

143

sleeve and drag me over to them, making me touch them. Perhaps Cobweb was indoctrinating him already.

One evening, the event that I had been dreading occurred. At dinner, my father said, 'Later, Swift, I want you to come to my study.' I went cold from head to toe, unable to eat my food for the hysterical beating of my heart.

He offered me a glass of sheh, diluted by cordial, leaning back against his desk, Master of Galhea, my father, lean, commanding and terrifying. I was insignificance itself, sitting there, looking up at him, glass clutched in my lap, waiting for the fateful pronouncement. Terzian seemed blissfully unaware of my discomfort. 'As you know, Swift,' he began, 'for your Feybraiha, I have to choose someone I think right for the honour of ...' (here he had the grace to falter) '... well, you've been told about it, haven't you?' He waited for me to nod. 'Good, good. Well, I have talked about this with Cobweb and he agrees with my conclusion; it seems obvious to me that the warrior har Leef should be the one.' My heart sank; I don't know why. I'd been expecting that hadn't I? Who else was there? My father looked at me strangely.

'That was why I had him promoted,' he said. 'I did hope you'd be pleased about this, Swift.'

I shrugged helplessly. My father raised one eyebrow, stroking the edge of his desk with light fingers. 'After I heard about your little escapade in Galhea with your young friend Gahrazel, I naturally assumed you had some interest in Leef ...' My squirming was enhanced by savage blushing. 'Nothing *ever* escapes my notice, Swift,' my father chided gently.

I was choked by my own silence. Terzian carried on.

'I believe at Festival time and also in the garden some weeks ago, you indulged in some – er, petty frivolities with Leef. Is this so?' He was becoming impatient with my dumb stupidity. 'Well?'

I nodded. Yes, it had been Leef. There was no-one else.

'Cobweb thinks you'll be ready in a week or two. Shall we say two weeks? I will arrange everything.' And that was it.

Sensing my dismissal, I stood up. I wanted to say to him, 'Can't you see that all this isn't just a case of "being ready in a couple of weeks" for me, as if I was only being fitted for new shoes or something? It's my body! My life!' but he had already turned his back on me, sorting through papers on his desk, and anyway, I was too scared to speak.

'Oh, Swift, on your way out, could you find the Kakkahaar for me? Tell them where I am.' He smiled wolfishly at me, but I could see he was already frowning by the time he looked back at the desk.

The weight of despair descended like a black cloud once I had closed the door behind me. Why hadn't I said anything? What could I have said? I knew Leef would be pleased and that annoyed me too. I did not dislike him, but I resented being handed over to him on a plate. It made me angry; I wanted something else, something more, but what?

When I delivered my father's message to the Kakkahaar, Aihah paused as he passed me and lifted my face with his hand. 'I would like to speak with you later,' he said.

'I'll wait for you here then,' I answered.

Cobweb was sitting by the fire, on the floor. 'It will do you good to listen to Aihah,' he said, and by that I knew that they'd been talking about me.

'What is going to happen Cobweb?' I asked, curling into his arms. 'It's all taking so long.'

'What is? Your Feybraiha? Is your head hurting you again?' He pressed his palm against my cheek.

'No, not that! That's got nothing to do with me, has it! I mean about the Gelaming.'

Cobweb sighed. 'Oh, that! I don't know, I really don't. Perhaps they are playing with us. Perhaps they really are wary of the Kakkahaar. We can only wait.'

'I wish it wasn't happening! What with that hanging over us and what my body's doing to me, sometimes I feel like … I don't know … like running or burying myself … Cobweb …' I clung to him. 'If only we could go back!'

'If only!' he agreed.

By the time Aihah came back to us, my head was pounding with the inevitable nightly headache. Just when I felt so exhausted that

145

sleep seem ineluctable, my body would wake up with a host of excruciating symptoms. I would ache and itch and boil inside. That night I wanted to cry and scratch myself raw. Aihah touched my brow. 'Come to my room,' he said and offered his hand. When I took hold of it, I felt a comforting coolness seep into my arm.

His room smelled alien, as if he had invaded it with his own scent and substance and made it Kakkahaar. I sat on the edge of the bed and he said, 'I think you should weep. You want to. There is nothing to be gained by holding it back.'

There was no way I could stop myself after that. He busied himself about the room while I lay on his bed and gave myself up to a maelstrom of howling. After a while he shook me gently. 'Here, sit up, drink this.'

'I feel wretched!' I said, sniffling into the glass.

'Of course you do,' he said softly. 'Back home we give that drink to our own harlings. It should make you feel a little better.' I had never tasted anything so strange. Later, I learned it was a distillation of the putiri plant, whose effects played a rather dramatic part in my life in the future. Aihah was critical of the way I'd been treated. 'Here in the north, hara appear to know (or care) so little about Feybraiha. I'm not surprised you're suffering. It is not something you should have to cope with alone. There's a host of things that could be done to ease your discomfort.'

'I've forgotten what it's like not to be like this!' I said.

Aihah laughed softly. 'You are so distressed,' he said. 'I don't like to see it. I don't like it at all.'

'My father has chosen for me,' I blurted, incapable of stemming the fresh tears building up inside my eyes.

'Not a welcome choice?' Aihah suggested.

I shook my head. 'Not really. I can't tell. Once I thought ...' I looked at him helplessly and he brushed my cheek with his thumb.

'Who is it now then?'

'There is no-one.'

Aihah sat down beside me. 'Now, you must never lie to yourself, Swift. That is perhaps the worst of Varr mistakes. Be truthful; who is it? Your body knows and it wants that one special flame that only one special person can give you. That is the way of Feybraiha.

If not, well, just about anyone would do; like animals or (darkly) *men*. This will be your first time, Swift, and it is very important. It is something you will carry with you for the rest of your life and because of that, it must be perfect. Now, come on, don't let me sit here and lecture you' (he gave me a little shake) 'search your soul and admit it.'

'I can't!' I cried. 'My head is too full. I can't see anyone. There is no-one!'

'You are afraid. Is your choice perhaps a controversial one?'

'There is no-one!' I was weeping again, my body heaving in great, agonizing spasms. I felt so much grief and I could think of nothing that would relieve it.

'Swift, look at me!' I thought I'd heard Aihah's voice but it had been only in my head. I looked at him. 'Into my eyes ... deep.' He put his long-fingered hands upon my face, lightly rubbing the sore spots above my eyes. 'Open up to me, Swift. Let your mind go blank ...'

It was so easy to let go. I had been holding myself together by great effort, now I could relax and the Kakkahaar would be there to catch me if I fell. I acknowledged his unobtrusive presence in my mind. He calmed me and caressed my thoughts, and then, with gentle, painless thrusts, he began to search my feelings. Each soft probing brought a picture to my eyes and it was like dreaming. I could see Forever, huge and black and white like an old photograph. A younger me running through the snow. Gahrazel smiling. Talismans on a gate. Was that Ithiel there? I ran right past him. He looked away from me. Then I was mouth to mouth with Leef and we were great black birds, spiralling upwards and the trees were lifeless and the nests were empty. I twirled and spun, reaching up for the white, white sky. His face was there. He said, 'You are the special one here, I think ...' and then I had a glimpse, so quick, so brief, of a shining canopy lit by stars and the eyes of my dreams, my nightmares were there with hair all around them. But it was Cal who pulled me back.

I felt a real cry echo in the room around me and the force of Aihah's mind poured into me, compelling me to calm. 'Face it!' he commanded and I sensed his awful, primal power held back. If he

147

wished to he could have unleashed it within me, trusting as I was, joined to him by mind, unleashed it to swallow me whole, but he only ordered, 'Face it!' and I did.

'It is impossible!' I cried. 'My father would never allow it!'

Aihah sat demurely with his hands in his lap. 'Terzian is Wraeththu. If he was doing his duty towards you correctly, he would have realized this for himself. It is not a question of what his feelings will allow. That is for humans, that indulgence! You must tell him, Swift.'

'I can't!' Even though I was pacing around the room, wildly throwing my arms about, I knew that the grief had left me. I knew why. Once, beside the lake, I had let Cal into my head and his presence had lodged there. My body had fixed itself upon him. No other would do.

'Will you tell Terzian for me, Aihah?' I begged, but he shook his head.

'No, I won't. You must tell him yourself.'

'But what if he says no?'

'He won't. He is Wraeththu. Although our differences from humanity seem little but an inconvenience to your father at times, he will understand this, Swift, I promise you that.'

'Hmm. Maybe I'll ask him tomorrow.'

The Kakkahaar laughed. 'Why wait that long? Go and see him again now before he arranges anything. Tell him that you've talked to me ...' (Ah yes I thought. They know we are afraid of them.)

Just as I was steeling myself to go and face my father, a horrible thought came to me: Cobweb. I grabbed Aihah's arm. There was no need for words.

'Ah, your hostling,' the Kakkahaar said. 'I realize this might cause friction. I will speak to Cobweb for you; I can do that at least.'

'Why do you want to help me?' I asked, wondering what he had to gain.

'Why? Well, that is simple. We don't know what will happen to us in the future, do we? If I am to die, then I hope someone will do the same for my own son. Every action has a reaction.'

'I see.'

'Not entirely. Your education has been sadly neglected. You are unusual for a Varr, Swift. You owe it to yourself to find that knowledge. Don't leave it too long. Now, go to your father.'

Terzian was surprised to see me again, glancing impatiently at the clock on the wall when I walked in. He always worked very late, sitting alone, wrestling with his problems. The papers on his desk were covered in scratchy drawings, the odd word written thickly and underlined here and there. 'What is it, Swift?' he asked coldly.

'It cannot be Leef,' I said. It took a moment for what I said to sink in. He had probably already forgotten about our earlier conversation.

'What?'

I went closer to him. 'I've been talking to Aihah.'

Terzian rolled his eyes. 'Go on.'

'Well, it'll be my first time and I want, I need ... It has to be Cal, father.' I hardly ever called him that. I hardly ever spoke to him directly. He stared at me thoughtfully and I like to think that then he saw me properly for the first time.

'You are so like your hostling,' he said, lacing his fingers before him on the desk. 'Perhaps I have never spent enough time with you, Swift. Sit down.'

I had expected an outburst; now I had no idea what to say.

'How did you reach this conclusion?' he asked reasonably and I thought, My God, he is listening to me. He has actually heard what I said!

I related some of my conversation with the Kakkahaar and he pursed his lips.

'I had no idea you felt this way,' he said at last.

'Aihah said you would understand,' I murmured. Would that make him angry?

Terzian laughed. 'Understand? I can't dispute that Swift! Cal does seem to have a traumatic effect upon everyone he meets.'

'Are you cross with me? I asked carefully.

Terzian leaned back in his chair. 'Why should I be?'

'I don't know ... I thought ...'

He leaned towards me. 'Perhaps I should have realized, but I've had a lot on my mind recently. Your choice is a good choice, Swift, but there is one thing … Oh, Hell, I don't know how to say this! Cal is a very strong person; his personality is strong. It may swamp you. I hope you can cope with it.'

'I think I can,' I replied.

Terzian smiled thoughtfully. 'Hmm. It's as well you came to see me tonight. I was going to confirm the arrangements with Leef in the morning. He will be disappointed, Swift. I thought you liked him.'

'I do,' I said. 'But, well, he was just not the one.'

'I understand,' Terzian replied. 'You'll just have to make it up to him later.'

We laughed together like adults.

Cobweb was waiting for me in my room. Aihah had lost no time in telling him about my decision. I was afraid he would strike me, but he contented himself with grinding his long talons into my arms as he shook me.

'Are you mad?!' he raged.

I tore myself away. 'No!'

'He will poison you!'

'No!'

'What was it you said to me, Swift, that night so long ago? Wasn't it something like, "I'll never betray you, Cobweb"?' He made an angry, sneering sound. 'It didn't take you long to forget that, did it?'

'Alright!' I shouted. 'You're right and I'm wrong. You're right to want me to surrender my body to the wrong person and I'm wrong to want to surrender it to the right person!'

Cobweb suppressed a smile. 'He's really got to you, hasn't he? First Terzian, now you! Where will it end?'

'I wonder!' I rubbed my arms. My beloved hostling had drawn blood. Contrite, he drew me to him and kissed the claw marks.

'Hard to imagine you in Cal's arms,' he said shakily.

'Thank you Cobweb.'

His eyes were shadowed. He looked away.

I was so nervous of having to face Cal that I stayed in my room until the following evening. My head was aching and I could not eat.

All I wanted to do was sleep, but because my skin was burning I could only toss and turn on the bed. At suppertime, there was a knock on my door and my heart seemed to jump into my mouth. 'Come in!' I called, sweat breaking out all over my body, but it was only Swithe.

'How are you?' he asked. He had brought me some milk and a meat sandwich.

'I feel ill, of course!' I retorted irritably. 'How are things downstairs?'

Swithe smiled. 'Same as usual, I suppose. We haven't been invaded yet anyway! I heard that Ponclast is coming down next week. He'll probably still be here for your Feybraiha.'

'Already the event is enriched beyond my dreams!' I groaned sarcastically. 'Where's my father?' This was an oblique question, but its meaning was not lost on Swithe.

'Oh, he's been talking to Cal in his study. They've been locked away together for hours. Even had their meal in there.'

'Oh God!' I pressed my arm across my eyes, every muscle in my body flexing with self-conscious shame.

'Leef was here today,' Swithe mentioned lightly. 'Some say he left here in a fearful temper.'

Restless to the point of agony, I went down to the drawing-room with Swithe. Aihah and Shune and Cobweb were already there and they greeted me as brightly as if I were a lunatic, to be humoured at all cost. I was bored of constantly being asked how I was feeling. Cobweb offered me sheh and rubbed the back of my neck. 'It'll soon be over, Swift,' he said softly. Aihah smiled at me and his voice in my head said, 'All is as it should be.' Feeling nostalgic, I wanted to see Gahrazel, but he never came to the house nowadays, living with the soldiers in the town, being with Purah, no doubt.

When everyone was talking, Cobweb beckoned me to go and sit with him again. I had been wandering restlessly around the room, going to the window, looking for the moon with its vague face, its soothing radiance.

'Terzian is speaking to Cal,' my hostling said.

'I know.' We looked at each other and I was grateful that he did

151

not condemn me, as perhaps he should.

'You must know that from now on, you must not be alone with Cal, don't you?'

I nodded. 'Yes.'

I put my arms around him, soft and hard, lean and full; my beloved mother of mystery.

'You're shivering. You should go to bed,' Cobweb said.

I had often wondered how, during aruna, it was decided which har should be soume and which ouana, or if they could be both at the same time (an intriguing thought. I tried to imagine the mechanics of it endlessly). Swithe explained to me that the roles were interchangable and that, as far as he knew, no-one had attempted to be both at the same time. We both laughed at the thought of it. Apparently, the decision over who should take what role varied from tribe and tribe. For some, it might involve occult ritual; soume was the altar, ouana the blade of sacrifice, for others something that was resolved naturally. Among our own people, I learned that many hara (such as my father) had rejected the idea of submitting to soume and that they always chose to take aruna with hara that were content to let them take the dominant role. If this was not the case, foreplay to aruna often involved a battle of strength over who would submit to whom. (Varrs are never completely comfortable with the feminine side to their natures, hence the need for those such as Cobweb.) As I was so inexperienced, it was taken for granted that for my Feybraiha, I would be soume to start with. Swithe told me not to be alarmed if certain parts of my body withdrew into the safety of the pelvic cage while I was soume. 'It is to prevent damage,' he said. 'Sometimes, aruna can be rather energetic and you know what parts of you are easily hurt.'

'That will make me almost female,' I said, uncertainly.

'Not entirely dissimilar, I suppose,' Swithe agreed. 'Although our sexual parts are much more complex than man's or woman's. Our ecstasy is so much more intense, because it can be used to obtain power. That is why our bodies are so refined in this respect.' He smiled. 'I can still remember when I was incepted and the har who came to me first.'

152

'What was he like?' I asked. Swithe smothered the dreamy, faraway look in his eye, and I thought of Cobweb.

'It was a long time ago,' he said.

Moswell, thankfully sparing me any graphic details (which were bad enough from Swithe) was concerned mostly with teaching me about etiquette. I learned that it would be proper to avert my eyes unless told otherwise and to do exactly as Cal wanted me to. By this time, I was wondering if I'd made the right decision, being familiar with Cal's instinct to make a caustic joke out of any trying situation. The chaperoned meetings I had to suffer with him were a nightmare. It was very difficult to talk under such constraint for we already knew each other quite well, so it seemed utterly ridiculous having Moswell sitting there, watching us like a hawk.

'This has come as a shock, Swift,' Cal said and then laughed at my furious blush. 'Not an unpleasant shock, of course. But what a responsibility!'

'It won't be your first time though, will it?' I reminded him, meaning Pellaz.

'No. I must have an extraordinary talent for educating virgins.'

'Cal, shut up!'

'Well, I've had no complaint so far.'

It was impossible to suppress his carefree attitude and he was determined not to instil the slightest note of gravity into the proceedings.

The day before my Feybraiha, Ponclast and my father received momentous news that sent a hush and then a babble right through the house. Through Shune and Aihah, the Kakkahaar had communicated that they had achieved massive breakthrough with the problem of the weird barriers the Gelaming had constructed about themselves. Soon, a passage would be completed through which the Varrs' armies could pass. The time had come. Restlessness spread through Galhea like a plague. Terzian would be leading his hara south within a week. This time, I felt I would be sorry to see him leave. He had been surprisingly understanding about Cal and also, this time, I was not so sure he would be back as quickly.

Terzian organized a great feast for my Feybraiha. It was to be the Varrs' leaving party just as much as my own coming of age. Yarrow roasted a whole ox in the yard and managed to procure sparkling Zheera, which is an extremely potent form of sheh and supposedly aphrodisiac, which made my father laugh when he heard about it. All the eminent citizens of Galhea were to be invited to the house and Ponclast gave me a gift to mark my coming of age, a jewelled, curved knife. It was very beautiful, but would undoubtedly snap like matchwood if used to defend myself. Gahrazel had turned out better than he had expected and he must have been feeling grateful to my father, whom he considered to be responsible.

On the morning of the great day, Bryony and Cobweb shared the task of choosing my clothes, brushing my hair and discreetly painting my face. 'Not that you really need it,' Cobweb remarked, 'but it's nice to dress up for special occasions.' The image that faced me in the mirror seemed like a stranger. Cobweb had made me trousers of pale, soft material in his favourite colour, lightest green, almost white except in the folds. He weaved small, starry flowers into my hair and dabbed my skin with an expensive perfume which Terzian had once procured for him from some far place.

Bryony sighed at me and said, 'You look so lovely, Swift, like a woman, like a beautiful boy. I don't know whether to fancy you or feel jealous of you. I wish I could hug you.'

'But you can!' I said and opened my arms. She felt small and slim and helpless in my hold and when I kissed her lightly on the lips I could see tears in her eyes.

'You are so lucky,' she said.

On our way downstairs, I turned to Cobweb. 'We are all happy,' I said.

'For now, maybe,' my hostling answered, 'so we must enjoy it!'

All my father's friends were waiting for us in the Big Room. It was nearly midday and the sun was streaming in through the long windows in great gold bars. Everyone was dressed in finery, everyone was smiling. Red leaves blew along the terrace outside. 'Swift, you are beautiful,' Ponclast said, taking my hand and sweeping an exaggerated bow. I felt I could never tire of this attention. My childhood had been torn from me. Now I was adult and hara could

154

flirt with me without reproach.

Custom dictated that Terzian perform some kind of ceremony in my honour, although, Varrs being what they are, there was nothing written down to give him any guidelines. I think he made the words up as he went along. I remember him touching my shoulder and saying, 'This body blooms, this Wraeththu flower,' and before all our guests he joined Cal's hand with mine and told him, 'Bring this flower to fruit.' Terzian is an accomplished speaker. Even Cal could not bring himself to smile as my father delivered solemn words about deflowering. I was relieved when it was over.

House-hara mingled among the guests dispensing sheh and wine, and many people came to speak with me. I can remember nothing of what was said. At some point I saw Leef standing with a group of friends near the windows. He saw me looking and we both froze and quickly turned away.

The whole day was one of happiness and feasting and dancing. I was floating on air the whole time. All my discomfort had gone. All that was left was a tingling in my skin that was a yearning for the dusk and the time that would follow it. When my father pronounced me Kaimana at lunch, Cal, seated next to me, took my hand and kissed my cheek. (Why was it Leef's eye I had to meet across the table?) My body surged with untapped power. I felt capable of anything.

Gahrazel came to speak to me in the afternoon. 'It doesn't seem that long ago that it was my Feybraiha we were celebrating here,' he said. 'My God, Swift, you've changed since then!'

'It wasn't that long ago and you've changed more than I have,' I replied. 'When did we last see you? We used to be such friends.'

'I know ...' Gahrazel sighed heavily and looked at the floor. When he raised his eyes again, I felt he was trying to tell me something.

'Gahrazel?'

He shook his head and reached for my hand. 'It's nothing. Look, I'll come and see you before we go south again, I promise.'

'Forever used to be your home.'

Gahrazel looked at the room around him, beyond the faces, at the walls. I saw him shiver.

'And how is Purah?' I enquired, but Gahrazel only smiled.

'I'll see you soon,' he said. 'And good luck for tonight!'

In the evening, after dinner, all the long windows in the Big Room were thrown open to an autumn evening still warm with the memory of summer. Hara wandered out there to dance in the moonlight and the smell of cooking meat drifted in from the remains of Yarrow's ox in the stableyard. I had had to speak with so many hara that day, I had hardly seen anything of Cal. Now, in the dusk, he came towards me and took me out on the terrace.

'Can you believe this, I feel nervous!' he confessed. 'It's such a responsibility, what with all these hara here and everything. I hope Terzian doesn't ask you to write out a report for him tomorrow. What if I fall asleep?'

'I think I'm too drunk to be nervous,' I replied. 'Nothing seems real yet. I want to put my arms around you, but everyone's watching us.'

'Feybraiha seems to be a spectator sport, I agree. I expect they'll all cheer if you do.'

'I expect so too. Oh, what the hell!'

We embraced. They cheered.

At midnight, my father called us to the middle of the room and delivered another embarrassing speech, which everyone applauded with deafening enthusiasm. When he finished speaking and everyone was toasting my health and fortune, Cobweb came and touched my arm. 'I think it's time, Swift,' he said. 'Come with me. It won't be so noticeable if you and Cal disappear separately.'

I followed my hostling up the great, wide stairs to my room. Always, on those stairs, my mind is flooded with memories. That time was no exception. I felt that at the foot of the stairs was my past, a forlorn child looking up, while at the head, my future, as yet unknown, gaped before me.

My room had been strewn with ferns and smelled deep, dark and mysterious. 'It's like a forest,' I said.

Cobweb took me in his arms. 'Dear, dear Swift,' he said. 'If he hurts you, I will kill him!'

'Will it hurt me then?' I asked, alarmed.

Cobweb shook his head quickly. 'No, no. I shouldn't have said that. If it does, it will be a sweet, sweet pain, and short in duration.'

He dressed me in white and took the flowers from my hair. I said, 'My God, it's real, isn't it!'

Cobweb smiled. 'As real as anything can be. Don't be afraid.'

He folded back the sheets and I slid between them. The pillows were fragrant with perfume. Cobweb lit a dozen long, white candles and turned off the light. The room became an enchanted place. My heart beat fast and I was deep within the forest.

'It is like a dream,' I said.

Cobweb was at the door. 'Goodnight, little pearl,' he said.

I lay there for what seemed hours, drunk on my own heady turmoil and the rich scent of the room. I tried to rehearse what I would say to Cal when he came in, but none of the conversations had any end that I could imagine. Now it was real; now. Before that moment I could not visualize reaching it, even during the day. I remembered once sitting on the roof with Gahrazel when he had told me about aruna and how I had felt about it then, thinking of Ithiel. Now I was afraid, now I craved its consummation.

Cal knocked on the door before he opened it, probably to give me time to compose myself. 'Swift,' he whispered. 'Are you awake?'

I laughed nervously. 'I feel ridiculous.'

Cal crept stealthily across the room as if wary of others listening outside. 'I know what you mean. It's a bit like Grissecon, having everyone there watching us. Hopefully, they're all too engrossed in drinking and dancing again by now.'

'Grissecon ... Have you ever done that?'

He paused to examine himself in the mirror. 'Yes. Once at Saltrock. That was where Pell and I stayed for a while.'

'Why did you do it?'

'For magic, of course. There was a sort of plague, but it was man-made. Aruna is stronger than anything man can devise. We performed Grissecon to kill the plague.'

'Who ... you and Pell?'

'No ... it was someone else.' He smiled. 'I don't want to talk about that now. You look lovely, Swift.'

157

'Everyone keeps saying that today,' I said. 'But will they tomorrow? Is it just a temporary thing?'

Cal shook his head. 'I could keep on extolling your virtues, but it might make you conceited. Shall we have a drink?'

He poured us sheh and sat down beside me. We could hear the music from downstairs; the window was open.

'I wonder what will happen when Terzian goes south,' I said.

'It's best not to think about that now. You might end up as Master of Galhea sooner that you think.'

'God, Cal, that's awful. Don't say that!' I cried, appalled. I hated to think my father was vulnerable, but Cal was probably right.

'At least you'll be here if anything happens,' I said.

'And what could I do?' he asked, laughing.

'Not *do* anything; just be here. I'd feel safer somehow.'

He took the glass from my hand. It was empty. I tried to smile.

'Don't be afraid, Swift. Aruna is the most normal, commonplace, easily accomplished thing Wraeththu can do. We spend most of our lives being concerned with it.'

He stood up and carelessly pulled off his shirt. His skin was dark, his hair almost white. I looked away and after a while he said, 'Oh Swift, can't you bear to look at me?'

'Moswell said it would be indelicate to stare.'

'Nonsense, it turns me on. I want you to admire me.' I turned my head. His skin was tawny and soft with a sheen like fur. He turned round three times. 'Front and back elevation,' he said. 'What do you think?'

'Wonderful ... a bit frightening ...'

'You think so? Come here.' He held out his hand. I struggled from the bed in a knot of nightshirt. 'I don't like that. Take it off,' he said and I hesitantly pulled it over my head. 'I can't imagine anyone finding a garment like that erotic, but still, concealment is enticing, I suppose.' We went to the windowseat and looked out at the garden and it felt wild and magical to be naked. Anyone might have looked up and seen us. Cal put his arm around me, stroking my skin, staring out into the darkness. 'The Gelaming might have a price on my head,' he said.

'What, because of that Orien?' I asked.

'That Orien!' Cal mocked. 'He was a respected shaman, Swift. I have a feeling that Seel … that Seel won't rest until I pay for what I've done.'

'Who's Seel?' I felt I'd heard of him before.

'He founded Saltrock,' Cal explained. 'We were good friends once but I doubt if our friendship could weather my murder of Orien.'

'You were sick, though, weren't you?'

'That is not an excuse, though I wish it was.' He pulled me closer against him. 'You feel so warm … I have a feeling, I don't know, I feel as if Seel is … is *coming closer* somehow. Sometimes it's as if he's here in this house. I've woken up and smelled him in the room, smelled his perfume, his body. I've seen his eyes … Oh God, why am I going on like this! It's your Feybraiha.'

'It doesn't matter. I like you telling me things, I want you to,' I said and pressed my face against his chest. 'I never dreamed this would be possible.'

'I wish I could regret it properly, but I can't,' Cal murmured.

'Perhaps it's because you're still angry,' I suggested.

'Oh, I'll always be angry, but I know I shouldn't have done that, never, never … but in a way, I don't care that I did.'

'Well, *I* don't care,' I said.

'Swift …' His voice was a whisper and his breath called out to me. I could feel my heart; my eyes were hot. When his mouth touched mine, I could see his life, moving quickly, like a never-ending picture, unfolding before my eyes. He trusted me. There was nothing hidden. It was all there. I relived with him that first time with Pellaz; that was all he could think of. I wished I could have known Pell better, but I had been so young when they had been with us before.

'There will never be anyone like him,' Cal said.

'Don't be sad.'

'I'm not, really. Come on.'

He led me back to the bed and we pulled the blankets over us.

'I never thought I'd come back here,' he said.

'I'm glad that you did.'

'Mmmm. Me too.' He put his hand on my back. I could feel him trembling. 'Are you still afraid, Swift?'

'I don't think so.'

'Good.' We shared breath again and then he broke away and said, 'Come on, Swift, don't just lie there! It works both ways, you know. I'm yours to explore, feel free to do what you like.'

'But I don't know what to do,' I complained. 'Show me.'

He took my hands in his own, his eyes were laughing. 'Touch me.' He threw back the covers to let me see him and his ouana-lim had become a gold and jade sentinel, pulsing with moving colours. 'Vibrant, isn't it?' he said.

'It is a sword. It will kill me!' I cried.

'No, it won't. Your body will be surprisingly accommodating. I've never taken aruna with a pure-born before. I wonder if it will be different.'

I took his ouana-lim in my hands and its petals opened around my fingers. It was so beautiful, so mysterious, alive and radiant, a thing created for the sole purpose of pleasure. Shining trickles of luminous blue-green touched my skin. I had never seen anything like it.

'Look at yourself,' he told me. My colours were bronze and metallic blue, with the faintest hints of blood red appearing and melting away. When he touched me, a sun seemed to blaze behind my eyes. I was lost then, in the intoxicating splendour that presaged our union. Sometimes, it was if I was out of my body, looking down, sometimes I was inside Cal's head, looking at myself. Then the moment came when he pressed me back. 'Say a prayer Swift,' he said and seared right into me in one, long, tearing sliding movement. It did hurt, but I craved that pain, moving to meet it. I had visions before my eyes, oh, such wondrous visions. Other lands, alien and beautiful, strange people walking along azure dunes. Some time in that exotic landscape I felt a nerve awake within me, deep inside, where he could not reach, and it wanted so desperately to be touched. I called his name, feverish and despairing, and just when I thought the torment would go on forever, I felt a snakelike movement within me and something shot out and made contact with that vibrating nerve. I could hear a scream, it may have been in my head, but a universe imploded in my body,

160

all my limbs shuddering and twisting to a nameless ecstasy. Hot, glimmering liquid spilled onto the sheets, aflame like opals. Light flared behind my eyes. I was released.

Afterwards, he wanted to talk to me again. It was all Orien, Saltrock and Pell. No matter how much he tried to hide it, he was obsessed with it all.

'It was not me,' he said, 'and yet it was. I can remember it all perfectly, yet it was another mind that moved those events, not mine.'

I learned that Cal and the one he called Seel had known each other for a long time, their relationship went back to before either of them were har. 'Saltrock is a special place. It's a Wraeththu sanctuary. Madness rarely touches it,' Cal told me warmly. 'One day you must go there. I think you will anyway, Swift. I can't see you living here forever, in Forever.'

I laughed and put my arms around him. 'Remember I'm a Varr,' I said. 'Do you think I'd be welcome there?'

'Of course, why not? Can you help who your parents are? Anyway Seel's people are unique. I think they'd surprise you.'

'Ah, the Wraeththu who call themselves the knowledge-seekers,' I said, not without sarcasm.

Cal sighed deeply. 'Again I've betrayed them,' he said obliquely.

'How did it happen?' I asked. 'I mean Orien and all that. I want to know. I want to know everything.'

'What, everything about me? How charming. Alright, if you really want to, although it may bore you.'

'It won't. Say it all!'

'God, that would take forever!' He snuggled down against me and his voice was low. The candles were guttering away; soon we would see each other only by starlight.

'I found Pell in a wilderness; an unearthly child. He was so beautiful I could hardly believe it and wild like a scared, sleek animal. I would have kidnapped him to make him har if he hadn't wanted to go with me. I had to have him. It was almost sick! I took him to Saltrock and Seel had him incepted. That was just the beginning ... I should have known that there was something not right, even then. It was Thiede, you see. It was Thiede that incepted Pell, gave him his Wraeththu blood. You have to understand that Thiede is ... God, what is he? It's so hard to explain. He's powerful, frightening, awesome. Perhaps beyond good and evil. He wanted Pell for something (who didn't?) but Thiede's desires are obscure, incomprehensible. I still don't know the reason, but I'm sure Orien did. Orien ... He was perhaps the kindest, wisest person I ever met. He was Saltrock's shaman, high priest, whatever ...'

'If he was that wonderful,' I butted in, 'why did you kill him?'

'Why indeed!' Cal sighed and pressed his face into my neck. 'Why ... I'll have to go back, Swift, to when Pell and I were in Galhea before. It's not easy. When we left here, all those years ago, we were planning to travel back towards the south. I wanted to find a way to Immanion, the first city of the Gelaming. I knew that was where it was all really happening, where Wraeththu had organized themselves, found order ... It seemed the logical place to head for. I had no idea where it was. Now I know it's farther than I realized, across the sea, a long way away. Anyway, we had only travelled for a short time, a few weeks maybe, when ...' For a moment he could not speak. His silence made my chest ache. After a while he swallowed. 'I watched him die, Swift, all his life running out of him. I couldn't do anything, just watch. Afterwards, I must have wandered around half crazy. I can't remember ... Somewhere along the way I lost the horses. It was like, like, how can I explain? My body was moving, feeding itself, sleeping, looking after itself in a way, but I was buried deep inside my own head, unaware of what was going on around me. One day I woke up and I was back at Saltrock. I don't know how I got there. They didn't know how to cope with me. I was out of my head, and when I wasn't I wanted to be. Anything I could get my hands on to escape reality, I shovelled it into myself. Seel must have been at the end of his tether trying to sort me out. It was all because of Zack too, you see. I thought I was being punished for what happened to him. I thought that losing Pell was the divine retribution for my sins. I couldn't face myself. My life was a series of lies, conceit and pride. I was unfit to live, a blight on Wraeththukind. It seemed that everyone I got close to

162

was destroyed in some way. The fruit of my self-hate was the murder of Orien. Perhaps it was the worst thing I could do, and to do it would prove to myself how utterly loathsome I was. I don't know. At the time, I blamed him for Pell's death. Now I can see that was ... not stupid ... just wrong.'

'Oh, Cal,' I said. He looked at my face and his fingers touched my cheek.

'Oh, don't weep for me, Swift,' he said. 'You see, the worst thing is, I haven't changed. I learned nothing from all that. I'm still selfish. My path is uphill. I don't struggle to climb it, I don't even slip back or seek the easy path. I just sit down where I am and think, "Oh, to Hell with it!" I'm too human; I shouldn't be har. Look at what I've done here. Don't think I'm not aware of it and don't think I don't enjoy it.'

'But do you still hate yourself?' I asked.

'Inside myself ... perhaps.' He pulled away from me and lay on his back, with his arms behind his head. 'Swift, I've never spoken to anyone like this, not even Pell. I don't think I ever will again ...'

'Maybe you had to,' I suggested.

'Maybe.' He smiled. 'This is depressing. Here I am again bringing up reeking stomachfuls of confessions all over you! I *am* here for a purpose ...'

He leaned over me and I closed my eyes. Already my body quickened for the feel of him, desire of him.

'No,' he said softly, and stroked my stomach with the gentlest possible touch. He pulled me against him and lay back. I looked into his lazy, violet eyes. This is too incredible, I thought. This is too much; it is a dream. So close. His beauty almost withers me. Perhaps I shall be turned to stone ...

'Swift,' he said, 'I want you to –'

'Hush!' I answered. 'I know.'

It was frightening, like going into a dark place full of unknown things. I could feel his strength, the great, beating pinions of his spirit. It was so different. Before, when he took me, I had lived the ultimate of visions, now I was part of his vision. He was an abyss and I was falling, a never-ending fall. When I reached the end, I would fall again. His head was thrown back, one arm pressed across his eyes. He murmured as if in pain, fretfully, then his arm lashed back and hit the pillow. His eyes were blazing, I reared up to escape them, but he caught hold of me, so strong, lifting himself. His mouth found my neck; he wanted blood. I remembered for a fleeting moment what my father had said: 'He may swamp you.' Of course, Terzian was speaking of this, not Cal as ouana, but the devouring, lashing female side of him, like a python, crushing me. For a moment, we were still, staring at each other. Then it happened. That secret part of me snaked out to ignite his pulsing nerve. He did not cry out, just hissed like a cat, threshing around me. His hands, like claws, tore at my shoulders. He lunged to bite me, snarling and crazed. Almost panicking, I hit his face and he flopped back among the pillows. There was blood around his mouth.

'Cal?' I said, tentatively, feeling all my muscles shaking. I felt him laugh around me; he opened his eyes.

'Pure-born, it *is* different!' he said.

In the morning I felt as if I'd been fighting for my life all night. My shoulders had actually stuck to the sheet with blood. Cal fetched a cloth from my bathroom and bathed my back. 'Oh, Hell, I'm sorry,' he said. 'I must have got a bit carried away but it was pretty amazing, wasn't it? So much stronger. God!' He laughed and stood up, throwing the cloth into the air.

'I've decided to become Varr hostling stock,' I said. 'If being ouana means being torn to bits, I'll opt for submission any day.'

'Oh, come on,' Cal coaxed. 'It's just me! You know how weird I am! Terzian isn't exactly unscarred either.'

'You enjoy being weird,' I grumbled, wincing as I tried to get out of bed.

'Yes, I have to agree with you there,' he said cheerfully. 'They'll have finished breakfast, won't they? I'm starving!'

He was gorged on my vitality. I could hardly move.

I walked through the day in a daze. Everyone gave me very strange looks, except for my father, who probably understood. 'Takes it out of you, doesn't it?' he said, and I felt he was glad to have someone he could say that to.

A Deception
Swell upon sham
The autonomy of mosquito wings
Embarks on the spoor of a celestial
bandit
Erudite killer, more stupid
Than peevish, human, monster freaks.

I had not really expected Gahrazel to come and see me before he left, and was therefore very surprised when he shook me awake the following morning. 'I thought you were dead!' he said. 'You used to be such a light sleeper.'

I pushed my hair out of my eyes, still half asleep. 'You're here early, Gahrazel.'

He walked up and down at the end of my bed and the constant movement, made me feel sick. 'Sit down, for God's sake!'

'It's not that early,' he said. 'Remember, I lead a soldier's life now. Gone is the luxury of lying in bed in the morning.' His voice was bitter.

'Is everyone else up?'

'Yes ... Swift?'

'What? Pass me my clothes, will you?'

He sifted through the pile on the floor and tossed bits of it over to me. 'Swift, I've neglected our friendship,' he said, not looking at me.

'What's happened to remind you of that?' I asked, pulling on my trousers.

'Oh, nothing ... Good God, what's happened to your back?'

I wasn't sure whether to feel proud or ashamed. I said nothing.

'Oh, I *see*,' continued Gahrazel, suddenly much more like the har I remembered. 'If Ithiel had done that to me, I'd have blacked his eye.'

'Oh, would you!' I retorted. 'Just think about the fact that Ithiel didn't feel the need to illustrate his passion so emphatically.'

'My little Swift!' he cried. 'It seems you follow in your father's footsteps as a wielder of power.'

'So it does,' I agreed.

'I think I shall miss Swift the child,' Gahrazel said wistfully.

'I get the feeling you're here for a reason,' I said. 'You're upset.'

'No, no,' Gahrazel denied quickly. 'Not upset ... perhaps I *am* here for a reason, though. I need to talk to you.'

'After breakfast,' I decided.

'If you like.'

We went down the stairs together, laughing, joking, pushing each other around, as we had done so many times before.

'I've just realized how much I've missed you,' I said.

'Blame Terzian,' Gahrazel said caustically.

He was offered breakfast, but refused, just drinking coffee and messing nervously with the cutlery, always glancing at the door. Terzian had already left the table, and in a strange way I was relieved. There was only Swithe left in the room, poring over a report my father had given him to read. I could see Terzian's mark of black humour in this, but Swithe just held the papers with distaste, totally ignorant of any intent.

'The Gelaming will annihilate them!' Swithe declared, throwing down the papers.

'That does seem likely,' Gahrazel agreed. 'But who can know for sure?'

'What do you think?' Swithe asked intently.

Gahrazel would not commit himself. He spread out his hands and shook his head. 'I'm not paid to think, just to skin the hides off any Gelaming we might meet.'

'You never used to keep your opinions to yourself,' I said drily.

Gahrazel shrugged.

After breakfast, I took him up to the long gallery. I knew we would not be disturbed there.

Gahrazel took a slim packet out of a top pocket. 'Cigarettes,' he said. 'Do you want one?'

'What are they?' I asked, eyeing with interest the slim, white stick he put between his lips.

'Smoke to combat nerves,' he said, inhaling deeply.

'Oh, like hemp,' I said knowledgeably. It was something I knew about, but I'd never tried it.

'Not really,' Gahrazel said. 'Do you want one or not?'

I shook my head. 'No. You always know more than me, don't you, Gahrazel?' He made me feel young again, too young.

He pulled a face. 'Do I? I don't mean to.' He smiled at me, and it wasn't totally without condescension.

'Well then, Gahrazel, what's the matter?'

He sat on the floor, his back to the window, and once again inhaled deeply off his cigarette. 'I trust you,' he said, blowing smoke rings at the ceiling.

'Should you?'

'I think so.' He looked at me intently. 'Swift, I hate what your father's done to me.'

'What's he done?'

Gahrazel stared at his hands. There was a moment's pause before he spoke. 'What he's tried to do. Among other things, make me like him, like my own father. I'm not at all like them, you know.' His eyes bored into me, full of words he could not speak.

'I've always known that,' I said and squatted down beside him. 'But I did think you'd adapted quite well. As we'd seen nothing of you ...'

Gahrazel made an irritated sound. 'Don't be stupid!'

'Don't speak to me like that!' I snapped, stung.

He sighed and rubbed his face with his hands. 'Sorry Swift.' His voice was mocking.

'What is it then?' I asked, standing up.

He looked up at me and squinted. 'I can't stay here.'

'I didn't think you would. You're going south again, aren't you?'

'I can't do that either.'

'What do you mean?' I asked apprehensively. I suppose I knew already.

168

'If I tell you ... you might have to lie to your father later.'

I nodded. 'Alright, alright, what is it, Gahrazel?'

He took a deep breath. 'I'm not going south with Terzian again. I can't! There are so many reasons, Swift ... I'm going to the Gelaming. I'm taking Purah with me.'

I shut my eyes and turned away from him with a sigh. 'God!'

'You'll wish I hadn't told you.'

'Your father!'

'I know. I had to tell you, Swift.'

'Why?' I demanded. 'Why didn't you just go?'

'I think you know the answer. Someone had to know. The chances are ... well, perhaps we'd better not dwell on the possible consequences. I had to tell you, Swift. There was no-one else I could trust.'

'When?'

'Ah, well, that's something I think it's better you don't know about, don't you?'

'Yes, I suppose so,' I agreed. 'Gahrazel, do you know what this means ... if you're caught?'

'Oh yes,' he said softly. 'More than anyone, I know *that*.'

I thought of Leef. Were there many of them, feeling as Gahrazel did now? True Wraeththu perhaps?

'Gahrazel,' I said. 'You're not alone, are you?'

He looked around quickly, furtively, as if suddenly chilled. 'What do you mean?'

'That you're not alone. There are others, aren't there ... others that perhaps lack the guts at present to ...'

'If I succeed Swift, it may give others the courage to follow me, yes.'

'Oh God!' I pressed my forehead against the long window. Surely my father couldn't be so ignorant of the dissension among his hara. Now I, Terzian's son, had been told. Terzian's son. Forever, my home. I looked down the long gallery, at its beloved, warm, worn, familiar length. 'You shouldn't have told me,' I said. 'I wish you hadn't!'

'Swift!' Gahrazel stood up behind me and put his arms around me. 'Remember, I once told you that we'd both know all of this

169

house some day. Maybe I meant more than just the bricks and stone ...'

'Let go of me,' I said. He didn't for a moment, but I did not warm to him. He sighed and his arms dropped away from me. I felt cold.

'There's so much you don't know, Swift,' he said.

'I don't want to know! Just go, Gahrazel!' I could not look at him.

'Not even "goodbye", Swift?'

'Goodbye, Gahrazel.'

'Will you wish me luck?'

'I can't!'

I heard him sigh. 'Farewell, my friend,' he said.

I listened to him walking away from me, numb to my innermost heart. 'Gahrazel,' I whispered to the window, watching it mist. 'Gahrazel.'

It was a turning point in my life. I had to decide where my loyalties lay. If Gahrazel had told me everything, as he should have done, my decision might have been different, but, as he said, I knew so little. One thing I was sure of, if Ponclast's son successfully defected to the Gelaming, there would be many willing, if not eager, to follow him. At that time, I thought the reason was mainly fear of the Gelaming, rather than sympathy with Gelaming ideals. After Gahrazel had left me in the long gallery, I stood for a while thinking about what he had said. I wanted advice from someone I too could trust. I couldn't keep my mouth shut, could I?

I found Cal in the drawing-room, lazing like a cat. He was idly tormenting Limba with a rolled-up piece of paper (Limba is trusting, but stupid.) I imparted my news with a suitable note of dread in my voice. 'Oh, Terzian will kill them,' was all he'd say. I made an exasperated noise, annoyed that he was taking this revelation so lightly.

'And if he doesn't find out until it's too late?'

'Do you care?' Cal asked me in a tired voice.

'Care? Oh, of course I don't! Let all my father's hara desert him and run squeaking to the Gelaming! Let them destroy us all. Let

170

them destroy this house!'

Cal smiled indulgently at my outburst. 'Oh dear,' he said, stretching. 'And how many of Terzian's hara are you expecting to make a run for it?'

'Enough,' I answered stiffly.

'If you *really* think it's such a threat, there is nothing to worry about,' Cal continued, spreading his arms.

'What?'

'Terzian will kill Gahrazel before he gets away.'

'Oh!' I shouted in exasperation, turning away from him. Cal came to stand behind me. He put his hands upon my shoulders.

'He will know,' he said.

'How?' I demanded angrily.

'How? Well, that is obvious. You will tell him.'

'Cal!' I cried, turning round, striking away his hands. He looked surprised for a moment. 'How can I do that? I am not even convinced that what Gahrazel is doing is wrong!'

'Wrong for yourself, for us ...'

'I can't!'

Cal threw back his head and laughed. 'Ah, the grey spectre of betrayal!' he mocked. I would not speak. 'There is only one thing you should think of in a time like this,' he continued blandly, 'and that is yourself. In the end, there is only you; nothing else matters.'

'Cal ...'

'Master of Galhea one day, perhaps?' He took my face in his hands and I did not resist. I looked into his violet eyes and thought of all the things they must have seen. Was it caught within them forever somewhere? Could I see those things if I looked hard enough? 'Learn well the lessons of self-preservation,' he said. 'Be subtle, my lovely. Be so subtle that you do not even realize yourself what you are doing. Gahrazel ...' He sucked in his breath and shook his head.

'But it may be for nothing!' I protested. 'I may only be delaying the inevitable!'

'Nothing is inevitable!' Cal replied, smiling gently. I could not be sure that we were not speaking about completely different things. 'Your Kakkahaar friends should have told you that,' he

171

continued. 'The path of our lives divides endlessly before us. We only have the power to choose which road to take, but even that road may be forked ...' He led me out into the garden, through the long windows, to let me see it, to let me look back at the house. 'This is where you belong,' he said and blew a fleeting vision of his breath across my face.

'Gahrazel is a fool!' I said bitterly, still torn, gazing up at Forever's glistening face.

'He is more than a fool ... He should never have told you his secrets. So stupid! He is weak. I think his downfall can be blamed on that!'

'Are you saying that he deserves to die?' I asked chilled.

'We all deserve to die,' he answered.

It is not enough! I thought. All morning I agonized over what to do, avoiding everyone, sitting among the trees, where it was cold and the sun could not reach. I had so little time. Gahrazel would not have told me if he wasn't planning to leave very soon.

My father was not present at lunch, and later I saw that his study was empty. In the peaceful, sunny afternoon, I went in there and sat down in his worn leather seat. Master of Galhea one day, perhaps? A consort of my own, all these halls mine? I closed my eyes, shook my head. Which is the right way? Would it be my father's blood in my mouth that would make me betray a friend? Subtlety, subtlety, that was the key. Cal knew all about that, and he knew all about betrayal. If the Gelaming should win ...? We dwell in Forever ... I smiled. My father had been young once. Hard to imagine, but true. Had he ever doubted himself? 'I do not want to lose you,' I said aloud to the empty room.

It is a terrible thing to make your heart go cold; terrible because it is so easy. Every day, a couple of hours before the evening meal, a messenger comes up to the house from Galhea, bringing papers and notes for my father that may have collected in his town office during the day. It is the messenger's custom to stop by the kitchen for half an hour or so for refreshment and to exchange idle gossip with the house-hara. During this time, he generally leaves his leather bag of papers on the table in the hall. Then either Terzian or Ithiel take the day's mail out and put back anything to be taken down to Galhea. A plan formed in my head.

In the privacy of my room, I wrote a note in block capitals using my left hand. It said, PONCLAST'S SON IS A TRAITOR. HE GOES TO THE GELAMING. THIS I OVERHEARD. My fingers were damp as I wrote it and it was with shaking hands that I stuffed it into an envelope. At any moment, as I stealthily scuttled across the hall, I expected the kitchen doors to swing open and someone to catch me fiddling with the messenger's bag, but luck was with me and I completed the task without detection. As I ran back to my room, I was thinking. Now I am truly a Varr. Now I have learned how to kill. It had not been an easy decision.

In the night, voices woke me from a nightmare of accusing eyes. Lights downstairs had thrown a spectral glow over the garden. Between my half-open curtains, I could see the waving shapes of the trees and hear the gusting lash of the wind. Someone ran up the corridor towards my room and threw open the door. A voice called my name and that voice was deeply troubled.

I shivered, still half asleep. 'Ithiel, is that you?'

'Get dressed!' he snapped. 'Quickly! Now! Come on! Terzian wants you!'

My blood seemed to cataract to my feet. Could he know I'd written that note? I didn't want him to know it was me. I didn't want anyone else to know that Gahrazel had spoken to me about his plans.

My father was in the hall, looking up, still wearing his wolfskin coat. His anger was contained, but I could sense it clearly. He said nothing, but pointed at the floor by his feet. I ran down the stairs, robe flapping, hardly daring to say, 'What is it?' He blinked at my question, turning his back on me, beckoning me to follow him. In his study he shut the door firmly behind me. There were just the two of us.

'My son,' he said softly. I was quaking, grinning fatuously, and went to sit down. 'Stand up!' he bawled. I nearly shot back to the door.

'What's wrong?' I asked him, innocence itself. Now, I realized, it

173

was vital for me to be innocent.

'Don't you know?' he sneered. I shook my head. He stared at me until I dropped my eyes. 'Well then, Swift, I shall tell you.' He paced around the room a few times. I could tell he was longing to go absolutely mad, but that was not his way. 'I've just returned from Galhea,' he said. 'Tonight, I find our enemies are nearer to us than I thought. Much nearer. Not in the south, not even beyond the fields of Galhea. No, it is closer than that!' His fist slammed down on the desk top. 'Here!' he cried. 'In Galhea, perhaps even in my own house!' I thought, If he shouts any louder my eyes will roll out onto the floor.

'I don't understand,' I said, striving to inject a certain amount of indignation into my voice.

'Don't you? Don't you!' my father raged, lunging towards me. I toppled backwards into the chair behind me. His face was inches from my own.

I thought, My God, he will kill me too! and at that moment I could have confessed that it had been me who'd sent the note, but all I did was splutter, 'I don't know! I don't! Whatever it is ...'

His hand gripped my throat. I tried to writhe, swallow. With a wordless exclamation, he let me go and went to sit in his usual seat, putting his feet up on the desk, tearing and scattering the papers that lay on it. He rubbed his eyes with one hand. I felt as if I was swallowing acid. 'Gahrazel,' he said, and that one word froze my flesh.

'What ...?' My voice was barely a squeak.

'Gahrazel,' Terzian said again. His hands clasped on the desk. He looked at me, directly. 'Surely you remember Gahrazel, Swift. Ponclast's son, in *my* care? Surely you know the one!'

I stared at my hands. 'Yes,' I said.

'Well, apparently, he wants to leave us,' my father continued.

'Leave us?' I peeped. 'I don't understand ... What do you mean?'

'What I said. Perhaps I should add that his intended destination after departing Galhea was the south and the Gelaming!' His use of the past tense did not escape me. I managed a pathetic laugh.

'Gahrazel? Never!'

My father looked at me with an expression that was nearly

dislike. 'Never, Swift?' My mind was racing. All I could think was, I shall have to be clever ... Terzian sighed deeply. 'Let's not waste time, Swift. I know you were Gahrazel's closest friend. He must have talked to you. I can only assume you knew something of what he was planning. Look, I hardly ever spoke to him and *I* could see how dangerous he was becoming, his strange fancies! Don't tell me you knew nothing! Are you such a fool?'

I lowered my eyes. 'I ...'

Terzian snorted angrily and stood up. Papers flew everywhere. One fell at my feet and I bent to pick it up. My vision was blurring; I stared at the paper blindly. Terzian snatched it from my hands and I almost cried out. Did he relish the terror in my eyes? 'Swift, nothing that happens in this house escapes my notice; nothing! You can be sure of that! I know Forever inside out. I know its deepest secrets, but ...' He squatted down before me and took my shoulders in his hands. I was shaking uncontrollably. His voice was quieter. 'But ... there are two things, Swift, two things that I shall never know, never understand, completely. And those two things are Cobweb and yourself ... You're closed doors, both of you. Too much Sulh blood in you, too much magic. I am ... wary of that, my son, very wary. If either of you should ever want to betray me ...'

'Terzian! No!' I cried and his name felt unfamiliar to me. 'Never, I swear, never!'

It was the truth, in a way; I think it was the truth.

'Swift,' he said and there was pain in his eyes. 'I have seen Gahrazel. This afternoon someone, I don't know who yet, gave me a message that implied something of what Gahrazel was up to. When confronted, he tried to deny it at first, but then his quarters were searched and all the supplies he'd been hoarding were found. He was taken into custody and ... after a while admitted the accusation was true. I asked him one thing only and that was "Why?" All he did was laugh and the one thing he said to me was, "Ask your son, Terzian!"'

I tried to look away, but his hand caught hold of my chin.

'What did he mean by that, Swift?'

'I ... I don't know!' I stammered, squirming in his hold, feeling

175

my face fold and twist. At that moment, I hated Gahrazel more than I would have believed possible.

'What do you know?!' Terzian demanded.

'Alright!' I said, still trying to free myself. 'Let me go. Please!'

He stood up and leaned against the desk, arms folded.

'I've never wanted to know about what Gahrazel believes in, father,' I babbled helplessly. 'We've drifted apart. We're no longer close friends. I don't *know* him. Not any more. Not since Purah came ... Once, once he did try to tell me something, but I didn't want to know. I told him that. I wouldn't listen ...'

'When?'

I shrugged, resisting the urge to wring my hands in my lap, but only just. 'I ... I can't remember exactly.'

'Swithe tells me that Gahrazel was here at the house yesterday,' my father prompted. I could feel a laugh, uncontrollable and stupid, building up inside me. Swithe! All his high and righteous beliefs. The only truth is his own hide, I thought.

'Yes,' I said, biting the inside of my cheek until the laughter went away. 'Gahrazel was here.' I looked at my father with Cobweb's eyes, huge and shadowed, hoping to melt him. 'He came to say goodbye to me. By that I assumed he meant because he was going to go south again, with you ...'

My father sighed and looked up at the ceiling.

'And why did you take him to the long gallery?' Why? I started to panic. Did he know everything already? Was he only tormenting me to hear my confession? 'You needed privacy, Swift, that's obvious. What did you talk about?'

'Nothing, nothing important!' I insisted. I was so scared, reality started to shift. There was a buzzing in my ears.

'Why there? Why?'

'Because ...'

'Why? Because why, Swift?' The whole house must have been able to hear him. I could imagine Yarrow and Bryony quaking in the kitchen, all the pots rattling around them, but of course, they were curled up in their beds asleep.

'Because, because ...' My mind suddenly cleared with inspiration. 'Because we ...' I lowered my eyes modestly and made my voice quiet. 'He didn't want anyone to know ...' I looked up again beseechingly.

'What?'

'That ...' I touched my brow with one hand trembling. 'He wanted to take aruna with me. He said I might never see him again ... but he didn't want anyone to know. Because of Purah, because of Bryony ... oh, I don't know!'

'Because of me ...' Terzian whispered softly to himself.

'I just went along with it. It was like a game ...' I sighed deeply. My father must have been holding his breath. Now he let it out in one long, shuddering gasp. He rubbed his face with his hands. 'So Swift, Gahrazel really didn't tell you he was thinking of running away ... or anything else? You knew nothing. Can you swear to this?' From his voice, I could tell how important it was to him. What was it he feared Gahrazel might have told me?

'I knew nothing,' I said softly. 'His mind was closed to me of all but memories of our friendship. Nothing else ... at all.'

Terzian went to the cabinet where he kept his liquor and poured us both a glass of sheh. His hands were still shaking slightly. So were mine.

'I'm sorry,' he said, clearing his throat and handing me a glass. His fingers, where they touched me, were cold. 'I had to ask you, Swift. I hope you understand.'

'Of course,' I replied. 'I should have told you at once, but ... What will happen to him?'

Terzian sucked in his cheeks, staring at the floor. He sighed. 'I'm afraid I can't say. I don't know. Ponclast went to a settlement further north two days ago. He's not expected back until the end of the week. Of course, I've sent messengers. Obviously, I can't make any decisions about this. It's his problem, I would say, wouldn't you?' He refilled his glass.

'Who do you think sent you the message?' I asked.

He did not even glance at me. 'I don't know. Someone who's well known to Gahrazel, I'd have thought. Someone loyal to his tribe, who would prefer to stay anonymous because he had to be disloyal to a friend. I think it's best to leave it at that, don't you?'

I nodded vigorously.

'Swift, there is one thing I'd like you to do for me. You're friendly with the girl, aren't you?'

'Who, Bryony?' (Bryony was always 'the girl' to Terzian.)

'Yes. Well, I had to have Gahrazel's accomplice shot. I don't need Ponclast's permission for that. I believe he was related to the girl.'

'Brother,' I said.

'I thought so. She's a good worker, I've no complaint about her work. She's good for the house. Cobweb likes her.'

'You want me to tell her Purah is dead?'

'Yes. It would be better coming from you.'

I stood up and put down my empty glass. Terzian touched my arm. 'Swift, come here.'

I found myself in the totally unexpected embrace of my father's arms. 'I'm very proud of you,' he said and kissed my hair. 'Don't ever-'

'Terzian!' I interrupted gently. Was there strength in me he did not have?

'You must ... you must take care of your hostling and little Ty when I'm gone,' he said, with difficulty.

'I will, but of course Cal will be here too.' My father's arms tightened around me.

'Yes, I know, but ... Cal is not of our blood, Swift. It's different for him. I leave Forever in your hands. Soon, in a few days ... I shall be gone. You must progress, Swift. Ithiel will help you. He knows. Realize what is important. I have to trust you! You will have to be wise beyond your years.'

I understood then just how afraid he was, that he doubted whether he would ever return to us, yet he had to go on. 'I hate them!' I cried. 'The Gelaming; I hate them!'

'Yes, yes,' he murmured. 'Hate them, Swift, hate them with all your strength. That is something they have no control over ... perhaps the only thing.'

That day I'd learned two important lessons. The first, as I said before, was how to kill. The second, perhaps even more insidious, was how to lie. It didn't matter to Gahrazel which way I chose to betray him, but it did to me. I had not told my father what he'd said, not in words. Gahrazel had been right. I did have to lie to my father, but not in the way he'd thought.

In the morning, Bryony came to the drawing-room in response to my summons, smiling and carefree, chattering until I wanted to scream. Obviously, gossip concerning events of the previous day had not yet filtered through to the kitchens. I looked upon this as my first act of responsibility as Terzian's son. I leaned against the mantelpiece as my father would have done. I began to speak and watched her as all the colour and gaiety gradually drained from her face and a look of bewildered anguish came to take its place.

'We can only assume that he knew what he was doing, Bryony,' I said. 'He must have known the risk ...' She shook her head and would not speak. Her eyes were dry, but I could see the muscles moving in her jaw. 'It was Gahrazel!' I exclaimed. 'He did this! It was his idea!' There she sat, small and hunched on the edge of a chair, while I tried to convince her that a terrible act was not terrible. All I wanted to do was shift the blame in her eyes, absolve my people, heap Gahrazel with culpability because he would never be able to speak for himself.

'Is Gahrazel dead too?' she asked at last.

'No ... His fate has not been decided yet,' I answered.

'No, of course not,' she said bitterly.

Once again, Forever held its breath. Terzian carried on making preparations for the trek south, grimly waiting for Ponclast to return. I had word that Gahrazel had asked for me, but I turned my back on him. I felt he had tried to drag me down with him, and wondered if this was because he suspected it had been me who'd betrayed him. Nobody had a good word for him any more. Suddenly, everyone had been suspecting something like this happening for ages, even Swithe. Cal made a half-hearted attack on Swithe one evening over his rather abrupt change of heart, but was not interested enough to pursue it. I could see that Swithe had been thoroughly shaken up by what had happened. It was one thing to moan about Terzian behind his back, but it was something else entirely to stand up and be honest and face Terzian's wrath.

179

Gahrazel was being held captive in Galhea. He never set foot in Forever again.

When Ponclast returned, an emergency meeting was held in the house. I saw Ponclast once in the hall. His face was grey; he looked right through me. I felt quite sorry for him. Obviously, both Terzian and Ponclast were aware of the detrimental effect it would have had on their warriors' morale if Gahrazel had got away with his defection. The whole affair was seen as high treason and the punishment would have to fit the crime. Terzian asked me if I would like to be present at the meeting. This was an honour, but I declined. Terzian did not press it. He was still under the impression that my last moments with Gahrazel had been spent aflame with the ecstasy of aruna. It is a sacred act, even to Varrs. 'This must be hard for you,' he said.

Ithiel had been sent some miles east on some errand or another. I heard my father say to him before he left, 'Take the girl with you.' I was surprised by this act of understanding. I knew that he looked upon humans with the same amount of respect as he looked upon dogs. I don't think Purah had ever ceased to be human in his eyes, but because Bryony was part of his staff and had proved her worth, she was less human than honorary har. Terzian always looked after the things he valued, or so I thought.

On the evening following the meeting, Leef came to the house to report to my father. Now he had been promoted again, to Ithiel's second in command, and was currently carrying out all Ithiel's duties while he was away. Perhaps his second promotion had been some kind of consolation because he had lost the honour of taking part in my Feybraiha. It seemed likely. We passed each other in the hall as he went to my father's study and he gave me a curt greeting. I suffered a pang of remorse, being only too aware of how once I had led him on to believe I desired him. Still jumpy because of Gahrazel, I decided I'd try to smooth things over between us. Secure in a new sense of power, I summoned one of the house-hara and told him to wait outside Terzian's study until Leef came out. 'Take him to the red salon,' I said. 'And have someone build a fire in there.'

It was a room we hardly ever used and all the furniture was uncomfortable in there. It was a room for formality, perhaps not the best that I could have chosen, but I knew there would be no privacy anywhere else and I shrank from asking Leef to go anywhere upstairs with me.

Fortifying myself with several glasses of wine in the kitchen, not even sure why I wanted to see him, I made Leef wait for ten minutes before I went in to him. 'Oh, have I kept you waiting?' I asked, pausing at the door, with what I hoped looked like magnificence. Leef smiled uncertainly, standing in the middle of the room, awkward as ever. He never liked being in Forever. He never relaxed there. Now I too had seen a little of the Terzian he knew and feared, so I was more sympathetic.

After a few minutes' stilted conversation, I said, 'So, now that you're Ithiel's second, you won't have to go south with my father again, will you?'

'No,' he agreed warily. 'It was rather a surprise. Unexpected. Ithiel never paid me much attention before.' I could see him wondering what I wanted, what he was doing there.

'In a way, it was because of me that you were promoted,' I said, hoping to make him think better of me.

'Was it?' he said, wondering whether he should thank me or not. His pride won; he didn't thank me. I offered him some wine, one of Yarrow's best, and he sat down hesitantly in a stiff chair, appraising the room, no doubt thinking how horrible and unfriendly it was. 'Why did you want to see me?' he asked.

'I don't know,' I admitted. 'When we passed each other in the hall, I thought ... You're cross with me, aren't you!'

'Cross with you? Why should I be?' he asked defensively.

'I'm not teasing you,' I said.

'No?'

'No. My Feybraiha ... it was something I had no control over,' I said.

'Look!' Leef stood up hurriedly. 'I don't want to discuss anything like this with you.'

'Don't go! I just want to apologize ...'

'Apologize?' For a moment he relaxed enough to be angry. 'For

181

what? Maybe I presumed too much. Hints dropped by you, then by Ithiel. Next, I'm told that circumstances have changed. I need no explanation other than that! Now, if you don't mind ...' He put his glass down clumsily on a spindly-legged table that rocked dangerously.

'I didn't know they'd actually asked you!' I exclaimed helplessly.

'They didn't! I made a fool of myself, that's all!' I envisaged how he must have told all his friends. It must have been excruciating for him, even more so, having to be at the house attending the celebrations.

'I'm sorry,' I said inadequately.

'Is there anything else?' he asked, with the coldest of eyes.

'No ...'

'Then if you'll excuse me ...'

He sidled past me as if I would strike out and bite him.

Later, my father summoned me to his study. I was still feeling distressed over the incident with Leef. Terzian looked very tired, his face white, his hair dishevelled. It seemed to me that he was in no condition to begin travelling. From his appearance, it looked as if he hadn't slept for a week.

'It's over,' he said, as soon as I'd shut the door behind me.

For a moment we just looked at each other. I thought he was upset because he'd been wondering about what it would have been like if it had been me and not Gahrazel. I reached to touch his hand.

'What happened?' I asked.

He closed his eyes and curled his fingers over my own. 'Poison,' he answered, as if he had a mouthful of it himself. 'They ... they made him drink poison.'

'Were you there?'

He nodded. I had never seen him so distressed, but then Gahrazel's death could not have been a pleasant spectacle. Few substances are lethal to Wraeththu. Only the tribe of Uigenna have the art of it and what deadly elixirs they possess are death in its most agonizing, terrible form. Ponclast had obviously considered the bullet or the blade too quick a release for his traitor son.

I went to Cal with my grief. 'This has been one of the worst days of my life,' I told him.

'It is only the beginning,' he replied mercilessly. 'Just a foretaste of horrors to come. I know. Life just works that way.'

CHAPTER

9

Destiny
Callasity gaping through the gashes
At tender, childhood dreams,
Can no longer recognise the fruit
Disfigured on indignant vines.

I began my training in earnest. Once the Varr armies had headed
south once more, amid pomp and sorrow, Ithiel started to teach
me how to fight, how to defend myself, how to kill. I applied
myself to my studies once more. Aihah, the Kakkahaar, had left me
several books to look through; far from enough for me to gain any
great benefit, but at least it gave me something to build on.

Sometimes, Cal would come to my room at night. Sometimes
we would only sleep together, needing company, but other times,
we would scream and struggle and tear at each other until the
dawn. He was voracious and the merest touch of him kindled my
responsive frenzy. I knew that it didn't have to be that way, but we
needed that rage somehow. We had so much pent-up energy, there
was no other way to release it yet. Once, while we were feeding
upon each other like vampires, howling like animals, Tyson woke
up in the next room and started to cry in terror. For a moment, we
were still, staring wide-eyed at each other. Then we began to laugh.
I seemed to have changed so much, the sensitivity of my childhood
dulled, a new hardness flowering within me.

News rarely reached us from the south. The supernatural mist
of the Gelaming seemed to have closed around the Varrs. They had
found a way through, but nothing could follow them. Could
anything come back out? Once, I tried to communicate with the

Kakkahaar, but could not manage it. Either my art was too feeble or the Gelaming's power too strong. Most likely, it was a combination of both. With Cobweb's help, I could achieve the right state of mind, but where there should have been light was only a grey, impenetrable void, and I shrank from that.

Dreams of greater power began once more to prowl through my sleeping mind. Often, Cal would have to shake me awake, alarmed by my muffled cries. Now, I could rarely remember the events I dreamed, even though I longed to. I knew I dreamed of a face that both scared and thrilled me, but I could never recall its appearance on waking. Cal would pull me from sleep and cry, 'What is it?' and all I could reply was, 'Eyes! Eyes!' Such haunting. It filled me with grief.

At Festival, the household tried to carry on as usual. Cobweb invited Ithiel's hara up to the house and Yarrow began to prepare his customary, sumptuous fare. We got most of what we needed from Galhea, but the other things, more exotic foods and drink, which had once been obtained from further afield, were no longer available to us. Two days before Festival night, we all gathered branches of evergreen from the gardens and decorated the house. That was when my father's presence was missed most. It was the first time since I had been born that he had not been home for Festival.

We had a small, miserable party in the drawing-room, where everyone drank too much and didn't get happy. Leef was there, but he barely looked at me. Bryony sat by the fire and, after her third glass of sheh, began to weep silently. Cobweb went to comfort her and I saw Cal looking at him.

'Do you still think about the ivy?' I asked him.

'Most days,' he admitted. I laughed and everyone looked at me.

When everyone had gone home or gone to bed, Cal and I lay beside the fire, sharing our cynicism. Some part of him was strangely distracted.

'He hasn't slept much recently, has he?' he said, unexpectedly. 'Haven't you noticed?'

'My hostling, I presume,' I answered acidly. 'No, he looks tired. He misses Terzian, I suppose, in spite of everything.'

'In spite of me, you mean.'

'Yes, in spite of you.'

'Do you think he knows something?'

'He tells me everything,' I said. 'What can he know that we don't?'

'You know him better than I do.'

'Oh, I don't know. What with your constant and careful study of Cobweb ...'

'Are you jealous?' he teased.

'No, of course not.' I rolled onto my back.

'He must be lonely.'

'Cobweb is always lonely!'

Cal stood up and looked at himself in the mirror above the mantelpiece.

'Swift ...' he said.

I sat up. 'I wouldn't advise it, Cal.' I could see clearly what he was thinking.

'Now or never,' he said, cheerily. He went to the door.

'Will I see you later?' I called.

'I hope not!' he replied.

For a while, I just sat staring at the shapes in the flames, shadows leaping beyond the hearth, thinking, what is happening to us? We are slipping, we are slipping ... Had Terzian ever said to Cal, 'What is mine is yours'? Had he? Wood popped in the fire. I threw on another log. Behind me, stretching away, the house was silent. My ears strained to hear through that silence. There was nothing. I went out into the hall and stood looking up the dark stairs, one hand on the bannister, one foot on the bottom step.

Bryony came out of the passage that led to the kitchen. 'Shall I turn off the lights down here?' she asked and I must have nodded. Her footsteps died away, into the house. The hall was full of the smell of greenery; ivy hanging down from the lights, softly moving with the chime of glass, torn ivy on the red stair carpet.

Cobweb's room was empty but his chair had been knocked over and there was a faint hint of outrage in the atmosphere. I ran up the corridor, up the few stairs that led to Cal's room, thinking that Cal had dragged or led Cobweb there, but the door was wide open and the room beyond in darkness. I was experiencing a strong sense of *déjà vu*. This had happened before. I looked in on Ty, but he was sleeping peacefully. All the doorways looked hostile and silent, sealed mouths. Behind any one ... A single, slight, echoing noise reached my ears. Prickles of cold broke out all over my skin. I prowled back down the haunted corridor and paused outside my father's door. Was anyone in there? I reached to knock, then hesitated. Perhaps Cobweb did know something. Were they in there? My father's room ... Gahrazel's face was suddenly before my eyes, laughing. I could see him young again. Again, almost inaudible, a muffled sound reached me from within the room. It could have been anything; fear, anger, pain or submission. We shall know all of this house one day ...

Before I realized what I was doing, I was pelting back along the corridor, towards the steep, forbidding stairs that led to the upper storeys. Winter lived there, my breath was steam and the eerie, violated darkness was terrible. But instinct guided me and horror of the waiting dark could not touch me. I could almost hear the echo of our voices, Gahrazel's and mine, so long ago, a lifetime away, scampering through these forgotten halls. His voice was so real to me. 'Do you know nothing, Swift?'

I found the room quite easily. Something flaked from the handle when I turned it. A supernatural rod of yellow light pointed upwards from the floor within. I went towards it and bent my face into its glow. Travelling down this ray of light, I saw below me, through a splintered hole that had waited here all this time for just this moment, my father's room. There were leaves everywhere as if the garden had burst in through the windows; a feeling of cold. I could sense the sparking presences of Cobweb and Cal, facing each other like unleashed elementals, but I could not see them. I heard Cal cry, 'What will happen to us?!' and his voice lacked its usual confidence.

My hostling, when he answered, sounded chill and distant. 'I have seen it ...'

'Seen? Seen what?'

Cobweb's voice was merely a whisper. 'I saw a great smoke. You went into it. Swift was with you ...' There was a pause and then he spoke again, ragged with haste. 'You must go that way. It is your destiny ...'

Cal moved into my line of sight. He had hold of Cobweb by the wrist, which was bloodless, the hand curled into a dead claw. 'Don't speak in riddles!' Cal cried impatiently.

'That's what I saw.'

Cobweb's dead voice made me shiver. I steadied myself and bent lower to the floor.

'When?' Cal demanded. He did not get an answer. 'Oh yes, of course! This is what you've been waiting for, isn't it? Have you made it happen? You will be glad to see me gone! Is this a lie?'

'No, I have not lied.'

'But you hate me!'

'I speak the truth!' Cobweb wriggled away from Cal's grasp and put his taloned hands on Cal's shoulders as if to shake him. 'Their Tigron is with them!' he cried, and his face was unbelievably white. The white of marble, of death. He crumpled into Cal's arms, so utterly without design, and it seemed Cal was nearly weeping.

'What do you mean? Tell me! Who are they?'

'Gelaming,' my hostling rasped. 'I have seen them ... Not here ... in the smoke, in the mist above the lake. You will go to them, both of you, through the forest of fear, into the mouth of your sin, where the beast speaks, where the beast walks and his blood is our blood. Oh! There is no escaping ...'

I too wanted to scream, 'What are you talking about?' but it was Cal's voice, not my own, ringing in my ears.

'Soon ...' Cobweb straightened up and his hands fluttered to his face. 'You want to bind me, but I am bound already,' he said.

'Cobweb ...?'

My hostling backed away, very slowly. 'You must take me; flesh to flesh, soul to soul. I have seen that too ... many times.'

'Is it something that you want?'

Cobweb frowned, shook his head. 'It is just something I have dreamed of.'

'Tell me about the dreams.'

'Not yet. Oh ...' Cobweb sat down on the edge of my father's bed. 'I shall be left alone and there will be a time of glass, like shattering, like shards of light, and the past shall come back like a shimmering veil ... I shall be left alone, but not for long ... Cal?'

Cal did not even bother to conceal the fear in his face. Mostly I could see only the top of his head, but his body was held rigid as if ready to flee.

'I want you now,' my hostling said, with bizarre sanity, and held out his arms. I denied the vision of sanity. He is mad, I thought, quite mad.

'I remember you, how you were before,' Cal said to him.

Cobweb shrugged. 'Faces from the past are always with us. They follow you too, Cal.'

'Is it Seel?'

'You are obsessed with that. Too much is hidden from me; I cannot say.'

Silence settled around them like dust. They were both staring at the floor deep in thought and then their heads rose like snakes, their eyes met.

'I don't like this room,' Cal said, rubbing his arms. 'It is cold.'

Cobweb tried to stand and faltered, his body trembling, shivering, his breath misting. Cal lifted him up, trying to gather, control, the sprawling, shuddering limbs. Cobweb appeared to have sunk into a trance. His head lolled over Cal's arm; his eyes were open, but blank. Cal held him reverently, gazing with undisguised tenderness into his empty face. They did not know they were being watched.

I heard them leave the room. The light went out and I was left in darkness, conscious only of the wind-sounds beating at the house, windows rattling. Gahrazel was in this place, poisoned and bitter. I shuddered and ran quickly to the door.

I didn't think I'd be able to sleep. What were Cal and Cobweb doing? Did they share aruna or anger and bitter words? I surprised myself by waking up and realizing that half my thoughts had been dreams.

Cobweb came to my room soon after. I had never seen him so radiant, but it was under the surface. Superficially, he was nervous and harried. He didn't know how to tell me, yet he felt he had to. I made it easier for him.

'So, what happened with you and Cal then?'

Cobweb grimaced at me and then came to sit next to me on the bed, plucking restlessly at the covers. It was hard to believe that we were not the same age, harder still to believe that he was my hostling. He shook his head and said, 'Oh, Swift!'

I touched his face. 'Jealousy and desire are not the most comfortable of friends,' I said.

Cobweb smiled ruefully. 'It must always have been there, of course. Strange, I don't often deceive myself, only other people. Now I remember I am not only soume, but ouana too. Perhaps I have woken up, perhaps some part of me shall die.'

'We've had enough talk of death!' I remarked sharply.

Cobweb stood up and shook out his hair. 'Strange that someone else should find me real,' he said.

Later, Cal told me about Cobweb's visions. I could see how much he thought of my hostling by the fact that he would not speak of anything else that had happened between them. 'It seems that one day we'll be heading south together,' he said, corroding a certain dreaminess with cheer. 'I wonder when.'

'We must enjoy this Festival,' I said dubiously. 'It may be our last.'

Cal laughed when I said that. It was just the kind of thing he liked to hear.

It took some months for something to happen, however. Spring was approaching and our lives had lapsed into a regular, if tentative routine. I thought that my brother should begin his education far sooner than I had done and spoke to Moswell about it. Tyson might not be allowed a proper childhood. His would certainly be nothing like mine had been, whatever happened. I used to think that, but for the threat of the Gelaming, we could have been truly happy at that time. There seemed to be no hatred in the house any more. All the disruptive spirits had left it. But we all knew how temporary this contentment might be. My father had been gone for so long and we had had no word from him, not even rumour. It was as if the Varrs had simply vanished into the mist, as if they had never been.

190

It all crept up on us stealthily. I, and Ithiel too, had expected messengers, torn and wounded, galloping madly, riding north to bring us news. But it was nothing like that.

One evening, Ithiel came to me while I sat in my father's study. I liked to spend time in there, for it seemed to bring me closer to Terzian. Also, I found it interesting to read through his notes and books. I learned much about how he ran Galhea and how he had organized his war-torn people when they had first arrived there. Already the days were getting longer and the house was full of sunset, sleepy and relaxed. I was sipping coffee, feet up on the desk, gazing out at the garden. One thing that I had initiated since my father's departure was that intruders were not to be shot on sight as Terzian had once ordered. I gave the excuse that more could be learned by interrogating strangers than by butchering them, but the truth was that indiscriminate killing appalled me. Perhaps it was because I always imagined being in that situation myself. Anyway we had no other way of getting news.

It seemed I'd had to change so much and in a short space of time. Galhea needed my father; he was not there. I was all they could have, the only son. Daily, I would go to the administration office my father used in Galhea and listen to his people's problems. I was not a trader or a farmer and had complained to Ithiel that he was surely far better equipped to deal with the people's queries and settle their disputes than I. Ithiel only smiled and patted me on the shoulder. 'Trader, farmer, you certainly aren't,' he said. 'But you are *fair*, Swift. That's what they need. You are Terzian's son and I shall help you as much as you want me to, but it must be your mouth they hear the words from, not mine.' Help me he did. It was obvious why Terzian relied on him so much.

Now Ithiel came into the study and smiled, amused at my unselfconscious imitation of my father. 'Intruders have been found in the forest,' he said. 'They were making for Galhea ...'

'Human or hara?' I asked.

'Well, both actually,' he replied. 'A band of wanderers, like gypsies. They call themselves Zigane, which I understand means gypsy anyway. Tribeless people banded together. Their leader is a woman ... she is what they call a pythoness, a sorceress and ...' He looked uncomfortable. 'Swift, she has asked to see you.'

'By name?'

He nodded. 'Her name is Tel-an-Kaa.'

'How strange,' I said, more to myself. 'You had better find out what she wants of me, and who sent her!'

Tel-an-Kaa, the pythoness, would not speak to anyone but me. To Ithiel, she would only keep repeating that her message was for Terzian's son alone; when I sent Swithe to her, she would not even acknowledge his presence. Something about the Zigane commanded respect. They had hara among them; Ithiel's soldiers were loath to use aggression against them; it was a superstitious fear, more than anything. I held my ground for three days and at the end of that time, sent Ithiel to the pythoness with word that I would visit her at midday.

The Zigane were indeed gypsies, or at least had modelled themselves upon gypsy appearance. They had set up a camp in the middle of the town, already selling trinkets and cloth to the Varrs. They lived in gaudy, decorated caravans and affected a matching mode of attire. We were told they worshipped snakes and that the pythoness could scry in reptile tongue.

It was not easy to tell the humans and hara apart. Both races were lean, tanned and sinewy, their clothes entirely similar. Ithiel conducted me to Tel-an-Kaa's caravan. It looked no larger than the rest, although it was bigger on the inside than it appeared on the outside. I ducked into the perfumed gloom of the interior and had my first glimpse of her. She was sitting on the edge of a couch, like a girl, her velvet gown worn and shabby, long, pale hair falling over her shoulders like rags, yet I could tell in an instant that I was looking at a queen. Her small face was serenity and splendour, half smiling, full of secrets. It is in the blood, true royalty. Perhaps we recognized that feature in each other.

'Greetings, son of Terzian,' she said and her voice was low and clear.

I motioned for Ithiel to leave us and he shut the door behind him. Now we were in another world, contained and silent. 'What is it you wish to say to me?' I asked.

She grimaced. 'Please, sit down. Would you like wine?'

I sat beside her and she handed me a long-stemmed glass.

'I was sent to find you,' she said.

'By whom?'

She smiled, shaking her head. 'We are not fond of this land, but we were persuaded by the fact that Terzian and his executioners would not be here ...'

'Who sent you?'

'I regret I cannot answer you. I bring news.'

'Of my father?' I asked quickly, noting my voice rise uncontrollably in timbre.

'It may not be welcome ...'

'Not ... is he ...?'

She shook her head before I could speak the word. 'Not that. He went into the mist.'

'I know that!' (Was that all she had to tell me?)

'Of course. They may have taken him, Swift. I don't know. It would be so easy for them, so exquisitely easy. He just went right to them, didn't he?'

'The Gelaming!'

She reached to touch my face with one small, white, childlike hand, and I thought, This must all be a dream. I shall wake up in a minute.

'You must not wait here for them, Swift,' she said.

I looked into her eyes, which were hesitant and grave. She was old-young, as Wraeththu are old-young. She was tired and she was powerful.

'Tel-an-Kaa, you must come to my house,' I said.

Tel-an-Kaa: a name of power, a sound of mystery. I never found out how old she was or her origins, or even how she had formed her band of wanderers. Perhaps it did not interest her to tell me, perhaps she only guarded the shroud of her enchantment. She was naturally wary of going with us alone to Forever, but adopted a pose of being too polite to suggest that any of her people should accompany us. Out of courtesy, I invited five of them to make up her party. 'We rarely have guests now,' I told her. 'Our cook is one of the best in the country and he will be pleased to be able to show off his art again.' Ithiel and I had arrived on horseback, and as it would have appeared improper for her to walk beside us (none of the Zigane horses were exactly what you'd call riding stock), Ithiel ordered some of his hara to bring a cart. Once more I reflected upon the indefinable quality of the pythoness that demanded respect. Even Ithiel felt it and he had never admitted to a great love of humankind.

On the way back to the house, I trotted my horse beside her. 'Why is it that you have sought me out?' I asked.

She smiled her careful, cat's smile. 'Oh, but I have already said, I had a message.'

'Someone has paid you well then?' I suggested, but she would not answer. I caught Ithiel's eye and could see that he was sharing my suspicions. Varrs are the most feared of Wraeththu in Megalithica, yet this outlandish gypsy queen had wandered insouciantly into our lands, without precaution or defence. It was uncanny. Perhaps more uncanny was the way in which we treated her. Was it just my influence? Because of Bryony, women fascinated me for their mercurial minds and their unpredictable disposition, but I would never have imagined that I would come to treat a human with such deference.

Tel-an-Kaa appraised my home with a critical eye. She bowed before Cobweb and said, 'Your name is known to us,' which, as she had anticipated, pleased him greatly.

Yarrow prepared us a sumptuous lunch, which the Zigane consumed with undisguised enthusiasm. 'It is some time since I have eaten as well,' Tel-an-Kaa confided to Cobweb. She resisted all attempts by our household to draw her out about the message she carried for me, light-heartedly mocking all serious questions. Cal watched her steadily and I could tell that she was conscious of his dislike.

'You are lucky our noble lord is absent,' he said to her. 'Only Swift is against the slaughter of strangers. Perhaps you owe your life to him.'

Only when Cal spoke to her did the Pythoness look uncomfortable. 'We would not be here if Terzian had not been away,' she said. 'His leaving is the sole reason for us being here.'

'Oh?' Cal said archly. 'And perhaps you'd like to expand on that sole reason …?'

'What I have to say is for Terzian's son alone,' she replied, but she did not touch her food again after that.

After lunch, I took her to the conservatory, where it was warm and private. Bryony brought us wine and honey cakes. I could see that she was not impressed with Tel-an-Kaa either, but that was probably just Bryony being female and territorial.

'I am surprised to see a woman in this house,' the Pythoness remarked. I decided not to answer her. Perhaps she was here to gather information about us. I resolved to reveal as little as possible.

'I think, perhaps, you had better tell me the real reason for your being here,' I said. 'You spoke obliquely of my father being taken by the Gelaming, but I doubt if you can produce proof of that. You spoke of messages, while telling me nothing. If you think I am unlike my father in some ways, you are right, but my patience is not limitless. If I decide you are a danger to us, I will not hesitate to order your extinction.'

She inclined her head graciously. 'But of course! I respect your position, Swift. In your shoes I would think likewise. I admit I have walked into your home with only a handful of vague hints and rather too much bravado, but I too have to be cautious. You are spoken well of and we expected to feel safe coming here, but I could not be entirely sure. You are Terzian's son after all and I am convinced his blood is thicker than most.'

I smiled, relaxing enough to sit down.

'Well then, why *do* you want to see me?'

'Why?' Her eyes swerved away from mine with the grace of flight. 'You will be annoyed when I say that some things I cannot tell you …'

She looked surprised at my laughter. 'Oh, I have grown up with that sentence ringing through my head!' I explained. 'Throughout my life I have had to put up with hidden things. That you should say it now seems only natural.'

'It is true. I cannot tell you who sent me. My master would remain anonymous,' she said. Her fingers idly traced patterns in the

195

wrought-iron table at her side; the honey cakes were untouched. 'In the south ... there is a great strangeness in the south. Magic, conflicting magic has warped the land. Time and space have been injured. It is true that your father went straight to the Gelaming. Although the desert tribe, the Kakkahaar, breached the Gelaming's defences, the Gelaming still had the power to choose where that breach should be ... Through my master, Swift, they have asked for you. They have no love of war, no desire for pain. Through you, pure-born as you are, they hope to unite the northern tribes-'

'Wait!' I interrupted quickly. 'I can never speak for any people other than my own, here in Galhea. It is true that I too have no love of war, and I would like to see peace restored to our lands, but the hara further north have never seen me. They have probably never even heard of me. How can I speak for them? They are Varrs. In Galhea, our way of life has maybe made us soft, but I can assure you, that is not the case in Ponclast's domain. The har who can cold-bloodedly order the murder of his own son will not listen to me. I can do nothing!'

She nodded thoughtfully. 'You are right. Perhaps that is not exactly what I meant ...'

I stood up. 'Have the Gelaming sent you, Pythoness?' I demanded. 'Is this their way of defeating us? Are you here to worm your way into Galhea's heart and set poison there?'

'No,' she replied, unruffled. 'I told you; my master sent me. Let us say that, in this matter, he adheres to neither side. As for the Gelaming's motives, I am not qualified to say ...'

'You must agree,' I told her, 'that this all seems highly suspicious. Only a fool would trust you. Only a fool would ride south into what is literally the unknown, because you suggest it.'

She rubbed her forehead. 'Yes, I suppose so ... I realize I have to convince you. I would be held in contempt if I could not succeed.'

'Convince me then.'

She looked up at me wearily, leaning on her hand. 'Convince you? How? All I have to say is that you must ride south and trust in Fate. Perhaps your father's life depends on it ... perhaps. In your heart, you must know you are irresistibly drawn to what is waiting for you. Your dreams will have been forewarning you for quite some time, I think. Remember them now. Do you sense danger? You don't, do you! You think you ought to, but you can't. You are strong, Swift, strong and good. I can see that for myself. Galhea seems like yours now. It seems like a place untouched by the horror beyond its fields. I speak from experience. It would astound you.'

'It seems you know me,' I said, wondering.

'I feel I do,' she replied. 'Give me your hand.'

Her female flesh felt no different from mine, yet we were worlds apart.

'See this,' she said stroking my palm. 'This is the line of destiny. It cuts deep; so straight, so true. Heart and head without blemish. The line of head is separate from the line of life; this symbolizes your intellect, your early development. You are passionate, but not governed by your passions. The only difficulty is ... now.'

'Now!' I exclaimed.

'An artistic hand,' she said, thinking aloud.

'Is it really possible,' I said softly, 'what the Gelaming believe, human and hara sharing this world; the concept of harmony? Is it really possible?'

The Pythoness pulled a wry face. 'They do not doubt it,' she said, 'but if it is possible, it will be sanctified by blood.'

'Fighting is a dream to me,' I said. 'I have only heard of it. I have never seen death ...'

'You will,' she answered. 'Long ago, I have heard, maybe in a saner, more aquatic age, when a temple was built, it demanded a life. Perhaps the temple that the Gelaming seek to build is so great, so beyond our grasp, only a thousand lives will make it live; I don't know. I'm only a poor girl after all.'

We both laughed and I took her hand. 'I do believe you,' I said.

'Your instincts have not failed you,' she replied.

So, my destiny would lead me at last to the south and the wild magic that lay there. In my heart, I was afraid that I could never be ready to face whatever might be waiting for me, yet I heeded the call, like my father had done before me, perhaps. Would I find him there? He had been gone for so long without us hearing news that it was as if he had already died. Perhaps he had. Would we have

197

known? Could Cobweb's intuition penetrate the barrier that kept him from us?

After my talk with the Pythoness in the conservatory, my mind was already made up. Hadn't my hostling known this would happen? It was Fate, and there could be no other way. Even so, I was nervous of telling anyone. I anticipated their scorn, their amazement, their anger.

In the evening, we ate out on the lawns, the smoky aroma of cooking meat drifting around us, the light of torches eating at the sky. I could smell the vitality of spring in the air. It was a smell of something rushing in, a focusing, and great excitement. Something was waiting for me. Now I turned towards it and the pull was stronger. I wore a fur coat draped around my shoulders, but could not eat. Two of Tel-an-Kaa's troupe were musicians, and soon the darkness was alive with the fairy music of their strange echoing strings, the rhythmic mumble of a speaking drum. Shapes swayed in the leaping light of the torches, hissing fat spat down onto the glow beneath the meat and I could hear laughter. It was as if I was somewhere else, looking through a window at the lawns of Forever. Fighting disorientation, I walked towards the lake.

There is nowhere on this earth so eerie, so haunted or so beautiful as that spot in my father's garden. Moonlight touched the uneven surface of the lake, around me tall cypress trees nodded their lofty heads in a slight breeze and I could see the flicker of white that was the summerhouse between the branches. I had not been there since that time when Cal and Cobweb had been there. When I tried to open the door, it was stuck, but eventually, in a sigh of flaking paint, it gave in to my demands and squealed open. I sat down on the lip of the lily bowl. Pale light fell in through the glass across the tiled floor. My heart was heavy. I was grieved and exultant at the same time. (Is that possible?) No-one could tell me exactly what Fate had in store for me. Would I go to my death?

I reached down, under the rim of the stone bowl, searching for the tap that would turn on the fountain. I shivered as webs brushed my skin. Resisting, as the door had done, the fountain tap gradually turned and life spurted into the ancient mechanisms. With a shudder and a few abortive bursts, water finally shot upwards out of the stone animal's mouth, turning its scaly flanks dark with moisture. I watched it. Everything was black and white, or grey. I listened to the water sounds. I dipped my fingers in the pool.

When I heard the door to the summerhouse scrape open, I looked up, thinking it would be Cal, or Cobweb. Only they knew me well enough to know where to find me. Instinct guided the three of us in scented circles around each other. But it was neither of them. I saw Leef standing there and knew immediately that this was just another intrinsic rightness of the whole situation. Leef and I had had our differences in the past, it is true, but circumstances, even roles, had changed in Galhea. Maintaining a worn-out atmosphere of resentment and bitterness was something none of us had time for any longer. I smiled and said, 'Come in, come in.'

'What are you doing here, all alone?' he asked. His voice was slightly slurred.

'Oh, just thinking,' I replied. 'Did you follow me?'

'Mmmm. To my cost, no doubt.'

'Ah, there speaks a sore heart!' I said lightly.

Leef pulled a face and leaned against the doorframe. 'There is no shame in wanting only the best, is there?'

I shook my head. 'No, but I feel that what you say is only flattery.'

'It's just my opinion, of course.'

We both started to laugh, the fountain sounds seemed to fade right away, and he walked across the floor towards me.

'What's going on, Swift?'

'What do you mean? Is this why you followed me?' I asked, playing for time.

'One of the reasons … Zigane! A woman demanding to speak with you and then you allowing it, even inviting her and her ragged followers into your home … What did she tell you, Swift?'

199

'A message, that's all. Come here. Sit by me.'

I didn't tell him everything, of course, only what was necessary. He made a few indignant noises, but did not interrupt me. After I had finished speaking, he said, 'And of course you've decided to ride south now.' I ignored his dry tone.

'Yes. What else can I do? Wait here forever ... or until it's too late? I'm not sure I have anything to lose. I'm not sure.'

Leef shook his head at the floor. 'Are you going alone?'

'I don't think so ...'

'Swift, it will be dangerous!'

'Yes.' I stood up, pulling the fur closer to my body. For a while we argued half-heartedly, he pointing out the dangers, me justifying the cause. I told him that Ithiel had taught me how to defend myself; I was not completely helpless. Leef pointed out that I would never know how to fight until I had had to put it into practice.

'Look, I'm going! There is nothing you can say to dissuade me!' I shouted.

'I don't want to dissuade you, but you have to be made aware of the pitfalls.'

'Cal will be with me,' I said airily, not yet sure if that was true.

'Just the two of you?'

'Yes, I suppose so.'

'That settles it,' he said.

'Settles what?'

'I shall have to ride with you.'

'You!' I exploded. 'You can't! You'll be needed here.'

'Needed? Maybe. But it seems to me that the fate of Galhea is to travel south. I'm a fighter. I'm well trained, and I also know the way.' He paused and smiled. I could see his teeth in the pale light. 'Perhaps you are concerned I am not ... *har* enough to travel with you and the celebrated Cal.'

'I don't doubt your ability, Leef.'

'Then trust my maturity too. You have nothing to worry about. What is done is done. The flower of Galhea rides south; he needs an escort. Much is at stake, Swift.'

'Well, if you're sure ... Thank you, Leef.'

He stood up and came to stand behind me, circling me with his arms.

'You are braver now,' I remarked.

'Terzian is not here, and you're no longer a child.'

'But I'm the beast that rejected you. I may do so again. Are you so confident or is it just the enormous amount of liquor that you've consumed, whose odour is now overpowering me?'

I could feel his laughter. 'Liquid courage,' he said. 'I want to take aruna with you. Shall we go back to Forever or shall we ride into town?'

'You are impertinent!' I snapped. 'Town, I think.'

Since his promotion, Leef had been given his own house and staff to care for his needs. It was not a large house, but comfortable and warm. We drank wine beside the fire downstairs, sitting on hairy deerskin rugs.

'This may sound a bit well-worn, but I have waited a long time for this,' Leef told me with a grin.

'Your hair has grown,' I said and reached to touch it. I could smell his desire, which is indescribable and different for everyone. He took my hands and kissed them. 'You're always losing weight,' I said. 'You look even thinner.'

He shook his head. 'No ... Swift, was it marvellous?' I thought he was still teasing, but when I looked at his eyes, they were serious.

'Yes, it was. I'm not going to say it should have been you, because it shouldn't ... I want you now; is that enough?'

'Enough? Let me answer that properly. Come here!'

Aruna with Leef was nothing like the way it had been with Cal. He was gentle and lazy and loved to be fussed. When I stroked him, he could purr like a cat. For a while he was content to lie there and be pampered, but once I began to show signs of being more ouana than soume, he laughed and threw me onto my back, lying over me so I could not move. 'Swift,' he said, 'let me at least pretend I am the first! Be scared and shy and compliant. Be water to quench my heavenly fire!'

His hand slid down my back, competent and caressing. I smiled in the firelight.

201

'Look at me; already I am yours.'

Later, we went up to his bedroom and we sleepily began to make plans.

'Tomorrow I shall have to tell them,' I said, glumly.

'I shall come with you.' Leef decided. 'It might make it easier.'

'No, I shall have to tell Cobweb, at least, alone. I suppose he knows already, but ... half of me still doesn't want to go but I can't waste my life here.'

'Ah, all the action's in the south and you want to be part of it!'

'Yes, if you like. I'm curious as well. What are they like? I know their culture is different from ours. Bryony says that Varrs are more like men. Perhaps the Gelaming won't even look anything like us.'

Leef took me in his arms, seeking my neck with his mouth. I could feel his tongue on my skin. 'Are you scared?' he asked in a muffled voice.

I thought about this for a moment. 'Scared ... scared ... Not really, strangely enough. If the Gelaming have really asked for me ...'

'If! Has it occurred to you that you may be a threat to them in some way? Perhaps it is a trap.'

That thought had already occurred to me. 'I shall soon find out,' I said.

I went home early to find Cobweb and Cal conversing furtively in the drawing-room. My absence had been noted and considered. Cobweb took in my rather bedraggled appearance with one chilling glance

'Well, when are you leaving?' he demanded. I looked at Cal, who smiled and nodded.

'It's up to you,' I said to him.

He shrugged. 'As soon as possible, I suppose. We don't want to deprive the jaws of fate unnecessarily, now do we?'

'Leef is coming with us.'

'How cosy.'

There was a moment's silence. I wanted to run to both of them and hold them to me.

Cobweb leaned back in his chair. 'I hope you're ready,' he said ambiguously.

'It's more than dreams,' I said, and when our eyes met, I could tell he knew what I meant.

BOOK TWO

BOOK TWO

1

Phantom Evil
Panopy, ardour, ritual, pain,
Death-stench, blood-stain,
War-magic, music-thrill,
Weary limbs, love and kill.

Our day of departure was warm and cloudless, acid green mantling the trees to herald our way. 'Once more into the jaws of chance!' Cal exclaimed in a weary voice. It was a sentiment he was fond of, but I guessed he was not too sorry to leave. Our goodbyes on the previous evening had been emotional and wearing. Most of our household shared the suspicion that we would never return and probably cursed our folly.

I had asked Tel-an-Kaa to remain in Galhea for a while, thinking that Cobweb might find her presence a comfort. Some of the Zigane obviously welcomed a chance to rest, and I suspect that the Pythoness was one of them. As she had said, life beyond the fields of Galhea would astound me.

I had appropriated three of my father's best horses (his stables were always well stocked) and a packhorse from Ithiel. We were bristling with weapons and had a large tent so that our nights could be spent in comparative comfort. Cobweb loaded me with charms and packets of healing herbs. Tyson gave me a stick to ward off devils, casting mournful glances at Cal as we mounted our horses.

Leef said that we would have several weeks' travelling before we even began to approach where the Gelaming's defences started. We set off at a brisk trot, westwards to avoid the forest, across the cropped fields. Herds of animals lumbered from our path, birds shrieked a warning of our intrusion. I could not accept that I was really leaving. It did not feel like it. Behind me, on their tree-mantled hills, the windows of Galhea sparkled in the rising sun. I could still make out Forever on the steepest slope, outlined against the sky. Bryony and Yarrow would be in the kitchens. Tyson would be waking up. Life would go on, as always.

Leef knew of several Wraeththu settlements to the south. We anticipated being able to restock our supplies there, all of us agreeing that to strangers we would no longer be Varrs, but just three travellers of no particular tribe, making for the Gelaming. We had tried to make our clothing as anonymous as possible, shrouding ourselves in grey, hooded cloaks, concealing our weapons.

For the first three days our travelling was uninterrupted save for sleeping. We were lucky that my father's horses had been kept in prime condition and that we could keep up a steady, consistent pace. The first night we had some trouble in erecting the tent. Leef found out that some vital part was missing and we had to improvise. We made ourselves a small fire and cooked some of the meat we had brought with us. I had been wondering about the night-times, that time for starlight and stirrings. Neither Cal nor Leef was a stranger to me physically. I wondered what would happen should either of them approach me. We had only the one tent after all. This, of course, was yet another aspect of my inexperience. For the first two nights, we curled up separately in our blankets, too tired to think of the solace or the fire of aruna, and I began to think that this was the way it was to be for the entire journey, a thought which I found strangely comforting for it avoided awkwardness.

On the third evening, we camped on the edge of a dense pine forest; rustlings behind us in the darkness. I kept having to look over my shoulder. Leef crept off into the trees in search of prey for our supper, while I untackled the horses and brushed the dust and dried sweat from their coats. Cal came over to watch me for a while. I knew he had something to say; I just brushed and waited. Eventually, he said, 'Tonight.'

'Tonight what?'

'Oh, just arrangements,' he replied. 'Up till now there has been slight reticence, mostly coming from you, I think. This is the world of adults, little Swift. This is the way we do things from now on. The lifeblood of Wraeththu, remember?'

'Oh,' I said dubiously. I carried on brushing the horse vigorously. Cal reached out quickly and covered my hand with his own to stop me.

'You're not in Galhea now,' he said. I tried to smile at him, but his eyes were too dark.

'You must do as you think is right,' I said.

Leef brought a large rabbit back to the fire, which he skinned and gutted and spitted on a stick. Cal shared out bread and cheese from our supplies and we drank wine from a bottle. Yarrow had only given us half a dozen; we had no room to carry more.

After the meal, Cal stretched out on the springy turf and said, 'Ah, Paradise! Imagine this is Eden and we still have all our ribs!'

Leef laughed. 'Hail, Lucifer!' he said. 'Fallen angel.'

'Angels have wings,' I said.

'Six!' Cal propped himself up on his elbows. 'Mine must have been burned off in the fall to Hell. Where are yours, Swift?'

'Oh, in my heart.'

'And yours, Leef?'

'Hidden; as all Wraeththu organs of magic. If you have no wings, Cal, I could take you flying.'

All of this conversation was conducted with much grinning and laughter, but there was no denying the undercurrent.

'We must all fly,' Cal said coolly. 'We must fly together.' He stood up, in the purple gloom lit by firelight, and shrugged away his clothing as if it had no substance. He stretched towards the sky, throwing back his head, a slim, white flame in the dusk. Leef's eyes gleamed with hunger, but the feast was before him. Cal reached for the moon, swaying, humming beneath his breath, summoning forth his inner strength. 'Moon of radiance,' he whispered, his hands twisting like moths. 'Pale swimmer of the skies, I entreat thee by the elements to sanctify our communion in thy name. Before thee, I sacrifice my fire. Before thee I am aquatic. Hail Ofaniel, angel of the moon! Shine upon us.'

Only the sound of the crackling fire broke the velvet silence. The waning moon shone back impassively at Cal's prayer. He shivered. Leef leaned forward on the grass. There was only one mouthful of wine left in the bottle. He threw it into the fire and murmured, 'Ofaniel.'

I too leaned towards the flames. They fought with the wine that had sought to smother them. I blew softly and the red glowed brighter. 'Ofaniel,' I said.

Cal looked over his shoulder at us. 'Beyond Galhea,' he murmured, 'we must abide by the rules. We are in another land. It is safer.' He reached out his hands and we took them in our own. 'Complete the circle,' he said. 'Feel the current. I am soume. You must be fire. I am the altar.'

This was something I had never experienced. Aruna as it was meant to be; an act of magic. Leef and I shared breath above Cal's body and when Leef slid like a fish into the soume sea, I covered Cal's mouth with my own, filled with his sighs. Watching them, the fire of desire consumed me from within. I was almost delirious by the time Leef guided me gently into the moist folds, slippery with his seed. Cal's body shone beneath me and his hair was wet. This was true soume; he did not fight me. Afterwards, he collected our mingled essences in a cup and dug a hole in the earth with a stick.

'What are you doing?' I asked, too exhausted to move. I saw his eyes glow in the last of the firelight.

'We must bury our sacrifice,' he said.

We had been travelling southwest. In the morning, Leef consulted his compass and we turned true south. Banks of thick cloud filled the sky before us, untended fields and defiant stands of trees undulated away from us to the left, while on our other side, the skirts of the great forest hugged the cracked surface of the road we followed. In places the surface had been burst asunder by the roots of trees; we passed bundles of rag that looked too hideous, too suggestive to investigate. Sometimes, we passed dead, burned out vehicles, sagging and rusting at the edge of the road, long abandoned. I wondered why they had been left there. Had men died in the rotted seats? Had the fuel just run out? I tried to open the door of one but was greeted by a puff of evil air, so did not look further.

210

I learned how quickly the earth takes back what humankind had taken from her. Buildings like empty skulls could be seen amid riotous growths of weed and grass. A field of corn surged unchecked across the neglected yard of a farm. We passed a crossroads where something hung crucified, its legs hugged by clinging vines, white flowers blooming among the rags of its rotted belly. Cal was quite impressed by that sight. When the wind blew from the south, we could smell magic, the hairs on the backs of our necks would rise and we would be filled with dread and joy. Overall, the countryside seemed deserted.

One morning, as we packed up our belongings at the side of the road, half hidden by a scrubby copse, a galloping troupe of hara thundered past us on large, glossy horses. They wore long feathers in their hair, their faces were painted to look like demons; they paid us no attention. Cal looked at Leef and said, 'Kheops?'

Leef nodded. 'Probably.'

They had no interest in us.

We came upon an inhabited town quite unexpectedly. Leef ordered us to halt. 'We'd best go around. Into the trees,' he said. Someone fired one or two warning shots over our heads, but no-one came after us. Whether humans or hara occupied the town was impossible to guess. Leef made us keep going for another two hours until he considered it safe enough to make camp for the night. I thought he was being too wary and mentioned it to Cal, who declined to comment.

We set up our tent among some thin, widely spaced trees. Noisy birds squabbled in the darkening foliage above us and feathers fell down into our fire. Leef organized us to keep watch for enemies throughout the night. When it was my turn, (in that dreadful cold time before the dawn that is truly the dead of night), I wrapped myself in my blanket and sat hunched by the fire, occasionally feeding it with small sticks and leaves and watching the sparks spiral and burn. I could hear Cal's gentle snores behind me; now and again Leef would mutter something incoherent. He had wanted us to put the fire out for, he said, the light might attract unwanted guests, but I had argued that the night was too cold for that. We were miles from anywhere and we hadn't seen a living soul for two hours. Eventually, if only so he didn't have to listen to my moaning, Leef relented and the fire stayed lit. Resting my chin on my raised knees, nursing a long-barrelled gun between my legs, I smiled to myself as I thought back on our conversation.

I must have been dozing; there's a vague memory of a dream even now, for suddenly I found myself thrown backwards with sickening impact. My mind immediately tried to rationalize: What is this? Has a branch fallen? As quickly as I thought that, rough hands covered my mouth; I had no time to call out. A voice said 'Freak!' quite sanely and something punched me between the legs. Sparks seem to shoot right out of me, pain contorted my spine and the reek of foul breath blew over me like the stench of death. They covered my head with the blanket; I tried to struggle, but whatever had hold of me was too strong. There was a taste of vomit in the back of my throat; they were still kicking at me. I was facing death. I was powerless. Then there was a shout behind me, a sound as low and clear as a bell, followed by musical laughter. Had these attackers thought I was alone? Gunfire rolled across the night air in an echoing peal; there was a sound like a sack falling to the ground, guttural curses. Suddenly, not so many hands seemed to be pinning me down. On my back I tried to wriggle away, fighting with the blanket that filled my eyes. Another lightning crack and something heavy fell across my legs. I cried out as my groin reminded me of the assault it had suffered. In an instant the air became full of the sound of bullets flying, ricocheting off trees; horses jostling and groaning in panic. I heard Cal swear and Leef shout, 'To your right, Cal!' 'Oh, the sweet wine of blood!' Cal exclaimed lightly. Another heavy thud. Then he was untangling me from the blanket and laughing in my face, his eyes shining like stars. 'You OK, Swift?' he said.

There was little to see really. A vile creature, quite dead, lay by my feet, gaping at the stars. Two others were sprawled over the remains of our fire. Cal was leaning forward, his hands braced on his knees. 'God, I'm out of condition!' He did not look it.

'One to you, two to me,' Leef observed cheerfully, counting bodies.

'You fight like the devil,' Cal remarked, bending to retrieve his knife from one of the corpses.

'I'm a Varr.' Leef looked at me. 'Swift, you were supposed to be on watch! Be more vigilant next time, will you? We were lucky; it could have so easily gone in their favour.'

It had been men who'd attacked us. Now I had the chance to appreciate what Moswell had once told me about ugliness. The bodies were filthy. Inside their open mouths, I could see the blackened stumps of splintered teeth. The smell was abysmal. We dragged the corpses some yards away from our camp and covered them with branches and leaves. Leef decided we should leave the area straight away. It was possible that others might be near.

After that, we were much more careful, avoiding any signs of habitation, veering away from plumes of smoke above the trees.

'I think the settlement of the Amaha lies this way,' Leef said, as our horses plodded along through a pelting rain.

'I hope so,' Cal replied drily, 'otherwise we starve.'

We had used up the last of the food from Galhea two days before and had been living off the land as best we could. Because of the time of year, there wasn't any fruit around, but we raided a field of root vegetables (tough and stringy, but still nourishment), close to a town we passed, and loaded our packhorse with them. I congratulated myself on my first kill. It was only a small animal, but it gave us a meal.

The Amaha are only a small tribe, and while not warlike, vigorous in defence of their own property. They professed to have little time for the Gelaming, mainly because they were more interested in getting on with their own lives, tending their fields and caring for their animals. Their existence seemed simple, but I envied their contentment. The Varrs had traded with them for some years, as Amaharan cured meats and cheeses were regarded as a culinary delicacy in the north. The steady affluence such transactions had encouraged meant that the Amaha could decorate their most favoured hara with gold and defend the walls of their town with weapons more effective than knives and spears. Not all the town of Ahmouth was supplied with electricity for they had only one generator, which, by the sound it gave off, seemed none too reliable. The buildings were single-storey and sand-coloured; many had thatched roofs and carved lintels. I was impressed by the neatness of the few short streets that composed the town.

Leef had been to Ahmouth a couple of times before and was familiar with Hiren, the Firekeeper, ruler of Ahmouth. Hiren was surprised to see Varrs abroad at this time, but did not ask too many questions. The Amaha had heard of Terzian's foray south but told us that, as travellers north had dwindled virtually to none, they had heard neither rumour nor truth about the Varrs' fate. They were not really concerned with the outcome but were interested in gossip. I heard Hiren muse aloud about whether the Gelaming would be interested in reopening trade with Ahmouth, should they take over Galhea. I think this, more than anything, made me realize that Varrs are not the centre of the universe as I'd been brought up to think.

We were lucky that currency from Galhea could still buy us supplies. Hiren offered us the hospitality of his house and then proceeded to name prices for the things that we required. He and his consort were like identical twins; both tall, fair and slim. They had three harlings, the oldest of which was about two years younger than myself. His name was Throyne and he seemed very interested in the fact that I was Terzian's son. Sitting next to him at the evening meal that first night in Ahmouth, I answered his questions as best I could, though there was a lot about my own tribe I was ignorant of. Throyne asked me what my caste was and what level I was on. It wasn't a subject I thought about often, but I was rather ashamed to admit that I was only first level Kaimana. Throyne thought my training had been neglected because of the troubles with the Gelaming and expressed condescending sympathy. I remember smiling thinly. 'My hostling has taught me many things,' I said.

Later that night, because we were feeling comfortable and rested, Cal, Leef and I took aruna together, sharing our strength. I was soume and it was almost too intoxicating to describe what it was like to have both of them caressing me and penetrating me, filling me with the blue cloud of their spirits. Cal laughed and said, 'Swift

214

is insatiable!' and Leef had added humorously, 'Swift is incomparable!' It was a happy time. Lying awake afterwards, while Leef and Cal greedily smoked cigarettes that Hiren had sold them, I found myself wondering if, on the road south, my father had sought company to relieve his spiritual and physical needs. I wondered whether, as the Varrs had eaten their evening meals beside their camp fires, Terzian had chosen someone and beckoned; whether that someone had been pleased or annoyed and whether I knew him. I told Leef what I was thinking (he would obviously know, if anyone), and there had been a moment's uncomfortable silence. My heart quickened its pace a little. 'Well,' I said, 'who was it? You'll have to tell me now.'

Leef reached over Cal to stroke my arm. 'I don't really know why I'm reluctant to tell you. How can it possibly hurt now?' (That meant it probably would.) 'It was Gahrazel. On that first time south, it was always Gahrazel. Sometimes we heard him cry out. Once I saw Gahrazel come out of Terzian's tent in the morning and take a knife and cut his own flesh. He watched the blood fall. It explains nothing, yet it explains everything. I was not surprised at what happened to Gahrazel.'

'Why didn't you tell me before?' I demanded. My flesh had gone cold.

'I didn't want to. Why should I? Gahrazel is dead now; another Varrish casualty. He was born in the wrong place, I suppose. He rarely spoke to me.'

I remembered the long gallery in Forever, morning sunlight coming in over Gahrazel's shoulder where he sat on the floor. 'I hate what your father's done to me, Swift ...' I shivered. It was merely the tip of the iceberg.

We stayed in Ahmouth for two days and, I must admit, I was reluctant to leave. Our quest had become unreal. Away from Galhea I was no longer sure if the threat of the Gelaming still existed or if it ever had. I thought about going home. Dark clouds still hung in the southern sky. I did not want to go towards them. Leef did not ask me what I was thinking. He just said, 'We must keep going, Swift; all of us.' Cal had spent too much of our currency on tobacco. We squabbled amiably as the Amaha watched us ride away from their homes.

We headed back to the old highway and once the fresh, crisp air got into my lungs and the horses were trotting nimbly through dew-soaked grass, my spirits began to lift again. Cal started to sing and eventually Leef and I joined in. Near noon, the grey ribbon of the road could be seen snaking across the countryside ahead of us.

'Soon we shall reach the city,' Cal said.

'What city?' I asked.

'A dead one.' Leef's voice sounded bitter.

'An amazing sight,' Cal remarked.

'Not the word I'd use,' Leef said coldly.

The road became wider, its surface more broken. The abandoned vehicles we rode past were no longer intact but scattered like insect shells across the tarmac. Buildings became more frequent sights, but they were all horribly vandalized, as if torn apart by frenzied hands. Disturbingly, some of them gave off a feeling of still being lived in. We kept our guns in our hands and quickened the horses' pace, which was difficult, for there were so many obstacles to negotiate.

'Few ever come here by choice,' Leef said. 'The city is close. We shall pass round it.'

'Is it safe?' I asked. 'Is it deserted?'

'Yes,' Leef answered shortly, but his eyes were never still.

'It was a man's city,' Cal told me. 'The reason it's now in such a sorry state can be put down to one cause; man himself. Unrest, poverty, bitterness. Bitterness that became anger and then hysteria. They tore it down themselves. Such a waste. Wraeththu consider it an unlucky place and sensibly shun it whenever possible. Some years ago, I passed this way and took a look around. I sort of liked it.'

We breasted a steep hill, and the road fell away into a valley before us, the contents of which took my breath away. Once, towers of glass must have reared towards the sky; now they were broken off halfway up, fingers of steel poking through concrete, strangely sparkling, heavy vines creeping over them like a shroud. Listing telegraph poles leaned drunkenly away from us in disordered rows, streetlights stood intact, watching mournfully over flattened rubble. I could still feel the life that had once bustled here, just a vibration of the past, the thousands of lives that had once filled its buildings. It could have been only yesterday or a thousand years before. I stared entranced.

'Do men still live here?' My voice was an awed whisper.

'If they do, I don't want to find out,' Leef replied.

'I never saw anyone when I was here before,' Cal said.

It took us several hours to skirt the city. I had never imagined a town could be so huge. It was scary, but the kind of scary that makes you want to explore. Cal and Leef wouldn't hear of it, and I was secretly relieved, though I pretended bravery. 'It's just wasting time,' they said, 'and it may be dangerous. It would be senseless to go in there.'

Before then, I had not thought that men had had real technology. I had only seen photographs and it was like looking at something out of a story. In that gaunt, sprawling ruin, I could see the vestiges of past greatness. Now it was too far gone for Wraeththu to rescue it. Cal said that Wraeththu should concentrate more on building their own cities anyway. They had stolen enough from men. It was too easy to do that. Nothing new could be gained from it. He began to speak, then, of Immanion, the Gelaming's city, that Thiede had built. He said that it was a true Wraeththu city.

'Thiede must be very strong,' I said.

'He is,' Cal agreed, suppressing a shudder, but not before both Leef and myself noticed it. 'He is strong, ruthless, clever ...'

'What does he look like?' I asked, and Leef repeated my question. Cal had actually met Thiede; to Leef and myself he was just a terrifying name.

'He looks like God,' Cal said grandly, but that wasn't enough. We pressed for more details. 'Well, he's very tall,' Cal continued, screwing up his eyes to remember, 'and he has red hair which is very long and spiked up over his head like a halo of fire. Naturally, he possesses unnerving beauty, and his eyes sometimes look yellow. He looks like a child and he looks a thousand years old. His fingernails are varnished claws that could take your eye out. He talks like an actor and pretends weakness. I must admit he scares the shit out of me!'

217

For a while we were silent, all of us thinking of the omnipotent Thiede. I was terrified that it would be him waiting for me at my journey's end, waiting to throw me my father's head before he killed me too.

Being on horseback all day and sleeping rough at night had been a great shock to my system at first. I never thought I'd get used to it. On the day after we'd left Galhea, my thighs had been rubbed raw, and the skin between my fingers. My horse was a headstrong yellow mare called Tulga. It amused her to fight with me constantly, tugging the reins through my fingers, never keeping her head still, walking sideways when the mood took her, no matter what instructions I tried to give her. It also grieved me having to feel dirty all the time. I was used to creature comforts and now it seemed I had only the comfort of creatures! Both Cal and Leef were used to travelling. They soon fell into a routine; it neither inconvenienced them nor did they appear to dislike it. I had to get used to eating partially cooked food peppered with soot and grass and leaf bits. I had to get used to feeling tired all the time. After some weeks, the discomfort did seem to lose its sting; I became inured to it. As we travelled towards the south, the air gradually became warmer; nights became more bearable.

Sometimes we faced hostility; it was impossible to avoid everyone. Once I had to fight for my life. I killed a man. It was not a momentous event for me, not even sickening. It had been either me or him; that simple. Luck had been on my side. Warm blood had touched my skin and I didn't even bother to wipe it off properly. Round about that time, we lost the packhorse. We never found out what happened to it, for it just disappeared silently one night. Someone may have stolen it, or its tether may have come undone and it wandered off. We never found out; but of course, a lot of our supplies disappeared with it. Leef was furious.

I began to dream of floating hair and beckoning eyes again. When I had those dreams I would always wake up craving aruna with a bitter taste in my mouth.

Cal and Leef did not pamper me. I learned how to survive and my conscious self forgot the Swift that had lived within the nurturing womb of Forever. I could feel myself maturing. I felt stronger and crueller. Travelling became my life until it seemed I had known no other. At first I had felt hungry all the time, but I became accustomed to that and started to smoke Cal's thin, acrid cigarettes. It helped me get over the hunger.

We stole, we fought off hostile strangers and we rode. Aruna was our only luxury. Through that we became close. Through that we became one unit, anticipating each other's thoughts, moving forward like a well-tended machine; it seemed nothing could touch us. We occasionally gleaned snippets of news about the Varrs, but never anything much. People had seen them pass. They had seen no-one return.

One day, Leef's horse broke its leg and we had to kill it. Impassively, we cut some of it up for meat and left the rest for the scavengers. Leef had to ride Tulga with me until we came across a small Wraeththu settlement where we could buy another horse. We had to pay much more for it than it was worth, for it was not nearly so fast or so fit as our Varrish mounts and it slowed us down. As we travelled, tension and strangeness reached out to us from the south. I could feel it most at night and we took more care with our rituals than before. Once, when we took aruna together, a spirit manifested itself in the air above us. Cal told us not to be alarmed even though it trailed us for about two days. Above the trees, the air seemed to shiver with electric currents; hair-raising noises, just audible, fingered the darkest corners of our souls. We could sense it. Unearthly power grew in strength around us, reached out tentatively to touch us. Plants along the way sprouted in giant abundance, dappled animals that we had never seen the like of before scuttled half seen through the foliage. If you gazed at the air in front of you for too long, faces would appear with gaping mouths and empty eyes. It was as if the land were cursed. Settlements of hara became less and less. What towns or villages we came across looked abandoned.

One night, as we made camp skittishly at the edge of a drooping forest, Leef said, 'Tomorrow we reach the marshes.'

'If they are still there,' Cal added drily. He drank deeply from a water bottle, grimacing at the staleness. His horse kicked gnats from its belly in the dusk.

As we approached the Gelaming, I could feel Cal's apprehension building up. He had once said that the Gelaming might have a price on his head, supposing there was some connection between Thiede, Seel and Saltrock. The land was in turmoil, nobody really knew what was going on, everyone was concerned only with their own survival, which generally meant leaving the area altogether. Only misfits, loners and rogues appeared to remain. If any hara ever came to share our fire, we were always on edge, for we had seen too many crazy eyes, too many death carriers. As far as Cal's fears of meeting the Gelaming were concerned, after all I had seen, I felt that his murder of Orien was just one more forgettable atrocity in a wilderness of atrocities. I knew how afraid he was, yet he had still agreed to ride with me, without reservation or question. I knew my mission, or part of it. Cal also followed a quest, but he had no idea what it was.

That night, I hugged him to me, his head on my chest, and he spoke of Pell once more. After some time, he also began to speak of Seel, somewhat disjointedly and nervously, but I learned how deep their relationship had once been.

'Seel was a dear friend whom I once tried to love,' he said with a sigh. 'But Seel's ideals are beyond that. I watched him change until the child I had once known died forever. That spirit in the air we saw, floating above us, tasting aruna with us, that is like Seel. Available, physical, but just when you think your arms are full of him for good, there is only mist. He is a true adept and I fear him. I fear we will meet again.'

In the morning, we woke up beneath a blanket of fog. The horses were jumpy and Leef spoke of heavy movement in the undergrowth around us, although we could see nothing. Since we had left Galhea, the three of us had got along together very well, but that day saw us arguing and snapping at each other; me bemoaning my discomfort, Leef getting annoyed at my moaning and Cal becoming fed up with the pair of us. 'Let's get moving!' he said. 'This place is dank; we should not have stayed here.'

By midday, a pale sun was trying to burn through the mist.

Ahead of us, huge, straggling tufts of waving reeds signalled the edge of the marsh.

'This is it,' Leef told us, 'Astigi, home of the Froia.' The Froia were a tribe that Cal knew very little about, although Leef was vaguely familiar with them.

'Here be magic, Swift,' he said, light-heartedly. 'I hope they'll be friendly. Most tribes are edgy nowadays and fear to welcome strangers.'

It was clear that we could no longer travel on horseback; most of the land was flooded and the roads were now dark waterways between banks of lofty reeds. Leef said that we would need a raft and that if we waited in the right place for long enough, hara of the Froia would come along. They habitually acted as guides through the marsh and accepted payment for providing transport. Leef only hoped they still provided the service.

The marsh was motionless and silent, but for the soft song of the frogs, unseen among the reed roots and the occasional rattle of a startled bird. We walked the horses for some miles along the edge of the waters, until we came to a rough jetty, poking precariously into the marsh. Here we would have to wait.

Cal was impatient; he could not keep still, insisting it was dangerous for us to sit out in the open. Leef calmly pointed out that we had no other choice. When he had last travelled south with my father, the Froia had still been hiring out their rafts. He did not *think* the situation would have changed, but ... Cal snorted and threw stones into the water. Our horses jostled and groaned behind us. I sat with my chin on my knees and tried to think of home, but it was like a dream. I didn't think we knew where we were going, perhaps Tel-an-Kaa's message had been false; we could die here waiting for the Froia.

Leef came to sit beside me. 'They will come, Swift, I can feel it. You will go into the marsh and out the other side. That Pythoness woman knew your destiny and I reluctantly agree with her.'

I smiled weakly at him, thinking, Oh, we are vagabonds, we are filthy. No-one can mistake us for Varrs, at least! We had not taken aruna together for over two weeks. Our bodies were wretched, our spirits low.

Leef laughed, guessing my thoughts. 'Yes, we are a sorry sight,' he said. 'I have only dragon's breath, but it's yours if you want it.'

'My dragon is lonesome,' I said and we embraced, clinging mouth to mouth, in an attempt to shut out reality. After some minutes, Cal kicked me on the leg.

'Break it up, we have company,' he said.

Sliding over the misty water like a wraith, a large raft sliced through the reeds. Two tall figures, swathed in concealing robes, poled it towards us. Leef jumped up and signalled them. One of them raised a hand in response. Our supplies were low, we were exhausted and needed rest; Leef asked for us to be taken to the Froia settlement of Orense in the heart of the marsh. We goaded, shoved and shouted our reluctant horses on to the raft. Tulga seemed obsessed with throwing herself over the edge into the weed-choked depths; I was hard pressed to calm her.

We travelled for about an hour, through narrow waterways and avenues of tasselled reeds, through whirring, hanging balls of mosquitoes, into unexpected lagoons thronged with white birds. It was a place of pervading stenches, hidden dangers and eerie beauty. Eventually, we could see humped dwellings rising up above the reeds; the floating town of Orense.

At the prospect of comfort, food and drink, our good humour was restored almost immediately. We had reached a new level of existence, where pleasures were simpler and easily gratified. Barrel-vaulted buildings constructed entirely of reeds glowed pale beneath the watery sun. Only the electric shiver on the horizon reminded us of absurdity. Orense was placid, a pocket of tranquillity within the boiling magic that existed beyond the marsh.

As was customary for visitors, we were conducted to the Braga, leader of the Froia. It was more than politeness or respect; they were naturally wary of strangers. His palace of reeds was roofed with mats of muted gold and pink, and carefully woven stalks formed a palisade at the front. All the time I was conscious of slight movement beneath my feet as the great platforms shifted upon the water below. We could smell pungent coffee. Voices called softly in the distance. Tulga stamped the ground behind me, nervous because she could not feel the earth. I was smiling with relief and

Leef put his hand on my shoulder.

The Froia are extremely reticent about revealing their skin and affect clothing of the most concealing nature. Only their hands, feet and faces are habitually visible. At the door to the Braga's house, we had jasmin water poured on our wrists and an aynah bud tucked behind our ears. This was to banish any evil we might be carrying with us. Inside, the light was golden. Tiny shafts of sunlight penetrated holes in the woven roof. Froia in hooded robes regarded us implacably from around the walls. Veils of pale muslin drooped to the floor and in the centre of the room was a wooden throne containing the august presence of the Braga. I was unsure what to do. Was some kind of obeisance required? Fortunately, Leef stepped forward, bowed gracefully and requested if he might be given leave to speak with the Braga. The Braga raised his hand carelessly: Leef may speak.

I looked at Cal and he smiled and shrugged. 'I hope all this ceremonial crap doesn't go on for too long,' he said. 'I'm starving and I itch and I can think only of cool water and hot coffee.'

'You have no respect for other people's cultures,' I replied lightly.

'No,' he agreed. 'What is culture, after all? It's like incest or inbreeding; everything gets too involved, too tight, too crazy. It bores me, actually.'

After only a few minutes, the Braga's attendants conducted us to a separate building, where we were supplied with warm (not hot) water for bathing and clean clothes and food. The Froia do not eat meat, except for fish on religious occasions. The brown goo we were offered for consumption looked disgusting, but its taste was savoury and pleasant enough. After we had eaten, Cal fastidiously inspected the robes we had been given. 'No chance of giving offence in this, is there!' he said.

Leef explained. 'The clothes we are wearing at the moment are looked upon as erotic. Among the Froia, the body is revealed only for aruna. While we are here, we shall have to abide by their customs. Imagine that you are walking naked among strangers. Now, put that robe on!'

The Braga requested the pleasure of our company for the

evening. We were now clean, fed and rested, but I thought this would hardly be apparent because of the enveloping robes we were wearing. The atmosphere in his reedy house was thick with the smoke of incense, curtains of smoke almost indistinguishable from the curtains of muslin. Young hara sat on the floor on cushions, playing music upon instruments of the strangest design. It sounded to me like the music of nature; the abrupt trill of a bird, the plash of raindrops or the echo of a storm that wakes you from sleep. Tame lizards stared out from the folds of the musicians' robes with eyes like jewels.

The Braga, seated on his carven throne and surrounded by acolytes, beckoned us to his side with an imperious gesture. I could see that he had dark skin with very bright eyes and a mouth that was used to smiling. His forehead was tattoed with intricate black lines, thin gold chains fell from his headcloth around his face and the rings that reposed upon his outstretched hand were like a swarm of brightly coloured insects. One of his teeth was gold.

'I understand that you are Varrs,' he said, 'and that one of you is the son of Terzian.' He was waiting for me to introduce myself, not wishing to ask directly.

I stepped forward. 'Terzian is my father.'

'He passed this way ... a character of strength and courage.'

I accepted this as a compliment and inclined my head. The Braga did not try to interrogate us about where we were going or why. He was used to strangers passing through his domain, perhaps his people's livelihood depended on it. He was wary, but he knew when to be discreet.

We were offered a drink distilled from honey, whose effects shot without hesitation straight to the brain. Gradually, it seemed that the noise around me became louder, the music more strident, the air thicker. Cal and Leef began to share breath, inexplicably, for normally they did not initiate anything between each other without including me. I turned away from them, and the Braga put his jewelled hand upon my face. 'Of royal blood,' he said. I smiled uncertainly, wondering whether that was some kind of oblique proposal. 'For your honour, there shall be dancing.'

He clapped his hands once and the clamour around us ceased.

Into the ensuing quiet, the Braga clicked his fingers once, and once again. Smoke rose lazily into the gently swaying gauze around us, sparkles like jewels or fireflies coruscating in the deepest shadows. One of the musicians stood up and walked to the middle of the floor. His instrument was curving, flutelike and made of wood. He raised it to his lips. Notes that rose from the dawn of the earth cut with purity through the curtains of smoke and incense. Every voice was hushed, while the young har swayed before us. His hood fell back. Beauty, I thought, and they keep this hidden! Beneath the haunting call of the flute a sibilant rattle rose and fell, rhythmic, beating, summoning. At first I did not see the figure emerging through the pall of smoke. Suddenly, it had solidified in front of me and the beating of drums vibrated the floor beneath us. Diaphanous veils concealed the body within them, but I could see a vague outline undulating and swaying below the folds. Even the face was hidden. Then two sinuous arms snaked out, glistering with heavy gold; bracelets and rings. When this happened, everyone in the room began to clap their hands softly in time with the music. The Braga leaned down and murmured in my ear. 'Does this please you?' I nodded. Something was reaching out to me; unseen and insistent. It was the rhythm of the drums, the heat of the room, a swaying, inviting phantom. There was a flash and a sound like gunfire or sharp thunder and I saw the veils float up into the air as if sucked away by a powerful wind. For a moment, I looked only at that ... spiralling, billowing, and then ...

The Braga's hand gripped my shoulder. 'For your blood, for your father, for what is to come; you shall be the first,' he said and his voice was a gasp. I almost turned round to look at him, puzzled by his words, but the dancer was revealed. That describes it, but it was more than that. These people were used to concealment. To them it was something powerful and secret and forbidden to reveal themselves. There is a word for it: 'veyeila', that is untranslatable to anyone who is not Froia. It means something like forbidden, taboo, desired, abandonment, frenzy; all these words and more. As I saw that har writhe barely clad upon the mats before me, I understood for just a while the eroticism they heightened within themselves by their austere code of dress. His skin was dark and oiled, his black hair curled to his shoulders, and he knew how to dance. All the invitation in the world reposed within his slender form. He danced before me, he smiled, his body gyrating inches from my face. His smell was amber and myrrh.

I heard the Braga's voice behind me. 'Swift, son of Terzian, this har is soume. His water must quench your fire. It must be now!'

I started to laugh, to protest, 'But I have no fire ...' but even as I thought it a flame was lit inside me, spontaneous as lightning, igniting desire; I had no choice. It is magic! I thought, and then the dancer was in my lap, straddling me, arranging my robes with experienced hands.

It was all so quick. One moment, I had been half-drunkenly watching a desirable har dancing in front of me, the next my back was pressed painfully into the carving on the Braga's chair and my ouana-lim was buried to the hilt within the dancer's body. My modesty was not forsaken, the robes saw to that. For several stulti-fying seconds he moved upon me, clenching muscles within himself, expertly bringing me to a quick and paralysing climax. Then he was gone, jumping up, flicking back the folds of my robe, dancing once more. For a moment, I could not move, but I could sense strongly the surprise in Cal and Leef as they stared at me. Had it really happened or had it been some bizarre hallucination, brought on by the strong liquor we had been drinking? Then I saw the dancer pick someone else from the crowd and I knew it was no dream. I felt the Braga's hand once more, squeezing my shoulder.

'He has brought you luck, son of Terzian. Good fortune will follow you out of Astigi. Speak to Nepopis later and he will tell you your destiny. You have my permission.'

I suppose it was a kind of Grissecon. The dancer was blessed and to embrace him worked a charm of good fortune. I learned that strangers were not often witness to the experience, let alone parti-cipants. Nepopis the dancer was 'theruna', a holy person, practised in the art of sex magic and held in the highest esteem among his people. He lived in seclusion, on the edge of Orense, coming forth only for the dance, but if he had a whim to, he would allow visitors to enter his home and speak their destinies for them.

Cal and Leef amused themselves by trying to embarrass me. I

realized the futility of trying to silence their remarks and turned my back on them. It was difficult not to get annoyed. At midnight, a Froia har came to take me to Nepopis, and I got up and walked out without a backward glance.

Nepopis lived in a single-roomed hut among a tall stand of reeds. It was surprisingly roomy inside. Now the dancer was thoroughly concealed by the customary robe, with only the hood thrown back. He bade me be seated and offered me coffee. It was as if the incident in the Braga's house had never happened. Nepopis was unselfconscious yet reserved. His smile was sincere, but guarded. As I drank, blinking into the steam, he stared at my face.

'You carry a burden,' he said, and I shrugged, wondering how much he could tell me. 'It is not yours to carry,' he continued. 'You would be advised to cast it aside. The past cannot be undone. Your father is beyond salvation – ' I made a noise of exclamation but he raised his hand to silence me. 'You must seek the path. You have neglected your training. Ah ...!' He closed his eyes and rubbed them with one hand, throwing back his head, as if seeking a message only he could hear. 'There is one ... I see blood and it is old, it is dry and there is fire that is not the fire of desire; it is something else. There is a cloud that is ... that is ... yes, it is emotion and it is seething. It will have to be ... *unmisted.* Two of you follow a destiny that is cut so deep. The third ... he is ... he is a follower, he is your follower ... he can be trusted. The time will come ... beyond Astigi ... first, beware the forest of illusion. The illusions are truth, but you will need strength to face them. You will understand the nature of the beast. He is still there ... in the forest ... echoes ... of ... no! In the future, you will see a face that you have known in dreams, and it will be burned upon you; you won't escape it; there will be no escape. You must follow your destiny, you must train because that is the only way ... His face. He has almond-shaped eyes and he is wise. He is held in high esteem. He bears the Tigron's mark ...'

Nepopis sighed and bowed his head, silent for a moment before looking up at me. 'I have held your seed within me,' he said, 'and I felt its destiny too. There will be a child of royal blood ...' He

227

shook his head. 'It is all so unclear, usually I find it easier, but the aether is disturbed ...'

'Can you give me a name?' I asked quickly, feeling the magic settling round me, back into the earth. Nepopis shook his head.

'I don't think so. It is guarded. I think they sense me.'

'They? Is it the Gelaming? Will I meet this person among them?'

Nepopis raised his hands. 'Enough. Enough. I've told you what I can.' He smiled. 'I'm sorry. I didn't mean to be sharp, but times have changed. What is going on out there affects my vision; it disturbs me, it leaves too much unseen.' He stood up and went to look out of the doorway. 'Swift, come here.'

I could not remember having told him my name. At his side, I looked out at a pink and cobalt sky, misting into the fronds of the reedbeds. Dark, winged shapes wheeled on the cooling air.

Nepopis reached for my hand and squeezed it gently. 'I have seen your home,' he said. 'I have seen your hostling and the long, dark gardens. All goes well with them. He is lonely for you, but ...' He turned to face me with a smile. 'I feel so many hara walk this earth bent double with the direst of destinies! It is a time for it; we live in a time of legends. Man had that time too, you know. I hope ours does not fade ...'

'It won't,' I said.

'You were born har.'

'Yes. I thought that you too ...'

He shook his head. 'No ... it was a long time ago that I was human, but I am not pure-born. It feels different with you, you feel so different; everything is stronger. It's like a weapon, that strength. Your seed is the colour of dawn, did you know that?'

'Yes, I know that.'

'It shines with force; I would like to keep some for the sake of its power. I will never use it against you.'

If that was a question, my reply was to take him in my arms, bending to taste his liquid breath of dark lagoons and deep waters.

At dawn, Leef came to the door of Nepopis's hut and requested entrance. He said that he and Cal wanted to leave Orense mid-morning. I'd only had about an hour's sleep and travelling was the last thing I felt like doing. After several minutes' argument, Leef bad-temperedly agreed that our journey could resume the following day. I didn't think that so short a delay could possibly have a dreadful effect on our progress, so I stayed with the dancer of dreams. Cal and Leef could do what they liked for the day; I wanted this time for I knew it would be the last chance I'd get for relaxation for a while.

'If only,' Nepopis said, 'if only this were another time and you did not have to leave. If only that mist wasn't waiting for you. The eyes in that mist have already claimed you as theirs, even though they have not yet seen you, even though they do not know ...'

I told him he spoke like my hostling, in puzzles. 'It is our way,' he replied. 'We must speak the way we think and we never think in straight lines.' He held me in his arms, a dancing snake, supple and strong. 'If you had not neglected your art, if you were Ulani as you should be, I would demand that you let me host your seed. But it is not to be. I know it would be pointless to ask you to return some day ...'

'I may do ... you never know.'

Nepopis laughed and stroked my face. 'Ah, but I do, Swift; I do!'

At dawn, the next day, we loaded our horses once more upon a raft and glided away from the floating pads of Orense. I looked back for as long as I could, until the reed buildings disappeared into a haze. Cal and Leef were surly with me. I think it was because for so long, it had just been us three together and they were a little put out that I had taken aruna with someone else. Probably, I would have felt the same way if it had been one of them that had been chosen. Not only had I neglected them for two whole nights, but I had held up our journey for an entire day! I apologized for this in a very scathing tone which brought a ghost of a smile to Cal's lips.

It took us two more days to cross the Astigi. Each evening we paused at one of the many floating villages where we were welcomed with food and drink, but no more exotic theruna. Occasionally, most often at dawn and dusk, something strange would cross our path and our Froia guides would elaborate signs of protection upon the air with rippling fingers. Once we nearly got caught in a loop of time, going round in circles that made our heads ache, but the Froia divined the weakest spot and we managed to break through into real time.

'What is most depressing,' Cal observed, 'is that all this messy, Gelaming hoodoo frolicking is going to get much worse beyond the marsh.'

'When I last came here, we wouldn't get much further than Astigi,' Leef told me. 'We got caught in time weirdness. I only hope we can get through this time.'

'Sadly, I think we can be assured of that!' Cal said bitterly.

The Froia helped us unload the horses at the brink of the marsh and Leef gave them as much currency as we had left. We felt that it would no longer be of use to us, so they might as well have it all. We rode away from the water into a liana-hung forest of dampness and haunting calls among the treetops.

'I wonder how long this place has been here?' Cal asked no-one in particular, and neither Leef nor I could think of a suitable answer. We followed the pull of the strangeness to its heart, and it let us pass.

Mystical Convulsion, Tender Caress

Bony frame's loathsome degradation,
Eyes seek the mark of wounds.
Palpating universe fallen unto me,
Membraneous skin expands into wilted
flowers.

It was like stepping into a dream. As that enchanted wilderness closed its green arms around us, reality faded and absurdity became the only truth. At first, we rode in silence, our horses pushing breast-deep through lush greenery. There was little sound and what sound there was existed high above us. I was lost in reverie, my skin becoming damp, brushed by a vague steam that rose from the soft ground. If I thought hard enough I could still feel Nepopis's slim, dark arms around me. Now that I had left him, his image began to crowd my head. I did not want to go back, but I wanted him here, now, before me on the saddle, pointing the way, unveiling his witchery of wisdom. Suddenly, I could feel flesh against me, fragrance all around me and Nepopis's low voice was in my ears. 'The eyes; they are blind … as yet!'

I thought I was falling asleep and blinked and sound rushed in; squawking, clamouring cacophony, and there was no-one on the saddle before me.

'Swift, are you alright?' Cal's face swam pale, disembodied at the corner of my vision.

'Yes. Yes,' I answered, still blinking, swallowing, gulping.

'Be strong, Swift.' Leef's voice was low and cautious behind me. He, more than Cal or I, had an idea of what to expect from the forest.

'I shall be afraid to sleep,' I said, with a shaky laugh.

'There will be no difference.' Cal clicked his tongue and hastened our pace to a trot. The swifter, jolting motion cleared my head a little; the branches of wide-leaved shrubs hissed around us.

We had no way to measure time and time was stretched and condensed in that place. Was it possible that we were not moving forward at all? The air around us became hotter and more humid, strong aromas of dark earth and rotting vegetation filling our heads, clinging to our clothes and hair. It seemed that we had been riding for at least half a day without stopping; we were tired but too scared to rest. We feared that by resting we would enable the forest to claim us completely and we would wander crazed for the rest of our lives. It was an unspoken fear, but I have no doubt that it was shared by each of us.

Half-seen figures flickered on the edge of my vision, half-heard voices whispered urgently in my ear. Grasping at sanity, I remember calling, 'Cal!' and my voice was deep and slurred, slowed down. Cal was ahead of me (we were riding in single file), and he turned on his horse, raising one hand. He did not speak.

'Swift!'

My eyelids jerked open. Where am I? The forest was hidden by jets of green steam, spurting with a putrid stench from the rotted ground. I was on my knees. My knees and hands were wet. I was alone. I could not remember what names to call out. Who were they? Had I always travelled alone?

'Swift!'

Louder this time, yet sibilant, like an echo. I tried to see into the viridian gloom, waving shapes that might only be leaves, shivering away into an inpenetrable blackness.

'Swift!'

I saw him. He was holding broad leaves about him, half concealed. He did not want me to see him. Was he naked? Was that it? I tried to reach for him. Where am I? I tried to speak his name; then I remembered he was dead. He smiled, threw back his head and laughed. 'Beloved friend! Do you remember our last meeting? Was I that good?'

232

'Gahrazel.'

I lurched to my feet and he backed two paces into the trees.

'Back!' he hissed. 'I don't want you near me!'

His hair was long and curling. He was eight years old. My father's training had not marked him.

'You betrayed me!' His voice was a thin scream, whose anguish and emptiness, both apparent, raised the hair on my head.

'No! I said nothing!'

'*He* told you to! Cal the devil, Cal the devil ...' His voice, sing-song, trailed away to nothing. His jaw hung slack, his eyes were two black stones.

'I didn't say anything!' My voice too had become high, the screech of a black crow, most deceitful of birds.

'You spoke of something, though.' Gahrazel's voice had become sly. 'To your father. I know about that. I know what you said. *Every word*. Did you wish that it was true?'

'I wish you had been different. I could not help you.'

'Not without endangering yourself perhaps ...'

'I could not help you.'

The Gahrazel that was not Gahrazel raised one pale hand to his face. He was weeping; his tears steamed like acid on flesh. 'I died ... they killed me.'

'Gahrazel ...' I reached towards him.

'No! No!' The foliage around him was shaking. He pointed at me with quivering fingers. 'You! You must hear it!' His words came quickly, their speed increasing all the time. 'Someone must hear it, that it died with me, dear God, that someone should know the truth. You! You! Terzian's brat, his blood, his seed, his damn eyes. His eyes! Steel they are, no laughter, no pity. When he killed me, when he killed me, my God, I saw his eyes, his eyes!' Gahrazel's sobs overtook his ability to speak. He pressed his trembling hands into his eyes.

'My father killed you?' Such a whisper, such a fateful phrase. Gahrazel stopped snivelling to look at me. His ghost tears were dry already.

'Yesssss!' Leaves scratching along the terrace in autumn; that was how he sounded. So dead. 'Didn't you know that, Swift? Didn't he

233

brag of that to you?' He laughed cruelly. 'Ah, of course, you know nothing, do you? The babes of Forever, wrapped in all that glorious stone. Stolen stone!' He flapped his hands at me. 'Now I'll tell you! Now I'll tell you! Your father, Terzian, he is the beast! He ate flesh, drank blood; mine! Ponclast poured the poison into an iron cup. It had to be iron; only iron can hold it. He handed it to Terzian and kissed him and told him to give me the cup. I took it. There was nothing I could do. Only pride left. They would not see me beg for life; I knew it was useless. So I drank it. In one draft. It tasted ... peppery, but not too bad. Only when it hit my stomach, then, you see, it began to work and the moisture in my throat, that helped it too. A cupful of poison and it began to burn. Burn me from inside out. I fell to my knees. The floor was cold. We were way underneath the ground. I was not afraid of death, but I hoped it would be quick. So strange it was, knowing I was dying. So inevitable, there is no fear. I was kneeling there on the floor, waiting to die, not moving much, for the burning was not pain exactly, only I knew that it was killing me, numbness spreading all through me, when my father said, "Now, Terzian." Behind me, he clicked his fingers, and hands were upon me, pulling me back. I lay there, my legs melting, and your father, Swift, he took a knife and slit my clothing, pulled it away from me, not smiling, but grave, looking at my eyes ... All the excitement of the world was condensed in his body. He opened his trousers, just that, not even naked, and took my melting flesh; he was covered in unguent to protect himself. How lucky I could no longer feel it! Even as he shrieked in orgasm and put his hand through my rotting chest, even as he tore my purple, gasping heart from my chest, I could not feel it. Of course my mind had gone completely, you can understand that. As I died I watched your father eat half of my heart and hand my own father the other. When my spirit left that place, what was left of my body was unrecognizable ...'

I was lying in the leaf-mould; I had vomited. My body was shaking. 'Weep now, Swift,' Gahrazel said.

He watched me weep. I thought, No, this cannot be true. This is illusion. This side of Terzian cannot exist. I would have known. Cobweb would have known. No! But even as I thought it, some deep, instinctive part of me knew it was senseless to doubt what I'd heard. Senseless.

After a while, I struggled to rise. Gahrazel was still a pale, insubstantial shape among the wide leaves. 'I died ... they killed me ...'

'Gahrazel, can I come to you?'

'No!' He retreated further into the trees. I could barely see him; his face, a white oval, that was all. 'You must not come to me,' he said. 'That must not be. Swift?'

'Yes ... Gahrazel?' My eyes ached with searching for him, my chest, my throat, with grief.

'Did you love me?'

'Once ... I think.'

He sighed, a faint breeze that shivered the leaves. 'You did not come. I asked for you, many times. I died alone ... quite, quite alone.' His voice was the sound of a bell, tolling over bare and shadowy hills, summoning nothing to a devotion that had lost its purpose.

'I'm sorry ...' How could I have said that? It means nothing. I could imagine him smiling, sadly. 'No-one is without sin,' I said. 'Not one of us. My sins are selfishness, fear and weakness. I was afraid, Gahrazel, not just of blame, but for my home, my people. Yes, I betrayed you; we both know that. I cannot apologize, because the consequences were so ... so ... beyond apology.'

'I'll forgive you, forgive you, only say it, say it now, the one thing I can take with me. Forever. Do you know what to say?'

I knew what to say. I closed my eyes. I summoned it up within me, a maelstrom of feeling, and let it spill from my mouth. 'I love you, Gahrazel.'

'Do you forgive me?'

'For what?'

'Do you?'

'Yes, yes; I forgive you ...'

All around me the greenness whispered and writhed. Darkness all around. I sank to my knees.

'Swift!' Hands upon my shoulders, shaking, shaking. I opened my

235

eyes. Tulga beneath me, half-seen sky above. Cal's anxious face. I shook my head.

'It was nothing. I dreamed.'

We came upon a clearing in the forest. Cal said, 'I have been here before,' and his voice was full of grief. All the ugly, dripping trees had become straight pines. Birds called. We found the damp remains of an old fire in the centre of the clearing.

'We are safe here,' Leef told us, but he did not sound sure. We dismounted and our horses began to crop the sward, unaffected by the atmosphere. Leef built a fire. I sat beside him, too shaken to move. Cal squatted some distance away from us, his face in his hands. Once timid flames began to leap from the damp tinder, we relaxed a little. The fire was comforting, normal. Leef unpacked food. 'Look, we have wine!' he said and held out a green bottle.

Cal sat down next to me and I took him in my arms. He was weeping silently into my hair. My eyes were dry, but my chest felt as if it was stuffed with sawdust. After some time, Cal sniffed noisily and said, 'What happened to you?'

I wiped his face with my hand, for a moment or two, unable to tell him. 'I saw Gahrazel. I spoke to him.'

'You too?'

'Gahrazel?'

'No ... not him!'

I held him to me tightly, afraid to let go, afraid of the contact. I told him what I'd seen, what I'd heard. Cal said nothing. Perhaps he had known already, but I didn't want to find out. I had once asked questions about my father, now some of them had been answered. Of course it was something I had to know. I wish I didn't. 'Gahrazel asked for me,' I said, 'and I turned my back on him. If I'd known what fate was awaiting him, would it have changed the way I felt? I hope so. Today, I said to him the things he should have heard before he died. His death was lonely, people there, I know, but it was true loneliness. Alone, unloved, unforgiven. Now I have said it. Was it real, Cal?'

'A spirit,' he whispered, 'or a conjuration of your own mind, or a conjuration of *theirs*; does it matter? If you have not appeased the shade of Gahrazel, you have appeased yourself.'

'Was it just within me? Was it guilt?'

'Pray that it was not guilt!'

If it was, perhaps we were all doomed. I whispered Cal's name and held him and shared his fear. This place was not just a place of the dead, no, never that.

We ate the food that Leef gave us. Leef was a tower of strength; the forest seemed to have the least effect upon him. His mind was ordered; he denied what was not real. 'There is no-one here,' he said, when I told him about my experience, omitting the details about my father. I did not want to discuss that with Leef. 'It was hallucination,' he insisted, 'that was all.'

Cal said, 'This place, this clearing ... I recognize it. Pell and I were here once. It was the last time we were together.'

'That's not possible,' Leef replied emphatically.

'It's the same country!'

'No, your mind is playing tricks on you.'

'That was our fire; it has always been here.'

'No!' Leef stood up, running his hands through his hair. 'Are you both cracking up on me?' he demanded. We stared at him silently. 'Look, this is Gelaming work. You must regain control! They will break you!' He shook a warning finger at us.

'Every sickly bloom has his face, every whispering leaf speaks with his voice,' Cal murmured. I reached for his hand. I understood.

'You will die here!' Leef exclaimed. 'Pull yourselves together, for God's sake!'

'There is no god here,' I said.

'Oh, there is,' Cal answered. 'He fights with the Gelaming. He's here, more than anything. They have his light, you see. They are his angels.'

'Have some wine, Cal,' Leef said drily, thrusting the bottle at him.

Cal drank, deeply. 'Was this from the Froia?'

'No,' Leef answered. 'I don't know where it came from.'

Night and day had no proper sequence in that place. We took turns at sleeping and rested well enough; we could not remember our dreams.

Once we had slept, we began our journey again, leaving the clearing behind. Cooling sticks and ashes cracked bleakly in a curl of smoke as our farewell.

We rode into the forest, down a steep slope carpeted with fallen pine needles. It descended into an inpenetrable gloom. Stark, black branches, fallen from the trees, littered the path, cracking abruptly as the horses stepped on them. It felt as if others had passed this way not long before us. I could sense life. After an hour, we came upon a ruined house, strangled and beautiful with flowering creepers. Its empty windows watched our approach. It was Forever. I made an exclamation, pointed.

Leef did not even turn his head. 'Ride past!' he ordered.

I had to look. Was this Forever's future? Was it doomed to die? The roof was nearly gone. At an upper window, I caught a glimpse of something pale, flitting quickly from sight. Was it Cobweb I saw there, haunted and sad, clinging to a memory blighted by truth? There was only silence and I was afraid of sound. I was afraid I would hear voices and that they would be voices that I knew.

It felt like afternoon, golden sunlight through the leaves. Laughter in the distance. My father stepped out in front of us. 'You are welcome, strangers,' he said and his smile was a predator's smile and I knew he held a gun behind his back. I looked away. Through the trees, human children scampered and screamed in innocent delight, through the sunlight, until the light was gone and inky blackness smothered their cries to whimperings of terror. Now they ran with white faces and gaping mouths, silent in their horror, bearing scratched limbs and torn clothes. Behind them, with grave expression, my father rode a heavy, black horse. The children ran from him in fear. He and Ponclast suddenly blocked the road before us, dining on human flesh, holding goblets of blood in their bloody fingers, toasting life. They had the faces of wolves and their long muzzles were red. 'The beast will come ...' Wolves' heads. A horde of Varrs with wolves' heads. A screaming town, running with red, people running. Human, hara. The Varrs had torches, setting light to the buildings, the people. Wolves' heads, forever grinning. On a broad road, under the streetlights, my father dismounting from his black horse, lifting the wolf helmet from his shining hair, brushing it back, handing the helmet to a soldier at his side, smiling. Ponclast striding over, embracing Terzian. He says the words, 'My star.' They kiss. Ponclast hands him a human heart and, staring into Ponclast's eyes, Terzian bites ...

I looked away. My throat burned; I retched.

Then a figure rushed out of the trees, light spiralling in, a euphony of birdcalls. It brought the afternoon back in. Someone grabbed Tulga's reins by the bit-ring. He looked up at me, smiling. 'I knew you would come!' His beauty was like gold in my eyes. So beautiful, after what I had just seen, I wanted to weep. He wore a ring that was like a seal. His ears were pierced with gold, three times on each side. Hair that was a luxury of blackness, lifting like wings, braided with pearls. His smile touched my heart. I knew him. It was Pellaz.

'Are you afraid?' He laughed. Tulga sniffed at him and he cupped her velvet nose with his hands.

'No ...'

He touched me, lightly, upon the leg and my flesh tingled beneath the cloth. 'What your friend Leef said was true; it *is* only illusion,' he said, 'but illusion of the truth nonetheless. It will soon be over. Look after him.'

'Who?' Of course I knew.

The vision shook its head, smiling sadly. 'My love, my tormentor, my dearest memory, my Cal. Calanthe; slayer and beloved. It will be some time ...'

'He has seen you.'

'Not like this. Only you have truly seen me and it will not happen again. Be strong, Swift. I have faith in you and I will give you such jewels as you cannot imagine ... when you find my people.' He was fading.

I reached for him. 'Pell, what is real?'

'You are. Remember that.' He was gone.

Cal urged his horse to my side. 'You spoke his name!' he cried, his eyes all wild as if I had spoken blasphemy.

'He was here,' I said. 'Cal, he was here. It was different. Cal, oh, Cal, I know it ... he ... Cal, Pellaz is not dead!'

Leef had to pull him off me. He was hysterical; he cut my lip.

Tulga neighed in terror. 'But it's true!' I wailed. Leef restrained a sobbing, broken Cal in his arms. How could he know what visions Cal had suffered in that place?

'Swift, for God's sake, shut up!' Leef cried angrily.

'What is real, Pell?'

'You; you are real.'

A sandy trail the colour of sandy hair, winding through a deciduous wood, whose trees are girded with moss. Green light everywhere. Fluting birdsong. 'You are real. You are real. You are real.' I am riding. Because Cal is in front of me, I realize quite quickly that this is his illusion, not mine. I am here as a witness; that is all. I can hear water. Cal's horse snorts and shakes its head. I can see Cal's clothes are torn. He is wearing a white shirt and the rips across his back are fringed with red. It is claw marks, a whip's teeth, the last desperate scrabbling of someone dying. He turns to look at me and his face is greenish, perhaps it is because of the strange light; he smiles and his gums and teeth are red. 'You are with me, Swift?' he says, and I nod my head.

'I am with you.'

I will look after him, Pell; never fear.

Ahead of us a spreading oak grows in the middle of a glade. Sunlight reaches it, but there are no birds here. Leaning with its back to the tree, a figure stares up through the leaves. It is robed in white, long brown hair around its shoulders. I don't think it sees us. I think it can't sense us. Cal's horse stops in front of me and bends its neck to begin eating. Cal slips from its back to the ground, over the neck; it's quicker. Would he dismount any other way? Tulga wants to eat and I let her. I see Cal lifting his ragged, soiled shirt over his head and his back is livid with long, angry weals. He reaches round and tries to rub them, but he cannot reach. I want to go to him, but I can't. I am frozen. I am mute. Observer; nothing else. Cal is walking towards the tree and the figure looks at him. It smiles sadly. It shakes its head; lifts its hands as if to say, 'Go back, go back.' Cal keeps walking. The figure says, 'You do not have to see this, Cal. You can turn around.'

Cal says nothing.

The figure says, 'Face the past.'

'Have I ever faced any other way?' Cal asks. The figure smiles and opens its arms. 'You seek absolution, Cal.'

'Never that. I have always been aware of everything I've done.'

'I know that. I had hoped ...'

'You have no substance to hope!' Cal says bitterly. The figure is still smiling sadly. Its hands are upon the neck of its garment. Cal's fists are clenched at his sides. I cannot see, but I know that he is staring straight ahead. I hear material ripping; a lazy, elegant sound. I think, it is expensive cloth, even though I can see what lies beneath. It is no longer red, no longer shining; just ravagement. Cal and the figure are inches apart. Cal raises one hand.

'Touch me within; touch your sin, Cal.'

It was once flesh, now it is nothing, a shell, nothing more. It is hard and dry. I can see the dull, brown bones of a shattered ribcage and I can see Cal's hand reach inside. Once he has touched, the spell will be broken; I know that. He reaches for the heart that no longer beats. He leans forward. The face; a dry mouth full of small, moving things that scurry upwards from the empty lungs. Their lips touch; one living, one who is beyond life. I see Cal wince; so slight a reaction. Corruption has him in its arms. It is pouring foulness into him. A head creaks back and there is no peal of godless laughter; just a thought. 'It is done.'

Like a fountain turned on, life comes back with a torrent of sound, wings in the treetops, whirring, whirring. Cal is alone and he is soaked in blood; blood in his mouth, his eyes, his hair. He shakes himself and red droplets fly through the air like bright, hard insects. He is sick with the taste of blood, but his eyes are dry, his back unbent. He comes back to me, fallen angel, evil incarnate, a spirit of love. He says one word as he remounts his horse. As he pulls up its head, one word. The word is this: 'Orien.'

In a viridian shift of time and space, we were riding through a forest of pines once more. Leef, leading, urged his horse into a canter. Ahead of us, bars of light were an avenue to the mouth of the trees. Beyond that, all I could see was hazy. Cal was behind me. I could feel him, but I dared not turn around. Faster. The horses galloped to the end of an enchantment. Colours flew past us, voices called, becoming fainter, birds spiralled upwards, their wings like metal. I wanted to cry, 'I am free! We are free!' but I could only laugh. My skin still burned where a golden hand had touched it. I could see his face in the haze. 'There is something waiting for you, Swift!' Like a bubble bursting upon the face of the earth, we exploded out of the forest, like bullets, like fear running. A sound of water, laughter, blazing light. Heat hit my skin. Perhaps I had been cold. My head swam. I had to believe it: I am real. The ground roared up towards me, like a green wave starred with white and amethyst. I melted into it, a green darkness; the peace of eternal green.

They let me sleep. When I awoke, it was night-time and Leef had built a small fire. The light was fading rapidly. I noticed at once that the air was clean, untainted. We had passed the barrier. Leef came to my side and offered me a drink of water. It was tepid, but I drained the cup. 'Nervous wrecks, both of you!' he said. Leef had seen nothing in the forest.

There was a river nearby and Cal had gone down there to bathe. I found him thoughtfully rubbing his skin with a handful of leaves, naked at the water's edge. He turned round when he heard me approach. We smiled at each other.

'Was it true, Swift?'

'Which part?' I sat down beside him.

'About Pell. Nothing else matters.'

'You are single-minded in your obsession.'

He laughed and rubbed at his arms. 'It was real blood, Swift. It's hard to get it off.'

'Here, let me help.' I ripped grass from the riverbank, moistened his shoulders with a handful of water and began to rub.

'I shall turn the river red.'

'Then it will be someone else's curse. The river flows away from us,' I said. His skin was cold.

'You have not answered me ..'

'About Pell? How can I? It was just a feeling. Leef was right; I shouldn't have said anything.'

'Could you be right, though?'

I shrugged. 'Anything is possible. That is one thing I've learned!'

Cal took the matted sheaf of grass from my hands. I took him in my arms. Just us two; it had been so long.

We were naked in the water together, ribbons of red flowing away from us. Beneath the surface, it was brighter, tangles of waving weed and dark, darting shapes. I clasped him in my limbs like something drowning, or drowned, and pulled him into me. It was all silver bubbles, in our hair, on our skin, rising, rising. No prayer. Were there angels under the water? I opened my mouth, delirious, forgetting where we were, and he had to drag me to the surface before I filled up with water. As my being ignited in an ecstasy of steam, I saw flaming stars scream across the blackest of skies above us. His breath still tasted of blood, but it was behind him now. The Gelaming had taken their price, or so I thought.

'So, where do we go now?' I asked him as we strolled back to the fire. The dark evening was still faintly pinky-red around us, fringed with insects and wings. We walked among banks of waving pampas grass.

Cal put his arm around me. 'Away from the forest — obviously! Straight on,' he said.

'You don't really know, do you! You are afraid.'

'They will come to us.'

'Can you be so sure? Will it be that easy?'

His hand dropped away from me. He reached for his eyes. Only the stained dusk around us and a feeling of imminence, unfightable and shining with power. Suddenly, I felt very small. I could feel the immensity of the world around me, seen and unseen. I was shoot-ing upwards into the sky and the body of Swift was becoming smaller and smaller, trees like pins, redness seeping into my soul. I had to shake myself to dispel the illusion. It was so close.

The glow of our fire was almost indistinguishable from the light of the sky above the forest behind it. But we could see it, as the tall grass parted before us. We could see it ... and something more. There were voices, muted like echoes. Cal made a hissing sound and pulled me down into the undergrowth. We looked at each other. His breath was sobbing. I tried to struggle. I think I said, 'Leef!' I was thinking of him.

Cal shook his head urgently. 'No, Swift, no!' His voice was high with panic as I broke away from him. I ran towards the fire and I heard a horse neigh, through the night air, high and shrill. I could see Leef, two figures holding him down, although he thrashed and writhed to escape.

He cried my name when he saw me, his face stricken. 'Swift, go back! Go back!' he screamed. Go back? I hesitated. Cal was behind me. I felt his hands land upon my shoulders and curl around them. I could hear his breath. It was as if we were frozen. We could not go back. Around our fire, maybe a dozen tall figures sifted through our belongings. Behind them, horses gleamed like marble and there was a smell, like jasmin, only stronger. One of them was kneeling by the fire, a hand stretched towards the flames, as if he had never seen fire before. He raised his head slowly and it seemed to take an eternity. I saw a curtain of tawny hair and a face that showed only curiosity. For a second, only curiosity, and then something like pain or fury made him turn away. He stood up and turned his back on us, shouting something incoherent to one of the others, who stepped forward. Cal's fingers spiked into my flesh like steel. I wanted to cry out or move, but I could do neither. The one who had stepped towards us spoke.

'Son of Terzian?' His accent was soft and fluid and he was very tall; his clothes were like nothing I'd ever seen before. I can only describe his dress as scanty but complicated. His neck was hung with chains and talismans and black beads, his ears with silver. His hair was also silver and shaved away from the sides of his scalp, but long over his shoulders. He smiled. I must have nodded or spoken — or *twitched*. 'I am Arahal,' he said. 'We are Gelaming.'

So, they had found us. And so soon. They had been with us in the forest, they had watched us in the water, they had waited by our fire.

'You are wet,' Arahal said with a laugh, flicking my hair. I could see his aura, all the colours of strength, yet they spoke like us, smiled like us. 'Calanthe, you were expected,' he said to Cal, with the slightest of coolness. Cal was still clutching my shoulders as if his life depended on it. I knew he had drawn blood.

'He is *different*,' he blurted. 'He ... his hair is different.'

The Gelaming looked puzzled for a moment. I had no idea what Cal was talking about.

'Oh, you mean ... I wouldn't know,' Arahal said. He shook his head and then glanced quickly behind him. 'It must have been some time ago, Calanthe.'

'It was.'

Cal withdrew his nails from my skin with a sigh. I wanted to crumple; I don't know how I managed not to. My fingers strayed to my shoulders, encountering moist warmth. It may have been sweat.

'Just wait here a moment, please,' Arahal told us. 'We would like you to accompany us back to our headquarters, where members of our Hegemony are anxious to meet you.' He made it sound like a request, but it was clear we had little choice. I could see them packing up our belongings, stifling our fire. Leef still stood between two Gelaming, now staring at the ground. He no longer struggled.

'Who was it, Cal?' I asked, in a voice that seemed to come from some distance away. 'The one by the fire. Who was it? Was it Pell?'

Cal laughed, but there was no humour in it. 'Don't be stupid, Swift! Another ghost, that's all. One that has haunted me for some years, one that I have been waiting for ...'

Something from the past then. I knelt on the grass, my hands on my shoulders, and I could feel it rushing in. The inescapable, the inevitable, a focus of time. It has always been here, I thought. Someone has always known this would happen, and yet I didn't know. How could I not have guessed, not imagined? Not enough magic within me, not enough hope ...

I looked for him; Cal's ghost. It would have been easier if he'd had no substance. It is hard to look at him directly. I could see that he'd been tempered by fire, by all the elements until the blade of his spirit was made deadly. His hair was smoother than the others'. He was not so tall. He must have felt my scrutiny. I saw him pause, as if in irritation or regret, before he turned to look at me. He had almond-shaped eyes. I could not see the colour; I never would. He was something of Cobweb, something of Cal, something, even, of Pellaz. I could tell he did not want to look at me; there was no

245

smile, his brow was furrowed.

Cal's voice came to me with bitterness. 'Just witchery, Swift, that's all. Don't let it get under your skin. He's so sincere, and his bland sincerity can dry the blood in your veins ...'

'But who?' I asked, and my toes and fingers were numb.

He turned away from us and his hair swung like silk. It was more than beauty. It was waking up and realizing there are things in the world so far from us, yet we yearn for them so, even before we've seen them, and when, if we're lucky, we finally do see them, it is a torment, because they are like smoke or fantasy, it is pain; you resent that they exist, yet they are your life, so far ...

Cal made a choking sound behind me. 'Same old magic!'

'His name?'

'His name is Seel,' he said.

The Gelaming had given their camp a name: Imbrilim. It was only an hour's ride from the forest. When we reached it, we found that it was more than just a camp, it was a city of canopies and gauze and soft lights. We heard distant, lilting music and the air was full of the scent of flowers. A fragment of Heaven, here on Earth.

On the way there, Arahal rode beside us, making desultory attempts at conversation, seeking to dispel any uneasiness, while knowing instinctively that he probably couldn't, as yet. However, out of the three of us, only Leef looked truly worried. These people were his enemies, more than they were Cal's or mine. He had sought them once before, with the Varrish army, his head full of anger and a thirst for blood. Now they had found him and he feared their justice. Cal kept a constant stare directed at the back of Seel's head, where he rode some way in front of us. 'I want to get my hands on him!' he said out loud, and it was impossible to guess exactly what he meant by that. Seel must have heard him, but he did not look round or even move farther away from us.

'What do you want of me?' I asked Arahal, hoping to divert his somewhat affronted attention from Cal.

'You sound weary,' he answered. 'After the forest, you must rest. The real answers can wait. Time has little meaning here.'

We rode through billowing avenues of silk, shadows gliding at

246

the edge of our vision. I saw hara who looked like gods and there was primaeval light in their eyes. Encompassed by fragrance, I was happy. It felt like happiness, anyway. A kind of relief. I wanted to laugh or weep or shout. It did not matter that tiredness had crept over me so deeply that I was at the point of hysteria. I had found the Gelaming and I thought that they were all that I'd imagined them to be. Hail, Ofaniel, angel of the moon, here on earth, riding a pale horse just ahead of us.

Arahal touched my arm, his knee touched my own as he brought his horse up against mine. I looked at him and his face was indistinct, but I knew he was smiling.

'Not far,' he said. 'You are yet young ...'

Gelaming always speak like that when they get the chance.

Imbrilim was usually noisy at night. The dark seems to bring the Gelaming to life. I had thought them to be an austere race of people, grave-faced and full of ponderous thoughts. Now all I could hear was music and laughter and hara calling to each other. I had never seen an army camp, but I would never have imagined one to be like this. Even Galhea was never like this. We came to a pavilion of pale, green muslin, a soft glow showing from within. Most of our escort rode on ahead, but about half a dozen hara remained with Arahal to help us from our horses and take away our luggage. As soon as my feet hit the ground, I began to feel faint. I think it was more the effects of the forest aggravating my exhaustion than shock at finding the Gelaming. Arahal murmured an order and two hara supported me as we passed under the muslin canopy into the pavilion. The room within was spacious and furnished graciously. We were led directly into the sleeping chamber beyond.

The next thing I remember was opening my eyes to find myself lying on a soft, low couch. Hands supported my head and offered me something warm to drink from a cup. It tasted of honeyed milk and alcohol. I don't know how long I'd been unconscious, but my clothes had been taken away and I was covered by a thin blanket that was surprisingly warm.

Arahal came and looked at me. 'It is important that you rest now, Swift,' he said. The effects of the drink I'd been given were gently making their way through my blood; I could barely keep my eyes open. Thiede's people. I thought that angels stroked my face. I could hear prayers whispered in a language I had never heard before, but that I could still understand. Drifting on the edge of sleep, I sensed several hara come in from outside, bringing night coolness with them. One of them said, 'Is the Tigron coming here now?'

'I don't think so,' another answered. 'I've heard he will send the Tigrina.'

'Ah, such a neat sidestep. Our Tigron delays the inevitable, I feel!' I recognized that voice. It had spoken to me always, in my dreams, in my soul.

'Perhaps, Seel, perhaps ... though a more charitable mind than yours might think that the Tigron only wishes to consider other people's feelings. These hara have been through a lot. You are too harsh.'

'Too harsh! I know him. I know Cal too. They are both too strong for that!'

'Be quiet, both of you!' another voice warned. 'The pure-born is yet awake.'

I could not open my eyes, I was drugged by fragrance, yet I felt him lean over me, almost feeling his hair brush my face. The angel with almond-shaped eyes, force beating out, that was stifled anger; stifled because he was a stranger to anger. He did not speak. I wished I was Cobweb, mystical, lovely and deadly; a creature to inspire, but I was just Swift, bedraggled, unkempt and unremarkable. When he stood up, it was like warmth and light moving away. A voice said, 'You are prepared to fight, I can tell.'

'Arahal, I was born fighting!'

I could hear them still talking as they left us. Someone extinguished a lamp and there was only darkness behind my eyes. I slept. When I woke, I would remember every word of that conversation, and remember it for the rest of my life.

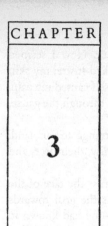

CHAPTER

3

Nor shall ye have faith …
Bewilderment envelope the observer,
The patriarch vanishes
Like fodder into aqueous entrails.

Is it mapped out for us from the start, our destiny? Does the supernatural agent who charts our life create us equal to our discoveries? Leef had once said to me that troubles were always relative. I had come to view inner strength in the same way. There is always something stronger than ourselves, no matter how brightly burns the flame of confidence and power. There is always something stronger, something waiting to damn us for our weakness. Round every corner of the forest another monster lurks in wait for us; sometimes we can laugh at its feebleness. It appears horrible, but its substance is tissue-thin. It can be torn. The worst monsters we encounter have the faces of angels and the grace of devils flirting among the cold flames of Hell. They can destroy us, merely because they scorch our souls unintentionally. Face such a creature and reason trickles out like blood from a cut vein. Is it decided before we are born whom we must love?

Filtered light falling through the floating gauze woke me with the softest of caresses. Beyond a curtain, lifted by fragrant morning breeze, I could see Cal and Leef curled up together on a low couch, childlike in the temporary innocence of sleep. Clothes had been laid out for us, new ones, essentially Gelaming in design. There was scented water and a bowl for washing; a mirror condemned me with brutal honesty. I had known myself once. Now I seemed physically a stranger. My hair and my eyes lacked lustre; my skin no longer seemed to fit me properly. Facing myself caused me pain. I threw a cloth over the mirror and walked out, through the gauze, under the canopy, into the light.

They had come as strangers, as invaders; strange to our land, unmistakably foreign in their height, their dignity, their dress and their supple grace. Gelaming: God's children.

To this end men had struggled in agony across the face of the earth for millennia, sterile millennia. This was the goal towards which all threads of survival had strained. No-one had known it. Those that had guessed were madmen; unheeded, derided. For that mistake, mankind had been swamped. To an outsider, such as myself during those first few days, Gelaming perfection seems almost an obscenity, something that cannot be, yet something that I felt the need to stare at until I was sure I could only go blind. To me, it seemed that all their blemishes of character and spirit had been polished away. I found myself wondering how they could possibly exist comfortably when they had nothing left to strive towards, no inner struggle, no contest. I should have looked deeper, but that did not come until later. As I walked among them that first day, I felt no fear, for the inspiration of terror holds no pleasure for Gelaming. It is merely another weapon, to be used only when the occasion truly merits it. They barely looked at me. To them, I was just another refugee, wandering wide-eyed among the angels.

Imbrilim was the size of a small town, and full of life. By day all the swaying canopies were held back and as I walked through the avenues of pavilions, I could see right into them. It was apparent that there were several places where all the inhabitants of Imbrilim went to eat. These seemed open for business all day, so it was rare that anyone took meals in their own pavilions. All this was paid for by the Hegemony of Immanion; the only things that hara had to pay for themselves were narcotics and alcohol. Tents for the consumption of beverages were set apart from those serving meals.

Everywhere, the flags and pennants of Immanion flapped lazily in the breeze. Their symbols were the double-headed axe, the scarab and two serpents entwined around a sword. All these signified the two-in-one; hermaphroditism. Above a huge pavilion of purple and gold (which I later learned belonged to the Hegemony) shivered the black and silver banner of the Tigron; a lion with a fish's tail shimmering against a dark ground. I lost myself entirely, but I couldn't stop walking.

Arahal sought me out. He found me eventually by the horses, corralled on the boundaries of Imbrilim. They were snowy creatures of myth, whose feet danced with the ache for wings. I reached towards them, my hand like ivory, and a dozen blue-black noses blew warmth upon my skin. They absorbed me and turned their heads to look at me properly. One tossed his snowy mane and threw up his head, nickering softly. That was Arahal coming; they knew him.

'I have never ceased to marvel at their magnificence,' he said.

I was too intimidated to speak. I could only smile in a way I'd not smiled since I could still climb comfortably onto Cobweb's lap.

Arahal insisted on taking me on a tour of Imbrilim; we passed many things that I'd already seen, but he explained a lot to me about the way the Gelaming conducted their daily lives. He pointed out a magnificent construction of sparkling white muslin. 'That is where we remember the Aghama,' he said.

'Aghama?' I queried. It sounded like an event.

'The first Wraeththu,' Arahal explained.

I had no idea what he meant. Yet another area of my education so sadly neglected. It was strange that I had never wondered about it, really. After all, Wraeththu must have come from somewhere. Now I learned the truth of our wondrous genesis. We had sprung from one mutant; born to a human female, a hermaphrodite child, whose special talents were seen by his parents as freakish abnormalities. Through his blood, he had created the new race; Wraeththu. To his people he had become the Aghama, revered almost as a god. I had known nothing of this, not even Cobweb had ever mentioned anything about this shadowy, part-mythological figure of the Aghama.

Arahal did not seem surprised. To him, Varrs were nothing but godless barbarians. He was prepared to educate me and took me inside the Fane of the Aghama. It was barely furnished; just a few polished benches before a table on which stood maybe a dozen slim, lit tapers. There was no representation of the first Wraeththu, either in paint or stone. 'We come here to think, to remember,' Arahal told me.

'Remember what?' I asked.

'Our beginning,' he replied, and in such a sombre tone, I shrank from further queries.

Out in the sunlight, I remember wondering aloud, 'What am I doing here?' Arahal only smiled. I recalled Cal once asking that question of my father, and Terzian's reply, 'Must you ask that every day?' I don't think Cal had ever truly known the answer; now I felt my own question was doomed to the same fate.

Arahal said, 'Megalithica ... It is a grand name. The hara that shall come to rule here will be equal in stature and their sons will possess the wisdom of the generations.'

What generations? As Arahal walked beside me, glowing with an inner light of pride, I thought about how the Gelaming had plucked their culture, even their cities, from the air and imbued it with a lustre of centuries. It was a lie. Their culture was still damp from its birthing, yet they talked as if they had owned the earth a thousand years. It had taken men so long to step away from the creatures of the forest and the plain, up from the slime, the first discovery of fire and shelter. Perhaps they had stepped too far, too far to get back, and their isolation had shrivelled them ... perhaps. Wraeththu are animals; they are not men, they will not call themselves human. I could say to myself, 'I am an animal,' and see something shining in the dark, powerful, sleek and close to the earth. My eyes can light up and my teeth are sharp enough to kill, yet now, it seems, I must fold away my fangs and claws and learn to lie down with the lamb whose flesh is so tempting. Gelaming taught me: there is no murder, just negative impulses to scorch the soul and a temporary destruction of flesh. The soul will always return. Only the murderer ultimately suffers from the act of killing. I wondered why they wished to educate me, what use I was to serve them, but my questions were sidestepped. Arahal would say to me, 'Do you not want to be full of feelings that are smooth and straight? Don't you want to be able to see round corners? We can help you to speak in colours, to see the pattern of sounds that are other hara's thoughts. This is the true mutation!'

Mutation: change. It seems my childhood fears would surface once again.

If they had come to Galhea, the Gelaming would never have killed us, or even sent us away from our homes, as we'd feared. We would just have been smothered quietly, our bewilderment soothed, the knives taken from our hands. Their conquering power was not violence, but no less effective because of it. We had been so wrong about them, and my father had ridden towards this without knowing. If he *was* with the Gelaming, I was sure he must be dead. If his body still lived, the Terzian I had known (and the one I had not) would be quenched from the fire in his eyes. Whatever I had learned about him, I had enough mercy within me to hope that he had *truly* died, and in the only way he'd have been proud of; fighting.

Back to that first day, strolling in the sunlight with Arahal, his hand upon my shoulder. The air around us was full of insects with wide, gossamer wings. They got in our hair and sparked there like gems as they fluttered to death. I felt disorientated, unsure of whether I was dreaming. None of this seemed real.

Arahal smiled benevolently at me. 'Ours is the only way, Swift, You will come to know us. You will see this for yourself.'

'Why me?' I asked him. 'What do you want of me? I'm not ready for it, whatever it is. My soul is too young. It does not crave this.' I did not even understand myself what I was trying to convey.

Arahal laughed. 'You are still in the forest, Swift. You must let go and come out of the trees.' Gelaming seem to hate answering questions. It's not that they prefer secrecy, they just expect people to find out the answers for themselves.

'I want Cobweb,' I said, helplessly. 'I want my hostling.'

'He is always with you.'

'No, not here.' I could barely remember Cobweb's face.

We passed a large pavilion, whose awnings were of palest pink and gold. Later, I found out it was a meeting place for those of high rank; the Hegemony and their closest staff. At its entrance, a group of hara stood in conversation, their hands gliding to complement their speech. Pain brought a bitter taste to my mouth. One of them was Seel.

Arahal called a greeting. Seel turned and looked and shook out his hair and smiled. I had not imagined him like this. Cal had described him differently to me. This was the har who had built a town from bare, corroded rock and blistered his hands tearing at the soda valleys in the south. Now he was just Gelaming, sanitised and unsoiled. He should have had snakes for hair. He did not look at me once.

I was not taken to the Hegemony for three days. During this time, Cal, Leef and I remained in our canopied home, emerging only to eat, when we would sit together in the quietest corner we could find in the nearest pavilion that served food. Once or twice, strangers came to talk with us, refugees from the north, as they supposed us to be. We were afraid of revealing too much about ourselves (all conversation seemed to turn to the Varrs and their atrocities), so shrank from responding to any friendly overtures. We amused ourselves by playing with the pack of cards Arahal had brought us and drinking vast amounts of wine.

Far from recovering from my weakness brought on by our journey through the forest, I seemed to be getting worse. It was an effort to do anything. I couldn't eat, but I was still the only one who ever went for a walk outside the pavilion. I liked the way nobody bothered me. I could wander half drunk for hours in total peace with people all around me. That was the best thing about Imbrilim, I think. Cal was on edge all the time, dreading further contact with Seel, while Leef was sullen and silent. It was a relief to get away from them occasionally.

'Why doesn't he come?!' Cal shouted out, unexpectedly, one evening.

'He will never come!' I answered, knowing that to be unbearably true.

Cal sat down on the floor. 'He's changed,' he murmured, to himself more than to Leef or me. 'Once he would have come storming in here, yelling at me ... now it's like, it's like he's been gelded or something.'

'Different fire, different fire …' I rambled.

Cal put his head in his hands. 'I *must* see him!' he insisted.

Seel never came.

In the evenings, I liked to stand at the entrance to our pavilion, taking in deep lungfuls of scented air that always smelt of nostalgia to me. Often, laughing groups of humans and hara would stroll past, lost in conversation, lost in friendship, perhaps on their way for an evening drink in one of the ale tents. Once Cal joined me. 'It's disgusting! I hate them!' he said.

Sometimes I could bear it no longer and would have to go looking round Imbrilim, looking for *him*. I usually found him. I seemed to have an uncanny instinct for sniffing him out. The best time was when I found him alone, in a field, beyond the camp. I don't think he was dancing, just exercising his body, but it was incredible to watch. There was no music, but I could tell he was hearing it. He was so slim, it seemed impossible that he contained all the right bits inside him. The thought of it was inconceivable. Such a perfect being could not be blood and bile and gut. Inside, he would be made of glass or crystal or cloud. Maybe all three. I watched him entranced, full of pain. Once he looked right at me and seemed to stretch just that little bit further. I hated him knowing I was watching, but he did not seem to mind. He was used to an audience.

Afterwards, I told Cal about it. He did not laugh, as I had expected. 'What is waiting for us?' he asked me. 'I can feel something breathing down the back of my neck, just outside, just above us, perhaps. Why do they make us wait?'

Miserably, I took him in my arms and we sat on the floor, among the silken cushions, in silence, tasting each other's thoughts without the contact of lips or flesh. After a while, Cal said, 'I get the feeling … I don't think I'll be around here for much longer.'

I could not answer him, for I knew that it was true.

In the morning, Arahal came for me. The sunlight beyond the canopies was hard and glittering, like Arahal's silver hair. He was dressed in skin-tight black trousers, with a confection of straps and silver chains adorning his chest and back. There were black feathers woven into his hair. He looked magnificent, a prince of legend. I was feeling horribly light-headed because of the skimpy meals I'd had over the past few days, but Arahal did not seem to notice or concern himself with my condition. I was sure that if I fell, he would just sling me over his shoulder and carry on walking, chatting amiably about things I would never remember or even hear properly.

He took me directly to the purple and gold pavilion and told me cheerfully that I was to be given an audience by members of the Hegemony. I was miserably conscious of my bedraggled and feeble appearance and knew I was in no state to present myself well. 'Does it have to be today?' I asked.

'I thought you wanted your questions answered,' Arahal replied.

An intensely beautiful har, dressed in floating grey gauze, with thigh-length platinum-coloured hair, conducted us into an antechamber. 'I am Velaxis,' he told me. I got the impression that was supposed to mean something. 'If you would wait here a few moments, Tiahaara ...' He swayed off into the curtains.

'Velaxis is a creature of renown,' Arahal said drily.

'Is he one of the Hegemony?' I asked.

Arahal shook his head and smiled. 'Oh no, but he is very close to them. Thiede gave him to them.'

This struck me as absurd, if not a trifle hypocritical. For a race who professed to believe so passionately in freedom, how could they countenance something that had more than a whiff of slavery about it?

Arahal noticed my expression. 'Velaxis is paid for his services,' he said. I must have looked even more surprised. 'He was once in Thiede's employ as a personal assistant,' he continued. 'No doubt Thiede realised the Hegemony would need efficient personnel here in Megalithica.'

Velaxis conducted us into the main chamber of the pavilion. We hadn't waited long. Our presence was announced. I was nervous, expecting formality of the severest kind.

In the middle of the room was a large table. A tall, half-dressed har was sitting on it, peeling a piece of fruit with a knife, his boots were scuffed, and long, fair hair escaped from a black ribbon at the back of his neck. He had a face that was used to smiling and very white teeth. Another, standing next to him, sharing a joke (they were both laughing), was combing out his hair, which was wet.

'Ah, the rogue Arahal,' said the one sitting on the table. That anyone should even think of Arahal being a rogue, let alone actually say it, was a revelation.

'Ashmael,' Arahal responded, bowing sarcastically. The fair-haired har put his knife down carefully on the table. He looked directly at me and I had to lower my eyes. 'And this must be the spawn of the mighty Terzian,' he said.

They offered me wine, which went straight to my head, and we sat on warm, wooden chairs around the table.

'Arahal, what have you been doing to him?' Ashmael asked, lifting my chin in his hand. His fingers were sticky with fruit juice. Arahal did not answer.

'Are you struck dumb or something?' Ashmael asked me. 'Can Varrs speak?'

'I am dying,' I answered.

Ashmael looked at Arahal and they grinned at each other. 'I think I should talk with him alone,' Ashmael said.

'As you think best,' Arahal answered and stood up. He and the other har (who had not yet spoken) went through the curtains to another part of the pavilion. From this, I gathered that Ashmael must be of higher rank than the others.

'Are you hungry?' he asked me. I shook my head, then nodded it, unsure, sick and starving. The Gelaming called for food and then sat on the table again, where he was obviously more comfortable. He looked at me in silence. His charisma was almost stifling. I could sense his power and his fame, yet he was effortlessly informal. I felt so small beside him, yet even in my helplessness, I wanted him to respect me a little.

'I want to know ...' I began, and then trailed off, confused as to what to ask.

'You want to know why you are here,' Ashmael prompted helpfully, still staring right into me.

I nodded and my head swam. 'I feel so weak,' I said.

'Then you must eat!' He reached for my face again. 'You're all bone! If it helps, I will tell you that this is only the effect of the forest; our little Purgatory. Your psyche has been wounded. I fear you will have suffered terrible revelations. Perhaps we should not have let you stew for so long, but we wanted to let you rest for a few days before interviewing you. It must be intimidating ...' He smiled and then made a noise of annoyance, standing up and striding to the entrance of the room. 'Velaxis!' he called. 'I believe I ordered food some time ago!' Even his sarcasm was charming.

'Are you their leader?' I asked, once he had sat down again. He laughed.

'No; their leader, as you call it, is a grand personage known as the Tigron. He is a phenomenon of phenomena ... oh, but of course, you've already met him, haven't you!'

'Have I?' I asked, thinking of Seel.

'Yes. To most he is only known as the mighty Tigron, but to his friends and those fortunate enough to share his bed, he is merely Pellaz.'

I should have known, I suppose, but even so, it took some moments for this fact to sink in.

'Pellaz! Then he *isn't* dead!'

Ashmael pulled a wry face and sighed. 'Just the opposite, I would say. Searingly alive! Even if he is Thiede's ...' He paused and shook his head. 'No, I must not speak out of turn. Such things are not for your ears, son of Terzian!'

All I could think of was getting back to our pavilion and being able to tell Cal about this. I wanted to go now. Suddenly, my head had cleared and I no longer seemed to be among strangers.

I must have tried to stand. Ashmael carelessly pushed me back into my chair with his foot. 'Where are you going? You haven't eaten yet and I haven't talked to you.'

'I must ... Cal ...'

Again, Ashmael shook his head. 'No, you mustn't. Cal has his own path to follow and I dare say it's a long one. There's no fiery reunion for him yet. Your paths must diverge for a while.'

'You're going to try and change him, aren't you?' I couldn't help saying it, but Ashmael didn't seem offended.

'We don't want to change anyone … well, perhaps … not Cal, certainly. He is a pawn in a mighty battle that concerns neither of us. Put him out of your mind.'

Velaxis brought in the food. There was cold, roasted chicken, a salad of crisp greens and nuts, and strong, aromatic cheese with blue veins. Once I could smell it, food was all I could think of. Ashmael ate off my plate, not really hungry, but too greedy to watch me eat it alone. He poured me more wine.

'Now then, the first thing we're going to do with you is begin your caste training, of which you've had none, I take it.' I shook my head. He smiled. 'After that, when you've settled down a little, perhaps the real purpose for your being here shall be revealed. For now, you'll just have to be content with learning how to be Gelaming.'

'Why is it all so secret? Why am I important? Until recently, my only claim to importance was the fact that I was Terzian's son. Is that still the reason?'

Ashmael shrugged. 'In a way. You must understand that the plans of the Gelaming are vast, and that you are only a small part of them, but an important one nonetheless. We all have our part to play. Soon, you shall understand yours.'

'You're not like Arahal and the others,' I said, suddenly. It was a thought spoken aloud.

'Not like them? What do you mean?'

'You're … I don't know … *real*. I can understand you.'

'Oh, don't let them decieve you,' he said, grinning. 'That's just their way. You'll soon learn. Terrific posers, all of them. Just remember; they all have to shit, they all sweat, they're all flesh and blood and bone. The rest of it they learned from Thiede, who is the archetypal cool person.'

'I think it's more than that,' I said dubiously.

He shrugged. 'Perhaps, but I helped shape Thiede's little kingdom for him and he values me, so I'm allowed to think as I like.'

I laughed with him. Whatever he said, Ashmael was not like the others. He had no time for trivia and was impatient with formality, but he could be a bitter enemy if you upset him.

He told me about the Hegemony, that there were three of them here in Megalithica; Cedony, who was here before with the wet hair, Ashmael and another, whose name was Chrysm. He told me that Thiede had kept them inactive for quite some time. All they had done since reaching Megalithica was provide sanctuary for refugees from the north and 'worry Terzian and Ponclast a little'. That was when I asked about my father.

'Where are my people?'

Ashmael looked me straight in the eye. 'I don't know,' he said, spreading his hands, 'truly I don't. I had nothing to do with that. It was a morsel that Thiede and Pell kept to themselves. We get so little news here. All we do is wait for orders that never seem to come. One day, we are told, "Terzian's son is coming to you and he has to be trained." It wasn't quite the earth-shattering event we'd been anticipating. I don't know why Thiede wanted you to come to us. It would have been much quicker for us to come to you at Galhea and bring you back, but that was the way he wanted it, so we couldn't argue. Thiede's fond of upgrading unsuspecting hara to greatness, as he did with Pellaz. I should imagine he has some grand scheme in mind for yourself. Better lie back and take it and make the most of it. There's little point in putting up a fight, believe me!'

'Perhaps my father is still in the forest,' I said, not wanting to be sidetracked from my original question, although what Ashmael had told me prompted a hundred more.

'I doubt it,' he replied. 'As I told you, dealing with the Varrish army was something that Thiede and Pell handled alone. It would have been tied up long ago.'

'Then where ...?'

'Leave it, Swift!' Ashmael warned and the tone of his voice silenced me utterly.

After a while, the other members of the Hegemony, whom I had not met, came to join us. At first, I thought it was Seel and my skin crawled. He had similar slanty, cat's eyes, but his hair was darker and he was taller.

'I can't stand it! The shower spits rust down my back and there's a dead bird in our water cistern!' he cried, raising his arms, rolling his eyes upwards. 'Ah, Immanion, I grieve for you!'

'Chrysm, this is Swift,' Ashmael announced.

Chrysm put his hands in his hair. 'Ah, at last, the Varr! Can we go home now?' he asked.

From the way I was treated by the Hegemony, I could tell that my status must be close to that of Arahal's. They spoke to me in the way that people of high rank do to those whose position is beneath theirs, but higher than most; the way that tries to convey equality, while still making it apparent that they are making a conscious effort to do so. I had always imagined the Gelaming to lack humour, to be utterly serious all the time, but as in most of my preconceptions about them, I was proved wrong. Apart from their stunning appearance, they were nothing like the way I'd imagined. I found I was rather drunk and told Chrysm of my earlier opinions of his kind.

'It is a strain being perfect, I suppose,' he said, grinning. 'For myself, I am not above the occasional orgy of bitching, which no doubt offends my guardian spirit to the point of apoplexy, but still … talking of which, is this rumour of the Tigrina's impendence rooted in truth or supposition or what?'

Ashmael shrugged. 'I don't know for sure. You know how these things get around. Pell won't come himself, I'm sure of that. Everyone's sure of that! Perhaps the Tigrina is bored, alone in his ivory tower in Phaonica. Pell might send him to us to keep him quiet.'

'Or to gratify his curiosity over certain people,' Chrysm remarked cynically.

'Mmm, that too, of course. However, I'm sure Thiede would have assured our gracious Tigrina that Cal is no threat to his position …' He noticed me trying to follow their conversation. 'I'd better explain to you, Swift, who the Tigrina is. His name is Caeru and he is the Tigron's consort. You will no doubt hear rumours that their relationship is not all it might be. It was Thiede's idea, of course. Pell never lets slip anything about his feelings, but it's no secret in Immanion about his relationship with Cal. Neither is it a secret that Thiede would do anything to prevent them resuming it.

I think it's sort of inevitable that Cal should come back into Pell's life. He could so easily have vanished forever. Just because he's here with us in Imbrilim must be bringing the Tigrina out in a cold sweat ... Something's going on, but no-one knows what it is.'

'Least of all Cal,' I said. 'He doesn't even know Pell is still alive.'

'I pity him, in spite of his sins,' Chrysm said, and for a while, we all fell silent.

Eventually, I had to ask some questions about Seel. I noticed my companions pause and grin at each other before Ashmael answered me.

'What about Seel? He's a born organizer, I suppose. He enjoys bringing order out of chaos. He's a close friend of the Tigron's and through that, the closest link to home. It is said they communicate frequently.'

'He's beautiful,' I blurted, inadequately.

'We are all beautiful,' Chrysm laughed, throwing back his head and gazing haughtily down his nose in a typically Seelish manner.

'Of course Seel has inner light,' Ashmael said caustically.

'Don't you like him?' I asked, appalled.

'Of course we do,' Ashmael answered quickly, patting my head. 'It's just that he's full of Pell's essence and finds it difficult to keep his feet on the ground nowadays. Few can aspire to embrace him. His nights are spent in solitary meditation, enjoying our Tigron's touch on the astral plane, no doubt.'

'No doubt at all!' Chrysm agreed, raising his glass.

At dusk I wandered back to the pavilion that had become my home, thinking about the afternoon's events. The visit to the Hegemony had been purely social, I could see that. They had wanted to put me at my ease and had succeeded effortlessly. I was no longer so anxious about my purpose for being in Imbrilim, for the Hegemony seemed as vague about it as I was, and that was comforting in a strange sort of way. Some of the elated mood that had accompanied my arrival in Imbrilim had come back to me. I had walked away from my pavilion that morning, afraid of what to expect and of no worth. Now I walked back a friend of august persons who had a definite place in the scheme of things, even if no-one was sure of what it was. I was full of Gelaming wine and felt like dancing. For the first time in ages, I felt once more like a son of a Wraeththu tribe leader. My shoulders drooped no longer and the effect was magical. Hara bid me good evening and waved. A woman carrying a child in her arms stopped to speak and told me she was glad I was feeling better. 'I am Shara,' she said. 'My people came down from the north some months ago, and after my father died, it fell to me to take charge of them. We were driven from our homes by the Varrs.'

I must have gone white. Shara immediately reached for my arm, flustered by embarrassment. 'I'm sorry. Please don't think I meant anything by that. We heard you were coming here. We know who you are. Did you suffer terribly at the hands of your father?'

How could I answer that? To say yes would be a lie and to say no might go against me. 'Many have suffered at the hands of my father,' I said and she nodded in sympathy.

'Our tents are in the eastern quarter of Imbrilim. My people are known as the Tyrells. Please come visit us sometime. You would be most welcome.'

I thanked her and she walked away from me. So humans too were forming into tribes, it seemed. As the Hegemony had treated me like an equal, so too had the human woman. There were many things I'd have to get used to. I also realized that everyone in Imbrilim seemed to know everyone else's business. I'd never seen Shara before, yet she'd known who I was and that I'd been feeling unwell. Isolated in Forever, I'd never known that communities can seem surprisingly smaller than they really are and that gossip travels faster than fire.

Leef was waiting for me outside the pavilion, staring anxiously up the avenue. When I saw his face, which was wretched, I was angry, because I could feel my mellow good humour melting away. 'Cal is gone,' he said.

He did not know where, only that Arahal had come back to our pavilion some time in the afternoon and told Cal to gather up his belongings. He had not owned much. 'Say goodbye to your friend,' he had been told, and Leef had watched helplessly as Arahal led Cal away.

263

'He knew it would happen,' Leef said, shaking his head. 'What's going to happen to you and me? What do they want with us?'

I put my hand over his and said nothing.

They would not tell me where Cal had been taken, nor what fate awaited him. I had to ask, I had to stand up and demand answers; Leef expected it of me.

I sought Arahal; I found him sitting outside a pavilion with a group of friends, sipping green liquor, absorbing the evening air, laughing softly. Never had a scene looked more inviting. He listened politely to my outburst, nodding at the end of it. 'You must not be concerned,' he said and offered me a drink. 'Please, sit down, Swift. Join us.'

'I had thought his suffering had ended,' I said, complying with his request and accepting the cool crystal goblet he placed into my hand.

'What makes you think Calanthe suffers?'

I turned away from him, angry at the evening for being so tranquil, annoyed at myself because I knew my anger was only superficial and that I only wanted to get this conversation out of the way so that I could enjoy myself and talk with Arahal about my conversation with Ashmael. It wasn't that I no longer cared about Cal's fate, just that I had accepted it. Before Arahal even told me, I knew that Cal's future, his path, was divergent from my own. If I sound cruel saying that, then it must be read as cruel, but it is how things were, nevertheless. When I turned round again, I realized Seel was sitting at Arahal's side. He was looking at the floor, one hand in his hair. As soon as he felt me looking at him, he stood up, excused himself to the others and walked away. Nobody commented on it.

'Where *is* Cal?' I asked Arahal.

He refilled my glass which I'd emptied too quickly. 'This is awkward, 'Swift. I can't answer you and you must stop wondering. There is no sense in it. It is Thiede's will, or the Tigron's, so you can do nothing.'

'Can you blame me for worrying?'

'Not at all!' He smiled and touched my face. 'If you are worrying … They said you had a look of your hostling about you. They are right.'

'They?'

He shrugged. 'Rumours, of course. Yet you have Terzian's steel as well. Let us hope you have not inherited his mania.'

I shivered at the possibilities in that concept. 'He was always a good father to me,' I said stiffly.

'And a considerate friend to Cobweb, no doubt.'

I squirmed awkwardly. 'Do you know so much about us?'

'Only what was necessary for us to know.'

I looked away, up the avenues of swaying silk, in the direction Seel had taken. I wanted to ask about him, but I couldn't. 'Is it true the Gelaming deny love?' I asked instead.

Arahal leaned back in his seat. 'Ah, love; what is it? Can we ever know? It defies analysis, I'm sure!'

'You have not answered me.'

'No. Perhaps I can't. The whole concept is a web of subtleties. Where is the dividing line between a close friend, who cares for your welfare, who shares the intimate pleasures of your bed, and a lover? Is there one?'

'Cal told me that the Gelaming scorn what they call "the passions of mankind".'

Arahal sucked his upper lip thoughtfully. 'Passion of any nature is to be scorned, of course,' he answered obliquely.

'You are evading me,' I said.

'Not really. I don't want to give you the wrong impression. Being Gelaming is a way of life, a state of mind; not just Gelaming either, but many other tribes. It is difficult to convey in words. If you had been trained, if you thought in the right way, then you would know and I would not have to explain.'

'But what if I don't want to think that way?'

Arahal smiled. 'Then you really are the son of Terzian, to the marrow of your bones, and we are wrong about you.'

Arahal became my tutor. For the next few weeks I had to undertake the training that would raise my level. It had nothing to do with warfare as Varrish caste progression did, but was no less rigorous because of it. I suffered gruelling sessions of painful self-examination, when Arahal dispassionately sifted through my innermost feelings and beliefs. It was only through severe concentration that I managed to keep my thoughts about Seel to myself. I dreaded Arahal becoming aware of them. It was obvious that he knew I was keeping something back, but he also sensed the embarrassment surrounding those thoughts, so for the time being did not press me to reveal them. All he said was, 'Guilt is a tool of destruction, Swift, remember that!' His voice full of dire warning. Some part of me really wanted to confess, but I feared Arahal's displeasure, more so because I thought he would not show it.

'Must you know everything about me?' I asked.

He smiled. 'You are missing the point, Swift. *I* don't want to know everything about you, but I want you to.'

In the evenings, I began to spend an hour in meditation. Everything seemed clearer then. I was pleasantly surprised how, when my mind was calm and ordered, it was so easy to summon up and control my innate powers. Now I could visualize with ease, which meant that I could now operate the special shields that the Gelaming used as a barrier at the entrance to their homes. I had only to visualize the force field to be there and no-one could pass through without my wanting them to.

After only a few days, Leef had moved out of our pavilion and gone to live with a group of hara he had made friends with, who, like ourselves and many other hara in Imbrilim, had come down from the north. I knew Leef was displeased that I had been absorbed into the elite of the Gelaming and he told me that he believed I had forgotten all about my old home and Terzian and Cal. He did not actually say it, but I'm sure he looked on me as some kind of traitor.

Perhaps I didn't think of my father and Cal as often as I should, but my mind was often full of Cobweb. I wanted to see him so much and he was so far away; our minds could not touch. We had always been near enough to each other for that, ever since I'd been born. Only now did I realize it and miss it. I used to wonder what he was doing and what Swithe and Moswell and Tyson were doing. Did Bryony ever think of me? Perhaps, in the garden, she could feel me near. At night, I liked to pretend I was back there, lying on the damp grass beside the lake; that place where things of importance had seemed to happen to me. Then I would feel like weeping, for I knew those times would never return. My innocence was lost to me and when I thought of that, I was swamped with loneliness, thinking, Nobody knows how to love me here.

A result or cause of these thoughts, of course, was Seel. Every day, my desire to see him became worse. I told myself I was obsessed and that obsession was dangerous and full of lies and that I must deny it. Then I would open my eyes and be full of tranquility and confidence, believing all my demons exorcised. Then I would see him again and a searing flame of longing would open up the wounds within me; I would want him again and more than that, want to tell him terrible things, terrible, wonderful things. I would imagine it again and again and again. The story would have one of two endings. The first ending was Seel smiling and saying, 'This was meant to be' and the other was his face convulsed with revulsion, backing away from me in distaste. Of the two outcomes, the latter seemed more probable. I kept my fantasies to myself.

One day Arahal said to me, 'Swift, it would be best if you did not take aruna with your friend Leef from now on.' I was so shocked by this that I did not think to mention that we had not been close for some time now.

'Is there any reason why?' I asked.

'Yes,' Arahal replied, but that was all I could get out of him.

I found that I could have a glittering social life in Imbrilim if I wanted to, for I was never short of invitations to other hara's pavilions. There were always parties going on. I had visited Shara's people several times, and although these occasions were never as sophisticated as those spent in Gelaming company, I always enjoyed myself. Most nights, however, I was simply too tired to go out and, once Arahal had called a halt to my education for the day, fell into an exhausted sleep, often without eating or even undressing. The intensive training was worth it, though, because after only five weeks, my level was raised to Neoma.

Arahal was quick to squash all my thoughts of relaxation. 'It is essential that your caste should be Ulani, at last,' he said. 'Once you have achieved it, then you can think about enjoying yourself more.'

'Why Ulani?' I wanted to know.

'Because I say so,' he answered.

I was curious about what the Gelaming planned to do with Megalithica now they were here. Were they eventually going to ride north and deal with Ponclast once and for all?

'Eventually,' Arahal conceded, in response to my enquiry. 'But not yet. Ponclast has constructed shields about himself. We shall let him think they are effective for a while.'

'I thought the Gelaming had no cynicism in their souls!' I joked.

Arahal shrugged. 'The time is not right; that's all. When we ride north, Swift, you will be with us. When we seize the reins of Ponclast's power, it will be to hand them over to you.'

I laughed out loud.

Arahal smiled. 'Ulani at least, you see ...'

My purpose for being summoned to Imbrilim was revealed as casually as that. Thiede had once groomed Pellaz to govern Wraeththu as their Tigron, and now he was having me groomed to oversee one of Pellaz's provinces. Swift the Varr, whom Varrs would find more acceptable than a complete stranger. Terzian's son, sharing his blood while not sharing his beliefs. Who else could have more chance of claiming Varrish loyalty except Terzian himself? The Varr now occupied virtually all the north of Megalithica and their influence spread even further than that. Even bearing in mind that the average Varr was little different from the average Gelaming of low caste, it would not be easy to overthrow Ponclast's dominance, for his people believed in his power, and their belief made his power real. I found myself wondering if Thiede had ever considered trying to win Terzian himself over, offering him sovereignty of the Varrs. Had that been the original plan? Terzian was worshipped by every Varr. He was a warrior prince, handsome, intelligent and fierce; a natural ruler. But the canker in his soul had run too deep and I knew he would never have succumbed to accepting Thiede as his lord; never. Whereas I was young and idealistic and half Cobweb's. The only conceivable substitute. I think the Gelaming's main problem with me was that I did not look more like Terzian.

'There may be violence,' Arahal said.

'I should expect so,' I agreed. 'I know what Ponclast's capable of.'

'We hope to avoid conflict as much as possible, but I'm sure you're familiar with the nature of your race. Distasteful!'

'Arahal, I'm lonely!'

'Swift, you must be patient.'

Sometimes, Ashmael would send for me and I would sit in his pavilion and listen to him talking with Cedony and Chrysm or other members of his staff. It was the best way to learn. Often, he seemed to forget I was there, but now and again, he would send the others away and talk to me. Once he asked me to massage his shoulders, complaining they were stiff. Beneath my fingers, they felt as supple as a puma's. He sighed pleasurably and said, 'What do you think of me, Swift? Do I please you?'

I was so surprised and embarrassed that I backed away from him. My answer was a shaky mumble. 'You are Gelaming, Lord Ashmael; that should be response enough.'

He laughed and shrugged, turning to look at me. 'Swift, I have told you about this before. You mustn't spend so much time looking up to us as if we were gods or something. When I asked you that, you should have just said yes and then seduced me. I was looking forward to it.'

After that, nothing happened between us. I think he must have been teasing me.

One evening, I was invited to a gathering at Cedony's pavilion. Arahal escorted me. It was quite an important occasion because everyone of note was there. I had seen little of Seel over the past few weeks and was surprised to see him there. I had thought he was away from Imbrilim for he sometimes went back to Immanion, although his journeys were amazingly swift; he was never away for long. I longed to touch him or even speak to him, but his unbearable loveliness was intimidating. He must have dozens of hara paying him compliments constantly. Whatever I could say to him would bore him. When he walked past us, he smiled and nodded at Arahal and then looked at me. I felt colour rise to my face, but thankfully he had gone before he could see it. Arahal threw me a shrewd sidelong glance, but said nothing.

Chrysm came over and asked me how my training was coming along. Arahal answered for me and told him it was coming along just fine, thank you.

'Your looks are improving,' Chrysm said to me, touching my arm, so that Arahal couldn't interrupt.

'No, my looks are returning,' I replied, somewhat coldly. 'It was the journey.'

'You are angry,' Chrysm said, smiling ruefully. 'Perhaps that was rude of me.'

'Not really.'

'Come and talk to me. Is that allowed, Arahal?'

'You are a stupid beast, Chrysm,' Arahal replied and walked away from us.

'Can he talk to you like that?' I asked, rather shocked.

'We know each other very, very well,' he replied.

'Oh, I see.'

'Mmm, I think you do, little Swift. I expect you hate being called that. You're not that little, are you? It's those enormous eyes. You always look so defensive, or defenceless; I'm not sure which.'

We went outside and walked in the cool, fragrant air. Because of the dusk and his shining hair, I could imagine Chrysm was Seel quite easily, but tried not to. It seemed impure to, somehow.

'Why doesn't Cedony live in the Hegemony's pavilion?' I asked. 'Doesn't he get on with the sumptuous Velaxis or something?'

Chrysm laughed. 'No, it's not that! He likes his privacy, I suppose. I take it you are unimpressed with Velaxis.'

'He looks down on me.'

'No, he doesn't! You are soon to be a mighty ruler, like your father. Why should he look down on you?'

'Oh, please! I'm not so sure about the mighty part or even the ruler, for that matter. Ponclast might take the law into his own hands and kill me.'

'Oh, come now, Thiede would never allow that! Anyway, stop being paranoid. In the words of mankind, Velaxis is merely a whore. If he really does try to look down on you, all you have to do is laugh at him. If you asked Ashmael for Velaxis' company for a night and Ashmael said yes, Velaxis would have to agree. Then let him try and look down on you!'

I laughed. 'Yes, I know. Sorry. I know I'm being stupid.'

'Oh, Swift.' Chrysm patted my shoulder and I reached to squeeze his hand.

We leaned upon a fence and I realized I was looking at the field where I had seen Seel exercising that day, which seemed so long ago.

'I once saw Seel here,' I said.

'You hardly ever mention him, yet why do I get the feeling he's always on your mind?'

'You are very perceptive, my lord Chrysm.'

'Swift, please! This is a forlorn shamble of tents out in the middle of nowhere. What is rank in a place like this?'

'It is part of Heaven.'

'Only one part is, I think.'

'You look like him.'

'I know. But I am not so self-centred as to think I am as desirable as the real thing. Well, not in your case, certainly!'

'Please don't tell anyone,' I said, turning to look at him.

'Why are you ashamed?'

'I'm not. It's just …' I waved my arms helplessly.

'No aspiration is too high.'

'You know that isn't true!'

'Mmm. Maybe.' He leaned with his back to the fence and spread his arms along it, his hair falling down towards the grass on the other side.

'How old are you?' I asked.

He raised his head. 'I don't care. It doesn't matter any more.'

'Don't you like having birthdays?'

He laughed. 'Birthdays? What are you thinking about, Swift, that you ask these banal questions? Can you say what you are really thinking?'

'No.'

He leaned over and took my hands away from my neck where I found I was clutching myself. He put my arms around him, his warm mouth touched my own and it was a taste of light and

271

swords. I pressed myself against him, appreciating the contact. It had been so long since I had touched anyone like this.

'Say what you are really thinking,' he said inside my head and I opened up my mind to him and let him see.

'You want me to be Seel,' he said, but he wasn't angry, just mildly amused, and I put my hands in his hair and dreamed.

CHAPTER

4

Magic Lost
Tears of anger flooded through pores,
Vulgarity stumbled cruelly across the
Tongue of jealous love.

Beyond the boundaries of Imbrilim, cool woodland undulates away towards the north. What magic exists within that tangle of trees is only of the most natural, unobtrusive kind. In the morning I went to walk there, looking up through the gently swaying branches towards a placid sky.

I had woken that morning, plagued by a black depression and numbing confusion. Yesterday, I had been in a good mood, now I was the victim of my own emotions. As I walked, I spoke aloud to my father, imagining him there. Unexpectedly, he was most sympathetic and I could almost feel his hand upon my shoulder. 'What do you expect of these people, Swift?' he said. 'Do you really think you've been truly accepted by them? Are you of equal rank to them? I once warned you about the Gelaming. Have you forgotten everything I told you? To them, you are merely a Varr; at best a novelty to be used as a pawn, and at worst an object of derision. You should not be here, not really. Don't you know this in your heart of hearts? Even their whores look down on you!' I tried to silence him, to block the scraping words out of my mind, but they would not go away.

'Terzian?' I asked him. 'Did you ever find an answer to your problems?' He never replied; it was something I could not even imagine.

I sighed and gazed up at the sky, visualizing freedom and flight, hoping to improve my mood. Now I was the beginning to understand my true nature, the possibilities within me, yet I was still plagued by doubts and teetering confidence. Arahal often upbraided me for this. 'You must believe in yourself, Swift!' he would say, but it was difficult. I told myself it would be so much easier if I was still at home among friends. It was too much to cope with, having to come to terms with a new lifestyle, living among strangers, while trying to discipline myself to be calm and tranquil. I was under too much stress. What I felt about Seel only made it worse. Frequently, I wished Cal was still with me; I needed his clear sight to guide me and sometimes I longed to speak with Leef, but something held me back from seeking him out. I condemned myself to solitude.

When I returned to Imbrilim, I could tell immediately that something had happened. The air was full of activity and restrained excitement. I approached the first person I saw and asked them what was going on. The young har was only too eager to tell me. 'The Tigrina is here,' he said. A shiver of anticipation ran through me. Straight from Immanion, Pell's consort. Would I get to see him?

One project that I'd seen initiated since my arrival in Imbrilim was the beginning of construction for a permanent Gelaming town, some miles to the south of where we were camped. Ashmael said scathingly that the only reason Thiede had ordered it to be built was that he needed an excuse to keep Gelaming personnel in Megalithica and was becoming tired of their impatience over their inactivity. Chrysm argued sanely that a proper town would have to be built because of all the refugees seeking sanctuary in Imbrilim. There were now too many to be comfortably coped with and it was clear that these people needed to become self-sufficient. Everyone seemed enthusiastic about the plan and labour for the building was not in short supply. Ashmael had taken charge of the operation and sometimes I went over to the site to work with him. I found it all very interesting. I had always thought a town was constructed simply by building a lot of houses and shops in one place, but Ashmael taught me that the precise site was very important, because of drainage, water supply and the fertile land that was needed for cultivation. Architects had been brought over from Immanion. Already I could tell that the new town would be a place of grace and spacious symmetry.

That afternoon, I planned to ride Tulga over to the site so I could speak with Ashmael. Maybe he could dispel some of my doubts. He had a soothing knack of making me feel important. It was there that I received my invitation to the presence of the Tigrina. Moments after I had walked into the low, roomy hut that Ashmael used as an office, a strange har knocked at the open door. I had just said to Ashmael, 'I've heard the Tigrina is here,' when the stranger interrupted us. He handed Ashmael a white envelope.

'What is this?' Ashmael demanded.

'The Tigrina requests your presence at an informal gathering in the pavilion of the Hegemony this evening, Tiahaar.'

'How charming. I live there. I do hope I can make it!'

The messenger inclined his head and turned to leave.

'No, wait!' Ashmael said. 'Have you any more of these?'

'Most have already been delivered ...' The messenger faltered, unsure of Ashmael's motive, no doubt familiar with his hectoring manner.

'Have you got one of these things for Swift the Varr?' Ashmael continued. I winced.

The messenger did not know who I was. He said, in a scathing tone, 'Why yes, I believe I have! I believe I have one for your dog, Lord Ashmael, as well. Perhaps the two creatures are included in the same invitation, I'll just see ...'

Ashmael snatched the bundle of envelopes the messenger had withdrawn from a shoulderbag. He leafed through them impatiently. 'Ah yes, here it is. Take it, Swift, and be sure to tell the dog not to dress for dinner!'

I accepted it and bowed gracefully towards the messenger. 'You must tell the Tigrina I accept with pleasure,' I said, 'but as yet I'm afraid I can't speak for the dog ...'

Ashmael and I both laughed and the messenger hurried away abashed.

'I don't want to go to this,' I said.

'Why on earth not? Such an opportunity to pose, my dear!' Ashmael countered. 'You must learn to cultivate your vanity, Swift. That's what will make you most convincingly Gelaming!'

I sighed deeply. 'I know what they think of me, Ashmael. I'm a Varr; less than a dog!'

Ashmael shrugged and then came to put his arms around me. It is a touch that never fails to electrify, however brief. 'Then show them, Swift. Let them think what they like, but we know better, don't we, and whose table will you be sitting at?'

When I got back to my own pavilion late in the afternoon, I found that new clothes were waiting for me in a carefully wrapped parcel at the entrance. Later, Arahal sent hara to attend to my dressing. The results were most pleasing. The sophisticated and elegantly dressed har who faced me in the mirror was my inner self-image expressed in flesh. Once I had not thought that was possible. The clothes, the painted face, the elaborately styled hair; these were a mask behind which I could try to hide my self-consciousness. No-one would see my heart beating quickly.

At sundown, Arahal came to collect me. He too seemed pleased with my appearance. 'I am honoured to escort you, Tiahaar,' he said, and courteously took my arm as we strolled into the evening.

'He has asked specifically to see you,' Arahal told me.

'Who, the Tigrina?'

'Yes, I'm afraid so.'

'But why?'

'As Tigrina, he does not have to give his reasons to me, a mere underling. Not that we can't guess at them, of course!' By this, I understood that the Tigrina was not wholly popular among the Gelaming.

The pavilion of the Hegemony was a blaze of coloured lights; loud music reached our ears long before we reached it. It seemed packed to capacity with milling hara, all dressed in the most exotic costumes you could imagine. The air was narcotic with perfume. How Cobweb would have loved Terzian to have given parties like this! He would have been in his element, gliding through a throng of social luminaries, being known by all who were worth knowing and lapping up the compliments. Gatherings I had been present at back home now seemed dull by comparison.

I was very nervous about having to speak with the Tigrina, though I said nothing to Arahal, and took it as a bad omen that the first person I saw when we entered the pavilion was Seel. He came straight over to us and pulled a face at Arahal. I was surprised by his vivacity; perhaps he had been drinking. 'Arahal, I have been regally stared at!' he said.

Arahal laughed. 'Then I hope you're ashamed of yourself!'

'For what?'

'Ah, such innocence! You know damn well for what! Pell's consort, remember!' Seel smiled; such a secretive, sensual smile. I could have wept. Arahal put his hand upon my shoulder. 'Seel, would you look after Swift for me for a moment? I shall go and ask his mightiness if he would speak with our Varrish protégé before or after the meal.'

He walked away so quickly, Seel and I could only stare at each other in mutual dismay. I knew my reasons (which I feared were written all over my face), but I could not understand his. I did not really know why Seel always wanted to avoid me. That he considered me beneath him was obvious, but I suspected he did not like to admit that, even to himself. He made an effort to smile (such radiance!), and we both began to speak at once. I apologized.

'Well, what do you think of Imbrilim?' he asked perfunctorily and gazed over my shoulder, taking a graceful sip of his drink.

I wanted to touch him so much, I had to clench my fists at my sides. I wanted to say to him, 'Imbrilim? It's very interesting, isn't it, but of course, I got used to this kind of life in Galhea. Ponclast's people were always coming down from the north; our house was always full. Get me a drink and I'll tell you more ...' but all I came out with was, 'Well, I ... I think it's ... um ... wonderful.' He looked at me then and gave me a caustic smile, leaving me cringing at my own banality. I wanted to look away, but I couldn't; his eyes were hypnotic. Perhaps our eyes locked for just a shade too long. All the time, I was bellowing inside myself for that fabled inner strength, but it appeared to have shot into hiding. I could think of nothing to say. The silence was unbearable and I wanted to sink into the floor. I visualized the thought, One day, wondrous Seel, you shall see me as I really am, and then you won't despise me! It was small compensation, but all that I could cling to.

'Shall I fetch you a drink?' he asked, and I nodded my head, babbling, 'Yes. Please. Anything.'

It was Chrysm who brought it back for me. 'Seel said to give you this,' he said with a knowing smile. I grimaced and drank, gratefully. 'I enjoyed our walk last evening,' Chrysm continued.

'I'm sorry about that,' I said.

'For what? You are too hard on yourself. You must learn to handle Seel in the right way. He is only har, you know.'

'Only!'

'He doesn't know what he's missing; that's all I've got to say about it. I only wish you'd wanted me to be me and not him!'

'Chrysm, stop it!'

He laughed at my flushed embarrassment. 'Well, Swift, have you seen the legendary Tigrina yet?'

'No, not yet.'

'You will have to prepare yourself for an interrogation, I fear.'

'Interrogation? About what?'

Chrysm touched my arm lightly. 'Don't look like that! Not that kind of interrogation. It will be about Cal. Probably his name will not even be mentioned once, but I swear you'll find yourself talking about him endlessly.'

'I'm not sure I understand you,' I said.

'When was the last time you took aruna with anyone?'

'Why? What has that got to do with it?'

'Nothing at all!'

'You are mocking me!' I thought about walking away from him, but could see no-one else that I knew. My glass was empty.

'Arahal means to keep you chaste.' Chrysm held a bottle made of lilac-coloured glass and was twisting it between his hands. 'Your body is sacred, Swift,' he said.

'Yes, it is!' I answered coldly. If I asked him questions, he would tell me the answers; he was trying to without the questions being asked, but at that time, I didn't want to know. I was afraid to or I just didn't care; it was hard to tell.

278

I was not given a seat on the top table as Ashmael had implied, but was placed next to Arahal on the next one down. The tables were laden with fragrant food, steam rising from roasted birds, their skins scarlet with spices, soaking in a marinade of tart berry juice. There were bowls and bowls of vegetables, aromatic with sprinkled herbs, and salad and baked fruit simmering in a salty sauce. The Gelaming are fond of food; their meals are always exquisite. It was difficult to keep my eyes off the splendid sight of the Tigrina, who sprawled elegantly in his chair like a god, bending his head to listen to what Ashmael, seated next to him, was saying. I had imagined the Tigrina to be dark like Pellaz, but his hair was the colour of white gold and teased out around his head like an enormous mane, tumbling over his shoulders like molten waves. I thought he seemed strangely vulnerable in a female sort of way, but Arahal brushed away my observation. 'There is steel beneath that velvet,' he said. 'There has to be!'

'Have I learned my lessons well, Arahal?' I asked. God knows what made me think of it then.

Arahal raised one eyebrow quizzically. 'I haven't taught you all that much yet, but I'm pleased with your progress so far.'

'Is there more than one purpose to my training?'

'What do you mean?'

I shrugged, but didn't continue. I could feel Arahal looking at me, wondering. I could feel the words trembling on the tip of his tongue. He curbed himself.

'There is more than one purpose,' he said.

Some time after we had finished eating, when I had relaxed enough to forget why I was there, the Tigrina sent someone to bring me into his august presence. Luckily, I had drunk enough by then not to feel too intimidated. Ashmael winked at me as I sat down. Close to, the Tigrina was an electrifying sight, his strong perfume was overpowering. He was dressed all in clinging black, with black jewels at his throat and in his ears and hair. His fingernails were incredibly long, lacquered to a sheen of lustrous jet and set with diamonds. Never had I seen a throat so long and curving and slim, or shoulders of such sculpted, precise proportions. Caeru was a vision and he knew it.

As I had expected, he spoke in a cool, measured voice. 'So, you are Terzian's son,' he said. I smiled weakly. 'You have travelled a long way to reach us.'

'It seems that way,' I said.

'The Tigron has spoken of you. I have heard about the time Pellaz spent in Galhea. Of course, you would have been just a baby then.' There was no mistaking the hardness in his tone. He turned away from me. 'Ashmael has been telling me of the plans they have for your future ... How privileged you are, Swift the Varr!'

Ashmael smiled fiercely at him. There was a moment's uncomfortable silence, during which the Tigrina sighed four times. I counted, unable to look away from him. I wondered what it would be like to be in his position; so high. Everyone knew who he was; his clothes, his jewellery were the best. His smallest whim must be gratified. He looked at me with dark blue eyes. 'Did you travel here alone?' he asked.

I shook my head. 'No, there were three of us.'

The Tigrina gazed over my shoulder at the crowd beyond us. 'Oh, and where are your friends now? You must point them out to me. I find Varrs most fascinating.'

I looked beseechingly at Ashmael, unsure of how to answer this request, but Ashmael would not help me, hiding his smile in a goblet of wine and scanning the room carelessly.

'There are only two of us left in Imbrilim, my lord,' I said. 'Leef and myself. The other has gone. I don't know where.'

'I see.' He snapped his fingers in the air, and Velaxis, who had been hovering behind Ashmael's chair, swooped to his side. 'More wine!' the Tigrina ordered. 'Be quick about it!' He turned his glacial attention once more upon me. 'Now, tell me about your home,' he said.

He listened to me for about twenty minutes. During that time, I consumed two goblets of wine. At the end of this time, Caeru raised his hand and silenced m: 'n mid-sentence.

'That's enough,' he said, and turned to Ashmael. 'Have one of your people bring the Varr to my pavilion later.' I sensed dismissal and stood up. The Tigrina smiled at me, but his eyes were still cold.

He raised his glittering glass. 'Until later, son of Terzian.'

'Well?' Arahal demanded, when I was sitting next to him once more.

'The Tigrina wishes to speak with me later on,' I said woefully.

Arahal made an irritated sound. 'Oh no,' he murmured.

I leaned over and drank from Arahal's goblet, which he fastidiously took from my hand. The linen tablecloth was strewn with crumbs and ringed with stains. 'You are concerned for me,' I said flatly.

Arahal smiled. 'Yes ... but I suppose you will have to gratify his curiosity. Do you understand why he wants to see you?'

'Because of Cal?'

'Not just that. Caeru knows why you are here and he will misbehave by trying to interfere with your progress. I don't suppose it will matter that much, though. Just don't give too much of yourself.'

'I don't like that warning, Arahal!'

'My only fear is that you will forget it,' he said, and toasted my health with a smile.

Way past midnight, when everyone was talking more loudly than ever and the musicians were playing with more abandon, I asked Arahal, 'About the other purpose of my being here; what is it?'

He pulled a face. 'Do you believe in destiny?'

'I'm not sure what I believe in any more.'

'Hmm ... well, it's something to do with that. The inevitable; what must be. Imagine a focus of two points in time; a focus of two lives at that point. Often, important things can be gained from such events.'

'You never answer me properly, do you?' I complained.

'Well, you must realize that enlightenment for you might change things. We have to be cautious.'

'Is something going to happen soon?'

'Something will happen tonight,' he answered evasively.

The Tigrina retired fairly early by Gelaming standards. Half an hour or so after he had left the party, Velaxis slunk over to where I was sitting, announcing rather bitterly that he was to escort me to the Tigrina's pavilion. Neither of us spoke as we walked through the cool night air. Moths fluttered blindly. There was a damp smell of grass. Some of the other tents were still glowing with subdued light; soft laughter and voices; shadows against the cloth. I was not nervous; I had some idea of what was to come. Both Arahal and Chrysm had hinted at it.

It was only a minute or so's walk from the pavilion of the Hegemony to that of the Tigrina and for all that time I was thinking about Seel. Since that first embarrassing exchange, when Arahal had left us together, Seel had managed to avoid me entirely. Perhaps I was reading too much into his behaviour, after all, there had been so many hara there, most of whom were probably known to him.

The Tigrina's pavilion was constructed of sparkling midnight-blue cloth and adorned with silver tassels that hung motionless in the still air. A single torch glowed blue-white at the entrance. Within, the only light came from a cluster of tall, black candles in silver clasps. Light reflected from spilled jewels, silken cloth and metal. The Tigrina was ready for us, carefully reposing upon a mass of dark, shiny pillows. He was alone, looking up when Velaxis and I eased through the door curtains and dismissing Velaxis with an imperious wave of his hand. Affronted, Velaxis swept out without speaking.

I wondered what had been going through this gilded creature's mind as he waited for me, what plans he had prepared. I could not tell whether it was through design or unease that he did not speak, but I watched entranced as Caeru slowly removed his heavy jewellery in silence. He laid the glistering stones down carefully upon a low table at his side, where they rattled into an untidy, treasure-chest heap. He stretched his neck and rubbed it languorously. I could see the scar of his inception on his arm. Arahal had told me the Tigrina bleached his skin with the juice of lemons. I could believe that; he was as white and luminous as pearl. I think he hoped I was afraid, but that was not the effect he was having on me. It was a kind of morbid fascination that kept me staring at him.

He offered me coffee, which I accepted, and poured me some himself from a tall, awkward pot, which had been steaming on the table. 'I expect you're wondering why I've asked you here,' he said, which I found to be a very predictable question. Perhaps this, more than anything, proclaimed that he was not truly Gelaming.

'I should imagine it's because you want to ask me about Cal,' I said. The Tigrina smothered his surprise. What did he think I'd say? I found it annoying that he expected me to be so utterly in awe of him, because I knew that Ashmael and the others were not. Did he really think that they wouldn't have spoken to me about him, and that their opinions, no matter how surreptitiously implied, would not rub off on me? I was not overly fond of Velaxis, but I had not liked the Tigrina's insulting attitude towards him. Ashmael, whom I respected intensely, never treated anyone like that, no matter how much lower in rank they were than him.

'You are just repeating what you've been told, of course,' Caeru said suddenly. I was alarmed, thinking he'd read my mind, but he was still talking about Cal.

'Isn't it true then?'

'Already, it seems, Ashmael has taught you how to be disrespectful,' he said.

I wanted to reply, 'Doesn't respect have to be earned?' but realized this would be going too far. No matter what the Gelaming might think of him, he was still the Tigrina, and commanded respect simply for that.

'I don't mean to sound disrespectful,' I said.

He smiled and leaned back among the cushions. The shoulder of his garment dropped away slightly, revealing more of that skin which was so perfect and pale. 'Can't you understand my fascination?' he asked. I smiled to myself, amused by the ambiguity of that remark, which I'm sure was unintentional.

'Yes. I understand.'

'Good … You look nervous, Swift the Varr, sitting hunched like that on the edge of your chair.' (I wasn't.) 'What have they told you about me?'

'Nothing.'

'Nothing at all?' He forced a laugh, throwing back his head, exposing that throat which seemed to have "bite me" written all over it.

'A little, then,' I conceded. 'But I would prefer you to tell me about yourself. If you fear you've been misrepresented ...?'

His mouth dropped open in amazement. 'How bold you are! How very Varr! Do you really want to know?'

'Yes.'

'How unusual! Very well, sit here beside me and I shall tell you.'

I stood up and removed Arahal's brushed leather jacket that I'd slung about my shoulders as protection against the cool, dew-laden air outside. The Tigrina watched me with interest. How I've changed, I thought. What Caeru doesn't realize is that this person here with him is as much a stranger to me as to him. I sank down beside him and he leaned away from me a little, as if uncomfortable having anyone so close. He tried to appear brittle and aloof, but now I could see the saddened, bitter creature that he really was. His eyes could not hide it.

'What do you want to know?' he asked.

I honestly think he was regretting having asked me to join him. This interview was not progressing the way he'd planned, although it was fairly obvious that some kind of seduction had been intended. I'd learned how to decipher Arahal's riddles enough by now to have gathered that.

'Tell me where you live.'

'In Immanion. Phaonica, the Tigron's palace. It is on a hill. It can be seen from any point in the city.'

'Do you like it there?'

'It's very beautiful. It is always warm.'

'How many servants do you have?'

'I don't know. A lot. I don't know them all.'

'You don't know their names?'

'No. Should I?' He sounded defensive. I suppose he hated his servants. Perhaps they despised him.

'Describe your bedroom.'

'It ... it is large.'

'Black and silver?'

He laughed nervously. 'Yes. I like those colours. The moon and darkness.'

I leaned towards him and he backed away an inch or two. 'What do you see from your window, Tigrina?'

'The lights of the city and beyond them, the sea. It is always moving. I look at it at night.'

'Is the sea black and silver?'

'Sometimes.'

My lips touched his neck. He was so tense, he could barely keep from quivering, but he did not stop me.

'Do you sleep alone, Tigrina, in that big, black room?'

'What?'

'Do you sleep alone?' I raised my head. There was hardly any space between us. His eyes darted everywhere but into mine. 'Do you?'

He closed his eyes, long lashes against his cheek. 'That question was impertinent. Why did you ask it?' I could smell his surrender, a smell like cut grass. I had asked the question that perhaps he had always wanted someone to ask, because then he could answer.

'Alone, Tigrina? Are you …?'

'Yes,' he said. 'Yes. Yes.'

There was only the slightest of resistance as I pulled him against me. I brushed his lips with my own and he opened his mouth, straining towards me. I raised my head and smiled at him so gently. I took his chin in my hand and pushed it back. He curled his fingers round my wrist, apprehensive. 'Isn't this what you want?' I asked, and put my teeth against his white throat, and bit down, hard.

His body arched against me, but he made no sound. I did not draw blood, but there were marks in his flesh when I raised my head again. 'Varrs do that kind of thing,' I said. 'You must have heard; we are barbarians.' He laughed and I held him tight against me.

'I will ask now,' he said. 'I will ask about Cal …'

'He has gone and I don't know where,' I replied. Caeru stiffened in my arms. He said nothing. 'One thing I do know, that I am sure of, is that either the Tigron or Thiede is responsible for his disappearance.'

'Are you fond of this Cal?'

I lifted his head. 'It can't be helped. He just has that effect on people. He makes them love him.'

'I know!'

'Such bitterness!'

'Such bitterness,' he agreed wistfully. 'I would like to meet him.'

'Would you?'

'Yes. Really. He can't take anything from me. I am Tigrina; Thiede made me so. That can't be taken away, and I have nothing else.' He did not sound self-pitying, only fatalistic. Cal would have found him irresistible.

He took my head in his hands and offered me his breath, which I drank from fiercely. He was panting as we parted. 'We are similar,' he said. 'Pariahs in the Gelaming camp.'

'Not I!' I exclaimed vehemently. 'I will not let them think of me that way!'

Caeru smiled. 'No ... I can taste your father in you.'

'I hope not!'

He frowned and shook his head. 'By that, I don't mean ... bad things, just strength and power. It is forming within you.'

'More so during the last few minutes,' I said lightly.

He smiled once more and put his fingers lightly on my chest. 'Have you met Seel yet?'

The sound of that name went through me like a javelin. 'Why?' I was too abrupt. Caeru nodded and smiled wryly to himself.

'Yes, I can tell you have. He is close to Pell.'

'I know.'

His hand slid under my shirt. 'Do you think I've brought you here for just this purpose, to touch you?'

I shrugged, but said nothing.

'Well, if you do, you are right, but it is more than that. I'm offering you a kind of protection. They have kept other hara away from you, haven't they? Nothing is coincidental, nothing!' he cried. 'You are in thrall, Swift, but you don't even realize it! I know these people. I know what their magic can do. You have a strong will and you shall be angry when you find out how they've manipulated you! Your innermost feelings are nothing to them!'

His fervour alarmed me and I put my hand over his mouth. 'Hush!' I did not believe him at all. He made a muffled noise and tried to pull my hand away.

'I am not a fool,' I said, releasing him.

'You are!' he insisted, but he knew I would not listen.

'No. Forget me; I want to talk about you. You are soume-har. I want to fill you.'

'I am Tigrina. You are insolent!' (Some vestige of pride perhaps?)

'Then why are you smiling?'

He shook his head, sighed, and lay back. 'Very well, Swift the Varr ...'

'Is that an invitation?'

He laughed, for the first time honestly, without control. 'Invitation? No, no; it is a command!'

For a second, some sober part of me was aghast. This being, this whole and shining being, was Pell's; he had done this once. The Tigron of Immanion had done this, held this in his arms, and I was just Swift, who until recently had entertained very few grand ideas. When had I changed? When? I remember thinking, Why couldn't it have been like this with Seel? What is it about him that weakens me so much? Tonight, with Caeru, I have said all the right things at the right time; I have been powerful. Is it just the wine that's made me so bold? Why, why, why, couldn't I have been like this with Seel?

As we writhed together, in a haze of sweat and tangled limbs, Caeru said, 'You will need this knowledge.' I did learn a lot from him. I learned how to prolong the pleasure until it becomes pleasure no longer and the final release is like dying and almost like pain. 'One day you will think of me with gratitude,' he said, and part of me could sense that time to come; formless and vague, a tantalizing presentiment.

Afterwards, I would not let him sleep. 'Now is the time,' I said.

'The time for what?' he asked drowsily.

'To tell me about yourself. I want to give you something in return. I want to give you my ears.'

He smiled lazily. 'You have given me enough ...'

'No, Caeru. Tell me. Tell me how it happened, how you became Tigrina, why it happened and what went wrong.'

He put his arms across his eyes. 'Do not call me Caeru. That is what *they* call me. It is the name that I was born with, it is true, but my friends have always called me Rue.' He sighed. 'Rue for sadness, who barely exists any more. Rue was happy; Caeru is not. Caeru is a slave, because Rue made a grave mistake ...'

'Go on.'

He sighed again. 'Very well. If you insist. Hold me, Swift.' He curled against me and I listened to the tale, the other side of the story. He began:

'Once upon a time a har named Rue lived in a very nice place called Ferelithia. It was a happy, rich town where humans and hara lived together and it was always warm. Rue was contented there. He earned his living through his voice; he sang. He had a lot of friends and life was kind to him. Only, one day, he fell in love with a beautiful face and a beautiful body, both of which belonged to an incomparable, mysterious har called Pellaz. Pell was just passing through Ferelithia and his relationship with Rue was destined to be a brief one. It would have been too, if Rue had not been so stupid and so naive as to let Pellaz take aruna with him to its furthest possible point. There was a child, and by the time I realized, Pell had long gone. It was so ridiculous, because at first, I didn't even realize what was wrong with me. I'd get strange feelings in my stomach, odd little movements and pains. I thought I was getting sick and tried to ignore it. Kate knew what it was, but she didn't tell me. She didn't have the guts to! Kate, by the way, is my friend; a woman, and perhaps my only friend. Pell had told her what he'd done to me before he left. Can you believe that I didn't realize? It's incredible, isn't it? One day, I just collapsed in the street. I thought I was dying because the pain was so bad. That was when Kate finally confessed what she knew. We had a raging argument that lasted all the way through my delivery of the pearl. I suppose it was good for me because it took my mind off the pain. "Oh, Rue, I wanted to tell you!" she said. As if that was any comfort!

'I couldn't understand why Pell had done it; made a child with me and then just vanished. What was the point? Our son was exquisite, beautiful and weirdly wise. I named him Wolf because it was a name of power and also how I thought of his father at that time. As he grew up, I began to see that ... he was different. I knew inside myself that he belonged with his father, because Pell had been different in the same way. What could I offer him? I loved my life in Ferelithia, but it wouldn't be enough for Wolf; he deserved more. At that time, I didn't know Pell had become Tigron. Maybe I wouldn't have made that decision if I had known. Kate agreed with me that Wolf should be taken to Pell. She said that Pell had left money for her, so that one day she could use it to visit him in Immanion. We scraped together a little more and the three of us set off across the sea on a wonderful, romantic journey to find Wolf's father. I think it was the last time I was truly happy.

'Of course, when we reached Immanion and found out exactly what Pell had become, all the Gelaming thought I was a callous adventurer, who had simply come to cash in on Pell's fame and fortune. They still think that, some of them. But it was only for Wolf. I didn't want to stay there. Thiede realized straight away that Wolf is a special child. It was Thiede who dealt with everything. Pell wouldn't even see us. He thought I was hounding him too, you see. There is only room for one in Pell's heart and that space is reserved for Cal; it always will be. I knew that. I've always known that. I didn't want to stay there; it was embarrassing. Then ... then Thiede suggested the worst thing of all. He came to me one evening, as I was trying to leave yet again. He made me sit down and he said to me, "Caeru, you are a shrewd har, you have common sense and you are beautiful enough to please any Gelaming. I want Pell to take a consort, for the people expect it. I have searched for quite a time to find someone suitable, but now I feel that search is over. I want it to be you, Caeru. I want you to become Tigrina of Immanion." He expected my refusal and listened to it patiently. Then he said, "I hope you've said everything you want to say, Caeru, for I don't want to hear anything like that again. You know who I am, you know that I have made my wishes plain. Out of courtesy, I have listened to your objections, but now you will have to forget them. It's unfortunate that you'll have to lose the lifestyle you are fond of, but you are destined for greater things, I'm afraid.

You will be Pell's consort and I shall conduct the ceremony of your bonding in blood to him."

It was obscene, wasn't it? The most sacred, intimate thing any two hara can experience; the sharing of blood. It is an unbreakable bond, and for me, because of that, a living hell. Of course, Pell went berserk when he found out about it. He came storming into the elegant suite of rooms that Thiede had put us in. It was the first time that I'd seen him since I'd been in Immanion. It made me weak; I couldn't help it. Some selfish part of me thought, I will do what Thiede wants because it will keep me close to Pell. I didn't want to lose him completely again. How stupid I was! Pell called me every foul name he could think of. How could I do this? he wanted to know. Hadn't he once confided in me how he felt about Cal? Was I mocking him now? He offered me vast amounts of money to leave, which I refused. I said that Thiede wouldn't let me leave. Pell called me a liar and accused me of plotting against him with Thiede. That was when Kate walked in and tried to intervene. She could see things were getting dangerously close to being out of hand. Pell roared at her. He called her an interfering human bitch and to keep out of it. Kate was horrified. She'd known Pell a long time. It's not like him to be like that, but he was furious. I'd never seen anyone so furious. It was like desperate panic. Eventually, during the shouting, he took a fruit knife off the table and cut his arm with it. He said to me, "Here! Here's my blood. Take it! Drink it if you like! Let's get Thiede to bless the act!" He smeared blood on my face; it was terrible. It made me as angry as Pell was. I'd had enough. I said I would leave but begged him to accept Wolf as his son and let him remain in Phaonica. Pell said nothing. He was just looking at his arm as if he was thinking, Oh hell, what have I done? I *did* try to leave, I really did, but of course, Thiede was waiting for me. Thiede knows everything. He told me not to be stupid, that Pell would calm down and get used to the idea. "You are going to be his Tigrina, Caeru, and that is an end to it. Go back to your room." It was impossible to argue with him.

'Well, as you see, Pell did agree to it in the end, but there is no affection between us. We are bonded in blood to each other forever, an insoluble link, and both of us hate it. Some part of Pell still believes I only went to look for him because I'd heard he'd become Tigron. It isn't true. We'd had a good time together in Ferelithia, Pell and I. I was fond of him. I still am. Now, he is courteous to me. Most evenings, he will come to talk to me. He says he doesn't blame me for what happened. He says he knew it was Thiede. I tell him he's lying when he says that but he only smiles. Sometimes, he wants to take aruna with me. He admires me as he would admire a well-sculpted statue. That's what I am to him, fleshless, but I can't refuse him. It's sick, isn't it? I think he has become genuinely fond of Wolf. They've given him another name now, one fit for a prince, but he is still Wolf to me. At least that turned out alright. Ah well, I have riches beyond imagination, I live in a palace and don't have to lift a finger if I don't want to. He touches me sometimes ... I should be happy, shouldn't I?'

So many people have said that Pellaz, Tigron of Immanion, is the kindest, most compassionate person they have ever met. He appears perfect. In a way, it is comforting to know that he is not. I listened to Rue's story in silence and I said nothing after he had finished it. Once I would have wept, as I had when I'd heard Cal's sad story, but now I expressed my emotions in a different way. I made love to him, sad Caeru; it was not aruna, but truly the warmth of love, because he needed it so badly, and I, soiled Varr of less than perfect character, knew how to give it.

At dawn, he bid me leave. We parted awkwardly; the magic of the previous evening had gone. Such things were meant to be brief. I wondered if Caeru, Tigrina of Immanion, had got what he'd come seeking for in Imbrilim. I would never know. By noon, his dark pavilion was empty.

CHAPTER

5

The Axiom
Sublimation through the spheres
Respect delivered by destiny.
Desire, desire with the beast of fire.

For some days afterwards, I could not keep the Tigrina from my thoughts. He had given me so much more than a mere night of pleasure; he had given me self-respect. Now I felt I could walk among Gelaming and feel equal to them; I felt taller, both spiritually and physically. Arahal noticed the change in me; I could tell by the way he looked at me, yet he chose to say nothing about it. My night with Caeru was never mentioned by anyone in Imbrilim, yet knowing as I did the way news flew around the camp, I was sure everyone must know about it.

During the next few weeks, I devoted myself to caste elevation, and found that in some ways, it was similar to learning to ride a horse. Once the simple techniques have been mastered, the more complicated and difficult parts seem to come naturally. Arahal praised my progress, admittedly with undisguised self-congratulation. 'It was hard for those of us that were born human,' he said, 'for the powers were not natural to us. We had to learn so much. I have never educated a pure-born har before, but it is obviously easier for you just because you are pure-born.'

'Well, Cobweb taught me things right from when I could first speak,' I said, feeling it was wrong I should claim all the credit. 'We could never speak of it openly, though, for Terzian would not have approved. He wanted his son to grow up to be a warrior like himself, not a secretive witch, which was how he thought of Cobweb. Anyway, he called it all mere superstition.'

'A foolishness which I should imagine he is regretting now,' Arahal laughed. His smile faded to a frown when he saw my face.

'Where is he?' I asked. There was a moment's pause, and then Arahal shook his head.

'I've already told you; I don't know, Swift. That has nothing to do with me.'

I wanted to believe him, for I looked on Arahal as a friend nowadays, but I knew he was lying.

One day, I woke up and knew I was Ulani. It was an instinctive knowledge. The ceremony seemed merely perfunctory, for it was inside myself that my caste was raised and no words or rituals could reinforce it, but, because of the Gelaming's love of celebration, Ashmael organized a grand affair to mark my ascension. Because my attainment of Ulani meant that now the Gelaming could plan their attack on Ponclast in earnest, the occasion was treated as a great holiday by the whole of Imbrilim. The atmosphere was intoxicating. Although the actual ceremony itself was brief and held in private in the pavilion of the Hegemony, the rest of the day was devoted to feasting, drinking and dancing. Leef came to congratulate me in icy tones, which annoyed me so much, I was rather peremptory with him. This brought a grim smile to his face as if his worst thoughts about me had been justified. Seel did not appear all day.

In the evening, Arahal said to me, 'Ashmael will speak with you tomorrow, Swift.'

'He speaks to me often,' I said lightly, feeling my heartbeat increase.

'He will *speak* with you, Swift.'

'Is it ... is it time to *know*?' I asked. 'The other purpose for my being here. Is that it?' Some of my forgotten fears fluttered at the edge of my mind.

'It is time,' Arahal confirmed grimly.

That night, I dreamed of the eyes for the first time in ages. I threw handfuls of dream mist at them, but they never blinked. In the morning, I woke exhausted.

'You are a prince, Swift,' Ashmael said to me. I looked in his mirror and saw him standing behind me, taller, his hands upon my shoulders.

'I am Cobweb,' I said and he smiled.

'No, not him; something else.'

My skin will never tan, my eyes will always look shadowed; that is Cobweb's legacy, I know that. I shall never be very tall as my father is, and I shall never have his frightening eyes. I am Swift, through and through, nothing more. I am Swift, and I have learned to like myself.

'Megalithica is ripe for the harvest,' Ashmael said, and I waited for him to continue. 'We shall take our power with us,' he said. 'It will be contained in a crystal and it will glow a dark blue-green. It shall be your power.'

'Where shall it come from?' I asked.

'Within you.'

I turned away from the mirror and saw that Ashmael's eyes were shining with a strange and terrible light, for he knew the meaning behind his words.

'How shall you take Megalithica?' I demanded. 'How shall you *really* take it?'

'What is least attainable is the most desirable,' he answered. A typically Gelaming evasive answer; it meant nothing.

'I will never get used to this!' I said.

He followed me across the room of dappled folds and stood with me at the entrance to his pavilion. 'It is the truth,' he said.

'If it is, speak it plainly. I am Varr, not Gelaming. I don't understand. You play with words!'

'Grissecon,' he said.

I turned and backed away swiftly. 'Me?' (The other purpose; of course. No wonder they were wary of telling me.)

Ashmael nodded silently.

'No!' I cried, already feeling publicly naked.

'You are inhibited.'

'Yes, I am. I've been told that before. I can't do this, Ashmael.'

He sighed. 'Oh dear! Must we have these problems? This Grissecon is essential. Only two people can do it to make it work and both of you are fighting tooth and nail to avoid it, one way or another. Both of you!' He threw up his hands.

Suddenly, I was cold and my arms were about myself and my flesh was chilled. Oh God, no, I said softly, weak with relief and sick with despair. In an instant so many things had become so clear.

Ashmael did not touch me. 'You know who it is, don't you,' he stated flatly.

I nodded, straightening up, though my arms wouldn't uncurl. 'Yes.'

'It is Thiede's will.'

'What an excuse that phrase can be! Everything it seems is Thiede's will. *Why*, Ashmael? Why not anyone else? I've never performed a Grissecon before.'

'It is a focus. Two essences that shall meet, and if Thiede has manipulated fate, it is inevitable; whatever happens.'

'Nothing has been coincidental, has it?' I said, remembering something Caeru had said to me. He had known about this, of course. 'It's all been planned, hasn't it? Everything!'

Ashmael had the grace to look offended. 'Not everything, no.'

Now I understood completely. Thiede had said, 'This shall be,' Pellaz had implemented it and there could be no argument. I was to be the one and I was everything to be deplored; Cal's friend, Terzian's son, a Varr. In other words, tainted. My father fed on human flesh and committed pelki against his own kind. His blood ran in my veins. No-one could be sure that such traits did not lie deep within me too. Except Thiede perhaps and Thiede always got his own way.

'When is this to happen?' I asked in a chilled voice that did not seem to belong to me. I was numb, totally without feeling at that moment.

'Oh shortly, shortly,' Ashmael answered. 'It shall be arranged and you will be informed as soon as we know the details. Swift, I can tell you're upset about this. I must say, you must not feel this way ...'

'What you mean is, I should not feel at all,' I added coldly.

'No, that is not what I mean, I can't understand your turmoil. The Grissecon will not be public; they have spared you that. Just look on it as aruna ... but there is more, I'm afraid.'

'More?' I asked in a dull voice. I could sense Ashmael squirming inside. This pleased me as I thought he could say nothing that could make things more unpleasant. I was wrong.

'Thiede wants a child to be made of this union,' he said quickly. I must have made a noise, like a screech or something. Ashmael jumped and even started to laugh.

'Can a child come from hate?' I raged.

'No,' he said. 'Of course not. But what makes you think it's there?'

'If it's not hate, it's something worse; indifference.'

'You are guessing.'

'No, I'm not! I know!'

'You don't, though! You read too much into things. Chrysm said so.'

What else had Chrysm told him? I could listen to this no longer. Without a word, I strode out of Ashmael's pavilion and walked back through the camp. It had started to rain; a fine mist. Ashmael did not call me back.

Arahal looked up, surprised, when I walked determinedly into his pavilion, unannounced. He noted my expression with apprehension. 'Ashmael's told you then?' he said, standing up.

'Damn you, Arahal!' I said, pointing a shaking finger at him. 'Damn you, all of you! You raise me only to humiliate me. This Grissecon, this person I must share bodies with, share seed with; it's Seel, isn't it?'

Sometime, someone had taken Seel aside and sat him down and told him. He had learned that Cal still lived and where he lived and how he lived, and then he had been told that Terzian's son was being summoned to Imbrilim and that Thiede had decided upon the vessels for the ultimate Grissecon; world power. The force within, blue-green, shining, barely controllable; sex as magic, to wield, to conquer. Seel and Swift, two small parts of a prodigious plan, our bodies connecting like live wires to allow the current to flow. I think he would have just shaken his head at first, in disbelief. He would have been smiling, that slight, wholly luminous smile. Maybe he said, 'Terzian's son? A Varr? Are you serious?' And then he would have realized just how serious they were. Then he would have stood up and let the bitter words flow out of him; Terzian, Varrs, Cal; all that was wrong with the world, that was blighted in the world. He might have said, 'Do you hold me in such contempt that my body should be used, possessed in this way?' Perhaps it had been Pellaz who had told him. I like to think that it was. His voice would have been soothing. Seel soothed to acceptance until the bitterness was deep inside him and he had nodded his head and agreed, 'Alright, if it *must* be so.' (Wouldn't that have struck a chord with Pellaz?) Seel would have thought to himself, I trusted you, Pell, and I could imagine his eyes looking at Pell's back, disillusioned and defeated. Then he must have thought to himself, as comfort, I will never speak to that creature; I will never like him. He is beneath me and it seems I must host his son, but I will never like him. No-one can make me do that!

One day I would have to touch him and his eyes would be veiled like cat's eyes and his head would be held to the side. I never had to be told all these things, no-one ever told me, but I knew them as surely as if Seel had told me himself.

Arahal stood up. He took my shoulders in his hands and shook me slightly. 'Stop this; you are hysterical,' he said blandly. Yet I made no noise. Perhaps my eyes were hysterical. How could I tell Arahal about my dreams that I'd had for years, the dreams that had been an intimation of the person to come? That person had been Seel; I knew that now. From the moment I first saw him, recognition had woken within me. Now, that one thing towards which I had been unconsciously striving all my life had become, indescribably, something terrible that I wanted to run from. What should have occurred naturally had become contrivance, Thiede's contrivance, and because he had accelerated everything all the harmony had been destroyed. I was numb. Maybe, if it hadn't been for this, Seel would have come to like me. I could have made him like me, but now he was angry and affronted.

Arahal's voice broke through my thoughts. 'Swift, be objective, for God's sake!' I looked up quickly, feeling my glance strike his eyes like an arrow. He turned away and poured me wine into a long, thin glass that felt temptingly shatterable when he handed it to me. I drank from it and tasted sourness; Gelaming wine was rarely sour. 'You are reacting irrationally,' he continued smoothly. 'You think you are obsessed with Seel, but that is only the effect of a powerful psychic attack. You were *made* to feel this way. Time was running out. Now you can stand back and view things calmly.'

His words sluiced over me like a stream of melted ice. Made to feel this way? It was laughable. They didn't have to do that. I was obsessed with Seel a long time before the Gelaming had even dreamed of their plans.

'I am ... confused,' I said. I couldn't bring myself to tell him what I was thinking. His hand rested lightly, for a moment, on my shoulder.

'Obsession is desire,' he said. 'Desire is the seed of power. You must fashion your thoughts into a cool blade. Focus your energy, Swift.'

'You speak of me and my behaviour,' I said, 'but what of Seel's?'

'What of it?' Arahal asked. 'Have you ever really spoken to him?'

'No,' I answered irritably, 'but I've sensed things. He doesn't like me.'

Arahal made an impatient sound. 'You must remember Seel is Gelaming,' he said, not without sarcasm. 'He is aware of his duty. His mind is trained to overcome personal preferences.'

'That's sick! This Grissecon will be impossible, and if it is possible, horribly humiliating for both of us.'

'Oh, Swift, calm down! There are ways of overcoming any difficulties that may arise.'

I shrank from asking him what they were. I put my empty glass down on the table. In a dish lay a lock of hair, shining, curled like a sleeping cat. Arahal saw me looking at it.

'Go back to your pavilion,' he said.

Sitting alone on my bed, I found my thoughts drifting towards my father and Cal. Both victims of the Gelaming, I decided uncharitably. Perhaps I feared I was being lost, misplaced, in a similar way. I tried to recall the way I had once felt about Cal, when my Feybraiha had come upon me. I tried to remember if I had felt like this, but the memory eluded me. I habitually banned all erotic thoughts of Seel from my mind, because I found them too painful to think about. Now I tried to imagine the feel of him, but all I could see were those unfathomable eyes, cold and distant. I imagined Grissecon and our bodies tangled together, his flesh hot beneath my mouth, damp with a mist of sweat; our craving, our energy. Then in my thoughts I took his face in my hand and turned it towards me. His eyes were dead, his mind untouched, even as his body moved around me. Could we make magic that way?

I lay back and put my hands behind my head, sinking into the soft cushions, going down and down. I was aware that I needed aruna, my body felt strange. I had rarely been denied it before, not when I needed it. I thought about Caeru; another of Thiede's puppets. I wondered if I would ever see him again. Did Pell know what had happened between us? I turned on my side and thought I would sleep. Then I was listening to the eerie chime that signalled someone was seeking ingress to my pavilion. I made the thought-forms that would open the portal and, after a moment, someone came to the inner chamber and lifted the curtains. I looked up, and saw him standing there. He said, 'I think we have to talk.'

'I think we do,' I agreed, surprised to find that I was not nervous at all.

He sat down on the end of my bed and looked at his hands and I wanted to say, 'Seel, you are the most beautiful thing I have ever seen,' even if it wasn't true, but all I said was, 'Well, what?'

'I think this will be difficult,' he answered, and I was not sure whether he meant this conversation or what was to come.

'I was told today,' I said. He did not turn round, just nodded. All that hair; it was unnatural. I wondered whether it had a life of its own and just lay there around his shoulders and down his back, for convenience. Perhaps it would stretch and crawl around if I touched it. He must have known my thoughts. Cal had once called him a true adept; thoughts might reach him like a scream.

'You must understand,' he said, 'that this ... *state* is alien to me. I

299

don't know what Thiede's done to me, I don't know ... I do know I dislike it!'

I made an impulsive decision and spoke plainly. 'You've known about this since I first came here, obviously. You've avoided me. I can imagine what you've been thinking.' He was silent. 'First, they must have told you about Cal.' His shoulders stiffened and he raised his head, but still he did not look at me. 'Don't think I'm not aware what I am to you. It's blighted Wraeththu, that simple. You don't want to soil yourself. Am I right?'

'Yes, you are,' he replied, somewhat in surprise.

There were a few moments of awkward silence and then I said softly, 'You should have come to see Cal while he was still here. You should have spoken to him.'

Then he turned round quickly. 'Killing to you of course is commonplace!' he said angrily. 'I suppose I should expect that! When I look at you, all I can see is Orien and Orien's blood on the floor and his guts hanging out of him. That's what I see!' He stood up, his arms waving. 'Oh, the Varrs! So sympathetic, weren't they! Who else could he have gone to, whining and beaten? Did you soothe him? Did you say, "Oh, never mind, Cal, what is one more death? It is nothing"? Is that what you said, all of you? As Terzian the murderer, your dear father, fawned over that perfect, demon body, was it all, "Oh, Cal, you are so good, so one of us"? Of course, there was you too, wasn't there! I expect with you Cal let the beast well out of the cave. Did he bite you? Did he tear at you? It's good, isn't it, that perversion? Some sick part of you actually enjoys it while it's happening; afterwards you feel disgusted. Only I don't expect you or your father, did!'

He glowered at me, colour pulsing along his cheekbones. I propped myself up on my elbows and stared back at him. He had made me angry. I wouldn't have thought that was possible. 'Sit down, Seel!' He didn't move. 'Sit down. There are some things I want to tell you.' He hesitated a moment, and then half fell back onto the bed. 'My childhood in Galhea was not the way you think,' I said. 'I want to tell you about it.'

I began with that time when my father had come home with the wound in his leg. I spoke with love, for my family and my people. I had to make him understand the way we had lived, that our lives had not been full of death and evil as he thought. I brought back the memory of Forever in the spring and the gaiety of Bryony's laughter about the house and the happy times we had had together, all of us. I went back to the beginning and told him about Festival and the snow on the ground. It was a story all about when the crows left the trees and two small harlings had trudged the boundary of Forever to keep the stranger out. Then I relived the pain of when Cal had first come to us, and made Seel live it with me, and all that followed, until I came to the part about my Feybraiha. Seel didn't want to hear it, but I told him. There were Cal and I, sitting naked on the window seat in my bedroom in Forever, looking out at the dark garden, he telling me things about Orien, Pell and Saltrock. Then I was talking about Cobweb and how Cal had released him from a prison he had made for himself. 'Good is disguised as evil,' I said, 'because some evil things have to happen to make the good things come about. There is no escaping that. Our world can never be that perfect, for then it would be out of balance and just fade away. What happened to Orien was abhorrent, for he lost his life, but Cal has lost some of his as well. He was a tortured being; still is perhaps.'

At the end of this Seel said, 'Cal is lucky. He is lucky that you all cared about him so much.'

'I thought our comfort was worthless.'

Seel smiled and shook his head and all his hair fell across his face. I could not see him. 'You are stormy creatures,' he said. 'You love and hate as men once did. I pity you.'

I laughed. 'Pity us? But why? Perhaps you should have come earlier, your people. You should have come north with your bloodless violence and taken all the weapons away. Why didn't you? You let death happen because you didn't come and stop it. I am pure-born and I have feelings and the only way the Gelaming will get rid of them is to beat them out of me. I am not ashamed of them. I am prepared to fight the bad within myself. It can be done without an emotional vacuum.'

'It's not like that!' Seel stood up again. 'The difference is subtle.

We have love in our souls, but it is not selfish. That is the difference.'

'You should see my people,' I said.

'Oh, I shall!' he answered. 'Hordes of them, with Ponclast at their head, all planning to slake their thirsts on Gelaming blood. They do that, don't they? Drink blood?'

I would not answer that. 'Where is my father, Seel?'

The pause was barely discernible. 'He's alive.'

'Does Thiede have him?'

Seel put his hands in his hair. He shook his head and then said, 'Yes. Yes, he does. Terzian is in Immanion.'

I wanted him to tell me more, but he would only shake his head. 'I can't. That's all I know. I can't tell you more.'

'I don't believe you.'

'Why not? Why should I lie to you?'

'Because I'm a Varr and because you don't like me that much.'

He shrugged. 'Hmm, I suppose so. But it is the truth. You'll find out about Terzian sooner or later, but not from me.'

He went to the door. He was going to leave and I wanted him to stay, even though I knew the strangling knots were only being wound tighter by his being here. He paused and looked back at me. 'You were right about one thing, Swift the Varr,' he said. 'I should have come and talked to Cal. You were right about that. Now it's too late.' He ducked through the curtains and was gone.

My heart began to pound. I relived the past hour a hundred times, seeking hopeful signs, but I was sure there were none. What had he come to say to me? All he had done was listen to me, really. I lay there on my bed, wistful and sad and exultant, and let a long, slow admission seep comfortably into my eyes, my brain, my heart. Admitting it was a relief, a burden lifted. It was as if I had shaken myself and a lifetime's mantle of dust had fallen away from me. I felt lighter and steeled to face the future. I was not ashamed. The admission was this: I love him.

The next evening, Chrysm came to visit me. 'You've been hiding in here for a whole day,' he said. 'Have you eaten? I've brought some food for you.'

I wasn't that hungry, but ate some of it anyway to keep him quiet. I had been quite happy in my solitude; I hadn't thought about food.

'What have you been doing here all alone?' he asked.

'Oh, nothing; just thinking.'

He carefully dissected an orange and handed me half of it. 'Ah, thinking! Ashmael tells me Grissecon will be performed on the first night of the next full moon. Only four days!' He shook his head. 'Is that something to do with what you've been thinking about?'

'Oh no!' I lied and we both laughed. Arahal had been to see me first thing that morning to tell me this news. I had thought of nothing else all day.

'Isn't it what you've always wanted?' Chrysm asked.

'Partly ... Has Arahal sent you here, Chrysm?'

He shook his head. 'No. They've finished with mauling your mind. I'm acting autonomously! Now, all you have to do is wait; wait and think. They want you to be alone. They want you to fast. They want you rabid with delirium, I suppose. More cheese?'

'Yes, please! Suddenly I am ravenously hungry!'

I told him about Seel's visit and he uttered an exasperated snort. 'Seel! I hope you knock some of his glib piety out of him! Still, you seem to have handled yourself better than in the past. It must be driving him scatty wanting you so much!'

'Chrysm ...?'

'It must be like being tempted by the devil for him!'

'Don't say that?'

'Why not?'

'Because it isn't true! I can't joke about it.'

Chrysm smiled secretively. 'It is true,' he said. 'You'd better believe it, Swift, but don't think too highly of yourself because of it. Thiede's sledgehammer mindgames have been thrown at Seel too, you know. Desire! Think of it! Thiede being thoroughly entertained watching you and Seel both squirming frantically, chasing your tails in a whirlpool of confusion. I could have told you that before.'

I should have been angry, I suppose. Chrysm had listened to me ranting on about my unrequited desire for Seel and he had known all along that Seel was suffering similar lonely throes of dark, unwanted passion.

'You should have said,' I told him abruptly.

'I couldn't. It might have interfered with the process of ... shall we say, enchantment?'

I ate in silence for a while, listening to the inner tumbling voice of my heart. I could feel Chrysm looking at me. 'The force you two will produce may explode the world,' he said hopefully. I smiled grimly. 'I'm sorry, Swift.'

'Don't be. Thank you for telling me. I'm not angry, just numb. I've felt like this before.'

'Has it made things easier?'

'Hard to tell yet.'

'You must treat him with compassion.'

'While knocking his piety out of him?'

'He is distressed.'

'Really?'

'Have you started to hate him?' Chrysm feared he was responsible. I put his mind at rest, only to worry him more.

'No. I've realized I am in love with Seel.'

Chrysm recoiled, not sure whether to laugh or remonstrate. 'Swift!' he cried and then softly, 'You are a Varr.' It was full of meaning.

'Yes,' I replied, smiling sweetly, 'It seems I am!'

The day came when the dawn was lemon and rose, the air sweeter than usual and the feeling of life stirring more noticeable. Before Imbrilim was truly awake, Arahal came to me, robed in purple and gold. He brought with him, on a silver plate, a lock of tawny hair surrounded by seven buds of the putiri plant. An attendant, veiled and silent, carried a flagon of water.

'It will be tonight,' Arahal said, perfunctorily.

'Yes.'

His eyes looked kinder than the last time we had spoken. 'I can see you have prepared yourself,' he said. I did not answer. He indicated the contents of the silver plate.

'These buds must be eaten at regular intervals during the day,

Swift. Their taste is not the most pleasant, but we have brought you plenty of water to wash them down.' He took one of the dull grey-green pellets between thumb and forefinger. 'You may as well take this first one now.'

'What will it do?'

'A slightly narcotic effect; a relaxant ... it will help you.' By his evasive glance, I gathered there was something more, which he would not tell me. I did not care. Obediently, I took the bud in my hand. 'Chew it well, Swift.'

The taste was bitter and rancid, reminiscent of a hundred foul things. Even severe chewing could not reduce the fibres to anything that was comfortable to swallow. Arahal offered me water. My eyes were running.

'Not too bad, was it?' he asked lightly.

I pulled a face of utter disgust. 'Delightful,' I said.

He smiled. 'We shall come for you later. Spend this day in tranquillity and purify your thoughts. Calm your body; be still.'

It was a long, long time to sundown.

At midday I forced down another of the nauseating putiri buds, eyeing my diminishing water supply with misgiving. I had been instructed not to leave the pavilion and to spend my time in serene meditation. I did, for a while, but then got bored and started to read instead. My stomach screamed for food, but after the second bud, it did not hurt as much. I began to feel light-headed and could not focus on my book any more. I lay down on my bed, staring up at the swaying canopy, and delightful shivers ran across my flesh. I put my hand to my face and could feel the contact of each pore, each atom. I sighed and could see the vision of my own breath. Two hours later, I ate another bud.

In the late afternoon, as I lay in a contented stupor, I became distantly aware that someone was requesting ingress to my pavilion. I could barely summon the energy to form the thoughtforms to let them in. I was wondering if it might be Seel, but I did not recognize the tall har that came in through the curtains. I would certainly have known if I'd met him before because he was like something from a dream or a vision, or, it must be said, a nightmare. In my drugged state, I could hardly see him; he seemed insubstantial, flickering, shining. His head was wreathed in flame and then I realized it was just his hair, bright scarlet and vivid orange. I decided I was hallucinating and just stared, my mouth hanging open.

Then the vision spoke. 'Well, aren't you going to welcome me, son of Terzian?' Such a sound can only be described as the voice of the world. The visitor must be real; perhaps another member of the Hegemony.

'Welcome, stranger!' I slurred and tried to raise my hand. The striking figure glided into the room. 'I'm afraid I'm unprepared for callers,' I continued in an unsteady voice. 'I have nothing to offer you ...'

'A seat will suffice.'

'I'm sorry. Please, sit down.'

He did so, crossing his legs, steepling his fingers.

'You must forgive me, no-one told me you would be coming, I don't know your name ...'

The stranger smiled. A predatory, weirdly inviting smile that for a second brought Cal's face to my mind.

'I think you may have heard of me,' he said. 'My name is Thiede.'

He waited a second or two to let the impact of this revelation sink in. He noted with satisfaction my gaping mouth and startled eyes. It is a reaction that will never cease to give him pleasure.

'I expect you are now wondering why I'm here,' he said and it did not sound at all predictable as it had when Caeru had said something similar. 'The reason is simple; I wish to talk to you. You don't have to say anything, Swift, for there is nothing you can say that I want to hear. I don't mean to sound harsh by that, but time is precious to me. Do you understand?' I nodded fiercely, aware that my stupor appeared to have fled. 'Now then.' He settled down and leaned back. 'You know that I had you brought to Imbrilim to have you prepared for the role I wish you to take in Megalithica. You are young, Swift, but flexible. I admire your spirit and your good sense. But that is not what I wish to speak about; Ashmael can deal with all that when the time comes. I am concerned with more immediate ventures. This Grissecon you are to undertake is very important and you must give it your best. I realize it might be a waste of breath to say this, but try not to let your emotions take control of you. There are two extremely crucial reasons for the Grissecon. First, the power of the essence. Its strength will be increased by the intensity of your pleasure. Seel will take care of that. It is your task to please him! Think of that; it may sound obvious, but don't be tempted to let Seel take control. Overpower him, Swift, drown him in his own desire, let the spirit come alive …' He grinned at the effect these words were having on me. 'No, you don't really need me to say it, do you. You *want* to give him your best; how well my plan has worked! Now listen. This part you must understand fully. When the time comes for you to plant your seed within him, you must leave this plane, travel to the upper spheres. It should be easy by that time. When you feel the pull, follow it. You and Seel as one individual. Once you have left this place, you may separate. You must seek the fields of lemon grass. On the horizon will be visible the golden pyramids of Shekh. You will know the place by them. Take aruna together in that higher place and call to the spirit of your son. It will hear you. It must be conceived there. Do you understand?'

I spoke at last. 'I don't know … I will remember the words.'

'Good. That will be enough.' He stood up. 'I shall leave you now. There is nothing more to say at present, but I shall look forward to our next meeting. Goodbye, Swift.'

Before I had finished my own farewell, the room was empty of his presence. One moment he was there, the next not, in the blink of an eye, so that I doubted whether I had ever really seen him. I could remember every word he had spoken exactly.

I ate another bud, thinking about what the mighty Thiede had said to me. My body was tingling. I felt so powerful, I laughed aloud. Thiede had spoken to me. My purpose, my importance filled the world. Outside, the sun dipped towards a crimson horizon and evening birds called above the canopies of Imbrilim. The air was full of imminence, tense as pulled threads, pulling me in. My future began here. This was the beginning. This was where it would all start.

Two hara came to bathe me and Arahal was with them, soft-voiced and sombre. As they sluiced my skin with salt, scented water, Arahal mumbled incomprehensible prayers above me, scattering dust that looked like ash. I was dried and clothed in white linen, my hair pinned up in a loose coil, my hands rubbed with oil. Arahal said, 'Take the lock of hair,' pointing at the plate where only two putiri buds remained. I took it. 'That is Seel's hair,' he told me. 'Absorb its vitality, tune in to his vibrations.'

'Does he have some of mine?'

'Naturally.'

'But how?'

'It was taken some days ago, when my attendant came to dress your hair.'

'I did not notice.'

'No.' I closed my fingers around that small part of Seel and the smell of him seemed all about me like a tantalizing ghost. A smell of spice and clean skin.

'Will we be alone?' I asked.

'Most of the time. Of course, the essences must be collected immediately, but your privacy will be respected. The first time you must not go too far, for the presence of yaloe in the essence may destroy its effectiveness. You will be tempted to break through the seal, but you mustn't. That comes later and is not Grissecon. I hope you understand.'

'Yes, Thiede told me,' I said. Arahal did not comment. He did not intend to be impressed by that.

'Come,' he said. 'We must leave now. The moon has risen.'

Outside, but for the light of the spectral moon, Imbrilim was in darkness. All the lights were doused, and everywhere was shrouded in eerie silence. 'They pray for you,' Arahal said. In the centre of the camp, in a place that was normally an open space of grass, a pavilion of dove grey had been erected. Multiple folds moved listlessly in the slight breeze. 'This is the place,' Arahal said. 'May the spirit of the Aghama be with you.' He placed two fingers on my forehead. 'Let this body be strength. Let this spirit be dominion.'

I watched as he and his attendants began to retreat, not walking, but simply receding, shrinking in size. For a moment I was afraid, suddenly sober and shivering in the cool air. It seemed I had stepped from the world of reality into one completely unknown to me, somehow threatening. Within the pavilion a siren was waiting for me and I was unarmed, save for the weapons the Aghama had bequeathed me that were supposed to subdue the monster that was the wondrous Seel's desire. My body was all I had and that seemed too frail, too unpredictable to trust. I stared at the place where I must enter, at that place where the gossamer folds writhed and curled. Imbrilim held its breath, waiting. I walked forward.

Lifting aside the drapes, I passed through a narrow corridor of hanging cloth until another door curtain blocked my way. I had to force my hand to move them. My palms were damp, my heart beating painfully fast. The room beyond was filled with the soft yellow-green radiance of two lamps, standing on the floor which was strewn with white fur rugs. In the centre of the room was a bed made of plump cushions, blanketed with furs. I walked straight towards it and looked down. He did not look at me; his eyes were closed, his hair spread out like floating seaweed all around him. He was covered by the blankets from the waist down, but by gazing at his chest, his shoulders and his arms, I could see he was as slim as I'd imagined him to be. Not skinny, but svelte with muscle while still softly curved, the hint of femininity. I thought, Oh God, I can't touch him; I can't! and then he opened his eyes and slowly turned his head towards me and I literally dropped to my knees beside him.

'So, we meet again, Swift the Varr,' he said softly and I could see his eyes were partly glazed from the effect of putiri buds. Some of his hair had stuck to his mouth and I reached to pull it away. My fingers touched his lips and I felt a shudder shoot right up my arm. He caught my fingers in his own and kissed them. I spoke his name.

'You are full of mystery,' he said.

'Mystery, is that it? I thought it was blight.'

He frowned. 'Don't say that. Not here. Not now.'

I felt as if I had never spoken to him before, yet at the same time felt that I knew him intimately. It was so easy to reach out and stroke his face. He rubbed against me like an animal. I put my hands in his hair as I had longed to do so many times. (Is this real? Is it?) 'I have never seen anything like you,' I said.

'Then see it all,' he answered and opened up the covering of furs as if it was his own skin. I stared, entranced. He seemed to glow. (I must be dreaming. I must be!)

'Do you hate me, Seel?'

'Do you have to ask that?'

'Yes.'

He shook his head and his eyes were shining like distant stars. 'No, I don't hate you.' He reached for me, his face like the face of a person who has seen the lights of home shining out to him through a storm. 'Have you waited a long time for this?' he asked.

'Yes, a long time.'

'You have searched?'

'I didn't know I was searching.'

He smiled. 'You were, though, you were. And now you have found.' He put his hand upon my face and brought my lips to his own. What I experienced within his breath is beyond words. It left me gasping, as if I'd been drowned, yet I wanted more. I wanted him so much, it was like pain. He laughed and sat up, pushing his hair over his shoulders, easing my arms from my robe.

'We are perfect, we are beautiful,' he said and bent to touch my throat with his mouth. His hair fell into my face and I breathed deeply of its fragrance. The touch of his hands upon my shoulders was like being burned; it was hot and it crackled with sparks. Seel, splendour incarnate, covering my body with kisses, dragging his wondrous hair across my chest, my stomach, my loins. His tongue, like a sinuous, questing reptile, exploring every pore of my flesh. As I lay there, shuddering, he raised his head. 'It must be the best,' he said. I opened my eyes. He looked so serious, his hands behind his head, staring down at me.

'It will be,' I answered. 'How could it be otherwise? You are the best in the world for me.'

I pulled him to me and pressed him back into the cushions. His face was all covered with hair and I tried to push it away. 'Open your eyes, Seel. I want to see them.'

'Why? Now?'

'This moment!'

I paused then, almost afraid of what I must do, still half convinced I was dreaming. Where would I wake up? Only slight pressure made him swallow me up; colour burst all around me. In his eyes, the pupils widened, but his face was so still. Then he said, 'God!' and laughed.

'Hush!' I told him. 'This is momentous.' And it was. It was comfortable, something simple, like slipping into a favourite chair and curling up there. We were perfectly matched, as Thiede had known we were, anticipating each other's thoughts and desires. Usually, during aruna, reality takes flight and it is all a world of dreams, but that time, I was wholly conscious the whole time of where I was, and the sensations were wholly physical. We never stopped looking at each other. I had never looked into another har's eyes at the moment of orgasm before; never. How I made him wait for that, using what Caeru had taught me. When the climax came, I saw colours pulsing inside his eyes, pulsing to the beat of his heart, and there were fires burning deep within. He whispered my name and we were quite still, in our heads, while all that wild sensation flooded our bodies.

We did not want to part, but as a hail of sparkling dust settled around us, on the bed, our skin, our hair, the curtains behind us lifted and Arahal padded into the room, accompanied by his attendants. I was so drained I could hardly move and it seemed it was coldly, without ceremony, that they lifted my damp body off Seel's and laid me aside. I had fulfilled my purpose in their eyes. Seel whimpered as Arahal milked our mingled essences from his body and I reached for his hand. His nails dug into my palm.

Arahal stood up and examined the glowing fluid he held in a glass bottle. 'Well done!' he said, which seemed somehow irreverent under the circumstances. Seel and I were in no mood for conversation and were glad when Arahal woundedly recognized this and left us alone.

'He has made me bleed!' Seel complained.

'Does it hurt?' I asked him, knowing that there was more required of us that night. He shook his head.

'I don't think so. Arahal isn't used to doing that; he shouldn't be so rough.'

I took him in my arms, longing to crush the life out of him. At times, his beauty sets my teeth on edge. He squirmed.

'I fought so hard,' he said.

I released my grip a little. 'Fought what?'

'Against you. One time, I nearly gave in. Do you remember?' I shook my head. Seel had never seemed the remotest bit interested in me before. 'It was in the field beyond Imbrilim, when you were watching me. I could always feel you watching me. I knew you followed me around. That time, I was thinking, "This is it. I shall go to him. In a little while, I shall go to him and we shall speak together." But when I looked again, you were gone. You had looked like something made out of smoke, so pale, yet I could see your strength. That time, I could not think of Terzian, nor Cal, nor Varrs; only you.'

'Strength was the farthest thing from my mind then,' I said.

He smiled and put his head against my chest. 'Oh Swift, I knew that as soon as we touched, there would be no going back. It is something I've feared for so long. If I ever tried to imagine the har who would do this to me, he never looked like you. More like Cal, I suppose ...'

'Most people's dream,' I added drily.

Arahal had left us a tray of food and drink. We pulled the bedcovers round us, for we were starting to get cold, and ate and drank. I was full of curiosity about Seel. There was so much I wanted to know about him, but I was unsure how much he would want to tell me. There was no way I wanted to risk offending him. Cautiously, I mentioned that I'd been told he was fairly close to the Tigron. He didn't appear reticent about it. 'I've worked with Pell from the beginning, when he first went to Immanion,' he said. 'And of course, we had spent some time together in Saltrock ...'

I wanted to avoid that issue. 'Tell me about Immanion,' I begged. 'Tell me about Phaonica and the people there.'

Seel laughed at my eagerness. 'I'm sure you'll see it for yourself some day,' he replied. 'It *is* a wonderful place, as you'd expect. Phaonica is incredibly huge; all the hara possess unnatural radiance there … Oh, Swift, I don't want to talk about that. I want to know about you. It fascinates me, how you lived before and the people you knew. Tell me about that.'

'Now I know how you feel!' I said. 'I don't want to talk about that either.'

'We have an eternity to discuss such things. Another time.'

As he said this, warmth and joy spread through me like a flame. I took him in my arms once more. He sighed against my chest and then said hesitantly, 'I have never hosted a child before, Swift. When you told me about Cal and your father, I couldn't believe it! Cal, of all hara! Still, if he can go through with it, there's no reason why I can't. But you must understand, it's hard for those of us not pure-born to feel comfortable with the thought of bearing life. It's not a function I was born with!'

In the small hours of the morning, while Imbrilim slept and all the lamps were out, I took Seel in my arms and pierced him and carried him with me to the higher spheres. We were in a world of lemon-coloured light and long fields of pale yellow grass stretched away from us on all sides. As Thiede had told me, on the horizon shimmered the vague shapes of spectral pyramids, which made our eyes ache to look upon. Seel and I sat down upon the sward, joined only by my hand in his hand. His skin was shining and his hair moved like feathers. He lay back and spread out his arms and I entered into him through the body and the mind and we called together to the spirit world, and presently a funnel of light appeared above us, rotating slowly. It drifted down to us and we were filled with the presence of our child to be. Within Seel's body, I nudged so softly the special seal that would open him up, and with utter compliance the muscles relaxed and I sought the star of his being, where life could begin. Nothing could part us now; nothing. We were joined inextricably, in convolutions of shining flesh; we were one. For a moment, we screamed together for the ecstasy was almost unbearable and light shimmered around us. Then I was lying across him in a room of silvery drapes that was filled with the pale glow that presages dawn, and our skins were cool and damp against each other. We both knew, in our hearts, that we were the makers of the true magic, that gift from the Creator, unparalleled, incomparable, the gift of life.

Destiny of the Pearl
*Barbarism thrives; such habits
Are frozen in time.
Perversity swallows up the world,
Goodwill to the mirror of crime.*

Seel and I spent two glorious days alone together and then, feeling thoroughly rested and exhausted at the same time, bid farewell to the small, grey pavilion where we had worked our magic. In response to an unspoken agreement, I moved that day into Seel's pavilion. From being utter strangers, we had become chesna, as close as Wraeththu can get, in the space of two days. It is something that has never changed, nor ever will.

As I was unpacking my rather small amount of belongings into a chest in Seel's bedroom, Arahal came to request my presence at the pavilion of the Hegemony. 'You too, Seel,' he said. 'I hope you've made the most of your holiday, for it's over for all of us now.'

All the high-ranking Gelaming were there, seated around the large table in the main chamber. Seel and I were the last to arrive. I was overpowered by uncontrollable pride as we took our places together near Ashmael at the head of the table. All of them knew that the splendid creature that is Seel was mine, and I his. Whatever Gelaming like to call it, I felt we were in love and knew that the radiance such feelings gave us were apparent to everyone.

Ashmael addressed me. 'Well, Swift, it is nearly time to get things moving. The crystal has been constructed and you and Seel have made the power to fire it. Soon, we shall have to travel north and sort this godforsaken country out once and for all.' He smiled around the table. 'Now, for the benefit of those of you who haven't been present at all the meetings we've held on the subject, Cedony will bring you up to date on our position.' He leaned back and gestured to Cedony, who was seated on his right side. Cedony stood up, trying to shuffle a rather unruly mound of notes into a single pile.

'Central and north Megalithica have been thoroughly surveyed, as I'm sure you all know,' he began. 'Our findings show that the majority of Wraeththu settlements have fallen under Varrish rule, or Varrish tyranny, which might be a more accurate way of putting it. Those who have maintained their independence are tribes who either have some kind of trading agreement with the Varrs, or those whom Ponclast views as irrelevant, whose property will not add to the Varrs' wealth and power. We have been rightly disturbed by the small amount of time it has taken Ponclast to establish his empire in Megalithica. It is known that he subjugates through fear, of course, and Varrish callous brutality is legendary, but it was always thought that the Varrs had turned away from the path, either black or white, and for the most part abandoned their natural abilities. Now, we understand that this is not entirely the case. While Ponclast has never encouraged development among his lower castes, he has certainly nurtured occult powers within himself and among his generals. He has created an elite company of dangerous, murderous maniacs, of whom Ponclast's ally, Terzian, is, of course, most notorious.'

Beneath the table, Seel reached for my hand. Through mind touch I asked him, 'Does it show then, my distress?'

'No,' he answered soothingly. 'Only to me.'

As if aware of our conversation, Cedony turned to me. 'We appreciate some of what must be said may cause you discomfort, Swift,' he said. 'Terzian is, of course, your father, but not all the company here have all the facts about him. We beg your forebearance over this matter.'

I shook my head. 'It's alright. Please continue.'

Cedony put his papers down on the table. 'In the extreme north lies Ponclast's citadel of Fulminir. It is a place feared and dreaded by both humans and hara in that part of the world. It was here that Ponclast and Terzian committed some of their worst atrocities. The Hegemony is aware that there are those among you who feel that the Gelaming should not seek dominion over the Varrs, that this is merely substituting one kind of tyranny for another. There are those of you who feel that some kind of arrangement suitable to both sides should be suggested to the Varrs, that whatever we feel about Varrish culture, to a certain extent we have no right to interfere. It is said that now the Varrs control most of Megalithica, the time for bloodshed and fighting is over and we should let the continent settle down on its own. What I am about to divulge may change your minds.

'The Varrs, or more accurately the Varrish government, will *never* lose their thirst for blood. We know this because we have learned that the Path they have chosen is involved with occult practices of the most black and evil type. From surviving victims, we have discovered that the Varrish elite feast upon the flesh of their own kind, the most prized vintages in their wine cellars being barrels of Wraeththu blood. They must have started these practices using human stock, I would imagine, but eventually discovered that much greater powers can be gained from consuming the flesh of hara. Another of their cheerful little pastimes is ritual pelki, usually simultaneously with the slow death through poison of the victim. What we are dealing with here, Tiahaara, is not Wraeththu of a more basic culture than our own, but demonic, heartless beasts who have tasted blood and will want more. Now is not the time for me to go into more detail about other crimes we know are regularly committed in Fulminir (there is a whole file on the evidence we have gathered), but I must urge you all not to vote against Thiede's design to thoroughly cleanse Megalithica of any trace of Ponclast and his acolytes. The name of the Varrs must be expunged from the memory of Wraeththu!'

Cedony sat down again heavily and for a moment or two there was silence in the room. I felt dizzy, as if Terzian himself had stood there and confessed his crimes. Then someone from the lower end of the table stood up.

'You have spoken well, Tiahaar Cedony. Later, I would like to examine the file you speak of, but for now, I'm sure I speak for all who you implied were prepared to argue against the Hegemony's plans, when I say that we defer our privilege to speak out. Please tell us Thiede's intentions ...'

Cedony looked to Ashmael and Ashmael nodded.

'My turn to speak, I suppose,' he said wryly, but did not stand up. 'We propose that a force of five centuries be sent to Galhea, which was previously Terzian's base and now left for the most part undefended, and establish a Gelaming base there. From that point we can launch our assault on Fulminir. Once Ponclast is subdued, we should have little trouble with the rest of the Varrs; *he* is their driving force and our main problem.'

'And what of Terzian?' someone asked, who was obviously unaware of developments in that area. 'Does Thiede have him or not? Where does he fit into this plan?'

'Terzian is no longer part of Megalithica's future,' Ashmael said coldly. He would not look at me. 'Are there any more questions?'

'Yes,' I said coolly.

Ashmael slid his glance over me warily. 'Swift?'

'There is something that hasn't been mentioned yet. The Varrish allies, the Kakkahaar. What do you propose to do about them?'

Ashmael looked surprised, then horribly sympathetic. 'The Kakkahaar have already been dealt with, Swift,' he said.

I squirmed with embarrassment. 'I see. I didn't know ...'

Chrysm rescued me gallantly. 'When we first set foot in Megalithica, Thiede requested a meeting with Kakkahaaran representatives. He made a deal with them. It is well known that they too are interested in the darker side of the occult, and perhaps under normal circumstances the Gelaming would have been as anxious to disband their tribe as they are the Varrs, but Thiede decided that in return for certain favours, he would grant them autonomy and a seat on the Council of United Tribes in Immanion. He did stress that the taking of life was still an offence in the eyes of God and har, and that any Kakkahaar convicted of such a crime would still pay the penalty, but that if their leader Lianvis was prepared to try to curb the Kakkahaar's more *beastly* activities, he would overlook past

318

crimes. Thiede and Lianvis have a certain respect for each other. We cannot allow the Kakkahaar's darker practices to continue without making even a perfunctory attempt to curtail them; we cannot, under any circumstances, be seen to *approve*, but of course we suspect that it is something we could never have complete control over. However, Lianvis is aware of Thiede's power and he won't want to put the future of his tribe in jeopardy-'

'And what were the "certain favours" that Thiede requested from them?' I butted in, fiercely. I had no right to be angry now, of course; I had forsaken my tribe, but betrayal still cuts deep.

'To appear to form an alliance with the Varrs, of course,' Ashmael put in smoothly. 'How else do you think we got so much information?'

'So Terzian was right,' I said softly.

There was a mumble of voices around the table and a small amount of shuffling. My anger discomforted them. Wasn't I supposed to be Gelaming now?

'I met some of the Kakkahaar,' I said. 'I did not like them. I was younger then; they frightened me.'

'Not an unhealthy attitude for a sensible harling!' Ashmael said cheerfully. 'Anyway, those of you whom we would like to travel north to Galhea will be informed over the next couple of days. You may warn your hara. It is safer to believe that Ponclast will know we are planning to make a move. Security must be increased around Imbrilim. Cedony, I believe that's your department; I shall leave the preparation to you. Now, I think this is a good time to pause and refresh ourselves, don't you? Velaxis! Wine and a sumptuous repast are in order, I believe.'

As we ate, I said to Ashmael, 'Are you afraid of Ponclast then?' He looked at me sideways.

'Don't underestimate him, Swift. He could damage us quite badly. That is why we needed the elixir that was produced during your Grissecon with Seel.'

'Can I see the crystal?' I asked.

'Of course, but not yet,' he answered.

Talks went on until well into the evening. It was mostly about small details for the journey north. Not much was said about what we'd do when we got there. I was in a daze. I remember saying to Seel, 'My God, I'm going home. I've just realized; I'm going home! Will they have been told there?'

Seel shrugged. 'You'd better ask Ashmael that. I would have thought so, though. It might cause problems having large numbers of Gelaming appearing from nowhere. When Ash spoke of Galhea being mostly undefended, I think he was probably exaggerating. What do you think?'

'He was. There are enough of the Varrish army still there to look after the place. I presume Ithiel is still in charge. If I were Ashmael, I would try to get in touch with him. He's quite rational!'

'Actually, Swift, we shall be leaving that up to you,' Ashmael interjected, having been eavesdropping on our conversation. 'But we shall leave that until we get there. You are our protection, my dear!'

We laughed together. A kind of excitement was building up.

'We shall probably keep quiet in Galhea for a couple of months,' Ashmael continued. 'Because, of course, Seel shall be with us and due to spawn at that time. An important event, as Thiede has impressed upon us.'

'There speaks the smug face of someone who does not carry a pearl!' Seel said caustically. 'Ashmael, sometimes you disgust me.'

That night, lying awake in Seel's arms I pondered aloud on what it would be like to return to Forever.

'I am Gelaming now,' I said. 'How will Cobweb react?'

'I should think he will just be glad that you are alive,' Seel replied.

'Oh, I don't know. To a Varr, being dead is better than being Gelaming.'

'I'm looking forward to seeing Galhea, Swift. Don't let premature worrying ruin that feeling for you. I know how much you love Forever, and Cobweb and all the others. Just think about seeing them again after so long. I'm sure everything will be alright.'

I was grateful for his optimism, but not convinced.

Cedony and Chrysm were going to remain in Imbrilim, but Arahal and Ashmael would travel north. As part of the preparation for the journey, Arahal taught me something about the nature of Gelaming horses. I had always thought them unearthly and had not been surprised when I learned that they had the ability to travel through time and space in a completely different way to any that I'd imagined. I had always been nervous of trying to ride one in that way myself, but now Arahal told me that I'd have to learn. It would be impossible for me to ride Tulga home and arrive months after everybody else. I knew that these fabulous beasts could take you out of the world we know somehow and take you flying through a mad helter-skelter of star-trails and aether. I knew that journeys of hundreds of miles could be accomplished in seconds that way. I knew that when you were brought back to solid ground again you were still drunk with the weirdness of it for hours afterwards. You can see why I was a little nervous.

The first time Arahal took me riding through the other-lanes and I found myself speaking mind to mind with a horse, it was as distant and as vivid as a dream, if you can understand what I mean by that, but disorientating because I couldn't wake up. It made my jaw ache. Arahal laughed at me. His hair still sparkled with static dust when we came back to earth again. I was sitting on a horse that was all white and glowing and prancing. Arahal said, 'She is yours now, Swift.' Her name is Afnina; I still have her. No har less than Ulani can travel in that way. It demands severe control of the mind to achieve it, and to lose that control in mid-flight would mean disaster. The horse could lose you in the vastness of infinity and it would be virtually impossible for anyone to find you again. Arahal didn't tell me this until after we'd reached solid ground. I was grateful for that.

Seel was worried about the journey, for he thought travelling in the other-lanes might damage the pearl within him. Ashmael said he thought Seel was being overcautious, but he communicated with Immanion to put our minds at rest.

'Why hasn't Pell ever come?' I asked, as we waited for an answer.

'Think you're that important, Swiftling?' Ashmael snapped, jovially.

'No, not me, but Cal was with me.'

He's not with you now, though!'

This was true, of course, but I still felt disappointed that Pellaz hadn't tried to contact me again. Even Seel hadn't seen him in any shape or form for some time. I wondered if this might have something to do with Cal, but shrank from discussing it with Seel. He was becoming edgy and restless and I knew that mention of Cal disturbed him. I would hold him in my arms at night, still incredulous that I could do that, and put my hand across his lean, hard belly. 'No womanish swelling!' he would say uneasily and tried to hide his pain if I prodded him too sharply. 'Where is it? What is it doing?' he once asked in a panicky sort of voice.

'Just growing,' I replied.

'Is it really there?' Seel mused to himself, as if he hadn't heard me.

We received word from Immanion that it would be advisable for our journey to be undertaken as soon as possible, in view of Seel's condition. No-one was really sure what the other-lanes would do to unborn harlings, but Thiede had said it was safe in the early stages, and no-one cared to argue with him.

The night before we left, Seel said, 'Home, Swift; this is it. I expect your family shall hate me.'

'My family of two. How awesome!' I pointed out rather glumly.

'Nonsense, Swift. From what you've told me, your family in Forever is quite large. They may not be related by blood, but they are definitely family! I can't believe that I'm actually going to meet the prim and fussy Moswell, the dreamy, romantic Swithe and the melodramatic, mad beauty Cobweb.'

'I believe you're mocking me, Seel!'

'No, I mean it. It will be like meeting characters out of a book, that I've read about. I can't wait!'

Seel had a feral gleam in his eye when he said that. Some mischievous part of him would welcome the havoc it would cause in my household when it was announced that a Gelaming hosted a pearl for me, especially when they saw him. I knew that Cobweb would probably loathe him from the start.

After the journey, swift as a dream, we burst onto the earth, in a spume of smoking manes and tails, onto the flower-starred fields beyond Galhea. The horses jostled against each other in excitement and I laughed at Afnina's elation. The air smelled damper here. Afnina pulled against my hands, rearing up on her hind legs so that her luxurious mane fell over my fingers.

It was another spring in the fields of Galhea. I did not really know how long I'd been gone. At least a year; at least. Cal, Leef and I might have travelled through the Forest for months, we had no way of telling. Leef was with me again now, although still rather curt and unfriendly. I knew he had been in two minds about whether to leave Imbrilim or not; there was not that much waiting for him back home, but I had personally requested him to accompany us. I knew it would look better if two of us came home. Leef made me wait for two days before he gave me his answer, which of course had been yes. I think he'd been surprised how easily he'd adapted to the way of life in Imbrilim. It had taken him a little longer than me but now I think he was as eager to forget he'd ever been a Varr as I was.

I could see the outline of Forever, high on its hill, all its windows catching the morning sun. Seel came up beside me. His face was pale. 'So, this is your home,' he said, with a brave attempt at a smile.

'You are tired.' I leaned to touch his face. The journey had seemed to have taken only minutes, yet I felt as if I had been riding for days. Seel looked exhausted.

'I am tired,' he said. 'I must rest.' He slid to the ground and leaned against his horse's flank. The animal turned its head and sniffed him curiously. I saw his hand reach to stroke its nose.

'Swift!' Ashmael skidded his horse to a halt at my side.

'Well, what do you want me to do?'

'Your hostling ... contact him.'

Now: I was home. Forever squatted like some vast, brooding beast on its hill, holding within its walls those people with whom I'd grown and lived and loved. I was afraid. I was afraid that by coming back I'd destroy the dream of my childhood, that Forever would seem different and my loved ones strangers.

I dismounted from my horse. Beside me, Seel could barely

stand; his face looked pinched and he was cold to my touch. I put my fingers against his neck, just below the ear, and tried to transfer a little of my strength to him. I could feel the pull; he needed more than I could give. I looked back towards Galhea. Nobody said anything. They were just waiting. I closed my eyes and called him: 'Cobweb...'

Once was enough. A blast, a surge of energy smacked into my brain, powerful as a hurricane and just as disordered. I could make no sense of it, but I knew it was him. Standing there, knee-deep in lush grass, I could even smell him. 'Cobweb, I'm home.' He withdrew a little, tentatively caressing my mind. He would be able to tell how different I was, what I'd become. I felt his puzzlement, vague at first. I formed the words, 'You must send Ithiel...'

'You are not alone...'

'No.'

'There are strangers with you, many strangers. Who are they?'

'Friends.'

'Friends? So many friends?

'They are Gelaming, Cobweb.'

'You have brought them here. I thought you would.' He felt weary and resigned; his anger would come later. He did not ask about Terzian or Cal. Before he withdrew completely, to find Ithiel and send him to bring us into Galhea, he said one last thing. He said, 'Thank you, Swift.' It could have meant anything.

I was walking with Cobweb in the garden. We had been fed, we had rested, and now Ashmael was talking with Ithiel. Ithiel had looked older; it surprised me. I took my hostling to the summer-house by the lake.

'Do you remember...?' I began to ask, and then couldn't say it.

Cobweb smiled and looked away. 'You have not lost your impertinence, I see!'

We walked in silence, evening all around us. Cobweb was so full of questions, he didn't know where to start and remained quiet. He reached for my hand.

'I'd forgotten how marvellous, how wickedly beautiful you were!' I said lightly.

324

He laughed. 'Me? All that? I'm surprised you say that now. After being with the Gelaming who are like ... like ... well, something like I've always expected.'

The door to the summerhouse was open, some of the panes were broken, others were greened by lichen. 'There was a great storm,' Cobweb said. 'All the lights went off in the town, some people were killed. I listened to it all night, all that howling. It was like angry spirits. I heard a tree fall in the garden. How it groaned! It must have fallen right through the glass here, some of it.' Stark, leafless branches littered the floor like black, broken bones.

'You should have repaired it,' I said, lifting a couple of the branches and tossing them out of the door.

Cobweb shrugged. 'Maybe, but I think I prefer it this way. It's symbolic.'

'You come here often, don't you?'

He didn't answer me, but went to sit on the edge of the fountain basin. I had a brief, painful flashback to that time when I had seen him sitting there before and Cal had come in like a zombie from the garden. Only now, the water in the fountain basin was choked with leaves, the orange fish long dead through neglect. Cobweb hadn't changed; for him that time could have been yesterday.

'I lost both of them,' he said to the floor and then looked straight at me. 'Thank God you came back.'

I went to him and put my head in his lap and he stroked my hair, but I could never be a child again. In a way, I hadn't come back either, not the Swift that Cobweb had known.

When we walked into Forever, through the great front doors, Cobweb had been waiting for us, standing on the stairs alone, a slim and tragic figure. His hair had grown; he seemed robed in hair. I had feared the house would look different, but it didn't. Perhaps a little smaller, but then I'd grown so much. Once I'd been a child in this place, in this hallway sat with Leef on the stairs at Festival, put that fateful note about Gahrazel into the messenger's bag, danced in the dust and the sunlight on my way to morning classes with Moswell. It all seemed so inconceivably long ago.

I felt huge and awkward standing there now, all in leather,

weapons at my hip, my hair shaved at the sides like Gelaming hair, smoking a black cigarette because I was nervous. Cobweb had looked at me. He recognized me instantly even though I knew I'd changed almost beyond recognition. I saw the muscles along his jaw ripple. Perhaps he saw something of Terzian in me then. But, hiding whatever emotions must have shaken him, he fell into his role of perfect host immediately, prepared to save all the questions until later; this was the role Terzian had given him. I was Terzian's son and because of that, Cobweb would not question my judgement about whom I brought into the house. My father was not with us; Forever was mine now. Cobweb ordered refreshment and ushered us into the drawing-room.

I had Seel, Ashmael, Arahal and about five others with me. Everyone else had been taken to Galhea by Ithiel, whom I'd instructed to find accommodation for them in the virtually empty army quarters. Like Cobweb, Ithiel did not question my orders, but his eyes were very cold. He did not approve of accommodating the Gelaming in Varrish barracks. I invited him to join us as soon as possible and he smiled grimly. I suppose it was absurd of me to invite him to the place he had probably been using as home for God knows how long.

Cobweb had embraced me briefly and scanned Seel with a chilling glance. Seel was hanging onto my arm, occasionally resting his head on my shoulder. I could feel him shaking. 'I'm going to have to lie down,' he said. 'Otherwise I might embarrass you and fall down.'

Cobweb sniffed and summoned one of the house-hara with a click of his fingers. 'We shall find accommodation for your friend,' he said. 'Is he ill? Would you like me to send for Phlaar?'

'Yes, if you could,' I said. 'I should have introduced you two before. Cobweb, this is Seel. Get someone to show him to my room.'

'Ty sleeps in there now,' Cobweb replied coldly.

'My father's room then,' I said irritably.

Cobweb raised his eyebrows and stared at me stonily. 'It isn't aired. No-one's been in there for ages.'

'That doesn't matter. Have someone light a fire in there.'

'As you wish, Swift.' He turned to the house-har. 'My son will be staying in Terzian's room. Have it prepared and escort Tiahaar Seel to it.' He made it sound as if we wouldn't be staying there long. I hadn't wanted it to be like that, but Cobweb just made it that way. Full of Varrish jealousy; another thing that now felt strange to me.

'You've changed,' he said, once Seel had left us.

'Of course I have!'

'That har is carrying your pearl, isn't he?'

'Yes. Still impossible to hide things from you, isn't it?' I said with a hopeful smile. Cobweb did not return it.

'Where's your father, Swift?'

I looked away. 'Not now, Cobweb. Please. Questions later.'

He snorted angrily and swept away, grinning ferally at Arahal as he passed him. Arahal sauntered over to me, bemused. 'An amazing creature!' he exclaimed. 'The stuff of legend!'

'Amazing, yes. Creature, yes,' I agreed. 'Arahal, you will have to tell him about Terzian. If you won't tell me, then at least tell Cobweb. I'll get no peace otherwise.'

Arahal looked uncomfortable. 'All shall be revealed when the time is right,' he said edgily.

I went to Seel in my father's room. It smelled a little musty in there, but there was a welcome fire in the grate, which had already taken any chill off the air. The canopied bed looked ancient and uncomfortable; I hoped it wasn't too damp. Phlaar was washing his hands at the sink, behind a screen.

'Seel, are you alright?' I asked. He was lying, half-clothed, on top of the bed. His face and hair looked damp. He smiled weakly.

'Apparently, my energy is drained,' he said.

'Will he be alright?' I asked Phlaar, who was watching us carefully, drying his hands.

'The journey here has taken too much out of him,' Phlaar answered. 'The pearl drains his energy enough as it is. It was foolish of you to travel this far in this condition!' Seel turned his head away from Phlaar's reproach. 'You need utter rest and quiet,' Phlaar continued.

'Like hell!' Seel snapped. 'I need an infusion of strength, that's all. Tell Ashmael, Swift; he can do it.'

Phlaar cleared his throat. 'Well, as you don't appear to be needing my services any longer ...' He moved towards the door. I thanked him and he smiled thinly. Later, he would tell his friends about Gelaming conceit.

Seel made a derisive sound. 'Varrs!' he said. 'They know nothing!'

'And you, being Gelaming, know everything of course!' I could never be angry with him. He held out his hand and I took it in my own.

'I'm sorry, Swift. I don't seem to have any control over my mouth nowadays.'

I sat on the bed and took him in my arms. 'It doesn't matter.' Seel laughed against my chest. My hands couldn't keep from straying over his skin; he was so touchable. 'Did that monster downstairs really host you?' he asked.

Living among the Gelaming, I hadn't really noticed myself changing that much, but now I was home, every mirror seemed to scream my difference at me, and every eye I'd known had become a mirror. I don't think Tyson recognized me at all. The last time I had seen him he had been such a baby; now he was a willowy harling with Cal's haunted, bony face and a glistening mop of fair hair. I could see a hint of Terzian in his eyes for they could turn very hard on you, but his spirit seemed wholly Cal's, unearthly and wild. He greeted me with reservation; we did not embrace. All he said was, 'You've been gone so long.' Two springs had passed in Galhea since I had last been there.

After my walk in the garden with Cobweb that first evening, I went to my father's study. It looked uncomfortably tidy; Ithiel had been using it. On the desk I discovered balance sheets for crops and supplies, with heavy pencil marks scored across them in places. I sat down in my father's chair and leaned back, gazing out of the window. It felt as if I had never left Forever. It felt as if Cal was in the house and we were still waiting for news of my father. Perhaps tomorrow the Zigane would come ... Cobweb had asked me about Terzian many times that day.

I found myself wondering how much my hostling actually knew about Terzian. I didn't think he was aware of exactly what had happened to Gahrazel, nor how close Terzian's relationship with Ponclast now seemed to be. How could I answer his questions without telling him what I knew? How could I stand there and say, "That har you loved, would give your life for, is a monster"? And yet, surely Cobweb would have known those things. Didn't he know everything about those he loved? Weren't all our minds open books to him that he could learn from whenever he cared to look? I did not want to talk about Terzian because it caused me pain. It was something I wanted to forget. He would hate me if he knew, he would call me a traitor. Could he then stand by and countenance what happened to Gahrazel happening to me? I shuddered.

Outside, the evening was fading into a red and purple sky, bare trees stark against the colour. Inside, warmth crept through the long corridors from well-tended fires, there was a sound of footsteps, the smell of cooking. I love this place. I was glad my father had gone from it.

I had learned from Cobweb that the Zigane had stayed in Galhea only until the autumn of that year. It was clear that Tel-an-Kaa had been a great comfort to Cobweb when Cal, Leef and I had first left Forever. Her optimism for my future, indeed for all our futures, had never been shaken. When Cobweb feared for my life, she would calmly argue against his fears. I knew that he was sorry when she left. She had given no reason for going. Perhaps her master summoned her, another errand waiting, another message to deliver.

'I think there must be a lot of female in me,' Cobweb said to me, seriously. 'For I could understand that woman. When she left, I was not surprised.'

'There *is* a lot of female in you, Cobweb,' I agreed, hiding my smile.

He shrugged. 'My fault, I suppose; laziness. Are women indolent, do you think?'

'No. I think it is more lazy to be predominantly male, but that is only my opinion, of course.'

Bryony was the only person in the house not too wary of me to come and throw her arms about me. 'Welcome, Swift, welcome back,' she said. I had gone to the kitchens as soon as I was able, again trepidly and a little nervous of what I would find. It twisted my heart with nostalgia to see the place. The worn table, the shining expanse of sink, the archaic stove covered in huge cauldrons of bubbling, aromatic Yarrow creations. He was still the same, strings of hair everywhere. We all drank a bottle of sheh together and I talked, with drunken enthusiasm, about my adventures. Strangely, it no longer seemed real. I found I was reluctant to speak about Seel, but Bryony had already heard about him and was armed with questions. Rather than answer them, I promised to take her to meet him in the morning. Bryony, no longer a girl, but now a strong, lean woman. Out of all the people I had known before, she had changed the most. She was human, she was older.

I slept with Seel in my father's bed; the room was free of ghosts. Lying in the dark, I searched the ceiling, trying to locate that spot where someone crouching in the room above could see in. I suppressed a shiver, thinking of Gahrazel. Was he still up there? Seel stirred in his sleep. I wanted to talk to him. I put my mouth against his hair. He twitched his face and mumbled some nonsense. I stared into the shadows, listening for smothered breathing, anything. All I could hear was Seel. I did not wake him.

Apart from the natural destruction of the summerhouse, it seemed time had not touched Forever. Perhaps it was the name that protected it: We dwell in Forever; dissolution could not mark it. My father's presence, even my own, had not been missed by the house. Only when within its walls did hara exist for it. Outside was death; I had grown up with this notion. I was anxious to establish some kind of rapport with Tyson, but he appeared to have little interest in me. As a child, I too had been content to experience only my own little world and had resented anyone trying to enter it with me. My brother resembled me in many ways and he clearly looked upon Cobweb as his hostling. He never asked any questions about Cal. That was how we differed; I had always been full of questions. Seel remarked on the fact that Tyson reminded him of

Cal. One day, my little brother would learn how to touch souls and break hearts. Already his eyes hinted at the knowledge of it.

The Varrs warily accepted the presence of Gelaming within their town. Over the months, they had isolated themselves from their brothers in the north, being concerned only with their own survival, bread upon their tables, and disregarding the concept of the War. Most of the soldiers had gone south with Terzian anyway. Now Ithiel found his time filled with the problems of administration, delivering justice upon petty squabbles and organizing the way our land was utilized. Strangers in our fields now meant extra mouths to feed that were not welcome, no longer a threat in quite the same way that they had been before. I was surprised that after the Zigane had left Galhea, other bands of humans had passed through. Some of them, bearing provisions, hardware or skills that were useful to the Varrs had been persuaded to remain in the town and had taken over empty houses in the southern quarter. The army had once lived there and it was now three-quarters empty. Human children and harlings played together in the gaunt buildings, where once a throng of polished horses had stamped restlessly, awaiting their masters' hands, awaiting a journey south. None of them had yet returned. It was accepted among the hara that they never might.

One afternoon, after we had been in Galhea for just over a week, I took Seel on a tour of the gardens. Life was stirring. Overnight, bare trees had become garlanded with a green mist of young leaves. I took him to the lake and he made me tell him again the story of Cal, Cobweb and the summerhouse. While I spoke, the summerhouse seemed to watch me mournfully from across the lake, perhaps remembering too.

Seel stared at the water thoughtfully. 'Did that really happen here?' he said aloud.

I looked around me. 'It is the setting, certainly ... but it *does* feel different.'

We went to investigate the fallen stones where I had found Cal. They were now nearly hidden beneath a growth of ivy (how relevant). I could remember the smells and the sounds and the feel of Cal's arm around me; that first magic taste of another har's

331

breath. I looked at Seel putting his hand against the stone, touching the moss and the leaves, and I felt as if I'd somehow missed half my life, as if that day of the storm and Cobweb's rage had only been a short time ago, and suddenly I was here again, full-grown, with a har who was remarkable in every way and had never known me untouched and shivering. What had happened to me? I felt disorientated, removed from reality. I sat down. Seel came to my side, smiling, pushing back that wondrous hair.

'Ah, time,' he said, sighing. 'When tomorrow comes, it often feels like there's never been a yesterday.'

I took his hand. He could always tell what I was thinking. 'Once it's past us, it's just like a story,' I said, 'like something we've only observed, or heard second-hand. How can I explain it?'

He shook his head. 'You don't have to. Remember here is a har who once found the dead body of a friend who had been murdered in cold blood. Did that really happen? Now I am here and it's another story, another person's life. I can't believe it happened to me. All those threads weaving in and out, bringing me here to you ...'

'Seel,' I said, 'you have never told me ... about Cal, about you and him. I want to know.'

He had been squatting beside me, now he sat down and turned my face towards him.

'I can remember the first time I met him,' he said. I didn't speak. Seel looked away from me, at the water. 'We were only children then. He was always ... *strange*. Popular, but the other kids were afraid of him. He fascinated me, he bewitched me ... We became har in our early teens, but had been lovers for some time before that. He went to the Uigenna, while I was incepted into the Unneah. I thought I'd never see him again, but he didn't stay with the Uigenna for long. When he came to the Unneah, I foolishly thought he'd come because of me, but then he had Zack with him. "You're too good, Seel," he used to say to me, as if that was something despicable. Zack wasn't good. He was mad and bad and beautiful. After I left the north and went to start the Saltrock community, they'd come visit me sometimes. I once took aruna with them and it was terrifying. They loved to hurt each other. But they did *love*, I am sure of that.' It surprised me to hear Seel say that, knowing how the Gelaming looked on such emotions. 'I don't often think of those times now,' he said and stood up, walking to the water's edge. 'Things happen, Swift, times change. We are conceited enough to think we can understand the future, even see part of it, but ...'

We looked at each other and an amazing flash of insight passed between us. Understanding of something infinite. Within seconds, it had passed. I held out my hand. Together, we walked back to the house.

We prepared for our final journey north. Arahal took me to his room and showed me the crystal, lying in a silk wrap of deepest indigo, pulsing with restless life, throbbing colours almost too painful to look at directly. 'It worked well,' Arahal said and smiled at me. 'Such power!'

'I can assure you the product was merely incidental,' I said.

Arahal laughed. 'It worked better than Thiede could ever have imagined.'

'I doubt that.'

'And soon your child will come into the world.'

'Yes.' I decided to confess an anxiety that had been bothering me for some time. 'Arahal, Thiede wanted us to make this child for a specific purpose. What is it? Will he want to take the child from us?'

Arahal clasped my shoulder. 'Don't be ridiculous! He won't take the harling away from you.'

'No, perhaps not the harling ... but the har?'

Arahal shook his head. 'A childhood; seven years. Later you must ask these questions again. I don't know the reason behind all this. That's Thiede's business. We have more immediate problems.'

'I want Seel to stay here when we leave.'

'Impossible; he will never agree.'

'But the child!'

'It will survive whatever happens.'

My hostling had already been approached about fostering the harling while Seel and I were away. It was a role he enjoyed, I suppose, and one to which he was entirely suited. I did not argue.

I could knead Seel's stomach and feel the hard growth that was the pearl within him. He complained of pain occasionally and was becoming more and more restless, but I could soothe him by stroking his back or combing out his hair. If he relaxed the pain usually went away.

Ashmael asked for the stableyard to be cleared and disinfected, the walls repainted. This was done without question. He had a pentacle painted upon the ground and wrote strange words all around it. Nightly, we gathered in that place and Ashmael, acting as shaman, began the preliminary entreaties towards the seventy amulet angels invoked at the time of childbirth. Cobweb would never join us, but I often saw him watching us from an upstairs window. Seel was anointed and blessed; he shone with a radiance that made me want to break the circle and take him in my arms. Later, alone with him in my father's bed, I would tell him he was perfect, again and again, until he'd tell me to shut up. 'If I was perfect, I wouldn't feel the way I do,' he said.

'How do you feel? How?' I asked urgently, pulling him against me, feeling his hard stomach hot against mine.

'That I want to be with you like this,' he replied. 'That I want you selfishly. I am worried my feelings will infect the pearl.'

'But they must!' I told him.

'Thiede chose me for my level head, among other things, remember.'

'Then it will be our son's secret defence against Thiede,' I suggested triumphantly.

'That is not the idea,' Seel replied with cynicism.

I am glad that it happened at night; daylight would have been too harsh. Ashmael wanted Seel to deliver the pearl in the yard, within the pentacle, but we both protested violently against that. 'I am not an animal!' Seel exclaimed. 'I will not give birth in a stableyard. I will not be watched scrabbling inelegantly around!'

'Since when have you developed such an exaggerated sense of vanity?' Ashmael snapped.

'Oh, and who is without vanity?' Seel argued relentlessly. 'Coming from someone who is so well acquainted with his mirror, Ashmael, I'm surprised you have the nerve to say that.'

'You were never this bothersome before, Seel.'

'I was never in this outlandish state before!'

Ashmael gave in reluctantly, but insisted that my father's room be prepared properly. Half the furniture was removed. Cobweb was far from pleased and watched the undertaking with a disapproving, beady eye.

I had tried to spend some time with my hostling each day, but he was still reserved with me. I imagined that Cal had spoken to him about Seel when they had been together and Cobweb made a great display of his loyalty to Cal and my father. I was shown up as a merciless traitor to my tribe, but because Cobweb is not essentially hard-hearted, he softened towards me eventually, especially when Seel argued with Ashmael over where to deliver the pearl.

'I cannot see how it will be beneficial for hostling or harling if Seel has to suffer being made a public spectacle,' Cobweb said to Ashmael.

'Your opinion is respected, Tiahaar,' Ashmael replied. 'But I don't think you quite grasp the semantics.'

'Perhaps not, but I grasp entirely the reality of what it would be like to deliver a pearl onto rough stone in front of a cluster of gawping idiots,' Cobweb replied, smiling.

One evening, Seel left the dining-room, halfway through the meal, without explanation. I followed him out, and found him half hanging over the bannisters, trying to get upstairs.

'Do you have to tell them?' he begged me.

I carried him to our room and laid him on the bed. He immediately curled up into a tight ball.

'I must bathe your face,' I said.

'What the hell for?' He uncurled, stretched, yelped and curled up again.

'You're sweating.'

'Never mind that! Tie my hair back.' I couldn't find anything suitable to do it with.

335

'I must fetch someone!' I cried. 'I don't know what to do! What if something goes wrong?'

'No!'

I remembered Cal once being in the same state and also that I had not been in the room when he had expelled the pearl. I hesitated for a moment longer, watching Seel moaning softly to himself, and then ran for the door. 'Swift!' Seel called after me, but I didn't stop.

Ashmael took control. He strode into that room and ordered, 'Seel, sit up!' Seel put his hands over his ears and Ashmael pointed at me. Cobweb was with me. Together, we lifted Seel up onto the pillows. By this time, Seel was almost delirious and did not object when we undressed him. Arahal paced restlessly at the end of the bed. Bryony brought us hot water and a cloth. I asked for a ribbon and tied up Seel's hair. He opened his eyes and looked at me.

'God, I don't like this. I don't like this!' he said. 'Hold me, Swift. Please.'

'Don't get in the way now, Swift,' Ashmael said.

Outside a wind had come up, howling round the weathered walls of Forever with an eerie shrill sound. Seel ground his teeth and whimpered into my shoulder. Arahal had set up a tripod supporting a shallow metal dish. Into this Ashmael threw dark, pungent dust to which Arahal applied a flame. With a gusting glow, the powder began to exude silvery smoke, whose thick perfume was so strong, Bryony, standing nearest to it, began to cough.

Ashmael began the entreaties: 'Yezriel, Azriel, Lahal ...' Cobweb and I held onto Seel's arms, while his body writhed in discomfort. 'Chaniel, Malchiel, Ygal ...'

As if his body understood that this was primarily a female function, all the masculine parts of Seel's body tactfully withdrew, as during aruna when a har is soume. He bit my arm. 'I am being destroyed from within,' he said.

'You must visualize it through,' Arahal instructed above Ashmael's invocation.

This is being conducted on two levels, I thought. On one level we have Ashmael and the Spirit, on the other we have the rest of us and the body.

336

'Tell Ashmael his voice hurts my ears,' Seel said to me.

It did not take that long, maybe fifteen minutes, but it seemed like an eternity. The room was full of incense, all silvery smoke, and Cobweb lifted the pearl from the damp bed and held it up. Seel was a dead weight in my arms. I offered him a cup of water and he said, 'One day, I'm going to make you go through this,' and we both smiled for the wonderful fact that it was entirely possible.

Seven days later, the shell of the pearl cracked and our son was real and breathing, mewling angrily at the world. I was disappointed that I missed it; someone was sent to fetch me from Galhea. Soon we would be going north and there were still many preparations to be made.

I ran into the house and up the stairs. Bryony and Cobweb were sitting on the bed on either side of Seel, and Tyson was prowling around the room, trying not to look interested. Seel smiled when he saw me. 'Look, Swift, look!' he exclaimed. Cobweb stood up to let me sit on the bed. I stared in joyous disbelief at what Seel held in his arms.

'Weird!' I said, which was all I could think of at the time.

The harling turned its head shakily at the sound of my voice. Its eyes were enormous; Cobweb eyes. Dark hair curled down its neck; its skin was flawless. Cobweb stooped and put his arm around my shoulder.

'You were once just like this,' he said.

'Take him.' Seel held the harling out to me. It was so warm. Its hands clawed the air and it whimpered once out of Seel's arms.

'He can't see that well yet,' Cobweb said.

Bryony's eyes were full of tears; she always seemed to weep when she was happy. Seel noticed and held her hand. He understood she was thinking about whether she would ever have a child of her own. There were no men in her life; she never mixed with the humans in Galhea, and even if she had a mate, there was no certainty that she was fertile. Many women weren't. I put my son into her arms and he seemed more comfortable there.

'You grew up so quickly, Swift,' she said.

'It didn't seem that way to me.'

Tyson strolled over to us. 'I remember when you were born and when you hatched,' I said to him.

His grave little face did not flicker. 'I remember *you*, Swift. I gave you ribbons and stones once.' It was the first time he had made any reference to having known me before. I put my hand on his shoulder and he did not move away.

'I am glad that your son was born here at Forever,' Cobweb said to me that evening. 'I am glad you came home.'

I decided not to tell him that it hadn't been my decision exactly. 'Tell me what you think of Seel now,' I said.

Cobweb lowered his eyes. 'He is exactly how Cal described him to me. I know I can't blame him for what has happened ...'

'Have you answered me?'

'I don't know. Have I?' he replied.

Some moments later, Arahal came into the room. 'Ashmael and I would like to speak with you now,' he said to Cobweb.

I knew immediately that it concerned my father. I stood up, deeply aware of an urge to flee.

'Sit down, Swift,' Arahal said sternly. 'We would like you to stay. We would like you to hear this.'

The Varrs had ridden south, into the mist, beyond Astigi. They had ridden into the forest, separating, getting lost, their minds wandering, panicking and helpless. Their weapons rusted away in hours. Their horses fell beneath them, mouldering away to bones in seconds. The sounds of their anguished screams had echoed around the treetops like the harsh calls of carrion birds.

In the centre of the forest, in a clearing, stands a lichened, white shrine dedicated to the Aghama. It is doubtful that anyone ever prays there, but it was in this place that Thiede and Pellaz waited for my father. It took him days to find them. I wondered what he had thought about, wandering into that sacred glade and seeing them sitting there. Did he have the taste of blood in his mouth. Had he remembered Gahrazel? Ashmael told me that Thiede and Pellaz had played dice to pass the time while they were waiting. Maybe they had diced for the souls of my people, like Death and Justice, looking up when Terzian staggered out of the trees, letting the dice fall one last time. Their ultimatum had been simple: change your ways, Terzian, confess your crimes, beg forgiveness, or go to your doom. His response had been inevitable: go to Hell! It was unfortunate for him that he did not understand what form his doom would take. Had he expected a sword thrust to the heart, a cup of Uigenna poison, a bullet to the brain? But it was not death; not that. Not any of those fitting punishments.

They had taken him to Immanion, capital of Almagabra, lush, green Gelaming country. In some place there, which Ashmael did not describe to us, the Gelaming stripped my father's soul and regressed him to the blackest, reddest times and made him face himself; his weaknesses, his faults, his sins. Oh, they'd known who would have been the best Varr to make Gelaming and turn against Ponclast. It had not been me. Not at first. It showed me that Terzian had not been beyond redemption; they wouldn't have bothered with him if he was. But he would not break, he would not turn around. Instead, he raved, he wept, he flailed his arms helplessly against the truth, but he would not recant. I had to sit in the calm, golden drawing-room of my father's house while Ashmael told us that Terzian had eventually begged Thiede's people to kill him. It had come to that. He would never try to kill himself and they knew that. They would not end it for him.

'Seek forgiveness from the souls you have wronged!' they ordered, but he still refused. Then they spoke about Gahrazel. Insidious voices. 'Didn't you once have fond feelings for Ponclast's son? Do you remember the first journey south that you made and what you said to him then? Didn't you promise him protection? You knew he was different, didn't you, Terzian? You knew he held, deep within him, the urge to run. You could have protected him, couldn't you? You had the chance. But instead you chose to enjoy his death. Did you enjoy it, Terzian?'

Terzian had shaken his head at them. 'No. I did not kill him. It was Ponclast. Ponclast did it!'

'You deceive yourself!'

'I never lie!'

'You took part in his murder.'

'I had to!' His cry had been despairing. He thought he would never speak these words, for it showed his weakness, and it was a weakness of the heart. 'My son was implicated,' he told them. 'They were close friends. Ponclast believed that Swift was involved in Gahrazel's defection. The only way I could protect my son was to comply with Ponclast's wishes. I always had to comply with Ponclast's wishes. There was too much he could do to damage me. I love my family!'

Did it bring me relief to hear that? It was an excuse, wasn't it? An excuse for all that bloodshed and bestiality. He had done it for love; for me and Cobweb. It sickened me. If Terzian had really felt all that, why, in God's name, hadn't he turned on Ponclast when he got the chance? I couldn't understand it then and I never will. Ashmael continued with the story of my father's imprisonment and my hostling and I sat apart on the sofa, listening with frozen faces.

They told us that most of the time, Terzian refused to eat, and he could not sleep. He was wary of drinking the water they brought him, in case it was drugged. Pellaz had spoken to him alone. 'For your son's sake, Terzian, let the evil go!' he had pleaded.

My father had simply replied, 'I am not evil. I merely did what I had to do.'

In the end, they realized that Terzian really would prefer to die than turn to the Gelaming. He did not want their absolution. They could not release him from whatever private hell he had put himself in. He wanted to die; nothing else. He could see no other future for himself. And so, they had taken him from the place where they had kept him for so long and put him into a suite of rooms in the palace Phaonica. They had given him attendants to see to his needs (to guard him) and eventually they had left him alone. It was then that Thiede had said, 'Terzian is finished. It does not matter what he's doing to himself.' And it didn't.

There was no moment of silence to let these words settle on the room. Cobweb had cried immediately Ashmael finished speaking, 'And what now? What now, for God's sake?'

Ashmael raised his hands. 'Be still, Tiahaar,' he said. 'Terzian will be brought back to you now.'

'What will be brought back to us?' I asked sharply.

Ashmael glanced at me quickly and then at Cobweb. 'Terzian. Your father.'

'Terzian is finished. You said that. What will be brought back to us, Ashmael?'

The room was full of darkness. I felt cold. Nobody spoke. Ashmael lowered his eyes. Arahal had been staring at his hands for some minutes. 'It is only right that your father should return to his family,' he murmured, with difficulty. He braved looking me in the eye. 'It is only right. He is dying, Swift.'

They left us alone. I took Cobweb in my arms and we watched the last of the light fade from the sky outside. Neither of us wept. When it was nearly completely dark, Cobweb said, 'I did not know about Gahrazel.' His voice was clear, thoughtful.

'Leef told me,' I replied huskily. I could not tell him about the forest. Perhaps one day, but not yet.

'It changes things, knowing that, doesn't it?'

(Knowing what, Cobweb? How much do you know?)

'It did for me when I found out,' I said. 'It did for a time ...'

Cobweb stood up and walked to the window. 'I'm not sure if I'll be able to cope with this, Swift. I'm not sure if I want to. In a way, I've got used to the idea of Terzian being gone. I think I want to remember him the way he was. I think I'm afraid of what they'll bring back to us.'

'We'll be together. I'll help you.'

'You're going north.'

'Then I'll tell Ashmael not to do anything about this until I return.'

'*If* you return.' He clasped his arms and sighed. 'You're telling me I should trust these people, Swift? You're telling me I have to let them live in my house after what they ...' He could not finish.

'You heard what they were trying to do.'

'Swift! That doesn't make it right ... does it?'

'I don't know. I don't know what I think, except that there are some things about Terzian, Cobweb, that *you* don't know about.'

He turned on me, snarling, 'Don't you dare to think that! Don't ever think you know more than me! I know what you're implying, I know all about that! I will never speak of those things, Swift, but just because of that, don't think I don't know about them!'

'Yet you loved him!'

'You think that's incredible?'

'Yes. You knew what he was, yet you loved him.' I shook my head in disbelief.

'You don't know what he was, Swift.' He stared out into the evening and there was utter, calm silence for a moment. I still did not think Cobweb knew everything.

'I can't believe that Pellaz did that,' he said, shaking his head. 'I was wrong about so many things, wasn't I? Right from the beginning. Pell and Cal. The light and the dark ... Which is which? Aren't they both a little of each? The Gelaming have destroyed your father, Swift; think about that. Think hard. All that strength ... Now they will not let us keep even our memory of him intact. They will bring a shattered husk back to us that might not even look like Terzian anymore. Even at the end, they will not let him keep his dignity. They could end it for him! They could! So easily. Painlessly, kindly. But no! They have to ... they have to ...'

He put his arm against the window and leaned his forehead on it. I had never heard him weep like that, loud, animal sobbing. His whole body shook. He had never wept like that. I went to him. Now we were the same height. I held him and kissed him, but I could not weep with him.

'Gelaming do not like to kill,' I said.

The Fall
*Deviation is the hidden dawn of
    daunt.
Phalanxes huddle in the kismet of
    deceit,
Profligate cortege of freedom
Mustered by the sanguinary evil.*

The sky is darker in the north; leprous clouds boil across it. When rain falls there, it smells bad, or maybe it is the wet earth that is noxious. Nothing is ever quite as you imagine it. Usually it is either worse or better. Ponclast's domain *was* different to the mental picture I'd formed when listening to Gahrazel, but the horror, the darkness, the sheer barbarity were utterly as I'd visualized them.

We broke through from the other-lanes onto a scorched plain. Nothing grew there; its surface was pitted and gouged as if by a great battle. In the distance the great black walls of Ponclast's citadel reared towards a turbulent sky. Fulminir, a gaunt and skeletal shadow, whose poison seemed to spread outwards, tainting the land. Above us, the clouds growled and crackled with subdued lightning. Above Fulminir, the sky was dark red. We rode to within a mile of its walls and from there we could see the raw light of naked flame upon the battlements and dark shapes that might have been vigilant hara. Ashmael was leading us. He pulled his sparkling horse (so out of place in that land) to a halt and raised his hand. The only noise behind him was the jangle of bits against teeth and metal, the occasional snort. No-one in our company felt like speaking. We numbered maybe three hundred. Sighting Fulminir, many of us realized how few that was. Maybe thousands of fit, vengeful Varrs waited in the darkness and we still had no way of gauging Ponclast's strength. A biting wind plucked at our clothes, our hair, the horses' manes. Beside me, Seel sat tall in his saddle and stared bitterly before him. I wanted to touch him, but it would not have seemed right in that place.

'This is far enough,' Ashmael called, and the wind carried his voice away from us.

Arahal, just in front of me, backed his horse until we were level. 'We don't want to have to stay here longer than is absolutely necessary,' he said.

'That goes without saying,' I answered. 'But how long do you think this will take? Will it be a case of unleashing the power of the crystal and being back in Galhea in time for dinner, or are we going to be here for days?'

Arahal shrugged and gave me a hard look. My sarcasm was not lost on him. 'Ponclast must know we are here. He will have felt us approach. It is a good sign in itself that there was no welcoming committee. He's still not sure of us. We could have been finished off easily coming out of the other-lanes.'

'We must prepare now!' Ashmael shouted. 'We are losing time.' He gave the order for certain members of the company to dismount. We needed protection; they were to cast a web of power around us, which would hopefully repel any form of minor assault launched from the citadel.

I heard Seel sigh. 'Look, Swift, look around you,' he said with sadness.

'Mmm, grim, isn't it?'

'This was once a great city. All this black, barren soil. I can remember great buildings being here and thousands of people, and cars and televisions and cinemas and bars and ... oh, what's the point of even remembering. It might as well never have happened.'

'Seel, how old are you?'

He laughed. 'I was dreading when you were going to ask that! In old time, old enough to be your father, now —' he shrugged carelessly — 'ageless enough to be your lover.'

I raised one eyebrow, a trick inherited from my father. It is a

344

gesture which can put a pleasing emphasis upon words. 'Heresy!' I said.

'You have corrupted me, it seems.'

'Do I ever seem too young to you, too childish?'

'God! What a place to have this conversation!'

'Do I, Seel?'

'Often!' He smiled and reached over to touch me. 'Oh, it's not naivety; just exuberance! I can be a sallow, bitter creature if I get too wrapped up in the past. I'm still eighteen, my hair's dyed red, I smoke too much ...'

'You never smoke!'

'That's now. Where do you want me? Now or then?'

'Shut up; you're mad!'

'No, this is madness.' He indicated the land around us with a sweep of his arm. Cities once. Now a crater of despair. Hell had been there.

I wondered whether Ponclast was standing on the walls of his citadel, laughing at us. Three hundred Gelaming. Was he just waiting to see what we'd do before he unleashed his hordes? Did he know about the crystal?

The air smelled cleaner once the shell of strength had been constructed around us. Hara began to construct a tall tripod of black, gleamless metal. At its summit was a shallow dish waiting to receive the crystal. I watched Arahal take the simple wooden box out of his jacket. It was lined with velvet. Inside it, reposing in dull, dark silk, lay our only hope. I could see it shining through the wrapping, emerald green, mazarine blue; holy fire. Thin vapours coiled out of it like ice in warm air. Arahal would not touch it with his bare hands. He had put on leather gloves.

We spoke the prayers, intoned the invocations for spirits of protection. The crystal was raised into place and all our faces shone in the glow of its clear, fluctuating light. Ashmael clasped two legs of the tripod in his hands and gazed upwards. His eyes flared green like an animal's eyes. He spoke to the crystal, softly, encouraging. Its flickers ceased for an instant; *it listened to him*. Ashmael's voice was crooning. He used few words, but his meaning was clear. Within the glowing points, an entity writhed, a living form of the

345

essence of two bodies. Conceived in desire and focused by will.

'Turn your eyes to the walls, beloved. They are weak. They are weak but they obstruct you. What is within them shall burn you if you do not burn it first. It offends you and it hurts you. Reach out and remove it. Make it disappear. Breach the walls and fill the space within. Make them feel your power, beloved. Enter their minds and make them sleep. Take the fire from them and all will be quiet. The badness that hurts you will die away. But first, you must breach the walls ...'

Slow, lazy beams the colour of spring leaves and dawn skies rotated leisurely in the air above us. Powdery azure smoke fell to the ground. The crystal began to sing. At first, a careless, humming sound. The beams moved slightly faster, reaching further. We joined in its song and it seemed a thousand thousand voices rose in response. I shielded my eyes; the brightness was so intense.

'Go to the citadel!' Ashmael ordered. The power needed little encouragement now. It was acting independently of him, mindless, but eager to instill its song into any mind it encountered. We were immune. We knew the song already. For a moment, the light bunched and reared into a great, spinning column, black dust rising from the earth, forming streaks within it, and then, with a great, shattering howl, the power surged towards the citadel, rolling like waves, cataracting, bounding, half-seen creatures riding its crests. There were shapes like vast wings, long, lidless eyes and lithe, clawed fingers within it. A peal like laughter or water.

It hit the black stone with a sound like the earth splitting and a massive crack snaked sedately through the walls. I was expecting foul ichor, black blood, to come pouring out of the breach, but nothing like that happened. As the greeny-blue light of our power crawled over the walls of Fulminir, something rose up beyond it. Something sickly yellow, high into the sky. It leaned towards the light; a column of leprous, evil smoke. When it touched the spirit of the crystal, a terrible sound brought the taste of blood to our mouths.

Ashmael shouted something. His eyes were wild. Everyone was tense, staring upwards, towards Fulminir. Seel was at my side, quite calm. He said, 'Ashmael will now panic.' I could only stare at him in horror. In the sky above Fulminir, the light, the child of our crystal, and the oily, black smoke demon that was the child of Ponclast's sorcery were entwined in combat. Horrible, deafening scrapings and squealings ripped the air.

'It will beat us,' I said. 'It will beat us.' I felt Seel's hand take my own.

'Never. Come with me.'

We stood beneath the tripod, looking up. The beam was weakening. We could see that. I was trembling. Seel put his hands on my arms and turned me to face him. His eyes were the eyes of a stranger. His hair was moving, as I had always expected it could, of its own volition.

'That is another of our children,' he said, jerking his head upwards. 'The child of Grissecon.'

I was numb. 'Don't say that ... it is *hurting*. Oh, Seel, I can feel it!' I could. It was like being ripped apart. Seel made that happen. He made us be in tune with it. Hysteria raised my voice to a squeal. Seel shook me firmly.

'Shut up! Listen to me. We have the power; only us. Do as I say! Do you hear me?' He looked incredibly fierce; a Seel unknown to me. I nodded. 'Then be naked, Swift.'

'What?'

'Do it, Swift!' There was no way I could argue with him. He scared me. He was different. This was a Seel who could kill. Ashmael, wide-eyed, stared at us maniacally through the legs of the tripod. 'Seel!' he shouted. 'Seel! Seel!'

'It's alright.' That was all he said, all he had to say. Ashmael dropped his head. My fingers fumbled with fastenings to my clothes. 'Help him!' Seel ordered and hands were upon me, ripping, not bothering with fastenings. I had heard of pelki and I thought it must feel something like that. To lose control of your body. To have other people move it for you. I resisted the urge to struggle. Shivering, I was on my knees in the black earth, naked and defenceless, three hundred pairs of eyes upon me and God knows how many more beyond the walls.

Seel dragged me to him and we sat on the ground beside the tripod. His hair was across his face; I did not know him. 'Trust me,

Swift!' My leg was twisted beneath me. I could not move. Seel straightened it out.

'This is the most vital Grissecon either of us will ever have to perform,' he said. 'Do as I say. It will not be much. But concentrate!'

We sat facing each other. He arranged my limbs and pulled me onto his lap. I was not prepared; it hurt horribly Flashes of red appeared in the light around us. Seel held me against him and I could feel his heart beating and buried my face in his hair so I could not see them watching us. But I could hear the crooning. Seel threw back his head and screamed out in a language unfamiliar to me. It was like gibberish, but I understood the meaning. He called to the crystal, ordered it to feed from us, let our strength combine with its own. Seel's fingers pressed the base of my spine and he moved within me, seeking the special places so that desire flamed inside me; I had no control over it. I was mindless, like the power, just body, just essence. The pain made it like perversion. I was making noises and when I heard them, it was as if they came from somewhere else. I opened my eyes and saw a dozen greenish fingers of light tentatively reaching down towards us from the crystal. Seel bit my ear and I winced.

'Concentrate! Power!' he cried. 'Power! Power!'

I threw back my head, my eyes snapped open again and the radiance burned into me. I howled and felt the core of heat build up within me. I dragged it out of myself. I was rising. I was becoming stronger and stronger. Bigger; rising. We were so tall, we filled the sky. Like Gods, like angels; pure fire, nothing else.

The moment came.

Deep within me, the burning serpent bit the star and with a wordless scream, a great tide of energy burst out, like an exploding sun. Around us, the Gelaming fell to the ground, hiding their faces, curled up. I was ignited again (it so rarely happens twice like that), and in a glorious blaze of light, shaped like a towering figure with wings across its face, its feet, its back, so full of light, so ultimately wondrous, the child of our essence reached out one lazy arm and touched the walls of Fulminir. Ponclast's demon seemed piteously small beside it, quivering, shrinking. I was laughing out loud, crazily. Through tears of laughter, I watched as, like powdering rock destroyed by rain, the walls of Fulminir crumbled. Great chunks of stone rolled earthwards, revealing the dank innards of the citadel, spiked towers, curving walkways and squat, blackened buildings. The citadel was wrapped in the blue-green radiance of aruna power. Frothing, fizzing, the child of the crystal jetted up into the air and exploded in a million droplets of sparkling foam, drifting downwards like bubbles, descending like sleep on the streets of Fulminir.

Seel and I shivered together, spent on the ground. The light had left us. The bowl on the tripod was empty. Someone came over and wrapped us in cloaks or blankets; something. Rain began to fall and I looked up into it, blinking.

High above, through the blinding sheets of water, a crack had appeared in the cloud. Beyond it, the sky was blue.

I turn the pages of a storybook. It is old, its pages thumbed by many human children. I come to the part where the prince comes through a barrier of thorns and finds a sleeping palace. The thorns are everywhere. Perhaps it was difficult for him to see the people. They would have been dusty, almost insubstantial, frozen forever at that moment when the spell was cast. Birds hanging in the air; impossible. A bee poised motionless at the brink of a flower and all the bodies ... Are their faces alarmed? Are they looking skywards, feeling the awful power descending, one last moment of dread before their minds are numbed? The book does not tell about that.

In the story, a princess sleeps in the highest tower and only the kiss of the prince will awaken her. In this palace, the one before me, the one that brought back the memory of a childhood tale, the only possible princess, the king's only child, is long dead. Not a spindle-prick, not death through innocence, but a father's hand holding out the fatal cup.

There is a tower in Fulminir. It is tall and it is perpetually dark. No princess ever slept there, I'm sure, but I ordered it to be forever sealed and I had them plant briars at its foot, so that one day thorns and flowers will cover its walls. It is a tomb without a body. It is for Gahrazel and to show him that I did not forget.

When our horses picked their way carefully over the fallen stones of Fulminir's walls, I did not know what we would 'find within. Neither did I want to find out. I was dog-tired, my body ached and I was floating in a half-dream state that little could penetrate. I stared at the city around me and it was like walking through a painting. A child's painting of Hell; red and black too stark, gaping faces. Eerily, the only sound was the hungry crackle of flames and the occasional thump of falling masonry. We rode by Varrish hara standing like imbeciles, utterly immobile, staring at the shattered walls. They did not see us. Like the people of the fairytale, their minds had frozen at the last instant before the spell was cast. Tendrils of blue-green light still investigated the dark, labyrinthine streets. Streets that were like tunnels, some of them disappearing into the ground like open sewers. Everything was damp and stilled.

Transfixed hara were caught in attitudes of bursting from open doorways, alarm forever painted across their panic-stricken faces, arms raised as if to ward off a blow. We passed a young har dressed in fine white silk, curled up in the gutter, gold at his ears and throat, his back branded and striped with weals. In a square, three rotting corpses hung from a scaffold, their blind, white, ruined eyes staring down implacably at the tumble of enchanted Varrs lying on the cobbles around them. In another place we found beautiful hara tied up with their own hair, their bodies naked and bruised. Varrish torturers stood grinning like stone around them. Others, who had perhaps only been passing by, had stopped to spectate. Their faces showed only mild interest.

Arahal pulled his horse to a halt; it skipped nervously sideways. He dismounted and stared up at the victims.

'Will they ever wake up?' I asked. My voice was blown away from me.

Arahal took a knife from his belt and sawed at the shining hair. He spoke three words and the wind sighed. Three bodies fell, slipped silently to the ground and twitched there feebly. Arahal rubbed his face, groaned, squatted and lifted the nearest har in his arms.

This was only the beginning. Fulminir had many other darker, fouler secrets to disclose.

Ashmael trotted his horse up beside me, an absurd blur of movement within the tomb. 'Wake up, Swift,' he said, with obscene cheerfulness. 'This way. Follow me.' He reached over and took hold of Afnina's rein by the bit-ring. I clung to the front of my saddle and we cantered through the ensorcelled streets of Fulminir.

Not even by those who have the most bizarre tastes in architecture could Fulminir be called a handsome city. But its sheer size and ugliness do inspire a certain kind of awe. The buildings are built very close together and the majority of them are tall; narrow but with many storeys. Evidence of extreme poverty was everywhere; the further we progressed towards the city centre the more harrowing became the scenes we encountered. If ever I had doubted that Varrs ate Wraeththu and human flesh, now I was given ample proof. We found a harling crouched in a blind alley, gnawing on a dismembered limb, his eyes frozen in a glassy expression of defence.

Ponclast's palace squatted like a scrawny bird of prey at Fulminir's heart. We rode right into it. More scenes of darkness, more tableaux of despair. I tried hard to imagine the lively Gahrazel growing up in such a place, but it was impossible. There was a throne room, vast, black and vaulted. Seel and some of the others were waiting for us there.

'Is there anywhere here we can get hot coffee?' Ashmael asked, with abysmal cheerfulness.

Seel grimaced. 'Save thoughts of refreshment until we are safely back in Galhea,' he said. 'You must find Ponclast.'

Ashmael nodded. 'We will. Come along, Swift.'

We urged our horses up wide, splintered stairs, shadowy banners motionless above our heads. When we could ride no more, we walked. Ashmael dragged me. I was dressed only in a woollen cloak; my feet were bare, my skin still wet. I remember saying, 'Is this my kingdom then? Is this what Thiede's given me?'

'We must find Ponclast,' Ashmael answered, repeating Seel's words, pulling me forward by my wrist. We hurried along endless black corridors, shuttered doors punctuating them at intervals,

351

terrifying in their silence. No windows, no light. A young har swathed in diaphanous veils, forever lifted in a breeze we could not feel, pressed his back to the wall, looking backwards. We walked past. He could not see us. I don't know what he saw, but his face was frozen in terror.

At length, we came out upon the battlements. In the open air, beneath a boiling sky shot with clear blue, we found them, Ponclast and his staff. They were leaning on the stone, looking down into the city streets, perhaps beyond them to the walls. On the stone floor was chalked a rough pentacle; magical implements were strewn carelessly around. From this point had the oil-smoke demon arisen. There were smears like soot and black liquid along the walls of the palace. A vague charnel stench still hung around. Ponclast's wide black cloak was lifted up behind him like wings, petrified in that position. I recognized him immediately. The first thing I thought was, Gahrazel's murderer, and this was followed closely, as more uncomfortable thoughts began to crowd my head, by: my father's seducer.

Ashmael pulled me to face him. 'You realize I have to release him from the stasis, Swift.'

I nodded. 'As you must.'

He spoke three slow words that sounded and smelled like ashes and lime, and then suddenly Ponclast jerked upright. He was so surprised, he nearly fell forward over the battlements. He uttered an exclamation and turned. I was a stranger to him. He did not recognize me, but he knew immediately that we were Gelaming and that we had defeated him. In one swift, supple movement he reached for the gun at his hip, but Ashmael had anticipated that, raising his hand, calmly, languidly. It was enough. Now Ponclast's arms were frozen again, his legs paralysed. His eyes were wild. Any chance he'd get he'd try to kill us, and then keep on killing. He enjoyed it. Neither was he afraid of death.

Anger spurted through me in a hot, quick wave. 'What can you do with him?' I cried. 'You can only kill him! It's the only way to stop him!'

Ponclast looked at me directly for the first time. He almost smiled.

'Yes, I am Swift,' I said in a cold, low voice. 'I am Terzian's son. I am with the Gelaming and now your kingdom is mine.'

For a moment, Ponclast was expressionless. Then he laughed. It was the most mirthless sound I had ever heard. Had he laughed like that as his son writhed in the final agony of death? 'Terzian's puppy!' he boomed, tears of laughter running down his sooty face. 'I was right about you. Weakness on my part not to get rid of you when I had the chance. So now you dally with those who destroyed your father –'

'No,' I interrupted. 'You destroyed him! You!'

'You think so?' Ponclast drawled. 'I gave him everything.'

'Including evil.'

'Including a thirst for evil. He loved power and he loved what we would do together. You never knew him, puppy; he was always mine.'

I thought, I will silence you, pig! I could not bear the sound of his voice. Before Ashmael could stop me, I lunged forward, taking Ashmael's knife from his belt, swift, swiftly. I lunged forward and struck at that hateful smile and then there was another smile on Ponclast's face, this one gaping red and toothless. He looked surprised.

'Swift!' Ashmael pulled me back. 'That is not the way! Stop!'

I struggled away from him and threw the knife at the floor. 'There is no *way*,' I said bitterly. 'No right or wrong; not here.'

I turned away. I walked back into the palace. Ponclast shouted empty threats behind me. I did not look around.

It seemed I walked for hours, always downwards, seeking the throne room where I thought Seel might still be. I didn't know exactly what Thiede expected me to do with Fulminir, but at that moment I was planning a thousand ways of pulling it down, burning it and mutilating Ponclast's elite dogs. It seemed such an anticlimax to find Ponclast like that. We should have fought. I should have sent him plummeting over the battlements; sent him to a bloody, crushing death. Gelaming do not like to kill . . .

Eventually, I came out into a courtyard, down a narrow, snaking stairway. I looked around myself. I was lost. In the middle of the yard was a well. Sitting on the well's wall was a splendid figure. It was Thiede. In that place of utter darkness he shone like an angel. He was an angel. Uriel for vengeance, clad in silver steel and silk, his hair like a nimbus, his eyes deepest black. I could see his long feet in thin sandals, the toenails curved like claws and lacquered with the lustre of pearl. If ever I had thought our race resembled humanity, looking at Thiede dispelled that illusion. He smiled at me. For a face so beautiful, his teeth are quite long.

'Once upon a time,' he said. 'I lived in a city like this. It may even have been this city ... Do you like stories, Swift?' I limped over to him. My feet were cut. Thiede leaned over and hauled up the bucket from the well. 'Come to me,' he said. I sat on the wall beside him and he tore a strip of silk from his sleeve and, with the water, bathed the blood and soot from my toes.

'All lives are stories,' I said. 'To somebody, they're stories.'

He nodded thoughtfully. 'Of course, this is true. I enjoy making up my own stories, though.'

'As you made up mine?'

'Yes. I construct the plot, place the characters and then they tend to become headstrong and run away from me. I lose control over them. Usually, it is because of Love, a thing I once sought to eradicate in Wraeththu. Now I'm not so sure I can, or even if I want to.'

'It surprises me you say this.'

'It surprises me too, Swift the Varr.'

I shivered. 'After today, the name of Varrs should never be spoken again. The tribe should perish, the memory of it should die ...'

'Is this your first decree?' He wiped his hands fastidiously.

'What are you going to do with the people of Fulminir?' I asked him. 'And the city itself; what will you do with that?'

'Isn't that up to you now, Swift?'

'No, I don't think so.'

Thiede looked beyond me at the dark mass of Ponclast's palace rising around us. We were still nowhere near the ground. The wind was chill.

'Do with them?' he mused. 'Well, it is a problem. They are no use to us in this world, that's for sure, but neither would we be thanked for sending such black souls into the next! Come now, what do *you* suggest?'

'I suggest, Lord Thiede, that we make a deep hole in the Earth and freeze them all forever and throw them all into it. Then we should close the pit. I would enjoy particularly stamping down the soil.'

'But nothing would ever grow there.'

'We could pave it with stone.'

'Hmm … a possible solution, I suppose!' He smiled at me, which I returned. 'There is one place you have not thought of, Swift.' He stood up and began to walk across the yard, beckoning me to follow.

'Another place …?'

'Yes.' He put his arm around my shoulder. 'Another place. My forest, the forest of best-forgotten mirrors.'

'But would people be safe from them there?'

'You should know that they would. You've been there.'

'Then it should be properly named.'

'Of course. I have been pondering upon it, waiting for you here. What do you think of this: Gebaddon? A marriage of the realms of Hell. Not this world, not the next, but somewhere in between where the only things they can damage are each other. Of course, there is the possibility, however slight, that they might discover enlightenment there.'

'A possibility, I suppose,' I agreed, 'but it would be unsporting to deny it to them.'

Thiede laughed and squeezed my shoulder. 'I chose well when I chose you, my dear.'

'Chose me for what exactly, my lord? I still don't understand quite what you require of me.'

The darkness of the palace had swallowed us again. We walked along a narrow corridor where there were open doors to either side. I did not want to look into the rooms beyond. There was no sound.

'Your purpose, Swift, is to govern for Pellaz and myself in Megalithica. Of course, you will need a full-size staff which will come together in time, and also I suspect there will be quite a lot for you to learn. Seel will be a great help to you; he understands about these things.'

'Will we have to live in Fulminir?' I asked, aghast. It was the Varrish capital of Megalithica, after all.

'No,' Thiede reassured. 'Galhea must be expanded. We envisage that it will become the major city of northern Megalithica. It is more central anyway. Fulminir is best forgotten. I think you will have to come to Immanion for a short while. You may talk with Pellaz there ...'

'Thiede,' I said. 'Who are you?'

He stopped walking, surprised. He inclined his head enquiringly.

'What I mean is, Pell is supposed to be Tigron of Wraeththu. Where do you fit into things? He answers to you; that is obvious. What position is higher than the Tigron's?'

Thiede smiled. 'Only one,' he answered, and, putting his hand upon my back, propelled me forwards once more.

'Few know my identity,' he continued, after a while. 'It is best that way.'

'Greater than the Tigron?'

'Wraeththu is mine, *are* mine. I've been around a long time, Swift. Since the beginning.'

'The *very* beginning?' I squeaked, enlightenment dawning slowly.

'But of course!' he answered.

'But —'

'No more!' he ordered. 'In the presence of the Aghama, you must learn to hold your tongue.' He smiled again. 'Don't take me seriously, I didn't give myself that title. Now, I have good news for you. I have decided to give Seel to you. If you like, I will perform the blood-bonding ceremony myself.'

'My Lord Thiede!' I exclaimed. 'What will Seel think of this?'

Thiede gave my shoulder a little pat. 'Don't be ridiculous, Swift! That is a mere trifle. I thought we understood each other.'

We came out into the throne room, where the Gelaming waited. We were on a balcony high above their heads. Seel looked up when he felt my presence, and waved. Thiede raised his hand. It dispelled the shadows. Dust fell from the torn banners around us. The light was with us.

CHAPTER

8

Furnace of Hate
Pilgrim of love suffering repudiation
As though having conspired with the
beast.
Manoeuvres in the vestibule of the heart
Crumble to dust in the palm of aires.

The journey back to Galhea through the other-lanes was a nightmare; I wanted to sleep for a week and trying to keep up the concentration required was horrendous. Most of the Gelaming remained in Fulminir, allocated the none too pleasant task of cleaning up and sorting out. As well as the citadel, there were numerous pockets of Varrs dotted about the countryside in settlements and small towns. It was doubtful that they'd put up much resistance, but neither would they welcome the Gelaming with open arms. I questioned the wisdom of trying to conclude such an operation using only three hundred hara, but Thiede pointed out that to use more would make them seem like an army, which was an impression that the Gelaming wished to avoid. I was told that many more Gelaming personnel would soon be arriving from Immanion, but even then they would not travel around in large numbers.

'It is inevitable that some remnants of the Varrs will want to fight us,' Ashmael said wearily. 'There is also the problem of the Uigenna, who, we understand, have fled into the extreme north of the continent. It would be politic to weed them out now, while they are comparatively weak. News of Ponclast's defeat must have reached them by now.'

Thiede wanted to come back to Galhea with us. When we entered the house through the great front doors, with all the house hara and Bryony waiting to greet us and cheer our success, Cobweb's acceleration down the stairs towards a welcoming embrace was stopped dead. It was a passable imitation of running smack into a wall. Thiede has that effect on people. He looks ten feet tall, while being nowhere near that height, and wears his awesome power like extra clothes.

I introduced him to Cobweb and he smiled graciously. Cobweb was speechless, watching this apparition wandering round the hall, picking up our ornaments, gazing up the great sweep of the dark, polished stairs. 'You are back so quickly,' my hostling said, 'so much sooner than we imagined.'

'Taking Fulminir was a mere itch on the Gelaming skin which your son obligingly scratched for us,' Thiede announced.

Our bedraggled appearance must have informed Cobweb otherwise, but he made no comment.

Seel and I went directly to bed, without bathing, without eating, even without undressing properly. Before we slept, he insisted on apologizing to me. 'I hurt you; I'm sorry.'

'You never hurt me. I love you, Seel.'

He thought about what I'd said and then smiled. I wanted to tell him about what Thiede had suggested, about the blood-bonding, but something held my tongue. It must have been my guardian angel. Seel stroked my face.

'When I look at you now,' he said. 'I see so many things. Not death, certainly, not bitterness or revenge or any of those bad things. When I look at you now, I experience a kind of pain, and I know it's happened before, but a long time ago ...'

'Pain?' I said sadly. 'I cause you pain?'

'Yes,' he replied. 'It is a kind of disease that, as far as I know, is curable only by another dose of the same thing. It is a plague that's scoured this small, helpless planet since life first crawled up out of the slime. A phenomenon that cannot be explained.'

'What are you talking about?'

I knew what it was and knew also that he was struggling to say it. To a Gelaming, because of his training and his beliefs, it was difficult.

'You have infected me,' he said.

359

I laughed and pushed him back and grabbed his wrists. 'Say it, Seel! Say it, or I'll break your arms!'

He howled and struggled and laughed and said it. 'Alright, alright, don't! I love you, Swift.'

We slept well into the following day and it was the smell of food that woke me. I spent a few, treasured moments gazing at Seel, who was still fast asleep and would not wake for some time. His face was dirty, his hair tangled and his clothes wrapped around him in knots. He was beautiful, and I knew I would never tire of gazing; never. Each time I looked at him, it was as if it were for the first time. With soaring spirit and singing heart, I took a bath and then ran down the stairs to the source of the delicious smells. Lunch was just over. Thiede had by this time thoroughly acquainted himself with my home and I found him sitting with his feet on the dinner table, indulging in leisurely conversation with Arahal and Ashmael. Moswell and Swithe were sitting there with dopy, sycophantic expressions on their faces, lapping up the pearls of Thiede's wit.

Thiede smiled brightly when he saw me, exposing those gleaming feral teeth. 'Recovered, Swift? I hope so. There's so much to be done. Unpleasantness to suffer, rapture to enjoy!'

I grimaced. 'Is there any coffee?' I sifted through the remains of the meal on the sideboard.

'We thought tomorrow ...' Ashmael began tentatively, raising his voice, leaning back in his chair to watch me.

I forked meat and cold vegetables onto a plate. They had not left me much to choose from. 'You thought tomorrow what?' The coffee pot was still warm at least. I began to pour.

'Your father. He will be arriving here tomorrow morning.'

I virtually dropped everything I was holding, lukewarm liquid splashed over my hands. I appealed to Thiede. 'Is this really necessary?'

Thiede raised an elegant hand. 'No, of course, it isn't, Swift. I can understand your feelings. If you would prefer it, I could arrange for your father to end his days in Phaonica, or even in Gebaddon with all his friends. It's all the same to me. Just give the word.'

I turned irritably back to arranging my meal. 'No ... this is his home. The point has been made. Pity it had to turn out this way though, isn't it?'

Thiede smiled at me ruefully. 'I hope you're not becoming hard, Swift.'

'Hard? Is there any other possible way I can face what's left of my father?'

Even Thiede could not answer that.

Mid-morning the following day, the rafts came out of the mist. It was something I'd never seen before, straight from Almagabra, something I could never imagine. Powered by crystals, aruna-fired, they drifted, alien and graceful, over the lawns of Forever, casting great oblong shadows. Hazy sunlight was beginning to burn through the moist air. Rain had fallen; soon the grass would begin to steam. From an upstairs window, we could see the huddled shapes of many hundreds of hara crowded on the rafts. They made no sound. This was what remained of the Varrish army, scooped up from Gebaddon. War veterans who had seen no fighting or whose battles had been wholly illusory among the dense foliage of the forest. Minds irreparably damaged, bodies wasted, they had the eyes of those who had looked into the abyss, the image of which was burned forever into their minds. If they were glad to be home, they did not show it. Perhaps they did not realize their ordeal was over.

Cobweb, Seel and I were in Cobweb's room. Tyson was playing on the floor, oblivious. We spoke in hushed voices. Cobweb called gently to Tyson. 'Your father is here.' The harling looked up briefly and flashed a Cal smile, presently absorbed once more in his game of make-believe. Cobweb had tied up his hair and dressed himself in dark, brushed doeskin. He was trying to make himself strong.

Bryony came into the room, holding my son in her arms. A worried frown creased her brows. She stood very close to Cobweb. None of us were happy that day, apart from Tyson, and he was half Cal's, so that wasn't really surprising.

I said, 'Seel, he has to have a name.'

Seel was in a world of his own, gazing out of the window. He looked blank. 'What?'

'Our son,' I said. 'He has to have a name. Now. For my father.'

Seel nodded slowly. 'Yes. I have been thinking about it.' He uncurled from his seat and stood up, taking the harling from Bryony's arms. 'Do you know, of those names, all those wretched names that were buzzing through my head when I delivered the pearl, there was one I liked. When Ashmael said it ... I think I knew then it had to be the one. It was Azriel.'

'Azriel ... A Gelaming name?'

Seel shook his head. 'Not really. It's very old ...'

'Oh, I see; an angel,' I said drily.

'Well, yes.'

I looked at the harling happily pawing at Seel's face. So innocent. Perhaps he would need a strong name. I had no idea yet what his future would hold, but I suspected that he would have very little control over it.

'Yes, I like it too,' I said. 'Hello, Azriel.'

The rafts settled on the lawns, their unearthly mechanisms sighing to silence. 'I suppose we must go down,' Cobweb said dismally. I reached for his hand and it was cold and clammy. Seel handed the harling back to Bryony and we walked down the stairs together. It seemed to take ages. Lingering behind the others, I looked back, thinking of the past. I was remembering running up those stairs to my father's room on the day they found Cal in the snow, and then it was the day of my Feybraiha, and I was coming down again with flowers in my hair and the smell of autumn all around. I shook myself. Cobweb was waiting for me. 'We are still together,' he said.

'All those times, though!'

'Yes,' he said with a sad smile. 'All those times.'

I wondered how the Gelaming had managed to round up all my father's hara. Had they really been wandering round Gebaddon all this time? I shuddered. The thing that struck me first was their utter silence. It was even more profound once we were outside. Beaten creatures, packed together like prisoners on those sleek, magical vehicles, shivering as if they were cold. It was a hot day, close and humid.

Ashmael came straight over to us when he saw us standing on the steps of Forever. He blinked at Cobweb. This was an unconscious appreciation of his beauty, which was at its most wondrous that day. My hostling was feeling tragic and it always gave him a special kind of bloom when he felt that way.

'We shall bring him into the house,' Ashmael said in a confidential tone. Cobweb nodded shortly and went back inside. He would go directly to the sitting room and put his back to the window and not come out again until Terzian had been secreted away upstairs.

The Gelaming seemed edgy, which I took to be proof of their shame. Who else had allowed these bewildered hara to wander forgotten in Thiede's hell forest? It was hard to imagine the broken creatures on the rafts ever having had a thirst for blood. They would never fight again. Hara had come up from Galhea, seeking lost, loved ones. Everyone milled uncomfortably, looking over the rafts as if they were open graves.

'Come with me,' Ashmael said. Seel put his arm around me and we strolled towards the rafts. My heart was pounding and I found myself chanting words of power that I had not used for years. I was conscious of eyes upon me; conscious also of their weary hostility. Heads raised. I could imagine the thoughts. 'There goes the one who sold us out to the Gelaming. Terzian's son, the traitor.' If I had been alone, they might even have mustered the energy to spit at me. Hara from the town just stared at me with unashamed curiosity. To them I was a celebrity and my part in what was happening now was just that I had initiated the possibility of it occurring at all. The Varrs of Galhea are really quite sheeplike. They need to be led and now they were happy to follow me. Wars cause discomfort, after all. Wouldn't peace bring prosperity? It was also the first time that most of them had caught a glimpse of Seel. If circumstances had been different, I feel they would have cheered us.

Seel said, 'Your warriors are home from the war that never happened. This should have been a day of celebration, but it feels more like a funeral.'

Terzian was on the smallest raft. Small, but provided with the greater comforts. Few hara were with him. I thought to myself, In a

363

few moments, I am going to have to look at my father, and found myself quailing, so I looked instead at the har who held Terzian in his arms. I saw straight black hair and a white face; I did not recognize him. His clothes were torn and colourless, his shoulder scarred as if by claw marks. The expression on his face was something like that of someone who has reached the end of his tether, someone whose strength is gone and who faces horror, someone who will protect to his dying breath the thing he loves. He convulsively tried to shelter Terzian with his body as we approached. He could not have known who we were, only that we were Gelaming, the enemy.

I had dreaded my father being totally unrecognizable, aged and toothless perhaps, or slightly decayed in some way. The reality, while nothing like that really, was just as shocking. He was so thin, lying on the cushions, his head in the strange har's lap. His once thick hair was lank and lustreless, his face grey, all the skin stretched over the bones. But he was still Terzian. He still looked like the father I had known. That was perhaps the worst thing about it. I put my hands on the side of the raft and he stared past me. Seel was standing there. He looked at Seel. I said, 'Terzian.'

His gaze flicked over me, surprisingly quickly. He blinked.

'It is I ... Swift,' I said.

He tried to rise then, stretching out a hand whose veins bulged blue through the white skin. His companion snarled at me. Terzian spoke, a small sound. 'My son. It is my son,' he said. There was no inflection to his voice. He just looked at me. I could not tell what he was thinking. Did he remember, as I did, that time he had spoken to me in his study, so long ago? The night of Gahrazel's arrest; something I will never forget. I remembered Terzian making me promise to look after his family, our home, as if he feared he would never come back. Now I thought that his homecoming was not part of the future as it was meant to be, or that he had ever wanted.

Terzian painfully lay back among the cushions and closed his eyes. He shakily raised a hand to his face. There was silence; we all just looked at him. I could feel Seel's hand on the back of my neck. 'Bring him into the house,' Ashmael said.

I could not watch them do it. I could not watch them lift him, helpless, limbs sprawling, like an invalid. Terzian's companion was reluctant to leave him. I heard a scuffle. Without turning round, still walking back to Forever, I ordered that the har be taken to the kitchens and fed. I understood how he felt, that he had cared for Terzian for some time and wanted to stay with him now, but I could not risk offending Cobweb. They took him away, dragged him to the house, and I heard him cry, 'Terzian! Terzian!' My spine crawled with pain. Hadn't these people gone through enough? It hurt me to separate my father from his companion, but I felt I had no choice.

Seel did not speak to me. There was little we could say to each other; it was all so ugly. In the hallway of Forever, he made me stop walking. I looked at him fiercely and he took me in his arms. I pressed myself against him, wanting his mouth, his breath and the sweet taste of life, so fragrant, to eradicate the stink of death in my throat. Neither of us uttered a word.

I had already arranged alternative accommodation for Seel and myself, so that Terzian could have his room back. We could have had Cal's old room, but I settled for a smaller suite because I was afraid of ghosts. Seel took me there and laid me on the bed. He gently took off my clothes and massaged my skin with oil. I felt over-sensitive, too ticklish, and all my muscles ached with tension. Seeing my father again had made me fear that I hadn't really grown up. Perhaps it was an illusion, this power that had been given me. Could I really give orders in this house now that Terzian was home again?

Seel could see me thinking deeply. He sensed my distress. 'You will have to be strong,' he said. We both knew that anyway, but it helps to hear someone else say it.

I waited until I was sure that the house-hara had settled Terzian into his room before I visited him. It was late afternoon and I was feeling sleepy and tranquil after a long session of Seel's exquisite attempts to ease my mood. Terzian lay in the bed, staring at the ceiling, bars of sunlight falling across his hands where they lay on the coverlet. It seemed I could see the life draining away from him even as I watched, but I had made my heart hard and walked towards the bed.

He looked at me. I was afraid his intelligence might have been affected, but his eyes were still alert. The room was dark and full of a thick perfume, which could not totally mask the faint miasma of sickness.

'Don't come in here,' he said. His voice was reasonable and slow, almost emotionless.

I sat on the bed and said, 'Father.'

He turned his head away from me. 'They told me of your betrayal. Get out! You are no longer my son. Get out!' He looked at me again and his eyes were full of contempt. I could not speak. 'Seduced you, didn't they?' He nodded to himself, a peculiarly aged gesture. 'Yes ... mind you, the prize was worth it. I've seen him.' He was referring to Seel. I tried to interrupt him, but he would not have it. 'All my lands as well, eh? My house, my town, my people. Oh, you've a shrewd business head on that skinny body of yours, Swift!'

I pitied him so much I couldn't make myself angry, which was cruel because he wanted me to be. If I remained calm, he would think he didn't even have the strength left to unnerve me. I knew I must try to argue, but my head was empty.

'Where's ... where's Cal?' he asked. I heard the despair in his voice, as if he knew the answer to that already, as if he knew that I didn't.

'Cal? Oh, I betrayed him as well, father. I took him straight to the Gelaming. They have him. Didn't they tell you that?'

Terzian tried to smile. The effect was ghastly. 'My son, a true Varr. You know nothing about loyalty, do you, only self-preservation. I would have liked to see Ponclast's face when he saw who it was that had defeated him. You should have seen mine when I found out!'

Those words finally got to me. 'Me, a true Varr!' I exclaimed indignantly. 'Let me tell you, father, it was only recently that I realized fully what being a true Varr means. I've learned the truth about a lot of things, not least the Varrish concept of loyalty, and the details of certain executions. Gahrazel's, for example.'

How it sickened me to see the furtive wariness creep into my father's eyes. He could not look at me.

'And who told you that? Gelaming story tellers, I suppose. What lies have they filled your head with?'

'No-one told me exactly,' I replied. 'It was in the forest.'

He knew which forest; I didn't have to explain. He seemed to deflate before my eyes.

'I don't have to justify any of my actions to you, Swift,' he said peevishly. 'You don't know everything. You weren't there. You can't possibly understand.'

'I don't want to. I don't want to have the kind of mind that could understand something like that.'

'Is that why you betrayed me?' He sounded so pathetic, I had to grit my teeth.

'I never betrayed you, Terzian,' I said. 'You knew the risks yourself when you went south. I only did what you once asked me to do. Your family is safe and their future is safe. I did that. Forever still stands untouched and your blood will always flow in the veins of those that live here. By securing our position, I've immortalized you in a way. You don't deserve it.'

'Oh, don't give me that! That's Cobweb talk!' he spat viciously. 'The truth is, my son, that you have come out of this very well, while the demon Thiede has punctured my soul. My life is running out of the hole that he's made . . .'

'I know what they did to you. I know what they were trying to do.'

'Do you? Do you really? I don't think so!' He closed his eyes and I thought how transparent he looked, how impermanent. Talking had enfeebled him more than he wanted to let me see.

'The past is done,' I said. 'Nothing can be changed now. What is important now is the future. You have a grandson.' Terzian didn't move. 'His name is Azriel,' I continued doggedly. 'Seel hosted him for me. My prize, remember?' There was still no response. I stood up. 'I shall send Cobweb to you.'

'No!' It was a weak exclamation. His eyes were still closed. 'Not yet . . . Swift, come back later.' It was a child's plea.

'Of course I will.'

'Bring Cobweb with you then.' He could not face seeing Cobweb alone.

Bryony was waiting for me on the stairs. She was agitated because my father's travelling companion had vociferously refused the comfort she had offered and was currently threatening to search the house for Terzian. 'Cobweb must not see him!' she cried, sharing my concern for Cobweb's state of mind, which was as yet undetermined. Ashmael and Arahal were still outside, supervising the dispersal of the bewildered Varrs. Thiede would not want to be troubled with domestic incidents. I would have to deal with it myself, distasteful though it was to me. 'His name is Mengk,' Bryony told me, disgruntled. 'Oh, Swift, he will not go! What if —'

'Alright, alright,' I interjected, impatiently. 'I'll see to it.'

We found Mengk prowling around the hall. I walked up to him with what I hoped was an authoritative air.

'Terzian is comfortable,' I said. 'You must now go to Galhea.'

He turned on me like a frenzied animal, uttering every curse he knew, flexing clawed fingers dangerously close to my face. He was not prepared to leave. With horror, I saw Cobweb come to the door of the drawing-room. So did Bryony. She tried to push Mengk into the kitchen and he resisted fiercely.

'What's going on?' Cobweb demanded and came towards us, arms folded. We all froze guiltily. He addressed Mengk. 'What is it you want exactly?'

Mengk was momentarily silenced, faced with the commanding vision of dark loveliness whom he knew to be Terzian's consort.

'Well?' Cobweb looked at me. I shrugged helplessly. Bryony had the courage to speak.

'This har travelled back to Galhea with Terzian,' she said. 'Now he is concerned for his master's welfare. Swift was trying to explain that Terzian is comfortable ... and ...'

Mengk straightened up and shook Bryony's hands off his arms. 'I must see my lord,' he said. 'I have cared for him a long time. Only I know what he needs at this time.' I was rather awed by his nerve.

Cobweb raised his eyebrows and I thought, as I had thought so often, how it is never possible to anticipate my hostling's reactions. 'You are probably right,' he said. 'Swift, take this har to Terzian.'

I started to protest, but could see from my hostling's face the futility of such an act. Sullenly, I showed Mengk where Terzian's door was and left him to it. I felt ridiculed because Cobweb had overridden my order. Downstairs, I found him solicitously examining Bryony's cheek, which was beginning to swell along the bone.

'She was struck!' he said, with some surprise.

'Why did you do that?' I asked him angrily. 'Why didn't you have him thrown out? He insulted you!'

Cobweb didn't look at me. 'I don't think so, Swift. I didn't hear any insults.'

'Just by being here, he insulted you!' I insisted.

'Put yourself in his position, Swift, and then remember that all we can do for Terzian now is try to make him happy in small ways. That vicious little brute has been looking after him. Terzian is probably used to him. I won't say "fond" because Terzian is hardly ever fond of anything. We must be patient during this time and learn to bite our tongues. We must smile at each other and not raise our voices and let Terzian think he is still master of this house. Now we shall go into the kitchen and make sure Yarrow has put out enough sheh for dinner. I think we should sample it now, in fact. Tonight, I shall dress in black and take pleasure in the Gelaming Ashmael's attempts to interest me. Come along!'

We followed him.

The meeting that eventually took place between Cobweb and Terzian is almost too painful for me to relate. It gave me a glimpse of the private side of my parents, that side that most children never see nor want to see if they are wise. I think the whole thing was made worse because it contrasted too strongly with the very convivial meal we all enjoyed that evening. Hara came up from Galhea, and Forever felt very much as it used to feel in the past when celebrations were in order; relaxed and comfortable.

Braced by alcohol, mellowed by good food and conversation, Leef and I had the long-deserved talk about our differences. Some things I realized he would never agree with me over (namely the issue of Cal and his fate), but once he had reassured himself that

369

power had not gone to my head, our friendship was firmly reinstated. Now we could laugh at incidents in the past. I was so relaxed, I actually forgot about what lay in my father's bed upstairs. Then Cobweb caught my eye meaningfully and mouthed, 'Now,' and I felt a great deal of my euphoria disappear.

Mengk opened the door to us in response to Cobweb's peremptory knock, and we went into the room. 'It is time you ate something,' Cobweb told Mengk. 'If you would like to go to the kitchen, you will find that our housekeeper has prepared a meal for you.' Mengk nodded respectfully and left us.

Then I had to see my father's face as he watched the radiant creature of mystery that is my hostling glide towards him. He must have recalled immediately fragments of the past and the feel of Cobweb's cool skin and the caress of his cool eyes. Now they both knew that the room within their minds where the delight of their union had once thrived had been irretrievably shuttered and barred. Terzian the shadow looking at the light. Cobweb's face showed only a kind of pitying disbelief. I knew that he didn't really want to see this new, shrivelled Terzian, let alone speak to him. He felt ashamed to be so vibrant. This was ridiculous, as Terzian had wronged him in so many ways in the past. Cobweb had always wanted to shower my father with love, while Terzian had perfected the art of shutting Cobweb out of his heart whenever he wanted to. Now the tables were turned. Now who was helpless? I could see that something definite had happened to the love that Cobweb had felt for Terzian. It was not quite the same, still fervent in a way, but no longer essential. I suspected Cal might have had something to do with that, but it may just have been that Cobweb had been alone for so long and had got used to the idea of life without my father.

'So, we have you back again,' Cobweb said awkwardly.

Terzian's face was dark. It was in shadow, but then that room was always dark. 'You never *had* me, Cobweb,' he replied inscrutably, 'never.'

I felt that Terzian should have died right after saying that. They would have been very profound last words. More than that, he deserved to die for it, because he wanted to punish us for living, especially Cobweb, who was beautiful and whom he would have to leave behind. Terzian would still look on Cobweb as one of his possessions and would no doubt be gratified if my hostling offered to throw himself onto Terzian's funeral pyre. Terzian was affronted that Cobweb should have a life without him.

'Is there anything you want?' Cobweb asked stiffly, even though he must have known that Terzian's every need was being catered for. He showed that my father's words could not affect him; it was incredible.

'Want anything?' Terzian's eyes narrowed. The cue was irresistible. 'In this life there has only been one thing that I have truly wanted ...'

Cobweb and I looked at each other, both painfully aware of what he meant. If only Terzian could have known how the implication in his words, the sting he hoped would poison, could not touch us. Perhaps Cobweb would tell him. Perhaps he would say, 'Oh, you are talking of Cal. Of course. The one who gave meaning to your life and who came to my bed after you left Galhea,' but no, unpredictable as ever, my hostling knelt at Terzian's side and took one of his hands in his own. (Surely my father must be able to see how Cobweb had changed. He was no longer the bound half-har whom Terzian had manifestly tried to keep utterly female. Surely he must see the difference?) My hostling smiled.

'Terzian, if I could do that one thing for you, I would,' he said softly. 'If I could bring Cal back, I would.' He stroked my father's face. I could not bear it. My toes were curling in embarrassment. Tears began to run from my father's eyes, trailing unchecked over his gaunt cheeks. His body began to shake; he sobbed. Cobweb gathered him in his arms and kissed him.

'Cobweb, I ... I never loved you ...' Terzian said in a horrible, gulping, cracked voice. I wished it would end. I could not move, transfixed by a kind of fascinated horror. My father looked dead from the neck down. Could he even feel Cobweb's hands upon him?

'Hush,' my hostling murmured. 'You don't have to say these things. You don't have to. I will say them for you.'

'No!' I cried. I don't know why.

Cobweb smiled crazily at me. 'It's alright, Swift. He just wants to say that he gave me the best he could, that's all. I've always known that. Terzian lost his heart to Cal a long time before he met either of us. It was meant to be. Cal was just the one.'

'Cal is just "the one" to many people, it seems,' I said scathingly. They ignored me.

'Cobweb ...' Terzian's voice was almost nonexistent now. 'I never thought this could happen to me. I'm dying, aren't I? I really am ...' Bewilderment, weak frustration, envy of the living; what was really going through his head? Cunning, I thought, uncharitably. 'I never thought I'd say it, never,' he wheedled, flopping a helpless hand against the coverlet.

'We must all die eventually,' Cobweb soothed. (Pathetic! Could such an inane observation possibly help him?)

'No, no, no,' Terzian groaned. 'Not that. I never thought I'd say "I love you", not to anyone. Now I say it to him all the time ... only ...' He reached up, gasping, mustering his failing strength, and caught hold of Cobweb's clothes by the neck. 'In Immanion, it's all I thought about, what kept me going, just one more day, just one .. ' He trailed off, wilting visibly. 'I cannot die without seeing him again, not knowing whether he's safe or not. I've kept myself alive for that, for the hope that he might be here when I came home ...' He shot me a withering glance. I wanted to say, 'Any more clichés, you two? Oh, come on, there must be more! Please, don't mind me, just carry on!' but I said nothing. Cobweb turned the sad, sick face back towards his own.

'Terzian ...'

My father started to shake again, his eyes rolled maniacally. 'Cobweb, Cobweb,' he wailed. 'Your magic ... your magic ... how I've scorned you ... what I've seen! The Forest! The Forest! Oh, Cobweb!' To watch my father weep was an obscenity that nearly made me physically sick. It seemed the Gelaming (or his own guilt?) had destroyed everything within him but for his bitterness and his obsession for Cal. I wondered whether Pellaz had ever interrogated him about that.

Cobweb spoke my name. My father lolled in his arms, spent and shuddering. I said, 'What?'

'You may leave us now,' my hostling replied, and I saw his anger at the relief those words gave me.

Downstairs, I found Thiede in the drawing-room with the others, opened bottles of sheh on the carpet, the room thick with cigarette smoke and laughter. I found it hateful, yet I wanted to be part of it. I sat down beside Thiede and he thoughtfully thrust a full glass into my hand.

'Harrowing?' he enquired lightly. He was smiling, but I knew he understood exactly how I felt.

'Yes. Harrowing.'

'Behind you now, though.'

'Yes, behind me.' I sighed. 'My father needs Cal, Thiede.'

Thiede sighed as well, but theatrically and embroidered by waving arm gestures. 'Oh God! Must my life continually be plagued by love-sick fools continually bleating that particular demand at me?' he said.

There is little more to say now. The time of upheaval was nearly over. I have to speak of the end of my father's life, for that will truly end the tale. With his ending, there began a kind of peace for me. I had played my greatest part on Thiede's stage. For a while, he would let me rest. Fulminir was deserted, peopled only by winds and dust, her victims succoured, her cruel inhabitants transferred to the shadowy, make-believe land of Gebaddon. For them, the play was over, at least in this world.

Taking Fulminir, of course, was not really the end. Megalithica is a vast country and the Varrs were widespread. Suddenly, what was left of my tribe found that those they had looked on as allies had turned against them, their slaves had the courage to rebel, their own loved ones, sickened by bloodshed and cruelty, broke free and ran to the Gelaming. Of course, many lives were lost. We could not avoid fighting, much as Thiede and his Hegemony hoped we could. Magic is sometimes not enough. Some minds are too far immersed in darkness to recognize light even when it is thrown in their eyes. There are probably a thousand thousand tales to be told of my country at that time; the heroes that rose up, the monsters that were discovered, the legends that were born. One day, I might go looking for those tales, for even as a child I had longed to write, and as I have said before, Wraeththu have not yet had much time for making books of their history.

Seel and I mingled our blood beneath the heavy, shady trees in the gardens of Forever. Thiede's ceremonial blade made the cuts, Thiede's own hand pressed bleeding skin to bleeding skin. He smiled his long-toothed smile and blessed us. Cobweb watched us with wistful eyes, thinking of what might have been. His gaze flicked once to Terzian's window; that was all. My father would not even countenance my blood-tie to Seel. I offered to help him to the chair by the window in his room but he declined with scorn.

Later, I couldn't resist going to see him, brandishing my blood-stained flesh. 'Look, father, a different kind of inception!'

He winced away from me. 'And we were once accused of emulating men!'

'I pity you. You cannot understand.'

He smiled wryly to himself. 'Oh, Swift, must I bicker my way to the grave?' His voice was introspective.

I watched him looking at what was left of his body, hidden beneath the bedclothes. Half of me wanted to gather him into my arms as Cobweb had done, half of me didn't care about him at all. There was a few moment's silence, then I said, 'Why, Terzian?'

He sighed. 'Why ...' Looked up at me, his eyes young, sparkling with shadows of the past. 'What particular "why" do you mean? Is it why didn't I say what the Gelaming wanted to hear or why did I ride south in the first place, or why did I ever become Wraeththu to start with? Or is it the darker "whys", those best not spoken, eh?' He smiled and I thought his face was so much as I remembered it, and I recalled how it had sometimes frightened me and sometimes filled me with fire. Of course I have always adored him, always feared his displeasure, always craved his attention, yearned his respect. It was still the same har lying there, only the balance of power had changed.

I said, 'No, none of those things. The "why" I mean is, why are you killing yourself?'

374

I thought he would wince again, but he didn't. There was silence in the room, deep but not uncomfortable. My arm had begun to throb a little and I sat down on the bed and sucked at the flesh.

'Let me see that,' Terzian said. His hands were hot and dry, papery dry. He traced the line of the cut with one finger. 'By this mark, you have committed yourself to another har — for life. His welfare is your welfare. You are prepared to uphold each other, whatever happens. It is not a vow to be taken lightly.'

'I know that.'

'Of course you do, that's not what I'm trying to say. Some vows are made when you are very young, Swift, personal vows that might never be spoken. I cannot go back on promises that I've made to myself, whatever others might think of my beliefs.'

'Is it that simple?'

He shook his head. 'No ... nothing can ever be that simple, can it? I worked hard for Galhea, Swift, worked hard to make it what it is. Perhaps, in caring so much, I've done things that I shouldn't have. Bad, evil, whatever you want to call it. It was because I've always cared about my people, this town was mine and I didn't want anything or anyone to take it away from me. I thought that whatever I did outside Galhea could never harm it. Maybe I was wrong. I can offer no excuses for my life, Swift, and I don't want forgiveness, but I want you to know that I *did* care, even if the popular view of me in this house is of a hard-hearted monster!'

I laughed nervously and he squeezed my arm. 'I know you've always disapproved of the way I've treated Cobweb,' he said. 'Will it help you to understand if I tell you that I've always feared him and, because of that fear, envied him? Yes, I've envied him in other ways too. I know I tried to make him weak, but I could never do that for Cobweb's strength is pure, elemental. If I'd had a little more Cobweb in me, who knows, I might not be lying here now.' He sighed and lay back, blinking at the ceiling. 'Oh, Swift, I thought I was so strong! I saw defeat as going down in a blaze of glory with a curse on my lips, a curse and a smile. I knew we could never win, of course, that was obvious from the start, but I also knew I could never wait for the Gelaming to come here. Neither could I have done what you did, and joined them. Perhaps I'm not as sensible as you or too vain, I don't know. I travelled south seeking a noble death, I suppose, but what happened ...' He shook his head upon the pillow, his face twisted with pain as he remembered, as he went back in time.

'No,' I said. 'Don't say any more! Don't think about it! Let it wait for another time!'

'No! There might not be another time!' he said desperately. 'I have to talk to you, Swift! I have to tell someone! It's all inside me, boiling away, I've got to let it out! Does my distress upset you? Is that it?'

I felt I should apologize, but could only hang my head.

'They told you about what happened in the forest?' he asked.

'Yes. They were waiting for you, weren't they?'

'Years, Swift, years!' he said, his mind jumping backwards and forwards. 'In that place of Hell, and then in the towers of Immanion. They pulled me this way and that. All I could say was, "Why am I so important to you? Just kill me!" but they wanted me with them! They wanted me to confess my sins and seek absolution. But why? What am I to them?'

'They wanted to save your soul,' I answered.

Terzian laughed. 'Oh, is that it? Is that why they brought my thoughts into form and made me face them? Is that why I watched a thousand deaths a day, and torture and blood and despair? To save my soul?' (But didn't you watch it for real once, father?) 'Oh, Swift, let me tell you this. One day they starved me and gave me salt water to drink. They would not let me sleep. I was woken again and again and again. Then I was taken to Pellaz. He's so radiant now. They've made him a god. He had a pool for scrying, in a wonderful cool parlour with plants and birds all around, and lovely hara to bring him all the things he needs. He gave me a crystal flute of wine, ice-cold it was, and he smiled and touched my face. "Terzian," he said "drink the wine. Drink, and look into the pool with me." I drank. I looked. I saw a room. Forever. Two hara glowing with aruna fire. I had to look away. It was an invasion of something so private ... even though ... Pellaz the golden spoke. He said, "You see, Terzian, already they have forgotten you." Cobweb and Cal. Together. Of course, I realized it was only an illusion. I laughed at him. They could not break me that way.'

I pulled my hand from his hold and stood up, afraid my eyes would give away the truth. That was no illusion, Terzian. 'You are letting yourself die,' I said. 'You still haven't given me a reason!'

'Well then, do you want me to live, Swift?' he asked quietly. There was silence. A silence too long. 'There's nothing left for me,' he continued. 'I have no place in this new world you're all building, no function —'

'That's not true!' I said harshly. 'They wanted you, Terzian! It was you they wanted to run Megalithica for them, not me. I was second choice. You would have had Galhea for eternity then and you could have made it bigger and better; nothing would have been denied you. You are a fool! When you say you have no function, that's just a self-indulgent complaint. You were never one for self-pity before, Terzian!'

'Well, maybe I am now!' he answered with equal venom. 'Anyway, do you think I wanted to be another kitten chasing bits of wool that Thiede would kindly dangle for me? No thank you. I am my own master —'

'Liar!' I cried. 'What about Ponclast?'

'That was different.'

'Rubbish!'

'Anyway, you talk as if I had a choice of living or dying. How can I? This is Thiede's doing. He took me apart, he sapped my will to live. Blame him! Your friend Thiede! Or doesn't that suit you?'

It was pointless arguing with him. Neither of us could reach the other over this. We had no common ground. Perhaps he thought that his death would be the final insult for our allying with the Gelaming. That was the truth of it. He was blaming us, me especially, for his death. If he forgave me, he lost his reason for dying.

'I can't let you do this,' I said.

'What makes you think either of us has any control over it?' he responded.

'You, father, you make me think it!' I shouted. I walked out, slammed the door, and leaned upon it on the outside, shivering.

Elysian Song
The pillar has risen to infinity,
The pyre has cast his throne,
The gates of Heaven have sounded the
bell ...
Calling me back home.

Days passed. Sunlight on the fields, life stirring. People from afar. Nomad tribes were made welcome for the first time upon Galhea's lands. We sought to annihilate the memory of the Varrs and our tribe was given a new name; Parasiel. It is the name of an angel and he is the lord and master of treasures. We have found treasure within ourselves and this name seemed truly apt.

My father hung onto life, though daily he seemed to fade. I visited him every evening but it was hard to talk. Perhaps everything that could be said between us had already been said. It was as if he wanted to linger in this world for as long as possible, in a distressing state, in order to inflict as much pain as he could upon my hostling and myself. Day by day, he released a little more of his life force into infinity. Mengk was with him constantly; another devotee made to suffer. Cobweb behaved like a kind of tortured saint, full of self-recrimination, solicitous to Mengk, calm and understanding with Terzian, unshakeable.

Thiede left Galhea to return to Immanion, promising me a summons to Phaonica in the near future as official representative of Parasiel for the forthcoming talks concerning Megalithica's future. Ashmael had returned with Thiede, and Arahal had gone east to take charge of the Gelaming personnel in that area. At the

379

moment, only a handful of Gelaming remained in Galhea. Later, this would change, as their architects and builders and technicians came to get to work on the town, but for a while our lives were our own.

It was not spoken of, but it was clear that we in the house were all just waiting for Terzian to die. Perhaps it sounds harsh to say that, but for myself, I was mainly concerned for Tyson and Azriel, who could not but be affected by the heaviness in the atmosphere. All conversations seemed to be conducted in whispers; the harlings could not run or shout as harlings should. Outside Forever, my people seemed content to forget that they had ever been Varrs. Ithiel took his orders from me. I was Master of Galhea and Terzian still lived.

One night, a strong wind came up from the south, bringing heavy clouds with it that shook all the trees in the garden, and a faint, acrid smell of burning. Bryony ran around the house closing all the windows, for we expected rain. I had already organised a refurbishment of the upper storeys of Forever, for I envisaged a day that the house would be used to its full capacity and too long had those haunted rooms stood untended. Bryony came to us in the sitting-room, her face pale. 'I don't like the third floor,' she said, rubbing her arms. 'Something seems to watch you there!' We laughed at her fears.

In the night, with wind lashing at the walls, speaking in a fierce, incomprehensible howl, I was woken up by a sound. A sound within the house, whose echoes had vanished by the time I was awake. Seel groaned when I shook him.

'What was that?' I whispered hoarsely.

'Nothing,' he answered, and rolled over, pulling the blankets over his ears.

Nothing. For a while I lay awake in the dark with my arms behind my head, listening. Nothing. Perhaps I had been mistaken. Perhaps a dream ... I began to drift back to sleep, but just as I was slipping under, it came again. Low, booming. I was not mistaken. I was fully awake this time. Not bothering to tell Seel, I scrabbled from the bed, pulling on a robe, and crept to the door.

Outside, the corridor was in darkness. I could hear the wind all around me. Feeling my way to the stairs, I reached to turn on the light. The sound came again; deafening. A great, hollow thundering. The door. Someone demands entrance. Who ...? Someone. Three times. I had heard it three times.

Flooded with light, the hall beneath me looked tense and stark, the great front doors dark and solid before me. Why had no-one else woken up? I hesitated only a moment. My hands were upon the doors, pulling them open. Wind rushed into the house like an angry spirit, bringing a train of whirling leaves. My hair was blown up behind me, my robe flapped with life. Breathless, I cautiously narrowed my eyes at the garden beyond. Nothing. There was no-one there. Only the wind howling.

With effort, I pushed the doors closed again and turned the great key in the lock. It should always be locked, I thought. Then the back of my neck began to prickle. My hair began to rise. The hall was too quiet. For a moment, I did not turn round. My heart slowed down to a comfortable pace, I rubbed the back of my neck.

'Swift.' A single word. A single sound. A hundred memories flooding in; the past around me. I turned round. He was carrying a canvas bag which he dropped to the floor. He ran his fingers through his hair, which was longer than I remembered, and windswept. He looked very tired.

I said, 'Cal,' and found my back pressed against the door. There was no way out for me through them, though. 'How ...? How did you get here?'

'You're afraid!'

'No.' I made myself step towards him. He stepped back. 'How did you get in here?' I repeated. 'How ...?'

'No!' He would not let me continue. 'I'm here. That's all. That's all you need to know. I've been given time. Not much, but enough for what I have to do.' He looked stern, but he couldn't keep it up. His face softened. 'Oh, Swift, how I've missed you all.'

I found myself smiling. How could I help it? 'You're not a ghost? You're sure you're not a ghost?'

He shook his head. 'Oh no, no, I'm not. They'll never kill me, Swift. You know that. Now, will you take me to Terzian?'

381

'Can't we talk first? It's been so long. I want to know what happened to you.'

'I'm sorry ...' He shook his head again.

There was so much I wanted to say. I could only stare at him speechless.

'Please, Swift. Now.' He lifted his bag.

I led the way upstairs. 'Do you get a feeling, walking up here? Does it make you remember?' I asked him.

'Yes,' he said quietly.

Two steps from the top, I turned on him. 'Oh, Cal, is it bad? Are you alright? Where did they take you? Did they hurt you? Are you safe?'

He almost fell backwards in surprise at my outburst. 'Don't ask me questions, Swift, please. I cannot answer them.'

'Then let me touch you.'

'Alright. For a moment.' He held out his arms and I stood on the step above him so that our height was level. He felt cold, but it was only the chill of being out in the wind. His violet gaze was steady. 'Take this back to your lover,' he said. 'My taste.' We shared breath, but I could taste only blackness, like a veil. He would show me nothing. 'There's not much time,' he said.

At the doorway to my father's room, he touched my face and said, 'Don't come in with me, Swift.'

'There's so much I want to say. Will we see you again?'

He smiled that lazy smile. 'Oh, can I come back here? Will I be made welcome in Seel's house?'

I lowered my eyes. I had forgotten that.

Cal laughed softly. 'Oh, Swift, don't be ashamed. You are happy and I'm happy for you. Your life will be perfect. You have everything.'

'You must come back,' I said. 'What is done is done, but you are still part of us. Your son is here. For him, you must come back.'

'If I can, maybe. Personally, I think Tyson would be better off not knowing about me.'

I shook my head. 'Never.'

'I'll always think of you, Swift, you and your mad hostling. The changeling. I've thought of you all a lot recently.'

'Where have you been?'

'Places, that's all. This sounds dramatic, but I'm being followed. A har on a black horse. How symbolic! My trials are not yet over, I'm afraid. There are still ghosts snapping at my heels. They battle for my soul, you know. Succouring Terzian on his deathbed is a karmic point to me, I think.' He laughed again, his face lighting up as it always did. A summer smile.

'No-one will ever have your soul,' I said. 'Cal, about Pellaz. He *is* alive, you know.'

There was a moment's silence. His face shivered briefly. 'Yes,' he said, 'I know, Swift.' He pulled a forlorn face and shrugged. He would say no more. 'I'll have to say goodbye now, Swift.'

'I can't just let you go like this. Stay a while, it can't hurt, there's so much —'

'No! You have to let me go. It's out of our hands. Goodbye.'

He opened the door, walked inside, into the darkness, closed it. I stood there for a moment or two, wondering. All was silence. Outside, the wind had dropped.

In the morning, I learned that my father was dead. The house was full of peace. When I looked at the body, I could see tranquillity in that lifeless face. A faint smile. My father's spirit was free now. He had another chance.

I took Cobweb and Seel to the long gallery and told them about a dream I'd had the night before about Cal coming back to Forever. I half suspected that Cobweb was responsible, for he was a master of visualization, but his surprise was genuine enough.

'A dream, Swift?' he said.

'It may have been,' I answered.

We left it at that. Cobweb covered all the mirrors in the house and had someone stop the clocks. He was serene. We burned Terzian's body on a great pyre in the fields beyond Galhea and the ashes were scattered to the four winds. With their scattering, we all knew that the last of the Varrs had perished. The name was only a dark memory.

Most days, I like to walk in the garden. I can think there. In the evening, the summerhouse calls me and I go to it, although it is barely recognizable now. Ivy has covered it and the lily bowl is choked forever. It is there that I can talk to you best, Cal. For sometimes, I am sure that you are near. It is where I can tell you to come back to us, that hate is banished for good from our home and even you could not bring it back in.

In the autumn, Seel and I are going back to Immanion, but it won't be for long. We shall be coming back for Festival and Ashmael will be with us. Seel says it is because Cobweb has bewitched him and I'm sure you can understand that! It will be a good Festival, Cal. We will remember, but not with sadness. I want you to know that whatever evil you think is inside you (and I *do* know that you think that), it is only part of the essential harmony of the world; the world needs you. Without pain, there cannot be pleasure, without darkness, light cannot thrive. We need contrast, and the lone wolves who stalk the earth, like yourself, they bring perspective and objectivity into our lives. We need you, Cal, all of us. Angel or devil, you hold the balance. You begin the tales, we end them. It is time that you began your own. Every day, I look at Tyson and see your eyes. One day, he will ask me about you, for you are in his heart. The hostling who did not care. That is something you must attend to, for your son is innocent and your trials are not his.

I often wonder if you and Pell are together again, if you have met, even. Would that be the prize or the punishment? Perhaps, when I go to Immanion, I shall find out. When I get back … Remember, Cal, Cobweb and the harlings will be almost alone in Forever while Seel and I are away. That is the time. I am counting on it. We shall come back through the snow and the yellow lights of Forever will be shining out to greet us. The doors will be flung wide open and the house inside will be alive with celebration. We shall walk into the hall and I shall see you there. I think you'll smile in that lopsided way you have and stand before me and say, 'You see, I couldn't keep away. I've come home.'

It isn't long, Cal. Listen to me. The bewitchments of love and hate are perhaps the strongest magics in the world. Magic called you to us in the beginning, I am sure of it. I called your name in a dream. Now I'm calling you again. Listen in the shadows; I'm whistling in the dark.

Wraeththu caste system

Wraeththu Hara progress through a three-tier caste system: each tier consisting of three levels.

KAIMANA (Kï-ee-marna)

Level 1: Ara (altar)
2: Neoma (new moon)
3. Brynie (strong)

ULANI (Oo-lar-nee)

Level 1: Acantha (thorny)
2. Pyralis (fire)
3. Algoma (valley of flowers)

NAHIR-NURI (Na-heer Noo-ree)

Level 1: Efrata (distinguished)
    2. Aislinn (vision)
    3. Cleatha (glory)

Natural born Hara have no caste until they reach sexual maturity, when they are initiated into Kaimana. The majority of them rarely progress further than Level 2 Ulani: Pyralis. Wraeththu of Kaimana and Ulani caste are always known by their level, i.e. someone of Acantha level would be known as Acanthalid, of Pyralis, Pyralisit. Once Nahir-Nuri has been achieved, however, the caste divisions (mostly incomprehensible to those of lower caste), are no longer used as a title of address. Wraeththu of that caste are simply called Nahir-Nuri.

Caste Progression

Training in spiritual advancement must be undertaken to achieve a higher level. Occult rituals concentrate the mind and realize progression. Progression is attained by the discovery of self-knowledge and with that knowledge utilizing the inborn powers of Wraeththu.

*Wraeththu special abilities:
a comparison to man*

The differences between Wraeththu and humankind are not vast in number, and not even apparent (in most cases) to the naked eye. Biologically their functions are similar, although in the case of Wraeththu many basic design faults present in the old race have been removed.

A. Digestion

Wraeththu digestion is not wildly disparate from that of humankind, although it is unknown for Hara to become over-weight whatever amount of food is ingested. Their bodies are so well-regulated that excesses of all kinds are merely eliminated as waste. Perfect body-weight is never exceeded. This thorough system cleansing also extends to most intoxicants or stimulants. Narcotic effects can be experienced without side-effects. Because of this, few poisons are lethal to Wraeththu. It has been rumoured that the Uigenna tribe of North Megalithica are fluent with the use of poisons effective against their own kind, but this has yet to be proved.

B. The Senses

Wraeththu senses of touch, sight, hearing, smell and taste are marginally more acute than those of mankind. But the sixth sense is far more well-developed. This may only be due to the fact that Wraeththu are brought up (or instructed after inception) with the knowledge to glean full use of their perception. This is a quality which has become dulled in Man. Some Hara can even catch glimpses of future events or atmospheres; either by tranquil contemplation or in dreams.

Again, it must be stressed that this ability is not a fundamental difference from humanity, as all humans possess within themselves the potential to develop their psychic capabilities. Most humans, however, are not aware of this.

C. Occult Powers

This is merely an extension of becoming acquainted, through proper progression, with one's psychic senses.

Magic is will-power, will-power is magic. Self-knowledge is the key to the perfect control of will.

Obviously, this particular talent may be used either for the benefit or detriment of other beings. As all Wraeththu are firm believers in reincarnation and the progression of the soul (see *Religion*), most are sensible enough to realize the dangers of taking 'the left hand path'. Others, however, still motivated by the greed and baser emotions of human ancestors, are prone to seek self-advancement through evil means.

D. Life-span

In comparison, to Mankind, Wraeththu appear ageless, but this is not strictly the case. Har bodies are not subject to cellular deterioration in the same way as human bodies, but on reaching the age of 150 years or thereabouts, they begin to 'fade', vitality diminishes and the dignified end is welcomed as the release for the soul and the gateway to the next incarnation.

Wraeththu sexuality

A. Reproduction

Wraeththu are hermaphrodite beings, any of whom have the capacity to reproduce on reaching the caste of Ulani. This is mainly because Hara of lower caste have insufficient control of the mind, which is required to attain the elevated state of consciousness needed for conception. Experienced Hara can guarantee conception whenever it is desired.

Conception can only occur during the act of aruna (Wraeththu intercourse); Hara are unable to fertilize themselves. The inseminating Har is known as ouana (Ooow-ana), and the host for the seed, soume (Soow-mee). This corresponds roughly to human male and female, although in Wraeththu the roles are interchangeable. When conditions are propitious (i.e. when the desired state of consciousness is achieved through the ecstasy of aruna), ouana has the chance to 'break through the seal', which is the act of coaxing

399

the chamber of generation within the body of the soume to relax its banks of muscle that closes the entrance, and permit the inner tendril of the ouana phallus to intrude. This act must needs be undertaken with patience, because of the inner organ's somewhat capricious reluctance to be invaded by foreign bodies or substances. Aggression or haste on the side of ouana would cause pain and distress to soume (or possibly to both of them) caused by the impenetrable tensing of soume muscles.

Once the seed (aren) has been successfully released, the chamber of generation reseals itself and emits a fertilizing secretion (yaloe) which forms a coating around the aren. Only the strongest can survive this process, weaker seed are literally burned up or else devoured by their fellows. During the next twelve hours or so, the aren fight for supremacy, until only one of them survives; this is then enveloped by the nourishing yaloe which begins to harden around the aren to form a kind of shell. By interaction of the positive aren elements and the negative yaloe elements, a Wraeth-thu foetus begins to develop within the shell.

At the end of two months, the shell is emitted from the body of its host, resembling a black, opalescent pearl some 6″ in diameter. Incubation is then required, either by the host or any other Har committed to spending the time. After 'birth', the pearl begins to soften into an elastic, leathery coating about the developing Har-child. Progress and growth are rapid; within a week, the pearl 'hatches' and the young Har enters the world.

Wraeththu children, on hatching, already possess some body hair and have moderately acute eyesight. Familiar Hara can be recognized after only a few days. Though smaller in size, the Har-ling at this time is comparable in intelligence and mobility to a human child that has just been weaned. Wraeththu children need no milk and can eat the same food as adults within a few hours of hatching. Development is astonishingly rapid within the first year of life. Har-lings are able to crawl around immediately after hatch-ing, and can walk upright within a few days. They learn to speak simple words after about four weeks, and before that, voice their demands by exercising their voices in a series of purrings and chatterings. Sexual maturity is reached between the ages of seven and ten years, when the Har-ling is physically able to partake in aruna without ill effect. At this time, caste training is undertaken and the young Har is also educated in the etiquette of aruna. Sexual maturity is recognized by a marked restlessness and erratic behaviour, even a craving for moonlight. Aruna education is usually imparted by an older Har chosen by the child's hostling or sire. This is to prevent any unpleasant experiences which the young Har could suffer at the hands of someone who is not committed to its welfare.

(N.B. Those Hara who are not natural born, but incepted, are instructed in aruna immediately after the effects of althaia (the changing) wears off. This is essential to 'fix' the change within the new Har.)

A physically mature Har, when clothed, resembles closely a young, human male. Hara do not need breasts for the production of milk, nor wide pelvises to accommodate a growing child. They are, whilst obviously masculine, uncannily feminine at the same time; which is a circumstance difficult to describe without illustration.

B. Aruna

The act of sexual intercourse between Hara has two legitimate types. Aruna is indulged in either for pleasure; the intimate communication of minds and bodies that all Hara need for spiritual contentment, or else for the express purpose of conceiving. Although it is a necessity for Wraeththu, the amount of physical communion preferred varies from Har to Har. Some may seek out a companion only once a year, others may yearn for aruna several times a week. It is not important whether a Har enjoys most performing ouana or soume; again this varies among Hara. Most swap and change their roles according to mood or circumstance.

The phallus of the Har resembles a petalled rod, sometimes of deep and varied colours. It has an inner tendril which may only emerge once embraced by the body of the soume and prior to orgasm. The soume organs of generation, located in the lower region of the body in a position not dissimilar to that of a human female womb, is reached by a fleshy, convoluted passage found behind the masculine organs of generation. Self cleansing, it leads also to the lower intestine, where more banks of muscle form an effective seal.

C. Grissecon

Grissecon is sexual communion for occult purposes; simply — sex magic. As enormous forces are aroused during aruna, these forces may be harnessed to act externally. Explanation other than this is prohibited by the Great Oath.

D. Pelki

There are only two legitimate modes of physical intercourse among Wraeththu. Pelki is for the most part denied to exist, although amongst brutalized tribes it undoubtedly does. It is the name for forced rape of either Hara or humans. The latter is essentially murder, as humankind cannot tolerate the bodily secretions of Wraeththu, which act as a caustic poison; pelki to humans is always fatal. Because aruna is such a respected and important aspect of Wraeththu life, the concept of pelki is both abhorrent and appalling to the average Har. Unfortunately, certain dark powers can be accrued by indulging in these practices and this only serves as a dreadful temptation to Hara of evil or morally decadent inclinations.

At the time of Tigron Pellaz' reign in Immanion, the religious beliefs of Wraeththu were widely disparate.

Obviously, the faith of the Gelaming is the most widespread, and the most organized. They believe that the power of the deity is expressed within each individual, and that to lead a religious life, is to strive for inner peace, tolerance towards others and development of Wraeththu's innate powers. They are fond of ritual and extend their beliefs to the existence of unseen intelligent forces, who have direct influence upon the lives of earthly creatures. Other tribes practise pantheism, dualism and diabolism, depending on area and lifestyle. A separate volume could be written on the intricacies of each religious practice, but to summarize, it may be said that all Wraeththu religions revolve about the occult aspects of the Wraeththu race.

Glossary of Wraeththu terms and principal characters

Afnina (Af-NEE-na) Swift's Gelaming horse, given to him by Arahal. One of those beasts that may travel through the 'other-lanes'.

Aghama (AG-am-ar) The title of the first Wraeththu, worshipped as a god by some.

Ahmouth (AR-mooth) Settlement of the Wraeththu tribe of Amaha.

Aihah (AY-har) Kakkahaar har, who visited Galhea as an advocate for his tribe, and also advised Swift concerning his Feybraiha.

Almagabra Country of the Gelaming, across the sea from Megalithica.

Amaha Wraeththu tribe of Megalithica, who trade with the Varrs.

Ara See Appendix I.

Arahal A Gelaming har, one of the Tigron's generals, prominent in Imbrilim.

aralid See Appendix I.

aruna Sexual communion between hara.

Ashmael One of the Hegemony of Immanion.

Astigi (Ass-TEE-gi) The great marsh in Megalithica, home of the Froia.

Azriel Son of Swift and Seel.

Braga (BRAH-ga) Leader of the tribe of the Froia.

Bryony Human woman employed in the household of Forever.

Caeru (KY-roo) Tigrina of Immanion, consort of Pellaz.

Cal Second consort of Terzian the Varr, erstwhile lover of Pellaz.

Cedony (SED-on-ee) One of the Hegemony in Immanion.

Chelone (CHEL-on-ee) A Varrish warrior.

Chrysm (Krizum) One of the Hegemony of Immanion.

Cobweb A Varr, hostling of Swift, consort of Terzian.

Ferelithia Wraeththu settlement in Almagabra, home of the tribe of Ferelith, place of origin of Caeru.

Festival New Year's celebration in Galhea.

Forever See *We Dwell in Forever.*

Froia (FROY-a) Wraeththu tribe of Astigi.

Fulminir Varr city in Megalithica, stronghold of Ponclast.

Galhea (GAL-ay-a) Varrish town in central Megalithica, governed by Terzian.

Gebaddon (Ge-BAD-on) An enchanted forest of Megalithica, where Thiede banished the Varrs.

Gahrazel (GA-ra-zel) Ponclast's son, friend to Swift.

Grissecon (GRISS-uh-con) Sexual communion between hara to achieve power; sexual magic.

Har Wraeththu individual (pl. hara).

Harling Young har until Feybraiha.

Hiren Leader of the Amaha.

hostling Har who carries a pearl (Wraeththu foetus), who hosts the seed of another.

househar A servant.

Hegemony Leading body of the Gelaming.

Imbrilim Gelaming camp headquarters in Megalithica.

Immanion Capital city of Almagabra.

Ithiel Terzian's equerry, second in command of Galhea.

Kaimana See Appendix I.
Kakkahar Desert tribe of Southern Megalithica.
Kate Human woman, friend of Caeru.

Leef A Varr, who accompanied Cal and Swift to Imbrilim.
Lianvis (Lee-AN-viss) Leader of the Kakkahaar.
Limba Swift's black dog.

Mawn A Varr, one of Ponclast's aides.
Mareta Household cat in Forever.
Megalithica Western continent taken from the Varrs by the Gelaming.
Mengk (Menk) A follower of Terzian.
Moswell One of Swift's tutors.

Nepopis (Ne-POPE-iss) A theruna of the Froia.
Nahir-Nuri See Appendix I.

Orense (O-rence) A settlement of the Froia.
Orien A Saltrock shaman murdered by Cal.
Ouana (Oo-ARN-a) Masculine principle of hara.
Ouana-Lim Masculine generative organ of Wraeththu.

Pearl Wraeththu embryo.
Pelki Rape.
Pellaz Pellaz-har-Aralis, Tigron of Immanion, leader of the Gelaming.
Peter Bryony's brother. See *Purah*.
Phaonica (Fay-ON-icka) The Tigron's palace in Immanion.
Phlaar (Flar) A Varr, Terzian's physician.
Ponclast Nahir-Nuri, leader of the Varrs.
Purah Friend of Gahrazel, was once human, see *Peter*.
Pythoness title of Tel-an-kaa.
Parasiel (Par-A-see-el) New name given to the tribe of Varrs after the fall of Fulminir and vanquishment of Ponclast.
Putiri (Pewt-I-ree) A natural drug, affecting mind and libido.

Rue See *Caeru.*

Saltrock Wraeththu settlement in Megalithica.

Seel Gelaming har, associated with the Hegemony, consort of Swift.
Shara Human woman in Imbrilim. See *Tyrells.*
Sharing of breath A kiss of mutual visualization.
Sheh (Shay) A Varr liqueur.
Soume (SOO-mee) Feminine principle of hara.
Soume-Lam Feminine generative organ of Wraeththu.
Swift A Varr, son of Terzian and Cobweb.
Swithe One of Swift's tutors.

Tel-AN-Kaa Human female, leader of the Zigane.
Terzian Autarch of Galhea, Varr, father of Swift.
Thiede (THEE-dee) The first Wraeththu, most powerful of Gelaming.
Throyne Amaha har, son of Hiren.
Theruna (The-ROO-na) A holy har of the Froia.
Tiahaar Respectful form of address.
Tigrina (Tee-GREE-na) The Tigron's consort.
Tigron (TEE-gron) The lord of the Gelaming, Thiede's protégé.
Tulga Swift's horse on the journey to Imbrilim.
Tyrells A human family in Imbrilim.
Tyson Son of Cal and Terzian.

Uigenna (EW-i-GEN-a) War-like tribe of Megalithica, famous for their poisons.
Ulani See Appendix I.
Unneah (Oo-NAY-a) Wraeththu tribe of Megalithica.

Velaxis A follower of Ashmael, Gelaming har.
Varrs Wraeththu tribe of Megalithica, ruling body, known for their warlike mien.

Zack Uigenna har, once a companion of Cal.

Zheera Sparkling sheh.

Zigane (Zig-ARN-a) A tribe of wandering humans and hara.

We Dwell in Forever Terzian's house in Galhea.

Yarrow The cook in Forever, one of Terzian's house hara.

THE FIRST BOOK OF LOST SWORDS: WOUNDHEALER'S STORY

The Gods are dead, but the struggle for the Swords of Power continues . . .

Fred Saberhagen

Vulcan, forger of the Swords of Power, was the last God to die. Now humans possess all the Swords, some for good, some for evil.

Woundhealer is the Sword of Healing, and is said to be held at the White Temple, for the south. Mark, Prince Consort of Tasavalta, seeks it to help his son regain his sight. But Baron Amintor and the evil wizard Burslam are also intent on gaining the Sword, at any cost. Before the conflict ends, Mark and his nephew Zoltan will have seen far stranger things than the Swords of Power . . .

'Fred Saberhagen has proved he is one of the best' – Lester Del Rey

Don't miss:

THE FIRST BOOK OF SWORDS
THE SECOND BOOK OF SWORDS
THE THIRD BOOK OF SWORDS
EMPIRE OF THE EAST

FUTURA PUBLICATIONS
AN ORBIT BOOK
FANTASY
0 7088 8276 5

THE URTH OF THE NEW SUN

The triumphant sequel to
THE BOOK OF THE NEW SUN

Gene Wolfe

'And still I shot upward.

'The maintop came into view. I reached for a halyard. They were hardly thicker than my finger now, though every sail would have covered ten score of meadows.

'I had misjudged, and the halyard was just beyond my grasp. Another flashed by.

'And another – three cubits out of reach at least.

'I tried to twist like a swimmer but could do no more than lift my knee. The shining cables of the rigging had been widely separated even far below, where there were for this single mast more than a hundred. None now remained but the startop shroud. My fingers brushed it but could not grasp it.

'The end of my life had come, and I knew it.'

In the long-awaited sequel to his award-winning BOOK OF THE NEW SUN, Gene Wolfe sends Severian, ex-torturer, now Autarch of Urth, to Yezod, the Planet of Judgment. Arriving after a spell-binding voyage on a magnificently-described sailing ship of space, Severian undergoes examination. On this will depend both his future and that of Urth.

GENE WOLFE:
'. . . his language and imagery reach back to the roots of modern fantasy . . .' – *Publishers Weekly*

'A national treasure . . .' Damon Knight

'Our Melville . . .' Ursula Le Guin

Also by Gene Wolfe in Orbit
SOLDIER OF THE MIST

FUTURA PUBLICATIONS
AN ORBIT BOOK
FANTASY
0 7088 8268 4

ARCHON

Stuart Gordon

The Joyces seem at first an ordinary enough family. Sam is a moderately unhappy social worker, Diane a teacher and Chrissa a typically moody 13-year-old. But Sam is haunted by strange memories from his past, of an island that appeared from nowhere, and of a woman whose passage on a sailing ship provoked a sinister sequence of events. And Chrissa is haunted too – by dreams of a Burning Man, calling to her. Then, on a terrible day on a windswept Scottish hill, to Diane's horror both Sam and Chrissa vanish before her eyes.

For they are destined to be warriors in a war that has been raging for thousands of years. The crisis is at hand, which will determine whether humanity will survive – or perish, horribly and finally, in a cataclysmic pole shift.

Mystical, hallucinatory and sweeping in scope, ARCHON draws on a huge range of myth, legend and philosophy to create a wonderfully colourful story. It is the first in a major SF trilogy.

FUTURA PUBLICATIONS
AN ORBIT BOOK
FANTASY/SCIENCE FICTION
0 7088 3708 5

All Futura Books are available at your bookshop or
newsagent, or can be ordered from the following address:
Futura Books, Cash Sales Department,
P.O. Box 11, Falmouth, Cornwall TR10 9EN.

Please send cheque or postal order (no currency), and
allow 60p for postage and packing for the first book
plus 25p for the second book and 15p for each additional
book ordered up to a maximum charge of £1.90 in U.K.

B.F.P.O. customers please allow 60p for
the first book, 25p for the second book plus 15p per
copy for the next 7 books, thereafter 9p per book

Overseas customers, including Eire, please allow £1.25
for postage and packing for the first book, 75p for the
second book and 28p for each subsequent title ordered.